C000064318

THE STAMP COLLECTOR

COLLECTOR

There and Back Again

By D. Andrew Brooks and Farhad Kashani

PROLOGUE

The Persian Constitutional Revolution took place between 1905 and 1911. The intent was to establish a Parliament in the vein of Great Britain as a check on the power of the Shah. This was a pivotal time in the history of this country and region.

Persia and Afghanistan represented a security buffer and safe route to India for Britain. Access to a warm water port has always been at the heart of politics for Russia. For most of the 19th century these two nations competed for control over this region in what was known as "The Great Game". The Anglo-Russian Convention of 1907 split control of Persia into three zones, the Russian sphere of influence in the north, the British sphere in the south, and a neutral zone in the middle. All of these machinations made it more difficult for Persians to establish the democracy they longed for.

During this period Winston Churchill was the First Lord of the Admiralty, responsible for the entire British Navy. He knew that ships fired with oil could run faster and stay on the open sea longer than those fired with coal. If Britain was to keep its superiority on the ocean, then they would have to convert the entire fleet to oil. Unfortunately England had large reserves of coal and no oil. Most of the known oil reserves at that time were in the United States and Indonesia.

Oil was discovered in southern Persia in the early 20th century by an Englishman named D'Arcy. The company he founded was called the Anglo-Persian Oil Company, but it later changed it's name to British Petroleum. This discovery was the start of the geopolitical game that has continued to this very day.

The spelling of names in this work has been a challenge. Until 1945 Persians commonly used Arabic names, but often spelled differently in Latin based languages. We have tried to use the Persian, Arabic, and Turkish 'spelling' for names and places where appropriate.

The story you are about to read is fiction, but it is based on the life of a man who played an important role in shaping the history of this period.

INTRODUCTION

My name is Abdulrahim Kashani. I travelled to many places in my lifetime. I wore many hats both literally and figuratively. And I saw tremendous change in my native country of Persia from my birth in the 19th century to my death in 1931.

How can it be that I am speaking to you dear reader so many years after my death?

The reason will become clear over time. Telling my story is something I must do. Think of it as testimony in a trial, for in a way that's what this is. My testimony of a good life well lived in troubled times.

You must know the stories of a thousand and one nights. Stories of Aladdin and Ali Baba. Stories of Genies and Princes and Thieves. I am certainly no Scheherazade, but unlike her tall tales, mine are actually true. I have met several Princes and confronted many thieves. I even met one man who could have been mistaken for a Genie.

I am getting ahead of myself though. Forgive me. This is just the way I am.

In my life I was always looking ahead, always trying to find a way to change the future for the better. Now I have all the time in the world and no ability to change a thing.

I was a member of parliament and the friend of a Shah, but I never had much personal power. I was the cousin of an Ayatollah, but I was not a pious Muslim. I belonged to a trade guild and The Freemasons. I sold stationary in my shop, published a newspaper off and on, and even wrote a book, but my true calling was collecting.

I was a collector of stamps, but also a collector of people and their stories. Some of these people you may know like Reza Shah, Winston Churchill, and even Mata Hari.

But how do I start? Where does one begin one's life story?

Let me begin in the middle, with a journey I took in 1914 from my home in Tehran to Paris and back. Everything that came before that prepared me for this experience. Everything that came after was a direct result. When the divine judges examine my life for merit, I believe they will start here as well, because personal sacrifice for the greater good is one way to ensure a positive outcome in the afterlife. At least that's what we Persians believe.

So if you are ready to begin, then so am I.

TEHRAN

September 21st, 1913

The year 1913 was good for me. My business was doing well. I had four healthy sons. The youngest Mehdi was only a few months old. Sales of my book on Stamp Collecting had paid for my printing run and I was beginning to earn a profit, but most importantly, the streets of Tehran were safe again after years of unrest.

My book was a labor of love, but this book also connected me to some interesting people. One of those was the worshipful master of our Freemason lodge in Tehran, Alfred Jean-Baptiste Lemaire. Our lodge was affiliated with L'Ordre Grand Orient de France, the most important Freemason lodge in that country.

We Persians admire many things about the French. We even say *Merci* for thank you more often than we use the native phrase in Persian. Paris to us was the height of culture. The French were also more tolerable politically than the Russians, who we Persians have many reasons to detest. We in the north of Persia lived in the Russian 'sphere of influence' and they influenced us often. The French were more interested in Syria and the Levant, so we got along.

One morning in late September of 1913 I was at work in my shop on Nasserieh Avenue in the heart of Tehran when for the first time ever, Jean-Baptiste Lemaire walked in to my shop...

"Good morning Abdulrahim! How are you on this fine day?"

"*Bon Jour* Jean-Baptiste, what a surprise! Come in. Come in and have some tea! Let's sit over here where we will not be disturbed."

I gestured to the area of my shop that was tucked away in the corner. I had no idea what our Worshipful Master wanted coming here in the light of day, but I knew it was not to buy paper.

"Please don't go to any trouble..."

"No trouble for an honored guest. Please. Right this way."

I turned to my young assistant who was standing nearby. "Khalil, please fetch some tea for our guest and be quick about it."

We settled in to my private seating area which was furnished with western style chairs and a tea table. It wasn't as elegant as the formal rooms in the lodge hall, but at least I wasn't asking him to sit on the ground.

Khalil returned almost immediately with my best tea service and a tray of food. Just as quickly he was gone, leaving us alone to speak.

"You have a nice place here Abdulrahim. Your business appears to be doing well."

"You are too kind. We have been fortunate these past few years, but I am still a humble shop keeper just trying to earn a living."

"A humble shop... located across the street from the Palace" he said with a smile.

"It is a good location" I admitted. "Paper is after all a luxury item for the well-educated, so we must sell where we can find the customers."

He smiled and looked around, but I got the impression he was more interested in ensuring our privacy than actually admiring the shop.

"What news from home Jean-Baptiste?"

"Ah! Thank you for your concern. My Family is fine. Paris is fine, but there are rumors that Kaiser Wilhelm is beginning to assemble a vast army in the east of Germany and their proposed Alliance with the Ottoman Empire is a cause for concern, but these are only rumor and innuendos, no?"

We had our own problems in Persia and I was not a man to worry about trouble unless it was at my doorstep.

"Abdulrahim, would you allow me to come straight to the reason for my visit today?"

"Of course my friend. You are a busy man and I doubt you are here for stationary."

Jean-Batiste again surveyed the room and seemed to come to some decision.

"You are correct. I am more interested in your stamp collection."

"You are a Philatelist as well?"

"No. No. Not me. But I have several acquaintances who are very interested in meeting with you... to see your collection... of course and possibly to negotiate... a deal shall we say."

"But of course! I would be honored to host friends of yours either here or at my home ..."

He raised his hand and from the pained expression on his face I felt I was missing something.

"These colleagues are not in Persia and unfortunately they are not in a position to come here either. I am asking Abdulrahim if you might be willing to travel to Paris to meet with them."

"Travel to Paris? To trade stamps?"

"Yes. I know it would be a long and expensive journey. My friends would be willing to provide for your travel expenses on the road. This trip would cost you nothing."

"All that way to sell stamps?"

"Paris is lovely in the spring. You have always dreamed of visiting. You told me so."

"Yes. I would, but such a journey..."

"Once you arrive in Paris, we are hoping you could be... flexible... in your schedule. You may have an additional stop before coming home. We believe there will be interest... in your stamps... further west."

My mind was racing at this point to grasp his true meaning. We Freemasons are a secret society and so it is common to say one thing but mean something entirely different. The west could only mean England or America, but why would he ask me to go to Paris if his real intent was for me to travel to America?

"I see" I said still quite unsure, but this seemed to reassure my friend for his entire demeanor changed. He seemed much more relaxed now.

"I'm so happy you catch my meaning Abdulrahim. My friends in Paris would like to examine you.. and your collection of course, then they will introduce you to someone who will take you to the real.. uh buyer. Do you understand?"

"Yes" I lied. "Your friends want to fund an expedition to Paris. If they are satisfied with me ... and my collection... then they will introduce me to a representative of a third party who will take me to the ... buyer ... who would like to negotiate with me ... to purchase my stamps."

"Yes! Bravo!" Jean-Baptist was visibly elated with my answer.

So obviously my trip had nothing to do with stamps, but who would want to meet me badly enough to pay for my travel costs to Paris? My mind was racing with the logistics of such a trip. It was not a thing to consider lightly.

"I will need to make arrangements for someone to look after my shop. Provision a caravan... This is quite unexpected. I can't promise anything until I think this through."

"But you will consider it, yes? It is very important."

"Certainly. I will think about it."

Jean-Baptiste suddenly stood and offered his hand. I took it with the secret grip which is our custom in The Freemasons.

We made small talk as I accompanied him to the front of the shop and in moments he was gone, leaving me to process what had just happened.

I truly was one of the foremost stamp collectors in all of the middle east and my book had found buyers far outside of Persia, but the reason for this trip could only be related to my other work.

A few years before this visit I played a small part in the overthrow of our previous Shah, our constitutional revolution.

We Persians believe that our sovereigns govern with the consent of the people. By 1906 we had suffered long under a Shah that was more interested in lining his own pockets than the well-being of his people. That year I founded an organization called the Fatemieh Society to support the creation of a constitution for the Persian people and a parliament to check the power of our Shah. You could call our society a militia of sorts. We were not as well trained or as well armed as the Cossack Brigade, but we made up for that with our passion.

My friend Sattar Khan and his army of supporters from Tabriz did so much more than my small company of soldiers here in Tehran, but I'm happy to say that together we convinced Mozzafaredin Shah to sign the constitution later that year.

As fate would have it, the Shah was assaainated the following year and his son Mohammad Ali Qajar became the Shah. The years since then have been challenging, mainly due to interference from the Russians and the new Shah's refusal to abide by his father's agreements... but again, I get ahead of myself.

"Who was the Frenchman Uncle?"

I turned to see my assistant Khalil standing a few meters away. He was a cousin to my wife Farrokh Lagha, but had become close to me over the years.

"A colleague of mine from the lodge" I replied.

We were alone and Khalil was family, so I felt safe to speak openly. I would not admit to being a Freemason to anyone outside my family or the lodge itself. Even though our organization was more closely aligned with the French, most of my countrymen would consider me an agent of the British simply for being a member, especially since I had spent several months seeking refuge at their embassy and knew most of the staff there personally... but again I am getting ahead.

To complicate matters ever further, many of our members joined the Freemasons in Constantinople as part of the Turkish Grand Lodge and became members of our lodge when they returned home. Recently the Ottomans and Germans were establishing closer ties and the British and French signed a not so secret agreement of support. So being a Freemason was complicated and likely to make everyone suspicious. Best not to talk about it.

"He seemed very nervous to me Uncle."

"Yes Khalil. I believe he was. You are very attentive. You will do well in business."

"Thank you Uncle. You want to see what I found in the Bazaar today?"

Khalil was a bright young man who was constantly exploring new ideas.

"Of course", I said, welcome for the change in subject.

He turned and led me to the rear of the shop to the back room which served as his make-shift kitchen, workshop, and bedroom since he slept in the store.

Some sort of odd machine sat on his workbench. It had many keys that looked like buttons and a piece of paper seemed to be rolled around a rolling pin near the top.

"What do you have here Khalil?"

"It's called a *typewriter* in English. Sorry Uncle. Une machine à écrire."

He translated the name into French for me since my French was significantly better than my English. In the past few years Khalil had become fluent in both, without any formal training. He was truly amazing with languages.

"Let me demonstrate!"

He placed his fingers on the buttons and pecked at them as a bird would peck at their food. As he did the rolling pin seemed to shift from right to left and as if by magic, letters were marked on the paper.

"Isn't it wonderful ? This machine is for English, but I heard from the seller that they are available for French as well."

"I see. Do you know if they have one for Persian?" I asked.

"I don't know Uncle, but I can invent one if not! You know what would really be valuable is a delete key. When you make a mistake, if you could type delete and erase the previous character."

"Erase a character that is already printed? How would you do that?"

"Print over it with white ink! Then you can type on top of that. We'll be rich!"

Khalil was indeed a mechanical genius. I had no doubt that he would one day invent some important new device that would change the world.

"Perhaps we will buy a French ... typewriter ... when we are in Paris."

"We're going to Paris?"

"It is possible. My friend has invited me to prepare a trip early next year."

"And I would accompany you?"

"Of course Khalil. If I make the trip I will need your language skills along the way."

In addition to French and English, Khalil had picked up a working knowledge of Russian, Arabic, and the Turkish dialect used in Azerbaijan. I did not know at the time how I would make such a long journey, but I knew that with Khalil by my side, I had a much better chance of success.

"Does Auntie Farrokh Lagha know? Will she and Abbas join us on the trip?"

Mention of my wife and oldest son brought me back to reality.

"No Khalil. She does not know and I would never risk taking them on such a journey. You understand no matter which route we choose, we may find ourselves in danger along the way."

"I understand Uncle, but I am ready for this adventure. No matter what the danger!"

I looked out the front window of my shop and saw the Edifice of the Sun across the way, with all of its intricate tile and ornate windows. The actual sun was beginning to dip below the twin towers casting a shadow on the front of my shop. This time of year the days and nights are equally long, so I knew it was nearing time to close for the day. The towers were the tallest structure in Tehran when built and still dominate the skyline of the neighborhood into your time dear reader.

Nasser Al-Din Shah enjoyed the panoramic view of the city from the top of the towers in the nineteenth century. It is also said in my time that his grandson Mohammad Ali Shah's men use the high perch to keep an eye on its citizens. I have seen the sunlight glinting off of a telescope lens from time to time, so I believe there is some foundation to the rumor.

I left Khalil to close up shop for the night and prepared to ride home, not on a horse or even in a carriage as I used to do, but on my bicycle, one of the few in all of Persia. As I said, Khalil is a mechanical genius. He saw photographs of bicycles in a book from France and would not stop until he had constructed one of his own design.

Khalil is also too truthful for his own good. He mentioned to me that I was becoming quite plump and that I should consider riding his contraption for exercise. I am a large man, more than six feet tall using the English system, and I had put on a few dozen pounds after my militia broke up, but I wouldn't use the word plump exactly.

In my defense, prosperity and high social status have their downsides. My wife hired a most talented cook for our home and we were constantly invited to parties. It is considered impolite to turn down food at these events! And I am a most polite person… until I choose not to be.

So every day that summer I pedaled half a mile from my shop to my home in the Ilchi Garden. I was fortunate to have a home in such a nice neighborhood. The owner was Persia's envoy to Britain. He owned many houses and he allowed my family to live in this house for a very reasonable rent. Zero cost was very reasonable in my opinion. This was yet another reason that people assumed I had a relationship with the British. That and the location of the house.

Our neighbors were mostly foreigners. The British Embassy was right next door and the other legations not too far away. In your time dear reader, my former home is now part of the Tehran Bazaar. If you guess that this does not please me, you are correct, but as I said before, I am unable to do anything about this in my current situation.

Summers in Persia are hot. Most of the wealthy people in my neighborhood have homes in the mountains, where the temperature is mild. They were absent for most of the summer, but now they had returned and the streets were pulsing with people. As I rode I saw many of them catching up with mutual friends on the street corners. They couldn't miss me gliding down the street with my flowing robes. Each group pointed at me and laughed or some shouted out crude comments that I shall not share with you.

The heat is not the only challenge in summer. Even the posh streets of the city were usually full of the dust that is kicked up by the horses and mules. So I was pleasantly surprised by the light breeze and fresh, clean air that day as I made my way home. It was the first sign that summer was giving way to fall. Soon the mountains just outside of Tehran would be covered with snow once again.

When I reached the edge of the garden, I dismounted from the bike and walked beside it for the last few steps. Walking through the garden was always my favorite part of the day. There were Cypress, Pomegranate, and Plane trees interspersed with vegetables and melons. The fragrance was intoxicating and in the late afternoon sun the colors were hypnotic.

No matter how much stress I had felt from my work, by the time I reached my front gate I felt like the luckiest man on earth with not a care in this world.

I leaned the bike against the wall of the inner compound wall and entered the house to find two of my children playing backgammon on the carpet. Hassan was five that year and very energetic. His brother Ali who was four years his elder was teaching him to play on a set given to me by my father. From the look on his face, Hassan was not doing very well. He inherited a bit of my bad temper. I sometimes had to fight back my laughter when he lost his because he reminded me of myself so long ago.

My oldest son Abbas was curled up in a chair reading a book as usual. He was a dedicated student. A father could not hope for a better first born.

"*Salaam! Chetori* Kashani" My wife called to me.

It may seem odd to you dear reader that my wife would call me by my family name, but that was our custom.

"*Merci!* I am well *Khanoum.*"

She was holding our youngest child Mehdi but upon seeing me handed him off to the nanny and crossed the room.

"Come in and sit down. I suppose you rode that dangerous contraption again today?"

"Yes *Khanoum.* It's good exercise. You want your husband strong and fit, yes?"

"I want to keep my husband safe and clean! I saw the scrapes on your arm where you fell last week. Don't think you can keep things from me. I know everything that happens under this roof."

"Do you know how beautiful you are when you are angry Farrokh Lagha?"

"Stop trying to change the subject."

"Yes dear. Is dinner ready? I have worked up a huge appetite. Is that *Ghormeh Sabzi* I smell?"

"When has dinner ever not been ready for the Prince of *Bagh Ilichi* when he returns home from work? Are you insinuating I am not a good wife? You want another? I am not enough?"

I turned and looked at my boys. Each had a sympathetic look on their face as if to say 'we know father. We have been suffering all afternoon.'

"I have an announcement to make before we eat" I said before Farrokh Lagha could continue. "In the spring Khalil and I will likely be making a long journey to buy and sell stamps."

"A long journey Agha Joon?" Abbas asked. "Can I come with you?"

"Where are you going Agha Joon?" Ali joined in. "Can I come too?"

"You are not old enough" Abbas replied.

"I am only two years younger than you!"

"Boys! Boys! I am sorry, but neither of you can come on this trip. You both have studies and I will be gone for a long time. It will take me many weeks to reach Paris."

The words were out of my mouth before I realized it.

"Paris!" Farrokh Lagha shouted. "Paris? Did you fall again on that bicycle and hit your head? You saw the news that the Germans appear to be preparing for war?"

I turned to Farrokh Lagha raised a hand to stop her tirade.

"I heard that rumor, but Jean-Baptiste assures me that Paris is much safer today than Tehran was these past few years. Do you not remember the street fighting? The Cossack Brigades? The cannon firing on our parliament?"

"That was different and you know it. You were protecting our home and country from *Farangi*! Not traipsing across Europe to trade your *little pieces of paper*!"

My wife did not share my enthusiasm for stamps.

"We have plenty of time to discuss this topic since I have not yet made up my mind. It will be my decision however, so let's have no further discussion tonight. I am hungry."

I looked into my Wife's eyes and saw the fear, but I also saw the love and concern. I knew she was only worried about me. She was also a woman who knew her place in society. She would accept my decision, but that didn't mean she would like it.

"Go wash up! All of you! Dinner is getting cold."

A few weeks after the visit from Jean-Baptiste, another interesting man wandered in to my shop, asking about my stamps. A very unusual individual indeed.

He was short and broad, with a high forehead, a blonde mustache, and blue eyes that were constantly looking upward. He was a foreigner, but dressed like a Persian with traditional robes and a black turban.

"You must be Sayed Abdulrahim Kashani!" he said in Persian with a broad smile.

When he spoke, our language flowed out of his mouth like a native. There was the slightest hint of an accent, but only a hint. Unless you got close, you would never suspect he was not Persian.

He used my honorific title Sayed, which denotes a descendant of the prophet Muhammad. As I said before, I am not a religious man, so this title was not one I used for myself. In fact, our family always wondered how my father and grandfather could be Sayed, when my great grandfather was not. If we were descendants, then why wasn't he?

"I am Abdulrahim" I said. "You are?"

"I have read your book on stamp collecting and hope to discuss a trade."

He did not answer my question so I looked closer at his face and features. Even though he was wearing a turban, his light complexion and blonde mustache made me think he must be Scandinavian or perhaps German.

"You are a collector as well?" I asked.

"Not on your level Sayed Kashani" he replied as he stepped closer. "Is there a place where we might speak privately?"

He continued to survey the store but in his strange way of looking up towards the ceiling.

I led him back into the private area and asked him to sit while I went into the back room to find Khalil and the part of my stamp collection that I kept at the store. They were not the best part of my collection, but the ones I would be willing to trade if the occasion arose.

"Khalil, I need you to make tea for our guest, but take your time, there is no rush."

"Yes uncle. We have a visitor?"

"Yes."

Then I had an idea.

"Khalil, do you by chance know any German or Swedish?"

"A little German uncle. *Ein Bisschen.*"

"Good. When the tea is ready I'd like you to pour it for us. And please spill a little on purpose outside his cup. Tell him you are sorry in German. Can you do that?"

"Yes Uncle. I know that phrase."

"Good"

I stopped briefly at the door and observed the man for a moment. I had a strange feeling about him. He had the bearing of a military officer but the look of a politician or even an actor. And though I am not a good judge, I believe most women would find him handsome.

I considered for a moment that he might be Russian, but I have heard Persian spoken by Russians and their accent was very different.

Given that Tehran was still in the Russian Sphere of influence and they were not very friendly with Germany, it would be very strange indeed to see a German military officer wandering the streets of Tehran. Of course this in and of itself might explain his attire.

I returned to the seating area and opened my stock book on the table in front of the visitor.

"My assistant is preparing some tea for us. I am afraid the best pieces of my collection are stored at my home, but I do have some interesting stamps here."

He leaned forward in his chair to examine my collection.

"I'm sorry, but you never gave me your name?"

"My friends call me Will."

I knew a man called William at the British Legation who went by Will, but this man pronounced it more like 'Vill'.

He began scanning the pages of my catalogue with real interest, pausing now and again at a rare example and passing by the more common pieces. When he got to the Penny Black he stopped and looked up at me.

"You have a Penny Black?"

It was famous as the first stamp ever issued in Britain. A must have for any serious collector.

"It is as you can see not a very good specimen. It has been cancelled. I have a much better one at home which was never used."

"You seem to have many French and British stamps."

The way he said it sounded like an accusation.

"I am fortunate to have many foreigners as customers. Given the location of my shop I supply paper and supplies to many of the foreign embassies and the Persian government. Once people learn that I collect stamps, they seem to go out of their way to give me their envelopes from home."

"The entire envelope?"

"Yes. In the beginning they would try to remove the stamp themselves or cut off the postage, but they did such a poor job I begged them to let me do it."

"Interesting" he said. "I don't suppose you keep these envelopes after you remove the stamps?"

I thought it an odd question, but then he was an odd man.

"My assistant Khalil is working on a process to break down the used envelopes into a pulp in order to make new paper. So he has preserved many of them for his testing."

"I see. How many years have you been collecting?"

"Since 1906, so eight years."

"I don't suppose Sir George Barclay or Sir Walter Townley have contributed to your collection?"

The mention of the current and former British Ambassadors to Persia crossed the line for me. Now I was sure I must be careful.

"In fact Sir George was the source of my best Penny Black and a few American stamps you will see later in this book."

Khalil's timing could not be better. He appeared with the tea service and began to pour. If I hadn't asked him to do it, I never would have known he had spilled the tea on purpose.

"*Es tut mir Leid!*" Khalil said as if it were the most natural thing to say in this situation.

"*Kein Problem*" the visitor replied as he wiped the spill with his napkin, but then he stopped in mid-wipe and sat back in his chair laughing softly.

"Well done. Well done. Your assistant is clever indeed. I should never have underestimated you Sayed Kashani. Forgive me. Perhaps the direct approach will be better."

I motioned for Khalil to leave us and closed the stock book now that it was obvious it was not his true purpose.

"Wilhelm Wassmuss at your service" he said finally after a long pause. "My friends call me Will" he said with a warm smile. "I have recently come to Tehran from Bushehr on the Persian Gulf. Along the way I spent some time with a relative of yours, Ayatollah Abol-Ghasem Kashani. He suggested that I contact you when I arrive in Tehran and that ask about your stamps."

I never would have guessed my cousin Abol-Ghasem was the one who sent this man or that my cousin had ever spoken with a German.

"Thank you" I replied. "You will find the truth works best with me mister Wassmuss. It does not matter to me where you are from. You are all foreigners to us."

I paused to let that sink in.

"Ayatollah Kashani made it clear that he also did not care for *Farangi*, but he did quote a verse from The *Arthashastra* about the enemy of mine enemy."

"Is my friend" I completed the quote.

I was not as learned as my dear cousin, but I could see how he would be happy to use the Germans to get revenge on the British. Since oil was discovered in 1908, my cousin the Ayatollah had been very vocal about how little Persia received from the concessions.

"You wanted to see me, so I assume there is something you want?"

"I was told you were very direct. That's good. I can work with that."

I waited for him to continue for what seemed to me a long while.

"I understand you are planning a trip next spring to Paris."

How a perfect stranger knew this was beyond me, but by this time most of my close friends were aware.

"I am considering it. I have been invited to meet with a fellow collector. I am afraid it is difficult to expand my collection in my own back yard."

"Yes. I can imagine. That reminds me. I have something for you."

He pulled a small envelope from the sleeves of this robe and placed it on the table in front of me.

"A gift Sayed... with no strings attached as they say."

I picked up the envelope and opened the flap, for it was not sealed. Inside I saw twenty or thirty unused stamps.

"Please! Have a look."

I removed pair of tweezers from their storage compartment in the stock book and carefully emptied the new specimens out the envelope and onto the cover. I turned them all face up using the tweezers so I would not harm them. Most of the stamps appeared to be from Germany, Austria-Hungary, and Italy.

"I wanted to ... balance your collection so to speak. They are not very valuable, but I didn't think you would have many of these specimens."

The monetary value of individual stamps in a collection is not generally the point. Often it is more important to have at least one example from every country. Stamps from an exotic country like China or Japan were also desirable. His gift had just added three new countries to my collection.

"I am happy they please you" he said.

I was never very good at hiding my thoughts. Farrokh Lagha said that my face was an open book. She could read every detail.

"Thank you" I replied. "I do appreciate these. Let me at least pay you for their face value."

"No, no I could not accept. As I said, they are a gift."

I continued to examine the details of the stamps on the table before me and wished that my magnifying glass was near, but there would be plenty of time for that later.

"Do you know the route you would take to Paris?"

"Honestly I had not considered this yet. I assumed a ship from some port on the Mediterranean to Marseilles then by train to Paris."

"The Orient Express from Constantinople to Paris would suit a man of your status."

"Ah yes. That would be quite nice" I said.

Jean-Baptiste had travelled out on this rail line and could not stop talking about the quality of their service.

"Perhaps there is also a challenge getting to Constantinople now? The Ottomans and Russians are constantly battling along this frontier."

"True, but the route from Tabriz to Van is still open. The fighting is far to the north. Once you cross into Ottoman Empire there is rail service from Van to Constantinople as well."

I considered this for a moment. I had friends in Tabriz and the Russian presence there had diminished somewhat since the massacres in 1911. I also liked the idea of spending some time in Constantinople. There was still a large Persian community there and my connections with the Freemason lodge would open a few doors if necessary.

"Would you be willing to travel through Constantinople Sayed?"

"It seems a little farther north than necessary, but if there is rail service, it may be worth the detour."

"Excellent! In fact I am travelling there myself next spring. Would you allow me to introduce you to some friends when we are there?"

"When we are there?"

"You know Sayed... if we cross the frontier from Tabriz to Van together, I can help you with any problems you might encounter at the Ottoman border. My German passport would be very helpful I believe."

"Perhaps you are correct" I said.

"Wonderful. It is settled. We will meet in Tabriz next spring and I will provide you safe passage to Constantinople. I will be in touch soon to arrange the details."

A few moments prior I had not truly decided to go to Paris, let alone planned how I would get there. Now it seemed I had just committed to becoming the travelling companion of a German stranger. I didn't trust this man and I wasn't sure if I would go along with this plan, but much could happen before the spring.

He stood and reached out to shake my hand in the western style. I got the feeling he had accomplished everything he wanted and now was anxious to leave before I could change my mind.

As he left the shop and closed the door I began to wonder if this trip could get any stranger.

Khalil approached and brought me out of my thoughts.

"Why do you think he was so interested in the used envelopes?" asked Khalil.

It took a moment to recall that part of the conversation and then it came to me.

"The return addresses" I said. "He wants to know who is corresponding with the British legation."

"But why Uncle? They do not give us the letters, only the envelopes."

"Sometimes simply knowing that two people are corresponding with each other is helpful for spies."

"Wilhelm is a spy?"

"Most certainly. We must be very careful with him Khalil.

"But he seems like such a gentleman?"

"That is his talent. He is like an actor in a play. He is able to take on the role of any character and you will swear that this is who he really is. He is very dangerous Khalil. We must be very careful."

"Will we go with him to Constantinople?"

"You were listening?"

"Of course Uncle. I would never leave you alone with a stranger without keeping watch."

I smiled. I was so much bigger and stronger than Khalil. He was taller than me but thin like a rail. I had years of experience as a soldier and the skills to protect myself from most any threat. Khalil was still in school when the Russians bombed our parliament and Tehran was in chaos so he did not serve in my militia. Still, there was confidence in his voice. Given his intellect, I would never underestimate his ability to help.

"I need to investigate our new German acquaintance" I said looking at the stamps he gave me. "Too many people in Persia are willing to assign guilt by association, so best not to tell anyone what was said here today."

"Of course Uncle. I understand."

That evening I retired early to bed and told my wife of the visit but not of my sense that he was a spy. It is a husband's burden to worry about the minor details of life.

"You told him you will make the trip?" she asked.

"Not exactly" I replied. "He assumed. I am still undecided."

"You should go" she ventured.

I turned and looked at her in disbelief.

"You want me to go on this trip?"

"I do not *want* you to go, but I also do not want to watch you completely lose the passion for life that you once had. You haven't been happy since the end of the revolution."

"I have my shop. I make a good living for us."

"You are a good provider and a good husband, but you can not tell me that you are content to mind a shop for the rest of your life. You are a leader of men. I still don't understand why you turned down the seat in Parliament."

"I am far too honest to be successful in politics. You know that."

"From what I hear in the market, we need honest men to clean up the mess the others have made."

In early November the days were noticeably shorter and the nights were getting cold. That month we were invited to a wedding celebration for the eldest son of the new Minister of Finance. It was a formal affair and due to his high office, many of the foreign envoys to Persia attended as well.

It was for this reason I found myself in a conversation with the British ambassador Sir Walter Townley over a glass of whiskey that he called 'Single Malt'. I was not accustomed to strong spirit. It was forbidden by the Quran, but these are the sacrifices one must make in social situations.

"This whiskey is from the highlands of Scotland Sayed. The distilleries along the river Spey finish their scotch in Sherry casks from Spain and use very little peat in the malting process, so the finish is quite smooth. Just smell it."

With that he placed his nose deeply in the glass and inhaled. The expression on his face was pure bliss.

Even though Sir Walter was speaking to me in French, the terms he used might as well have been in Greek or Russian. I followed his lead though and understood his reaction. The fragrance seemed sweet, but still with the power of the alcohol. I could get intoxicated from only the fumes.

Sir Walter took a sip. Again I followed his lead, but this time it took all of my strength not to choke or spit out the whiskey. I never drank anything so powerful.

Sir Walter saw the look on my face and laughed.

"Slowly Sayed. It takes some getting used to I know. Let it swirl in your mouth before swallowing next time."

I took another sip and this time I did not choke, but I am sure that is because my mouth had been numbed by the initial experience.

We continued in companionable silence, he enjoying the scotch and me doing my best to survive. Eventually I decided to just enjoy the fragrance.

"Sayed, there is something I would like to ask you if I may."

"Of course Sir Walter. I am at your service."

"I ask only because I know you see many different kinds of people in your shop. I am wondering if any persons of the Germanic persuasion might have been in. There is an agent provocateur operating in the south and there have been reports of him in Tehran."

Thoughts of the telescope on the tower across from my shop came to mind and I began to wonder if Sir Walter already knew the answer to this question. Did the Shah share his surveillance with the British?

"A German spy in Tehran Sir Walter? I have heard no talk of that myself."

My answer was completely truthful. I had not heard any talk until now and he did not ask if I had seen him myself...

"He is a tricky character. He dresses like a Persian and even speaks Persian like a native I am told."

"Would it not be dangerous for him here? What do our Russian friends say?"

"Friends? Please Sayed. You can be frank with me. I have never met a Russian I could trust, let alone one I would call a friend."

This was the first time I had ever heard a British official speak so openly and wondered how much whiskey Sir Walter had consumed.

"What would you have me do if I see or hear about this German spy Sir Walter?"

"Get word to me that you have located a rather rare stamp that I might be interested in and I will send for you."

"Of course Sir Walter."

"Thank you Sayed. Might I also enquire of your cousin, the Ayatollah?"

Now I was sure the Ambassador knew more than he was saying.

"I have not seen or heard from Abol-Ghasem in years. We chose very different paths in life and he stopped trying to brainwash me years ago."

To emphasize my point I raised my glass of whiskey to toast Sir Walter who immediately seemed to understand the meaning.

Jean-Baptiste approached and saved me from further conversation along these lines. The three of us made small talk until Sir Walter said his farewell and retired for the evening leaving his bottle on the table behind him. When we were alone Jean-Baptiste led me to an even more remote corner of the room.

"Your preparations are in progress for Paris?"

"Yes. I was actually hoping I would see you here this evening. I am thinking to travel first to Tabriz and then on to Constantinople. From there a ship to Marseilles or the Orient Express."

"Constantinople?" Jean-Baptiste was visibly shaken. "That is unfortunate."

"Really?" I said. "So what do you recommend?"

"I was thinking to accompany you to Beirut. A lovely city. I miss it greatly. From there you could take a French ship to Marseilles, but now that you mention it, a friendly Persian in Constantinople next spring could be a very useful asset."

"Asset?"

"Forgive me. I misspoke. Give me some time to work out the details Abdulrahim. I think your plan of visiting Constantinople may be very timely. How is your Turkish Sayed?"

"I have no fluency in Turkish, but Khalil will be with me."

"Ah yes. Splendid! I should have guessed you would travel with Khalil. A fine fellow. You know he repaired my pocket watch for me last week."

"I am not surprised. My father is a watch maker and his father before him. Khalil studied with them before he came to work with me."

"So maybe you should be called Sayed Abdulrahim *Saati*."

"Your Persian is getting better Jean-Baptiste. Mehdi the Watch Maker works for my father but Abdulrahim *Tambri* would fit better for me, don't you think?"

"You are much more than a mere 'Stamp Seller' if I translate that correctly Sayed. Much more."

"I am happy to be known as Abdulrahim from Kashan. Even though I was not born there, my family has a long history in that city."

"Speaking of names, I have heard that your Parliament will create a registration office for birth and death certificates. Soon every Persian will be required to take a formal family name."

"Is that so? Why?"

"Taxes of course! How can a government know if the districts are collecting the right amount of tax when you don't have an accurate count of the population?"

To me it was not a bad idea. It would also help ensure proper representation in the Majlis.

Our host, the Finance Minister approached along with my friend Ali Ladjevardi and ended our discussion on names. I hastily withdrew my glass of whiskey into the sleeves of my robe where the host would not see it.

"Are you enjoying yourselves my friends?"

"Yes. Certainly ! Congratulations Minister on your son's wedding. You must be very pleased with the match."

"The girl is from a good family and my son is happy, so that is all I can hope for! Praise be to Allah."

"Praise Allah the merciful" Ali and I both repeated without

much fervor.

"And is your cabinet job getting any easier these days?" I asked but the topic seemed to instantly dampen his mood.

"It has been two years since the Russians dismissed the American William Shuster as Treasurer General of Persia, we are only now restoring normalcy to the office."

In my opinion, 'normalcy' in our government finance group was not acceptable. Payments to anyone with a connection for no value to the people was not a desirable state, but since we were at a party hosted by the finance Minister, I decided to keep my opinions to myself.

My good friend Ali Ladjevardi was not so tactful.

"I met Shuster Agha several times when he was in Persia and found him to be a most reputable man. I do not believe any of the rumors that were spread about him on his departure. And there is of course the matter of how the Russians are able to dismiss a Persian Official who was selected by our parliament."

"Of course my friend. I did not intend to demean that gentleman's good name, but he was very much an American, naïve in so many ways. He thought that he could change generations of tradition overnight, just because it was the right thing to do."

I wondered if the Finance Minister realized just how foolish that sounded coming out of his mouth. I quickly shifted my attention to Ali and changed the subject.

"Business is good Ali? I hear you now have a third company?"

"That is our burden Sayed, is it not? To grow our business and expand when possible. That is the way of nature after all. How tall does a tree grow?"

"As tall as it can?" answered Jean-Baptiste.

"*Exactement Monsieur! Exactement!*"

Our host engaged in gossip about the court for a while and

then moved on to the next group of guests as a good host is wont to do. Jean-Baptiste saw an old friend across the room and took his leave shortly thereafter leaving me alone with Ali.

"Do you intend to drink your whiskey or keep it hidden up your sleeve for the remainder of the evening?"

"You don't miss much do you Ali?"

"You don't survive in business if you do" he replied.

I took one last sniff of the aroma and deftly placed the glass out of view on a nearby table.

"I wonder if you might make a few connections for me when you are on your journey my friend. I will make it worth your effort."

"Please Ali. How many years have we known each other? I would be happy to help in any way I can. Of course one day, if I have a daughter and your demands on this trip are too great…"

I did not need to finish the thought. We had often spoken of joining our families when the opportunity was right. Ali was closer to me than my own brothers.

"I have been told your cousin Abol-Ghasem is in Tehran. My brother saw him at prayers last Friday. Are you aware?"

"I know only that Sir Walter asked about him this evening. Did your bother say more?"

"It seems Abol-Ghasem has become very passionate in his opposition to the Anglo-Persian Oil Company. He has aroused the interest of the Imams in the south and is creating a groundswell of support to rescind the concessions. There are even rumors that the extremists intend to blow up the refinery at Abadan."

"The British would never stand for that" I said in disbelief. "They need the oil for their war ships. Churchill's reputation is on the line."

"And Churchill has higher aspirations than running the Admiralty. He will not allow an uprising in the south."

This new revelation brought all of the pieces into place. I deftly reached for the hidden glass of whiskey and downed its contents in one shot then located the bottle Sir Walter had left behind on the table not far away.

"My dear Ali Ladjevardi, let me introduce you to my new friend from the Scottish Highlands, Mister Macallan. He is only 18 years old, but very mature for his age."

It was no surprise when the following morning my learned cousin appeared at my door in Bagh Ilichi.

"The peace of Allah protect you cousin" he said as I opened the door.

It was mid-morning on a school day so my older boys were away and Farrokh Lagha was instructing the cook on the menu for tonight so she could make her trip to the market. I was not feeling well this morning and decided to leave the store to Khalil.

"I called at your shop but Khalil said you were unwell. I hope it is nothing serious?"

I was not about to tell my cousin the Ayatollah of my experience with single malt whiskey. The subtleties of aging eighteen years in oak barrels and the sherry cask finish would be lost on Abol-Ghasem like pearls before swine. This quote I learned from Jean-Baptiste who tells me it is from the 'other' bible. Another item I did not plan to share.

"I am fine. It must be the change in the weather. It is getting cold here in the North Cousin. Please come in."

He raised his hand and motioned towards the garden. "I think it may be much better if we spoke in the garden. It is such a beautiful place after all."

I couldn't tell if he was worried about prying eyes and ears from our servants or if he did not want to bring trouble into my house. Of course it could be that our secular home was not suitable for a holy man such as himself.

I followed him in to the garden and we strolled past the now empty vegetable beds to a seating area among the Cypress trees.

"Did you truly send Wilhelm Wassmuss to see me cousin?"

I was not in the mood for more small talk after an evening full of polite conversation.

"I know you to be an open minded man who will stand on the side of justice even when the politics of a matter are contrary to the status quo."

My learned cousin studied literature, logic, and semantics in seminary and went on to receive his Jurisprudence degree when he was twenty five. A simple 'yes' was not his style.

"Your faith in me brings me honor, but I am a simple shop keeper."

"Did you not lead a company of fifty soldiers against an unjust Shah? Did you not sit in protest at the Ottoman Embassy in order to create support for a change in the policy of your sovereign? Did you not publish a newspaper to advocate for change?"

His logic was unassailable as I should have expected, but in my heart I knew there were big differences between the two of us.

"It's true, I have done my part to ensure our people are represented" I offered. "I hope we can change things peaceably. But I am not the one fomenting mayhem and unrest of the uneducated tribes in the south with the intent to destroy an oil refinery."

He nodded his head and pursed his lips to acknowledge my point before speaking again as if trying to decide which direction to go.

"I have counseled against these violent acts unless we see there is no other way forward. I will try to change things through the courts and through political persuasion if it is possible."

"But the 'enemy of thy enemy' may not be the right partner for this effort either Cousin. The Germans are not without their faults."

"I do not trust them either Sayed, but they are a convenient partner in our class struggle against the rule of the Bourgeoisie in this country. The elite Persians are lining their purses on the backs of the poor and the British are taking an even larger share of our oil without just compensation. We must not tolerate this."

I had heard that communism had established a foothold in our country but I had no idea my own relative was part of that movement. I did not have the strength this morning to argue on the side of democracy and capitalism with a true believer. I just wanted to go back into the house to lie down for a while.

"What would you ask of me Abol-Ghasem? How may I be of service?"

"Did you promise Wassmuss that you would travel with him to Constantinople?"

"I may have led him to believe this, but certainly did not give my word."

"That is what I thought. Will you promise me?"

"To travel with him to Constantinople? Are you sure that is all you wish me to do?"

"No, you are correct. There is more. Wilhelm will introduce you to friends once you arrive. Please stay in Constantinople as long as they require before moving on to Paris."

He then handed me a small book with a worn leather cover.

"This is a code book. The first few pages will explain how to encode and decode messages."

"This is excessive don't you think?"

"The Shah and the Russians monitor the telegraph lines and often read the mail as well."

"I am not a spy."

"And I am not asking you to spy. I am simply asking you to report to me from Tabriz, Constantinople, and Paris."

"Exactly what should I report?"

"Anything you think I would want to know. I trust your judgment. Send a telegram to Farrokh Lagha when you arrive in a new town to let her know you are safe. Include a short status for me at the end. Post letters for more lengthy messages. I am not asking you to betray your country or even your principles. It is because I do not trust the Germans that I want your reports. I need to know they are keeping their end of the bargain."

"And what might that bargain be?"

"I think it is best that you do not know the details."

"On that I think we can agree."

I was eager for the conversation to be over and lie down for a while so I needed to change the subject.

"Would you like to come in for some tea or a light meal cousin?"

"Thank you for your kindness Sayed, but I must be going. I will leave for *Qom* tomorrow morning. You can send me a telegram in care of the Mosque in Qom when you start on your journey."

He stood and bid me farewell. It was the last time I would see him until my return journey from Paris.

TABRIZ

April 28, 1914

K halil and I prepared through the winter to make our journey, fretting over what to take and what to leave behind. I found someone to look after my business and enlisted the help of Ali Ladjevardi to look in and audit the books. One can never be too careful.

There was no rail service yet between Tehran and Tabriz, so we prepared to make the first leg in the traditional way, by caravan. I bought a horse to ride and a pair of pack mules to carry our gear. Khalil decided to ride his bicycle. I hired two porters to travel with us and made sure that everyone had a rifle for protection. Even in times of peace, the roads are rife with thieves.

We had planned to depart a week after *Nowruz*, our new year celebration. The Persian year begins on March 21 of the western calendar, when the day and night are equal length and spring has just begun. Now I ask you dear reader, isn't this a much better choice for the first day of the year than some dark day in the midst of winter?

Nowruz is the most important festival for us Persians. It is a secular event, a time for families to celebrate and give thanks for another good year. It's also a time to look forward to the year ahead. For several days we feast on special dishes and watch traditional dances. I had much to be thankful for and there was simply no possibility that I would start my trip before this holiday was over. Besides, Khalil and I needed to pack on a few pounds for the road.

Unfortunately Khalil fell ill the day after Nowruz and it took almost a month for him to recover. We left Tehran near the end of April. That one month delay changed everything as you dear reader will discover.

On a good day we made twenty miles and on a bad day only ten. The four hundred mile journey north to Tabriz required almost four weeks all told. Along the well-travelled route there were way-stations and small villages every ten to twelve miles providing food and water. When we reached a larger village, we shared a room at an inn, but many nights we slept in our tents just off the road, taking turns keeping watch until the following day. With four armed men, we had no trouble.

We arrived in Tabriz in the middle of May and found lodging at a boarding house in the heart of the city with stables for our animals. Once we were settled in, I sent the requisite telegrams to my wife and illustrious cousin Abol-Ghasem. So far the journey was going well.

So it was that on our first full day in Tabriz Khalil and I set out for the home of Haji Mehdi Kuzeh Kanaani. Haji Mehdi was a rich merchant with shops in the Bazaar and a fervent supporter of democracy. A fellow Freemason in Tehran suggested that Mehdi's home was the best place to begin my search for my friend Sattar Khan. It was a gathering place for everyone associated with the Constitutional Revolution.

"Uncle, are you sure this is the house of a merchant? It looks like the palace of a prince!"

The front façade of the building was grand indeed, with ornate columns supporting arches two stories tall and stained glass windows adorning the entire second floor. I was confident we had the right place though so we proceeded to the front door where we were greeted by a servant.

"I am Abdulrahim Kashani from the Sadat Fatima Society of Tehran. This is my nephew Khalil Redjaian."

"Sayed Kashani!" a voice called from within the mansion.

I looked past the servant to see a well-dressed man standing at the top of a grand staircase. On further inspection I saw there were two sets of steps covered in marble. The banisters were made of the most intricate wrought iron. It truly was a home fit for a prince.

"I am Mehdi Kanaani. Welcome to my home. Sattar Khan has told me all about you."

He continued down the stairs and met us at the bottom.

"Haji Mehdi Agha, it is a pleasure. Let me introduce my nephew Khalil Redjaian."

There was something about this man. The force of his personality. He seemed to be more alive, more present than most people. He had the most intense look in his eyes like they could see things others could not.

"Of course Abdulrahim Agha. I assume you are here to pay a visit to Sattar Khan?"

"Yes, we are hoping to learn where he is staying."

"Here of course! We have the best doctor in Tabriz looking after his leg, but I'm afraid it hasn't improved since he was shot by Yeprem Khan's men in Atabey Park almost three years ago."

"Is he able to receive visitors?" I asked.

"Most certainly. Half of the visitors to my house come to see the great man."

"Without your funding and support for the revolution we

would never have prevailed" I offered.

"And without men like yourself, willing to lay down their lives for their country, my money would have been useless."

"My men played only a minor role in the success..."

"That's not what Sattar Khan told me" he interrupted. "Fifty well-armed, well-trained men made a big difference. He said your men showed discipline under fire and fought as a unit better than the professional soldiers of the Persian Cossack Brigade."

The look on Khalil's face made me feel a bit awkward. I never shared any of the details of that time with him. Now he was looking at me as if I were some kind of hero. It was time to change the subject.

"Is it too early in the day to see Sattar Khan?" I asked.

"Not at all" he replied. "Please follow me."

He smiled and turned back up the stairs. We followed him to the second floor and along the gallery to an intricately carved door that was at least ten feet high. He opened the door and we saw that the light through the stain glass windows gave the room an almost magical feeling. Sattar Khan was reclined on a chaise lounge reading a newspaper with his bandaged leg elevated on several pillows.

"Abdulrahim! What a pleasant surprise! Who is this you have with you?"

Before I could answer, Khalil stepped forward and launched into a speech in what I knew to be Azeri even though I don't understand a word of the language. He and Sattar Khan traded a few comments while I helplessly observed.

"Your nephew speaks fluent Azeri Sayed. You should ask him to teach you."

"I am too old to learn a new language. Besides, I have Khalil."

"He was just suggesting that he can construct a chair with

wheels so Sattar Khan could move more freely about the house" Haji Mehdi translated.

"Yes uncle. Do you think we have time before we continue our trip? I can use rubber wheels like my bicycle so it doesn't damage the beautiful floors of the house."

"Khalil, it took months for you to build the Bike. We only have a week and I am sure Sattar Khan does not want to be bothered..."

"Oh but I do want to be bothered" he said. "I have been stuck in one position, all be it a wonderful place, for two years now."

"Perhaps Khalil could make drawings and show my carpenter and blacksmith what he had in mind" offered Haji Mehdi.

"Please uncle? I would be so honored that a great man like Sattar Khan would use one of my inventions."

"Of course Khalil."

"Sayed Abdulrahim to the rescue once again" Sattar Khan replied with a big smile. "Did your uncle ever tell you he saved Bagher Khan and Haji Ali during one of our most intense battles?"

"My uncle never speaks of the revolution."

"The true heroes never do" said Haji Mehdi.

"What news of the Armenians Keri and Khetcho?" I asked trying to change the subject once again.

"Khetcho took a bullet in the jaw and retired to Switzerland" Sattar replied. "They have good doctors there. Almost as good as my doctor" he added at the last moment although it didn't feel like he meant it.

"Keri has returned to his home town Erzurum. There is some trouble brewing between the Armenians and the Ottomans. You know he found the people responsible for killing Yeprem Khan and made them all pay. I was happy the day I heard the news."

"But wasn't it one of Yeprem Khan's men who shot you?" Khalil asked.

"Yes, but he was just doing his duty and frankly we were in the wrong. It took a couple of years to realize this, but when you fight for democracy and the rule of law, you must also follow the rule of law. When Yeprem was made chief of police for all of Persia, he received legitimate authority to disarm and disperse my company. When we resisted we were breaking the law."

"So you don't hate Yeprem?" Khalil asked.

"Far from it. I loved the man like he was my brother. War is a terrible thing Khalil. I hope you never have to experience it. That is why your uncle never speaks of that time. It is best left to the past."

The great doors to the room opened again and the servant announced another guest.

"Ahmad Kasravi to see you sir."

A tall, slender man in his early twenties walked into the room. He was wearing a western style business suit and wore black rimmed spectacles. Overall he had the look of a college professor ready to give a lecture.

"Ahmad how wonderful to see you again!" Haji Mehdi said. "Let me introduce you to two new friends. Sayed Abdulrahim Kashani from Tehran and his nephew Khalil Redjaian."

"Abdulrahim fought with us in Tehran" Sattar Khan added. "And Khalil is a linguist like you."

With the last comment Ahmad turned to Khalil and asked a question in Azeri to which Khalil replied. I have no idea what the next language was, but again Khalil replied correctly given the look on the professor's face. A third time a question was asked and answered in a language that sounded nothing like the other two.

"How old are your Khalil?" Ahmad asked in Persian.

"Twenty three years professor."

"And how did you know I am a professor?"

"A man as learned as you must be" Khalil replied.

"And yet you understood everything I said in three languages, four counting Persian, and I expect there is more?"

"Only Russian, and English. Oh and French, but everyone speaks French."

Everyone in the room laughed at the last comment.

"So seven languages at twenty three years old and you think this is natural?" Haji Mehdi asked.

"You and Ahmad are both gifted" he continued. "Ahmad is only one year older than you. The only difference between you is that he is studying languages that are older than the Prophet."

"Khalil is also a mechanical genius" Sattar Khan said. "He will design a chair for me with wheels that will give me freedom to move throughout the top floor. I will no longer be an invalid."

"You are the one I saw riding the bicycle into town, yes?" Ahmad asked.

"Yes professor. I built that last year for my uncle."

"You must come to our school and make use of the machine shop we have created for the mechanical engineering classes. Perhaps you can provide the design and they can complete the chair as a class project."

"Ahmad graduated from the American Memorial School, the most prestigious secondary school in all of Persia."

"I still volunteer there from time to time. That reminds me... The carpet in honor of Howard Baskerville is ready. It is spectacular."

"Ah, I was going to ask about that" Haji Mehdi interjected.

"Howard Baskerville?" I asked.

"Yes. He was a teacher at our school and an amazing man. He taught English history and geometry to a mixed class of boys and girls. He even produced and directed a student production of the Merchant of Venice."

"He sounds like an amazing man" Khalil said. "Do you think I can meet him?"

"I'm sorry Khalil" Sattar Khan replied. "He was killed by a sniper while leading a group of a hundred student soldiers against Royalist troops."

"He was only here for two years before his death" Haji Mehdi interjected, "but loved Persia and fought with us for a free country. He was a true hero of the Revolution."

"The carpet bears his image and is a tribute to his sacrifice" Ahmad said.

An awkward silence followed as we thought about the friends they had lost over the past seven years. As I said before, it was a very chaotic time.

"Abdulrahim, you were a newspaper publisher, were you not?" Haji Mehdi said breaking the silence.

"Yes, with the help of Abdul Hossein the King of Historians."

We Persians often give prestigious titles to our politicians and heroes that over time come to replace their given names.

"We called our paper the Divine Mirror" I continued.

"You are a religious man Sayed?" Ahmad asked.

I wasn't prepared for such a direct question. The title Haji meant that Mehdi had made the pilgrimage to Mecca and Mehdi is a religious name, so I didn't know how our host would react to the truth.

"It's OK Abdulrahim" Sattar Khan interjected. "We are among like-minded friends here."

"No. I am not religious" I replied somewhat relieved.

"I enrolled to study as a cleric" Ahmad began, "but in 1910

Haley's comet returned. The preachers all said it was a sign that the twelfth Imam was about to reappear, but I had read about astronomy on my own, and knew the truth that this comet returns every seventy five years like the working of a clock. Then I calculated it has been in our skies twelve times since the beginning of the so-called Occultation. If it is a sign, it has been wrong eleven times before."

"What did the imams say to that?" asked Khalil.

"They tried to reason with me and said I was correct about the previous eleven visits, but that it was exactly because this was the twelfth visit of the comet that it was a sign of the twelfth Imam."

"And?" Haji Mehdi asked.

To that Ahmad pulled out his pocket watch and studied the face.

"And as of now he is three years late."

We all laughed at the comment, although since we were only a few hundred feet from the Jameh Mosque perhaps we should not have laughed so loudly.

"If you printed a paper Abdulrahim, then perhaps you would like to see our printing press?"

This interested me very much and delivered us from further blasphemy.

"I would like that very much. I understand from some of my friends that you also print night letters here."

They were the unsigned pamphlets distributed in the dark of night to influence the common people of the town.

Instead of answering directly, Haji Mehdi extended his hand as if he wanted me to shake it. After a moment I understood and used the expected grip of a Freemason. I was not disappointed. Haji Mehdi and I had yet another thing in common.

"We do print night letters. I can show you the set up we use for those as well."

I looked towards Sattar Khan and could see that he was tiring from the visit. Khalil, Ahmad, and I made our farewells and followed Haji Mehdi to the basement of the home where the press was set up. We talked about publishing and printing for a while but I did not want to impose on our new friend and host any longer.

Our new friend Ahmad seemed of a like mind. I gave Haji Mehdi the details of where we were staying then the three of us said our goodbyes at the door and made our way out of the mansion.

"You must come see me at the school tomorrow and I insist you bring the bicycle for everyone to see" Ahmad said.

"I'd be happy to" Khalil replied. "I'd like to show your engineering students how the wheels are constructed since the design for my chair will be similar."

He gave us directions and bid us farewell.

"That was a very interesting visit uncle. Why did Haji Mehdi shake your hand?"

"Haji Mehdi is a Mason" I answered quietly. "Let's discuss this in our rooms after we eat. I am famished!"

The following morning we rode the bicycle through the streets of Tabriz getting strange looks from the people as we went. Khalil had designed a second seat behind the first so a passenger could ride comfortably while holding on to the driver.

About halfway to the school we saw the Persian Cossack Brigade drilling in a public park. Khalil stopped at a safe distance and we watched them for a while.

"Why are they drilling in a public park Uncle?"

"To intimidate the local population. It is a message to the people. We are here and you will respect us."

"They are very impressive. You fought against them?"

"Yes we did, but they are only human beings. They just have proper training and support. Many of them had no choice but to join."

"What do you mean?"

"The first soldiers in the Persian Cossack Brigade were Muslims from north of Georgia. Russia conquered these lands in their push to the Black sea, but could never completely stop the rebels. So they struck a deal with the Ottomans to take the Muslim people from that region. They forcibly relocated entire villages hundreds of miles."

"But what if they didn't want to move?"

"Have you heard the term 'ethnic cleansing'?"

"No, but it sounds awful."

"The Chechens and other people of that region fought back but eventually they were overwhelmed. Those who escaped to the south joined the Cossack Brigade to get away and support themselves."

"So they must hate the Russians like us."

"I'm sure they do. Unfortunately they still serve under Russian officers."

"Like Colonel Liakhov."

"Like that bastard Liakhov yes."

Just thinking about the military dictator of Tehran brought back the oppression we felt across the city that year. We would never forgive him for bombing the Majlis, our parliament.

"I have heard that recently the Russian officers are being recalled to St. Petersburg. Tsar Nicholas the second is having as much trouble with his people as Ahmad Shah is having with us."

"The man in charge of the brigade appears to be Persian to me"

Khalil offered.

I studied the man who was reviewing the drills and as I did, he turned and looked directly at me. He was a large man and strikingly handsome. His uniform indicated that he was a Major. I didn't recognize him from any of my previous encounters, but I could tell from this distance that Khalil was correct. He was Persian.

I held his gaze, not wishing to give him the satisfaction of thinking I was intimidated. He smiled after a few moments and nodded his head in our direction before turning back towards his troops. I continued to stare at them, remembering my men and the few days I had to prepare them to fight. Not nearly as much time as I would have liked.

"Uncle" Khalil called, waking me from my thoughts. "Do you know if we will pass by the Palace of the Crown Prince on the way to the school?"

Tabriz is the capital of Azerbaijan province and was the second largest city in Persia during my lifetime. Throughout history, the Qajar Crowned Prince has lived in Tabriz and held the title of Provincial Governor. During my lifetime, they were all tyrants. I had no desire to go anywhere near the lion's den.

"I hope not. Let's go Khalil. There is nothing more I want to see here."

We pedaled on until we came upon the Arg of Tabriz, an enormous fourteenth century structure in the heart of the city.

"What happened to it" Khalil asked. "It looks like it was bombed or burned."

"The Russians again" I said with disgust. "They did that when Mohammad Ali Shah tried to come back in to power three years ago."

Five hundred years of history I thought to myself. What a waste.

"Let's keep going."

Twenty minutes later we arrived at the American School. As we pulled up into the courtyard Ahmad and several of the students poured out of the door as Khalil and I dismounted from the bike.

"You were not joking Ahmad, look at that thing!" one of the younger students called out. "Can I try?"

"Look at the wheels?" one of the older students said. "The spokes are so thin? It is nothing like a wagon wheel. How does it work?"

"The spokes are under tension" Khalil said in response to the older student. "They are each like a rope hanging from the top of the tire. The load is carried only by the spokes at the top of the wheel as it spins."

"The black material is vulcanized rubber, right?" the older student asked as he approached the bike and began squeezing the tire.

"Exactly. And it is filled with air to reduce the weight and absorb some of the shock."

"That is incredible. What a marvelous design."

"I want to ride it! I want to ride it!" the younger student called out again.

"Hop on the back and I'll take you for a ride" Khalil said.

The young boy eagerly climbed on board and Khalil took off.

"Ahmad, how are you today?"

"Fine Abdulrahim. Your nephew is quite good at that. I know it is not easy to ride."

"It takes some practice, but it's not that difficult after you get the idea."

Ahmad gestured towards a seating area near the door and I followed. We sat on a bench and watched as Khalil drove circles around the entrance to the school, picking up a new passenger each time.

"Abdulrahim, may I speak frankly about a sensitive subject?"

"Of course. You will find I am a very straight forward man. It is why I am not in politics."

He smiled at the remark.

"I'm told that you are the cousin of Ayatollah Abol-Ghasem Kashani."

Abol-Ghasem again! Has he turned up in Tabriz now? Was he following me?

"I am afraid that's true" I replied, "but we are not related in any way other than blood."

"You *are* direct. I like that about you Sayed."

"Why do you ask Ahmad?"

"When I left the seminary, it was not on good terms. Some of the Imams call me the Anti-Cleric."

Now it was my turn to laugh.

"Something big is going on in the religious community" he continued. "I don't know what it is yet, but I have heard there was a gathering of Ayatollahs and other well-respected clerics down in Qom these past few weeks. I was hoping you might have some insight."

"My cousin did come to see me without warning before I left on this trip" I replied. "Until that time I had not seen him in years. He didn't share anything about his plans other than his intention to visit Qom. I had no idea there was to be a conclave. I've heard they are trying to establish a divinity school there. Perhaps that is the reason?"

"Simply discussing a school would not require so many high level officials. I was also told they are meeting with a representative of the Ottoman Sultanate."

That was a coincidence that I did not like.

"He mentioned nothing to me about this meeting, you have my word."

"You are familiar with the Young Turk Revolution, I am sure."

"Yes. It seems like the Ottomans and Persians have much in common."

"Even China has overthrown their Emperor in favor of a representative democracy."

"When was this? I have not heard this news."

"No more than two years ago" Ahmad replied. "They are now the Republic of China. Czar Nicholas is dealing with his own trouble in St. Petersburg as well. It seems like the twentieth century will be the period that we finally overthrow the remaining Monarchs of the world and bring representation to the people."

Ahmad was correct, but neither of us foresaw the two world wars that would result from these changes and the further impacts to Persia from the cold war that followed. But that is a story for another time dear reader.

I turned my attention back to the students and saw one of them in a solo ride around the courtyard.

"You're doing fine!" Khalil yelled out. "Keep going!"

Ahmad stood up from the bench so I followed his lead.

"If you hear anything further about this you will tell me?" Ahmad asked.

"Of course. I would appreciate the same courtesy."

"Of course" Ahmad replied.

He shook my hand, but only in the normal way, simply to confirm our agreement.

"I think it's time we continue the tour" Ahmad said. "I want to show Khalil the drawings our students did for Sattar Khan's wheeled chair."

We walked over to the group of students and rejoined Khalil. He had a broad smile on his face as he watched the students taking turns with his Bicycle.

"Tim" Ahmad called out. One of the students turned and approached.

"Tim?" I asked. I had never heard that name before.

"My name is Timur, but the Americans call me Tim. Most of us have English names to go with our real names."

"Tim has something he wants to show you Khalil."

The four of us left the group of students to their fun and entered the school with Ahmad and Tim leading the way. We navigated though several turns and long hallways before entering a room set up with tables whose tops were set at an angle slanting forward. There were mechanical arms attached to the tops of each and what appeared to be a carpenter's square attached to the arms.

"This is our mechanical drawing classroom" Ahmad said as he led us over to a table with a drawing in progress.

Tim sat down at the table and pulled the mechanical arm out of the way to reveal a drawing of a chair with wheels.

"This is amazing!" Khalil said. "It is exactly what I saw in my head!"

Tim smiled and looked up at Ahmad.

"Ahmad came to see us yesterday and described your idea to me. I couldn't sleep until I got the basic design worked out."

"The wheels aren't quite right yet" Tim continued. "But now that I have seen the Bicycle wheels, I have a much better idea of how they will work."

"We also need to add an adjustable leg rest for Sattar Khan. He can't bend his knee, so we need to hinge these foot rests here such that they will straighten out."

Khalil and Tim were pointing at various parts of the drawing and debating the pros and cons of various changes to the design. Ahmad and I watched in silence for a long while until the two inventors ran out of steam.

"I think we have a plan" Tim said. "If you can give me tomorrow to update the drawing, we should meet again the day after and review the changes."

"How about it Uncle? Can I come back day after tomorrow to work with Tim?"

"Yes Khalil. I have some other business to take care of for Ali Ladjevardi that day."

We left Tim at the drafting table as he was preparing a new piece of drawing paper and headed back out to the front of the school.

When we arrived we found the students assembled in a group with several armed men standing in a line in front as if they were holding back a mob. An ornately decorated carriage was parked behind the soldiers and a young boy was sitting on the bicycle wearing what appeared to be a military uniform.

As we approached a man alighted from the carriage and turned towards us.

"You are the owners of this machine?" he asked.

"I am" I replied quickly not wanting Khalil to answer ahead of me.

"His majesty the Prince would like to thank you for your generous gift to his son."

"My gift?"

"What do you call this?" he asked.

"It is called a Bicycle" Khalil said. "I made it."

The man turned back towards the carriage and spoke to someone inside although we could not hear their conversation.

"It's the Prince's carriage" Ahmad whispered to me. "He's the brother of the Shah and that man is his secretary. You should not try to resist. The Prince's body guards will shoot with very little provocation. I've seen them do it myself."

The secretary backed away from the carriage and Prince Mohammad Hassan Mirza emerged. He was dressed in a military style uniform as well, replete with medals and a tall fez hat. He took several steps in our direction but stopped well short.

"My son was thrilled to see this bicycle on the main road as we passed by. Who can teach him how to operate this?"

I reached out my hand and pushed Khalil back a step as I stepped forward.

"I can your majesty. I am Sayed Abdulrahim Kashani from Tehran."

"Sayed Kashani, I require you to teach my son how to ride, but we must be on our way now. Please deliver the bicycle to the palace tomorrow morning. We thank you again for your generous gift."

With that he motioned to his son who let the bike drop to the ground as he returned to the carriage. The Prince, his son, and secretary climbed in to the carriage as the body guards climbed onto their stations on the outside. The driver cracked his whip over the horses and in no time at all were they gone.

Ahmad and I looked at each other in disbelief.

"We're so sorry Sayed! We were having so much fun that Kambiz and I took the bike out to the main road to see how fast we could go. The Prince's carriage was suddenly upon us and they called for us to stop. We never thought…"

The young man stopped in mid-sentence and simply stared at the ground.

I saw real tears in some of the students eyes, but when I looked back at Khalil I only found anger.

"The Prince is no better than a common thief" he said with his teeth clenched.

"Oh he is an uncommonly *prolific* thief" Ahmad said. "He and the entire Qajar family have stolen from this country for over a century."

"So what can we do about this?" Khalil asked.

"Nothing" Abdulrahim answered. "Even if we left town immediately, he would send cavalry after us and hang us for disobeying his order. He is ruthless."

"I am sorry Khalil" Ahmad offered. "Truly sorry."

"It's not your fault Ahmad" Khalil said. "How could you have known?"

The students returned to the school.

"We will be OK Ahmad don't worry. I will buy another horse for Khalil. We will travel by rail once we get to Van, so the Bicycle would have been a challenge anyway."

"I was planning to give it to the school" Khalil said with tears in his eyes. "To Tim and the other students."

Khalil picked up the bike from where the Prince's son left it and I climbed on the passenger seat.

"I will keep my promise concerning the other issue we discussed today Ahmad" I said.

We pedaled off towards our boarding house with less enthusiasm than we had when we arrived.

When we arrived at our inn, the proprietor handed me a note.

> *Abdulrahim Jaan,*
>
> *It would be my pleasure to host you for dinner tonight at my house. There are a few interesting people I think you should meet.*
>
> *Haji Mehdi Kuzeh Kanaani*

It was a short note and fairly intriguing. Given the connections he had, there was no limit to the possibilities of who the guests might be, aside from the Crown Prince. Of course we had already met him once today.

We took a rest that afternoon and cleaned up before cycling to Haji Mehdi's home. The entire house was lit up with candles and as we approached, the light spilling out through the stained glass windows gave the house a warm inviting glow.

We were met at the door by the servant and led into a large room on the first floor where I saw Haji Mehdi with several gentlemen dressed in traditional robes and a tall man in military uniform with his back turned.

"Abdulrahim! Khalil!, I am so glad you could make it. Let me introduce you to some of my friends."

As we entered the room the man in uniform turned and I immediately recognized him as the officer in charge of the Persian Cossacks from earlier in the day. From the smile on his face I could see that he recognized us as well. He was even more intimidating up close.

"Major" I said.

"Sayed Kashani" he replied. "Did you enjoy your bike ride today?"

"Very much. From our vantage point your company didn't seem to need the drills today. They were in complete synchronization."

"So you have already met?" Haji Mehdi asked.

"From a distance" the Major replied. "We were not properly introduced."

He walked closer and extended his hand to me.

"I am Major Reza, at your service."

I shook his hand and introduced Khalil.

"My nephew Khalil Redjaian."

They shook hands as well.

This situation was very uncomfortable and raised several questions. The Persian Cossacks put down the rebellion in Tehran under the leadership of Colonel Liakhov and it was not clear to me whether this man had been partly responsible. I lost many good friends to those bastards. Was this Major a friend or an enemy?

As if to sense my trepidation, Haji Mehdi stepped in with an explanation.

"I can see you are a bit confused Sayed. I can assure you that we are all among friends here tonight. I would not have invited the Major if he had been anywhere near the Majlis during the bombing."

Two of the other gentlemen approached and Haji Mehdi turned towards them. From their robes I could tell they were from the Bakhtiari tribes.

"Abdulrahim Agha, I would like to introduce two of our southern patriots Commander Assad Bakhtiari and Amir Ardalan from Bushehr."

I recognized the first name at once. Although I had never met him, Commander Assad and his Bakhtiari tribesmen were just as important as Sattar Khan and the men from Tabriz when it came to our victory in the revolution.

"Commander Assad I am honored to meet you" I said.

"Sayed Abdulrahim Kashani I have heard your name mentioned many times" he replied. "Let me introduce my friend Amir Ardalan. He did not serve with us in the Revolution. He is more familiar with Finance than weapons."

I looked closely at the second man and saw that he was closer to Khalil's age, yet still there was a confidence about him.

"Amir Kahn. Let me introduce my nephew Khalil Redjaian

from Kashan. He is my assistant and translator on this journey."

"Translator?" Amir asked. "Do you speak any Bakhtiari?"

"I have always wanted to learn one of the Lurish dialects" Khalil replied, "but never had the opportunity. I spent more time on the northern languages like Azeri."

"Well perhaps we can teach you a few phrases of Bakhtiari and you can help us with the Turkish dialects. I can't understand a word the locals are saying."

"If I may ask Commander Assad, what brings you to Tabriz?" Bushehr must be eight hundred miles south of here."

"It has been a long trip indeed, but we still have a long way to go. We are travelling to a meeting in Van. Eastern Anatolia"

"What a coincidence" replied Khalil. That is our next stop as well."

In the back of my mind a connection was beginning to form. Commander Assad's men were successful in the revolution to a large extent because they were the best armed men in the battle. They were well supplied with the latest weapons from Germany. In addition, when Sir Walter spoke of Wilhelm Wassmuss, he called him a provocateur from the south.

Perhaps I was becoming paranoid, but the Bakhtiari's trip to Van, Wassmuss suggesting the same route, Abol-Ghasem's connection to the oil refinery at Abadan and his insistence that we meet with Wassmuss. The coincidences were adding up.

"And from there?" Amir asked.

"Constantinople" I replied.

Amir turned to Assad and said quietly "*Sag ihnen nicht, wer wir in Van treffen*" of which I understood not a word. It certainly didn't sound like Bakhtiari though.

"Is Constantinople your final destination?" Amir asked.

"We are en route to Paris" I replied. "I have business there."

A servant approached and nodded towards Haji Mehdi.

"I believe dinner is ready" Haji Mehdi said to all in the room. "Please join me."

I placed my hand on Khalil's arm and he seemed to understand that I wanted him to wait as the others made their way towards the dining room.

"Did you understand what he said?" I asked quietly in French.

"It was German Uncle. They don't want us to know the purpose of their meeting in Van."

"Did it seem to you that Amir was in charge and not Assad?"

"Yes Uncle. I believe you are correct, although he is very much younger than Assad Agha."

I didn't want to call attention to ourselves so we quickly followed the group in to the dining room and took the last two seats at the table. I found myself seated next to Reza Khan and across from Amir. Normally I would let the host drive the topic of conversation, but I was deeply curious about our new friends, especially the Bakhtiari.

"I understand the new oil refinery at Abadan is at full production now" I offered.

"I believe you are correct" Assad replied. "I heard the same news."

The servant began serving food and pouring water into the crystal glasses.

"Have you seen the refinery?" Khalil asked. "I hear it is a huge plant with state of the art technology."

"Khalil is an inventor" Haji Mehdi offered. "A mechanical genius!"

"Technology!" Reza Khan said with disdain. "I have heard that the British are paying the workers substandard wages and making them live in unbearable conditions. They are reaping the profits from our natural resources and Persia is getting a fraction of what we deserve."

I decided to take the contrarian position to get the conversation loosened up.

"Not to disagree Major, but without a skilled petroleum engineer or Sir D'Arcy's substantial investment, we would never have discovered the oil in the first place."

He looked at me like I had lost my mind.

"Are you a British sympathizer?"

"I am not Major. I am on the side of Persia and of justice."

"From a businessman's point of view" Haji Mehdi interjected, "I would have to say that D'Arcy took a very large risk and deserves to recover his investment. His initial outlay of five hundred thousand pounds sterling was not enough to find the oil. He had to bring in more investors and even then it appeared they would come up dry. I heard he actually gave up and told his people to come home. The only reason they were successful is because D'Arcy's man in the field ignored the order."

"Ignoring orders is dangerous" Reza Khan offered. "You have commanded men in battle Abdulrahim Agha. You must agree with me."

"It is important to follow the chain of command" I agreed, "until the men at the top demonstrate they are not fit to lead."

"Which is the reason for our constitutional revolution in the first place" Haji Mehdi interjected.

"What say our new friends from the south?" I asked. "Have you been to the Oil Fields at Masjed Soleyman or the Abadan refinery?"

I looked directly across the table at Amir so there could be no mistake of who I was asking.

"I have been to both places" he responded. "The Major is correct. Wages are low, conditions are horrible, and our people are dying of small pox and other diseases."

"Perhaps there are others more deserving to blame" Reza Khan offered. "Mozaffar-ad-Din Shah gave up the oil rights and Emir Khazal Khan of Mohammerah gave Abadan Island to the infidel British for their damned refinery."

I was watching Amir's face as Reza Khan spoke and noticed an interesting reaction when he said the name of Emir Khazal Khan.

"Surely it is within the rights of the Shah and the Emir to sell these?" commander Assad finally weighed in. "As Abdulrahim has pointed out, the oil was hidden from our untrained eyes and we do not yet have the knowledge to refine the crude."

"*In Sha Allah* this will change!" Amir cried out as he pounded the table with his fist.

The sudden burst of passion startled everyone, none more than Amir himself who appeared slightly embarrassed by the outburst.

"*In Sha Allah!*" Reza Khan offered with a big smile on his face.

I couldn't tell if he was agreeing or making fun of Amir, but the net effect was to restore the mood back to normal.

"Major, I have heard it said that your men call you Reza Maxim" Haji Mehdi offered, changing the subject.

"Maxim as in Truth or Principle?" Khalil asked.

"Maxim as in the Maxim gun" I answered, finally putting the connection together. I had heard stories of the amazing Reza Maxim. I should have known this was the man."

"What is a Maxim gun?" Khalil asked.

"It is a fine weapon" the Major answered. "A rotating gun that can fire six hundred rounds per minute. A superior mechanical design."

"Like a Gatling gun?" Khalil asked. "I read about that design in a new magazine from America called Popular Mechanics."

"Yes, but much better. It uses the recoil force of one bullet to eject the cartridge and load the next."

"It usually requires a team of four to six men" Haji Mehdi interjected. "The Major here is able to operate one by himself with greater accuracy than a full team."

"You sound like a man we want on our side" Amir offered.

Amir then turned to Khalil. "You read English?"

"Yes Arbab… and French of course" he replied.

"And German as well" I offered just to watch their reactions.

"*Du sprichst Deutsch?*" Assad asked Khalil with an incredulous look on his face.

"*Ein Bisschen Jare Ehre*" he replied.

"Well this is unexpected" Assad half mumbled to himself in Persian.

"What my friend meant to say" Amir said "is that meeting you is an unexpected good fortune for us. How good is your Turkish Khalil?"

"His Azeri is almost fluent" Haji Mehdi offered. I would expect his Turkish is just as good. I have no problem conversing with the Ottomans myself."

"And you are both *en route* to Van?"

"Yes Arbab" I replied. "and then on to Constantinople."

Amir paused for a moment, then seemed to reach some decision.

"Would it be possible to call on you tomorrow Abdulrahim Agha? I have a proposition for you, but I am afraid the details would be inappropriate over dinner."

"I unfortunately have an appointment with the Crown Prince in the morning. Perhaps late in the day?"

"Mohammad Hassan Mirza?" Haji Mehdi asked.

"Yes. That Crown Prince" I replied. "He wants to appropriate Khalil's Bicycle for his son and commands me to instruct the boy in its operation."

Reza Khan moved forward in his chair. "He wants to take your bicycle?"

"He wants us to make a gift of it" Khalil said. "I guess that is not exactly theft."

Reza Khan sat back in his chair and shook his head. "Some day we will rid ourselves completely of tyrants like the Qajars. We need more than a parliament. We need to clear our house of the rats that infest the palaces and exterminate their lackeys while we are at it."

A long silence ensued as the guests digested this last comment. Little did any of us know that this man would fulfill his own wish in less than seven years from this night and become the next Shah of Persia.

"Please everyone enjoy your meal" Haji Mehdi said. "There will be plenty of time for more conversation after dinner."

We enjoyed a marvelous meal and continued catching up on the news from around the world, but the conversation never returned to such delicate subjects. It seemed we all had our fill before dinner began.

The following day Khalil set off on his own to explore Tabriz and I took my final ride on Khalil's bike. I arrived at the palace and was greeted by one of the Prince's security officers who led me around to the entrance used by the merchants who supplied the palace with food. I walked the bicycle through the delivery portal and followed the guard into an inner courtyard that was surrounded on all sides.

I stood in this courtyard for what seemed like an hour as I waited for the Prince's son to appear. The boy and a man introduced as his tutor finally appeared making no apology for their delay. I have learned to be a patient man though, especially in situations where I do not have much choice. So once they arrived I began my lessons.

To his credit, the child learned quickly and within an hour had mastered the machine as well as I could hope. I explained to his tutor that he was ready for an extended ride and we were shown to a part of the palace grounds that reminded me of my own garden back in Tehran. Of course this was on a much grander scale and could rightly be described as more of a private park.

The little prince wasted no time. He mounted the bike and took off through the pathways at a speed which was impressive for his age. From my perspective, my job was complete and it was time to find my way home, before my student suffered his first crash.

The palace guard escorted me back to the front of the palace and I made my way back to the entrance. Despite the fact that we had lost the bike, I was happy that I had escaped an audience with Mohammad Hassan Mirza. My patience only goes so far.

As I made my way to the main road to hail a Hansom cab, I saw an open carriage pull up with a passenger that I didn't quite expect.

"Sayed Kashani" Wilhelm Wassmuss said as I approached. "What a pleasant surprise."

He was dressed in robes as usual and still spoke to me in his fluent Persian.

"Is it a surprise?" I asked.

"Forgive me Arbab, I forgot that I can be blunt with you. I was told you would be making a visit to the Provincial Palace this morning."

This news could only have come from a few people so quickly following our dinner.

"I assume I have Commander Assad and Amir Ardalan to thank for the ride?"

"If you have no other commitments, you can thank them yourself. They are expecting us."

I had no other plans for the day so in half an hour we pulled up to a home almost as nice as Haji Mehdi's. We alighted from the cab and were shown into the house by a servant. I followed Wilhelm into a formal library to be greeted by our expected hosts.

"Sayed Kashani, I am so glad you had time for us" Amir began.

Salaam! Chetori Abdulrahim agha?" Commander Assad asked although something about his demeanor led me to believe the two men had been arguing about something. He was not as cheerful as the night before.

"My friend Wilhelm tells me that Khalil is exploring the city" Amir continued, not waiting for me to answer.

The comment could only mean that we had been under surveillance.

"Indeed" I replied.

"I am afraid I owe you an apology Arbab. I was not very forthcoming last night when we were introduced, but then there were several new faces in the room and one can never be too careful."

"Does this have something to do with the Emir of Mohammerah?" I asked.

"I told you he was clever" Wassmuss said.

"Why do you say that?" Amir asked.

"A lucky guess. I noticed your reaction last night when the Major mentioned his name."

"My grandfather" Amir continued. "I am not accustomed to hear anything negative said about him in my presence, but then how was the Major to know?"

"So your meeting in Van is related to your family's business?"

"It is. We are meeting with Calouste Gulbenkian of the Royal Dutch Shell oil company. Do you know of him?"

"I believe I have heard the name, but not much more" I replied.

"Mister Five Percent" Wassmuss interjected. "He always seems to own five percent of any deal he is involved with. He is fast becoming one of the richest men in the world."

"In this case he would own much more of the Turkish Petroleum Company" Amir continued. "He is trying to broker a deal between the British, the Ottoman Empire, the German National Bank, and my Grandfather to explore for oil in Mesopotamia near Kirkuk."

"Kaiser Wilhelm is very keen to see this deal consummated" Wilhelm said.

"I understand the Ottomans and Germany cooperating" I said, "but the British?"

"Gulbenkian is a British Citizen of Turkish Armenian ancestry" Amir said. "He traces his family back over a thousand years to the area around Lake Van. We will be meeting near his ancestral home."

"He was educated at King's College London as a petroleum engineer" Wilhelm continued, "but he understands finance and business just as well. It is no wonder he comes out on top of every deal."

"I see" I said trying to digest all of these new facts. "But why would the Kaiser want the British to gain access to new oil reserves while at the same time trying to shut down the ones in Persia?"

Wilhelm and Amir looked at each other for a moment as if trying to decide how far to go.

"You know we are building the Berlin Bagdad Railroad?" Wilhelm replied.

"Yes, but I understand you still have several hundred miles to go."

"That is true. After we completed service to Aleppo, we learned of the possibility of oil in Kirkuk and decided to re-route the line through Mosul and on to Bagdad to facilitate the transport of oil. It added some additional miles to the plan, but it will be worth the extra effort. Many of the details depend on the cooperation of the Ottoman Sultan and after last year's Coup, the Three Pashas."

"But the British?" I asked again, trying to get to the bottom of it.

"Once we have the rail service in place and the oil fields open" Wilhelm answered, "we will be able to transport directly into Germany and not have to ship through the Suez canal. We can destroy the refinery at Abadan and foment a revolt at the oil fields. This will starve the British of their oil."

"Our oil" Commander Assad barked.

Destroy Abadan? Foment a revolt? At least I was getting the unfiltered version now.

"So your grandfather needs to be part of this new deal with Germany and the Ottomans to replace the loss of the income from the Anglo Persian Oil Company" I said.

"Temporary loss" Assad interjected again. "We will take back what is ours and shut down Britain's route through Afghanistan to India. We will starve them of their oil and the riches they plunder from the subcontinent."

"And their share of oil and profits of the new fields?" I asked.

"You know how Persia never seems to make any profits from Anglo Persian Oil and how Churchill's ships are getting the majority of the oil at a discount?" Wilhelm asked. "Let's just say the tables will be turned for the Turkish Petroleum Company. No oil or profit for the British shareholders."

It was all starting to come together for me now except for one important piece.

"So how do Khalil and I fit in to this?"

"Last night at dinner I learned that Khalil spoke English and Turkish and German" Amir replied. "And I learned that you are an excellent judge of people. Your comments this morning have reaffirmed my judgment. I would ask the two of you to act as our advisors at the meetings in Van. Simply listen and observe. Khalil should not let on that he understands anything other than Persian and French. You Sayed should get to know the others and simply tell me what you think."

I understood that we were being asked in a way to spy. I had not quite decided if I wanted to help these men, but then I remembered Wilhelm's visit to my shop.

"Wilhelm asked us to join him on this route late last year" I said. It was not a question but my meaning was obvious.

"Our meeting with Gulbenkian was set after our visit in Tehran Sayed" Wassmuss said. "It was a happy coincidence that we planned to travel through Van. I need your help with a related situation."

I waited for Wilhelm to continue.

"It involves your cousin Abol-Ghasem. You see, the oil fields in Mesopotamia and the last leg of the Berlin Bagdad railroad are in a region claimed by Sunnis, Shias, and Kurds. Each group is claiming rights to the oil and to the concession required for the rail line."

I could just see Abol-Ghasem's face when he realized that funding for his causes could be ripe for the harvest.

"We need to construct a deal acceptable to all three of these factions that still enables Germany to get the oil it needs."

Finding a deal where the Sunnis and Shia would work together would be very difficult. Making the Kurds happy at the same time? Impossible.

"Sultan Mehmed has even bigger plans" Wilhelm continued.

"He wants to unite the Shias and Sunnis against the British and French. He has tried this before but now with the potential of oil revenues, he feels there is a chance it can work this time."

"But why me? I am not a religious man!"

"Exactly!" Amir answered. "Do you think for one minute a true believer would listen objectively to a proposal from the other side?"

"But I am just a simple businessman who sells paper and collects stamps?"

Commander Assad broke out laughing. "Sayed, you are truly amazing! A more humble man has never lived."

"Setting aside the fact that everyone involved in the Revolution knows and respects you" Wilhelm said, "You have established personal relationships with most of the important representatives in the Majlis and with all of the foreign ambassadors in Persia. They trust you."

"Not the Russians" I said. "I hate the Russians."

"As do I" Assad interjected.

"The most important people in Persia know you to be a fair and honest man who will keep the secrets of others as if your life depends on it. You are what we call an 'honest broker' Sayed. You know the whole story and even if you do not divulge all of the reasons, we know that when necessary, you will share the information that you feel will guide us in the right direction."

'The right direction' was an interesting choice of words. I did not intend to support any cause that would negatively impact Persia and my family. If that is what he meant by right direction, then I was on board.

"So after the meeting in Van?" I asked.

"Commander Assad and I will return to Mohammerah to confer with my grandfather" Amir said.

"You and I will board a train for Constantinople" Wilhelm said.

"And Khalil" I added. Visions of Khalil being 'appropriated' as Amir's personal translator made me wary.

"And Khalil" Wilhelm confirmed. We need him in Constantinople. If we are fortunate in Van, Gulbenkian will invite us to join him on his return trip.

"When do we leave for Van?" I asked.

"The day after tomorrow" Wilhelm replied.

That would allow time for Khalil to return to the American school and review the wheelchair designs with Tim and for the two of us to say our goodbyes to Sattar Khan. We also had to buy a horse to replace the stolen bike.

"We will send a message to your inn with the details tomorrow, but you should plan for 200 miles with some rough terrain over the mountains."

"We will be ready" I said.

"I will have my driver take you back to your inn" Amir said. "I have procured a Model T automobile for my Grandfather's collection."

I said my farewells and made my way out of the house only to find that Commander Assad was right behind me.

"You are not happy my friend" I said when we were alone.

"It's nothing important" he said. "I am too old for all of this intrigue and too proud to be the lap dog of that fool Amir. I am a Thane of my Tribe. I deserve respect!"

"He is the grandson of an Emir."

"An Emir who was knighted by the British and calls himself 'Most Sacred Officer of the Imperial Order of the Aqdas'."

"Aqdas?" I asked. "That is the bible of the Bahai faith is it not?"

"Many people suspect he is a Babi, which makes this deal between the Sunnis and Shia even more difficult. If they suspect an infidel is a part owner... I just need to get out of there and cool down."

"Why don't you escort me back to the inn then. We can forget about the present and talk about our mutual acquaintances from the revolution."

I had never ridden in an automobile before and I have to say it was a treat. We got more looks on the street than I did on the bike and went much faster as well. Assad and I got so caught up in our conversation that I didn't realize we had arrived until the driver interrupted us. As I watched them ride off into the crowded streets I realized just how interesting this day had turned out. I had a lot of thinking to do.

Khalil and I had a light supper as I shared with him the events of the day. He was more excited to hear about my ride in the Model T than the political details, but then he was still a young man.

The following day Khalil set off for the American school while I met with another old friend from the revolution and purchased the supplies we would need for the next leg of our journey.

When I returned to the inn, Khalil was back and gave me the note we received from Amir.

"We are to meet at the Bazaar just after sunrise Uncle."

"And so we shall" I replied. "What do you think of the Wheeled Chair design?"

"It is perfect" Khalil replied. "Tim is brilliant. He incorporated all of my ideas and added several improvements. It is much better than my original design."

"This is the reason it is better to collaborate sometimes Khalil. It is not a contest to see who is smarter. Sattar Khan will have a better chair because two mechanical geniuses combined their ideas into one superior product."

"He gave me a copy of the drawings."

"You don't seem very happy."

"I know we must leave tomorrow, but I wish I could spend more time working with Tim. I will miss working with someone who understands my ideas so easily."

"Maybe when we return from Paris, we can come back through Tabriz and you can stay behind for a while before coming home."

"I'd like that Uncle." Khalil's mood seemed to lighten somewhat. "We have a long trip ahead though and we have no idea what the rest of the trip will bring. Let's not think about the return until we reach Paris."

"Agreed" I replied.

We had no way of knowing all that would happen to us over the next few months. Khalil would never return to Tabriz. By the time he made that decision, collaborating with Tim on a new invention was the furthest thing from his mind. What happens to us in life is not always fair. We are judged by the choices we make along the way.

VAN

May 31st, 1914

Khalil and I rose before sunrise and met our porters at the stables. As expected, they had the mules packed and the horses saddled ready to go. We made our way through town to the Bazaar which was already coming to life with suppliers making their deliveries and merchants preparing their shops for the long day ahead.

When we arrived I was surprised to see the Model T parked beside the horses, pack mules, and a wagon made from a Russian style tarantass. This wagon design essentially used six young saplings as supports between the two axels to act as a shock absorber. The cargo bed was fully loaded with supplies and carpets for the journey ahead. Upon further inspection I saw a cache of rifles stored where they could be easily accessed.

I counted four porters readying the supplies. With my two men and our combined arsenal I was confident we would be safe from any run of the mill highway robbers.

"One last ride before the journey?" I asked Amir referring to the Model T.

"We are driving to Khoy Sayed Kashani. It's just over a hundred miles and flat, with a good road. My automobile will be much more comfortable for us than riding in a saddle all day."

'Good road' was of course a relative term. If the roads to the north were as challenging as the road south of Tabriz I expected the automobile might need a bit of horse power to get out of the ruts.

"But what about fuel?" Khalil asked.

"It has a range of about one hundred and fifty miles on a full tank. There is a container on the wagon with enough fuel to return home. The roads through the mountains are not suitable for an automobile."

I saw Assad checking on the gear in the wagon but did not see Wilhelm anywhere.

"Are we still waiting for Wilhelm?" I asked.

"He left yesterday to arrange passage across the mountains and frontier. He also felt it would be better if he were not seen with us on the road. Now that you are here we are ready to go."

As we were about to step into the model T we saw Haji Mehdi approach.

"Abdulrahim Agha! I am so glad I caught you."

"What's wrong Haji Khan? You look upset."

"It's the Crown Prince. He is very angry with you."

"But I have not seen the crown prince since the incident at the American School three days ago?"

"It's his son. Last night the doctor was at my home and told me that the boy crashed the bicycle and broke his arm. The Prince feels you did not give the boy adequate training."

"The Prince can't possibly hold you responsible" Amir said to me.

"Even I still crash occasionally" Khalil added.

"The boy's tutor claims that you spent no more than a few minutes showing the boy how to ride and then sent him off into the park by himself at breakneck speeds without the first lecture on safety."

"This is not true!" I exclaimed. "I was with him for a full hour before I allowed him to leave the courtyard and spent the first ten minutes telling him how dangerous it could be. I even showed him the scars on my arms from my first crash."

"The truth is whatever the Crown Prince says it is" Haji Mehdi replied.

"So what do I do?"

"You leave right away, but please be careful to stay out of plain sight until you are well away from the city. He may send men after you."

"Does he know Sayed Kashani is travelling with me?" Amir asked.

"Not that I am aware" Haji Mehdi answered.

"Then Abdulrahim and Khalil shall ride in the back seat where they will not be seen. Problem solved."

"Thank you for your warning Haji Mehdi" I said as I shook his hand.

"As much as I would like to see you again, I recommend you think about a different route home from Paris" he replied.

I couldn't believe that the Prince would hold a grudge for so long, but I could see the look of worry on my new friend's face.

We mounted the car with Khalil and myself safely hidden in the back and made our way out of the city on the main road north.

The first day we made good time and stopped almost twenty miles from Tabriz. We filled our water bottles and purchased supplies at a small way station but continued on a few miles before setting up camp. Amir's men and my porters set up the tents and began preparing our evening meal.

While Amir had never used a title in his conversation, his tent and furnishings bore witness to the fact that he was the grandson of an Emir. I understood the need for the wagon when I saw them fully set up. The tent must have been twenty feet on a side with carpets covering the ground. The pillows alone in his tent could have filled the space where Khalil and I were to sleep.

We ate our supper just after sunset on a folding table, the four of us sitting on folding chairs. Three kerosene lamps were hung from the canopy that covered the table, with yet another carpet at our feet.

With six porters in total there was no need for Khalil and I to lift a finger, let alone stand watch. This leg of the trip was certainly more comfortable than the first.

The night passed without incident and I slept well. We were off just after sunrise making good progress as we had the day before. We stopped mid-day at a small post station that was no more than a well and small hut selling hot food. The proprietor had a selection of kebabs kept warm on a grill and an assortment of flat breads that he cooked on a Bedouin style flat-top camp stove.

We didn't bother setting up the full camp, but given the heat of the sun and the lack of trees in this station, we did enjoy the shade of the canopy and the comfort of the folding table.

A porter called out midway through the meal and pointed towards the road from Tabriz. A cloud of dust could be seen on the horizon and a soft rumble of hooves could be heard which could only mean a large group of horses riding fast. The porters made for the wagons and distributed rifles to all as we waited for the first sight of the oncoming riders.

It was not uncommon to see riders in a hurry on the road, but as the horses approached we could see there were at least a dozen. A few moments later we could easily see they were in uniform. As they made the final turn into the station it was clear they were part of the Persian Cossack Brigade.

There was only one possible reason they were here.

As a group they dismounted, rifles and sabers at hand. Commander Assad and I looked at each other and realized that the six of us would be no match against twelve trained soldiers in an open field of battle. We signaled to the others to lower their weapons.

Their leader was bringing up the rear and not clearly visible until he walked through the company of men.

"Sayed Kashani! Commander Assad! Would you mind if I joined you?"

Major Reza Khan strode forward and removed his cap, the familiar confident smile on his face.

Khalil as the junior member of the group immediately backed away from the table and gave the Major his seat as the rest of us slowly sat down in our chairs. One of the porters poured a fresh glass of water and gave it to the Major who gulped it down with pleasure. He placed the empty glass on the table and pointed to it.

"Another please" he said. "It's been a hard ride."

The porter refilled the glass and the Major took a few sips. He was the center of attention and I could see clearly that he had a flair for the dramatic. Fifteen men were waiting to see his next move and he was in no hurry.

"It seems that your anger must have gotten the best of you Sayed Kashani, but I would never have pegged you as a man who would hurt a child."

"Hurt a child?" I asked incredulous.

"Do you deny that you broke the young prince's arm?"

"Now they are saying that I broke his arm?"

"Yes Sayed. Why do you think we have ridden so hard to find you. I was told by the Royal Tutor that during you lessons with the Crown Prince's son, you became angry at the thought of losing your bicycle. You suddenly grabbed the boy by the arm and threw him off the bike on to the ground."

"Lies!" Amir jumped to his feet and pounded the table.

The Cossack Brigade cocked their rifles and raised them to the firing position as one.

Amir slowly returned to his seat and the Major waved off his men.

"Sayed?" the Major asked politely.

"I went to the palace as instructed and met with the boy and his tutor" I said calmly. "I spent an hour with him, teaching him how to ride and explaining the dangers of trying to go too fast too soon. When I felt he was ready, we moved to the park and he took off like the wind. I told his tutor that all the boy needed now was practice."

"And then?" asked the Major.

"And then I returned to my rooms and the next day prepared for this trip."

"You never touched the boy?"

I looked at him in the eyes trying hard not to lose my patience. I was not accustomed to being accused of such lowly acts.

"I apologize Sayed" the Major finally said after it became obvious I would not answer. "I know that a man of your station would never do that. Obviously it is I that have been lied to."

The major stood and turned to his men.

"Stand down and go take your fill. We will rest before returning to Tabriz."

The men lowered their weapons and returned them to the holsters strapped to their horses. They led the animals to the watering troughs set up by the well and then dispersed to relieve themselves and fill their stomachs.

"I should have known that story was a complete fabrication" Reza Khan continued. "What is it you said at our dinner Sayed? ... Oh yes, that we should 'follow the chain of command until the men at the top demonstrate they are not fit to lead'."

I nodded.

"I believe you are correct. Please accept my apology Sayed Kashani."

"There is no need for an apology Major. We both know that it is time for a change in our leadership. I don't know if it will happen in my lifetime, but one day Persia will be free from tyrants who steal from the people to line their own pockets."

"Indeed!" Amir said as he raised his glass.

"So what will you do now Major?" Assad asked.

"We can't return to Tabriz so soon" he answered. "We must make it appear that we did our utmost to find you ruffians. Although I can't quite remember ever seeing a band of criminals dine in such style while on the run."

"Why don't you and your men travel with us to Khoy?" Assad asked. "We have ample space in our tents and plenty of food for your men."

I saw the slight wince on Amir's face as his elder partner made the offer. I also saw the smile on Commander Assad's face and realized immediately the pleasure he took at making the offer.

Reza Khan relaxed and sat back in his chair.

"The older I get" the Major replied, "the more I appreciate the finer things in life. I have heard that this road was dangerous. Please allow my company to ensure your safe passage to Khoy."

Amir was about to speak when the Major cut him off.

"I hope that when convenient, you will send word to your Grandfather the Emir that Major Reza Khan of the Persian Cossack Brigades sends his regards, and did everything in his power to ensure his interests were protected."

I had wondered if the Major knew who Amir was and now I had

my answer.

"Now if it is not asking too much, do you happen to have anything stronger than water in that wagon of yours?"

We didn't make many miles that afternoon but then we didn't really care. Khalil and I decided to ride our horses and leave the cramped confines of the Model T to Amir and Assad. It gave us a chance to get to know Major Reza Khan a bit better and it gave our two Bakhtiari friends a chance to discuss the recent turn of events in private.

Since we no longer had to worry about being discovered, we were able to make camp in the open at a small oasis. The horses had their fill of water and were corralled within a grove of palms and date trees. The porters set up the tents and the table as usual, but that night the main tent hosted a banquet of roasted lamb and strong drink in honor of our new security detail.

The next morning's ride was not very comfortable for Khalil and myself. Even though the members of the Cossack Brigade drank much more heavily than we did, they seemed to be unfazed by the experience.

The following night was a bit more restrained with the Major's men and porters dining on their own and the five of us enjoying a light meal in the main tent. We continued in that manner until we reached the outskirts of Khoy before sunset a few days later.

With our supplies restocked by the porters from the bazaar in Khoy, we enjoyed one final evening with the Cossack Brigade and Major Reza Khan. While we did not overindulge as we had the first night, we did continue on well into the night listening to stories of the Major's exploits in the Brigade.

The next morning Khalil and I awoke later than usual to find that the Major and his men had departed. I had come to like the Major and was disappointed that I didn't have the chance to thank him again for his trust in me before he left.

We found Commander Assad sitting at the folding table smoking from a *hookah* sitting on the ground beside him. The flexible hose on this water pipe was long and supple, making it easy to reach his mouth when he was ready for another drag. One of the porters was pouring a Turkish coffee from a *Ghouri*, the long handled copper pots traditionally used to make the bitter drink.

"Salaam! Chetori Sayed Kashani? Do you care for a coffee or a pipe?"

"*Merci*! I am well Commander Assad. Coffee would be welcome, but I do not smoke."

"Khalil Jaan?"

"Salaam Commander Assad! Coffee would be nice if we have sugar" Khalil said directly to the porter who retreated to the fire to prepare the order.

Khalil and I sat and made ourselves comfortable. I breathed in the cool morning air and noted the change in temperature. We hadn't seen any steep climbs since leaving Tabriz, but I knew we had gained altitude.

"I see our friends have moved on" I said.

"At sunrise" Assad replied. "I am sorry to see them go. I quite like the Major's company. We didn't exactly fight on the same side, but I can understand soldiers much better than politicians and Princes."

He glanced over his shoulder at the big tent.

"He is not so bad" I replied. "He's just young and privileged."

"Khalil is about the same age" the commander continued, "but he has worked and studied since becoming a man. I am afraid Amir is still a bit of an adolescent. I have spoken to him many times about his temper."

"I am not quite free from this challenge myself, so I am not one to judge" I replied.

The porter returned with two cups and two steaming czeves which he poured immediately with great skill. We sat in amiable silence for a while, Assad relishing his pipe, Khalil and I enjoying our coffee.

Reza Khan had been clear our last day on the road that the situation in Khoy was not always stable. The Russian Cossacks used Khoy as a garrison for their men since the last Russo-Persian war. A few years before our journey the Ottomans had pushed across the border and expelled the Russians, but now it seemed the Russians were back in control. We were now just fifty miles from the official border with the Ottomans to the west and fifty miles to Russian controlled Armenia to the north, but lines on a map mean nothing when you have a superior force.

"Do you think we will have trouble getting to Van?" Khalil asked as if reading my mind. "I wish the Major could have stayed with us to the border."

"Wilhelm will take care of our safety from here" Amir said as he approached the table.

"Salaam! Chetori Amir Agha?" Khalil asked. "Did you sleep well?"

"Well enough" he said.

The porter didn't wait for orders and hastily set out a tea cup, a plate of Lavash bread, and two small bowls with feta cheese and jam. Moments later he returned with a tea pot and a plate of prunes and raisins for the table.

"Wilhelm will meet us here with our new security detail and we will be off. Travel will be slow through the mountains, but we should be in Ottoman territory within the week."

It occurred to me that I should update *Khanoum* and Abol-Ghasem on our progress.

"Do you think Khoy has a telegraph office? I need to message my family on our progress."

Amir pointed off in the distance and I saw the line of tall poles leading in to town. So I excused myself and retired to my tent leaving the others to their breakfast.

I retrieved writing paper and my code book from its hiding place and began to compose the telegram. I wrote only that we had met with Wilhelm in Tabriz, arrived safely at Khoy, and expected to rejoin him today. I didn't think any of the other details would be important at the moment. If I had time later today would post a letter with more details about our travelling companions and our run in with the Crown Prince.

I mounted my horse and asked the others if there was anything they wanted while I was in town. It seems the porters had done a good job when we arrived the day before so I rode off to find the telegraph office.

The telegraph line converged nicely with the road into town. It was a simple matter for me to follow the wires to their termination point.

As I dismounted, I noticed armed Russian Cossacks patrolling the streets. I was glad that we would soon be on our way. The sight of these men was enough to make me angry. We were on Persian soil and they dared to police our streets like they owned them.

I entered the telegraph office, filled out the required form, made the payment, and waited for confirmation that my message had been sent and acknowledged. It still seemed like magic to me that I could communicate with my wife several hundred miles away and that she would get the message in hours.

As I exited the building I noticed a man standing beside my horse with his back to me and two Cossacks approaching him.

"That is not your horse" the first Cossack said in a horrible attempt at French.

I assumed they spoke no Persian.

"But of course" came the reply from the man in a perfect Parisian accent. "I am waiting for its owner."

"I am the owner" I replied continuing on in French.

The man turned at the sound of my voice. I was not surprised to see Wilhelm Wassmuss standing there, although I was taken aback by how well he pronounced his French.

"Sayed Kashani, how wonderful to see you again!" he said in Persian.

I looked over to the Cossacks who were not backing away.

"Thank you for your concern Corporal" I said in French to the senior of the two soldiers, "but my friend and I arranged to meet here today. There is no problem."

They continued to stare at me and I finally remembered the simple Russian phrases Khalil taught me on the road to Khoy.

"*Bez Problem. Spasibo!*"

I knew my Russian pronunciation was probably as bad as their French, but the look of disgust on the soldiers face as they turned away made me want to put them in their place. If the Czar stationed his soldiers in our country, the least they could do would be to teach them the language. The satisfaction would not have been worth the cost however and I had already been chased out of one town on this journey.

"You have a horse Wilhelm Agha? I asked switching back to Persian.

"Yes and a company of men ready to make way, but I think we are better served if we bypass the town. These men would not be welcomed by the Russians."

We retrieved Wilhelm's horse and rode southwest out of town towards the open desert. We found the twenty well-armed Turks camped behind an outcrop of rock that shielded their position from the town and provided their sentries with a good view of the approach.

Wilhelm spoke to their leader in German for several minutes and seemed to reach some agreement.

"They will wait here for us" Wilhelm said to me. "We can get half a day of travel in if we hurry."

Moments later we were off again for our camp.

When we arrived I was pleased to see that the porters had already struck camp and packed the mules for the journey. We dismounted from our horses and handed them off to one of the porters who led them over to the watering trough.

My three companions were having tea while they waited for us so I went quickly to the table to have a cup myself before the porters packed everything away.

"Hello Wilhelm" Amir said. "I trust you had no difficulties?"

"No problems at all Amir Agha" he answered. "Our security detail arrived yesterday with a message for you from Enver Pasha."

As Wilhelm handed the message to Amir I almost choked on my tea before regaining control. Why would the Minister of War for the Ottoman empire and one of the three top leaders personally provide a security detail for our caravan?

Amir opened the note and smiled broadly as he read it.

"Grandfather sent a message to the Three Pashas explaining the importance of our meeting in Van. Enver Pasha wishes us a safe journey and has provided one of the Sultan's palace guard units to accompany us across the border."

"Of course" Wilhelm said. "The Ottomans need oil as well and want to see that Turkish Petroleum is a success."

"Does that alleviate some of your concerns Khalil?" Amir asked.

"Certainly" Khalil replied then turned to me and said under his breath. "I wasn't *that* worried Uncle."

"Well then, let's be on our way!" Amir said. The arrival of the note seemed to rejuvenate the young man.

I surveyed the camp one last time and noticed the Model T was gone.

"Your Automobile?" I asked him.

"While you were at the Telegraph office I had one of my men take it in to Khoy for safe keeping. I will reclaim it after our successful meeting in Van."

I saw the look on Commander Assad's face and recalled his earlier remarks. Young men are indeed optimistic, especially when they come from rich families. They almost think of themselves as invincible. With a crack unit of Palace guards protecting us, it was doubtful we would run in to any trouble to dispel that belief. When we arrived at Van though, Amir would be negotiating face to face with one of the most successful businessmen in the world, who had more personal wealth than the Emir had in his entire Emirate. I would never bet against experience.

The table and remaining items were loaded on the wagon and we set off just before the noon hour. We met up with the Turks as planned and by sunset arrived at the start of the mountain trail that lead to the border.

We made our camp as usual, but the camaraderie we shared with Reza Khan's men was nowhere to be found. The Turks were all business and had no desire to engage with us on a social level, not even their leader.

It took three days through the mountains to reach the village of Qotur and another day to arrive at the border. As expected, we had no trouble crossing in to the Ottoman Empire and made good time on the relatively flat terrain that followed. Three days later we arrived at lake Van.

The guards suggested that we camp one last night by the lake shore and make the final trip to Gulbenkian's estate the following morning. After a full week on the road we all appreciated the early evening and long night's rest.

The next morning we bathed in the waters of lake Van and changed into our formal attire. Khalil and I both decided to don our western clothes for the meetings and continue wearing them from now on. Although we were technically still in Asia, we would soon cross over into Europe and it was time we adopted new customs. Wilhelm likewise made the transition and seemed to feel less comfortable in his suit than we did.

Amir and Assad were representing the Emirate of Mohammerah and as such were dressed in their finest Bakhtiari robes.

We rode the final five miles to the Gulbenkian estate and arrived mid-morning. Our security detail and porters made camp well outside of the gated property leaving the four of us to ride up to the main house alone.

It was a grand estate with manicured lawns and formal gardens that reminded me of the British Consulate in Tehran. Although the style was very different, I felt very much like I was back home in Bagh Ilichi garden.

Calouste Gulbenkian surprised us by greeting us at the front entrance as his footmen cared for our horses.

"Welcome Gentlemen" he said in French with a warm smile. "You must be Amir Agha?"

Amir climbed the steps ahead of the rest and shook hands with our host.

"I am Monsieur Gulbenkian" he answered in kind. "It is my pleasure to meet you. May I introduce my good friend Commander Assad from Bushehr."

"My pleasure" Assad responded.

"Monsieur Assad I have heard so much about you."

"Have you met Wilhelm Wassmuss Monsieur Gulbenkian?"

"I have not had the pleasure, but I was expecting you Herr

Wassmuss."

"Enchanted" Wilhelm said.

"And finally I would also like to introduce you to two of our new colleagues, Sayed Abdulrahim Kashani and his nephew Khalil Redjaian."

"What a surprise Monsieur Kashani. Jean-Baptiste Lemaire wrote to me and asked that I meet with you when you arrive in Constantinople, but it seems fate has brought us together much sooner."

"I am just as surprised as you Monsieur Gulbenkian. Jean-Baptiste didn't mention anything to me before I left Tehran. I am so pleased to see we have friends in common."

He reached out to shake my hand and immediately I realized the connection. I shifted my grip to the Mason's handshake and saw the confirmation on his face.

"My nephew Khalil" I said.

"It is a pleasure to meet you Monsieur" Khalil said as he bowed at the waist.

"Please, no formalities. You are all my guests. Please, come in."

We entered the foyer to see that the inside of the house was even more grand than the exterior. Black and white marble covered the floors in the pattern of a chess board. Large oil paintings with pastoral scenes hung on the richly paneled walls. Elegant French furniture and fine Persian carpets were visible in every room we passed through on our way to the rear of the mansion. We continued out through a pair of French doors and on to a veranda overlooking a manicured lawn which ran down to a dock on the Lake. The view was breathtaking.

Under a canvas canopy, a dining table set with six places awaited us.

How did he know there would be five of us I asked myself?

"Let's have a light meal before others return from sailing. If you approve, I will ask my butler to send for your personal items and have them sent up to your rooms."

"Sailing?" Assad asked.

"Yes. My other guests arrived over the past few days and I felt they might enjoy an excursion on Lake Van in my sailboat. They will dine on the boat and return mid-afternoon."

We were all seated at the table set with crystal, china, and silver utensils which were a step up from our previous week on the road. Instead of road weary porters serving our meal, a butler and pair of footmen catered to our every need.

"Monsieur Gulbenkian" Khalil said breaking the silence, "I understand you are a petroleum engineer by training."

"Yes Khalil. I studied at King's college Oxford."

"Can you recommend a book that I might learn a bit about this topic? It seems fascinating."

"Are you a student of geology?"

"I don't know much Monsieur. I can distinguish igneous from metamorphic and sedimentary formations of course. And I have learned a bit about the Rock Cycle... but I wouldn't say I had any deep knowledge in that area. Everyone knows about those things."

Gulbenkian laughed.

"Of course they do! Jean-Baptiste wrote that you were very bright and an autodidact."

"Auto...?"

"Self-taught with a voracious appetite to learn everything you possibly can."

"That's our Khalil" Amir said under his breath although it didn't sound like he meant it as a compliment.

"I should have one or two books in my library here that would be of interest to you. Let me look for them after we finish here."

Amir cleared his throat and I got the distinct impression he was not happy that Khalil was dominating the conversation.

"Have you heard from my Grandfather Monsieur Gulbenkian?" Amir asked.

"As a matter of fact I have. He has also posted a letter to you which you will find in your room. He is well and assures me that you have his utmost confidence and support in our discussions. Power of Attorney in other words."

Amir seemed to be pleased with that and the dour look on his face lifted somewhat.

I saw Khalil begin to say something again so I placed my hand on his leg under the table. I shook my head slightly when he looked at me and he seemed to get the message.

"Can you tell us about your other guests?" Wilhelm asked.

"Well, Gustav Müller is here representing Deutsche Bank. He was one of the founding members. Wilhelm, I am sure you are already well acquainted with him of course."

"We have two guests from Britain. The first is an old friend of mine Sir Mark Sykes. He is a member of Parliament and no stranger to this region. He travelled with his father throughout the Ottoman Empire almost every winter as a boy and even published a book called 'The Home of Islam' a few years back."

"I've met Sir Mark" Amir exclaimed. "I have never met anyone with as many stories and ideas as he. You will all like him immensely!"

"Indeed" Gulbenkian agreed. "You may know of our other British guest as well, Miss Gertrude Bell."

"*Al-Khatun*?" I asked. I knew of Miss Bell by reputation but had never met her.

"Miss Bell and Sir Mark are here together?" asked Amir.

Gulbenkian's reaction was quite interesting. He seemed to have trouble finding an answer.

"Ah, not exactly" he replied sheepishly. "Gertrude is on her way home after years travelling in Arabia. I asked her to be my guest, but she will not be part of the negotiations."

"Why do you ask if they are together?" I asked Amir.

"Because they hate each other!" Amir interjected.

"I wouldn't use that strong of a word" Gulbenkian offered.

"Sir Mark told my Grandfather that Miss Bell was a 'conceited, flat-chested, globe-trotting, rump-wagging, blethering ass'!"

"Well, Sir Mark is a bit excitable, that's true, but I would rather focus on the lady's accomplishments."

"Such as?" Assad asked.

"Such as earning a degree from Oxford, successfully climbing the Matterhorn, learning to speak six languages including Persian and Arabic. She even translated several works of Omar Khayyam when she lived in Tehran. She is an accomplished archeologist and was the first to map and document the Al-Ukhaidir Fortress."

"Two German archeologists were the first to *publish* on Al-Ukhaidir" Wilhelm noted as if keeping score.

"Yes indeed. Gertrude gave them copies of her map my dear Wilhelm. Otherwise they would never have found the site in the first place."

It surprised me that Gulbenkian would make such a direct remark. Perhaps his relationship with the Germans was not as tight as I first thought.

"All of this from a woman?" Khalil asked. "She sounds amazing! I can't wait to meet her!"

"She is a bit too old for you I am afraid" Amir scoffed. "Even if you do like flat-chested rump-waggers!"

Gulbenkian continued, ignoring the snide remark.

"We also have the French Consul-General from Beirut, Monsieur François Picot representing his Government's interests and finally I am pleased that the Ottoman government has asked Ahmed Riza Bey to represent the Empire."

"What is Monsieur Bey's position?" I asked.

"He is currently President of the Senate I believe, but more importantly he has the blessing of the three Pashas to negotiate for the oil rights in Mesopotamia. Without their consent, there is no deal."

I focused on eating my lunch as I tried to work out how Khalil and I came to be included in a meeting of such illustrious people. I was also curious to know how much Jean-Baptiste had said in his letter about my trip and about Khalil. I was sure there would be an opportunity to speak with Gulbenkian alone, but until then I would have to navigate as best I could.

As we finished our meal we saw the boat glide in to the dock in the distance and the crew scurrying around to secure it to the moorings. Before the activity stopped we saw someone leap off of the board and storm down the pier. Another person jumped off and followed, yelling something unintelligible at the top of his voice.

As the first person got nearer we could see that it was a woman wearing trousers and a blouse. She was obviously wet from head to toe, her red hair plastered to her shoulders. As she ran up the stairs I could see her green eyes fuming with fury. She was small in stature but the way she carried herself made her seem much larger than life.

Gulbenkian rose and moved around the table to the steps to greet her.

"Gertrude? Are you alright?"

"I've never been so furious in all of my life!" she shouted as she approached the house. "He pushed me into the water!"

"Who pushed you Gertrude?" he continued.

"That son of a dog Sykes of course!"

They were speaking in English and I was only able to catch a few words, but Khalil leaned in and gave me the gist of the situation.

She charged up the stairs and past the table taking no notice of our group. Without saying a further word, she disappeared into the house leaving a trail of wet footsteps behind.

We turned our attention back to the dock to see a group of four men walking up the pathway to the house. The youngest of the group was laughing and stopped every so often to throw out his arms to his side and pretend to lose his balance, which caused one of the other men to laugh even louder. Two gentlemen in the group simply seemed to be annoyed and appeared not to be enjoying the joke.

"You should have seen her Calouste!" the young man said. "She was absolutely livid!"

As they climbed the stairs the younger men regained their composure having recognized that we were about to be introduced.

Gulbenkian gestured to the group starting with the man in the lead. "As you might have surmised, this is Sir Mark Sykes."

Sykes was tall and slim with a bushy mustache but no other facial hair. He appeared to be in his mid-thirties with a mischievous smile and seemed to be enjoying the attention.

"Ahmed Riza Bey" Gulbenkian turned to a distinguished looking gentleman in his fifties. He had that stoic look of a lifetime government official and was wearing a Turkish fez, so there was no real doubt who he was. He nodded his head slightly to the group of us. Just enough to be polite, but not enough to lower his status.

The Frenchman Monsieur Picot was easy to identify as well when Gulbenkian pointed him out. Slightly older than Sykes, he also sported a bushy mustache.

"And last but not least Herr Gustav Müller."

The banker was the oldest of the group, appearing to be in his sixties. He was dressed conservatively in a three piece suit even though they had just come off of a boat ride on the lake.

"Herr Müller the famous astronomer?" Khalil blurted out.

I patted his leg again under the table.

"Alas, *nein*. I am ze *other* Gustav Müller" the gentleman answered.

"He's an astronomy expert as well" Amir said under his breath.

Gulbenkian quickly introduced the five of us and then suggested that we all retire for a few hours rest before we began the initial discussion.

We were shown to our rooms on the second floor of the villa. Mine was just at the top of the stairs. My small travelling bag was sitting on the bed as promised, so I took the opportunity to freshen up before knocking on Khalil's door which was just next to mine.

"I'm sorry I spoke out at lunch Uncle" Khalil said as I closed the door behind me. "I was just excited to meet such a brilliant man as Gulbenkian and then Herr Müller..."

"Don't worry" I replied. "You did nothing wrong, but you must understand Amir's position. We are here as his guests so you must defer to him in these situations."

"I understand uncle. It won't happen again."

"Be particularly careful in this meeting Khalil. You are not to say a word unless you are asked a direct question. Listen carefully and pay attention to the way people move. Sometimes you can tell more from the language of their body than the words they speak."

"So we are spying on them for Amir?" Khalil asked.

"We are spying for no one but ourselves" I replied quietly. "You and I will decide how much to share with Amir after we learn more."

"Is Gulbenkian a Freemason uncle?"

"Why do you ask this?"

"I was paying attention when you shook hands with him. I saw you change your grip."

"Yes. He is."

"If he is a Freemason doesn't that mean you must be on his side and not the Germans?"

"It does change things indeed, but I was never on the side of the Germans... or the British for that matter."

"Gulbenkian seems not at all like I expected" Khalil continued. "He seems ... like a good person. I sense a genuine kindness in him."

"He may well be" I said. "I will try to get him alone later tonight. I need to know what Jean-Baptiste has shared with him. Now get some rest. I'll come for you when we are ready to go down."

I returned to my room for a short nap. The bed in the room was more comfortable even than my bed at home in Bagh Ilichi so I was out in minutes. A gong ringing downstairs pulled me out of my sleep.

Khalil was ready when I knocked on his door and together we made our way down to the library where the meeting was to be held.

The room was lined with bookshelves that were filled with books of all sizes, shapes, and colors. A large fireplace with a carved stone surround dominated one wall and a set of French doors with wide sidelights dominated the other. Large windows admitted natural light into the room making it feel even larger than it was.

A round table was placed in the middle of the room with six chairs. On the table in front of each place was a stack of papers.

Three comfortable chairs were lined up on the other side of the table. A fourth chair was set almost perpendicular to those three. It was clear from the arrangement that Wilhelm would occupy the one chair, with Assad, Khalil, and I sitting in the three.

Gulbenkian was the only person in the room as Khalil and I arrived.

"Monsieur Kashani, I was hoping I might have a word with you later today."

"I was hoping for the same opportunity" I replied. "I have many questions."

He smiled and nodded.

"I'm sure you do. Rest assured I will do my best to answer them."

He walked to a side table near the fireplace and picked up three books that were stacked on top. He brought them over to where we were standing.

"I have two books from Albert Perry Brigham for you Khalil, his 'Textbook of Geology' and a more recent publication called 'Commercial Geography'. The latter is more about the economic issues of distribution and geopolitical impacts on trade. I thought you would find that just as interesting. The third book is an old text on Petroleum Engineering."

Khalil took the books from Gulbenkian as if he were taking a new born baby.

"I will take good care of these Monsieur. I promise."

"No need to promise me anything. They are yours now. Take them with my pleasure from one lifelong student to another."

"You are too kind!" Khalil said. "Thank you so much."

I could see the pleasure it gave Gulbenkian to give away these books to someone who wanted them. Perhaps Khalil was right about him.

The others began streaming into the room so Khalil and I took our seats. Soon all of the principles were present and seated at the table. Assad joined us and finally I saw Wilhelm taking the seat behind Gustav Müller.

"Thank you gentlemen for your long journeys to Van" Gulbenkian began. "We are here to consider the formation of a new company to be called Turkish Petroleum Company, with a purpose of exploring, discovering, and extracting the oil we believe to be available in the region of Mesopotamia around Kirkuk."

"In front of you on the table you will find a draft copy of the term sheet that will highlight the investment required, the oil and mineral rights being granted by the Ottoman Empire, and the proposed distribution of shares."

He continued on through the term sheet paragraph by paragraph, answering questions and making clarifications as they went. If I followed the math correctly, the British were to have a thirty five percent interest, the Germans twenty five percent, Royal Dutch Shell Corporation twenty five percent, and the remaining fifteen percent to Gulbenkian himself. The French didn't seem to be getting any of this deal, so I was curious as to why Monsieur Picot was sitting at the table.

"Now that we have finished the first reading, I would like to open up the conversation and get your feedback on our proposal. Please speak freely."

Gustav Müller was the first to speak.

"With all due respect Herr Gulbenkian, I don't understand why the German interest is being held so low? Are we not expected to provide the lion's share of the investment capital? Are we not also providing the funding for the Berlin Bagdad railway... which will be necessary for transporting the oil?"

"We could always build a line south to Abadan instead" Sir Mark interjected. "I'm sure if we gave the d'Arcy Group a significant part of our thirty five percent, the British government could use the remainder to build our own rail line as a joint venture with our friends in Paris. After all they built the railroad from Van to Constantinople that some of us travelled to get here."

Now I understood why Picot was in the room. I knew of the French interests in Beirut and the Levant. Even though these territories belonged to the Ottomans, the French had coveted the region for years.

Britain also seemed to control a much bigger share than thirty five percent. Gulbenkian was a British citizen, so he is subject to pressure from his government. The Royal Dutch Shell combine, formed only seven years before, was half-owned by the Samuel Brothers. Also Brits. Even the Dutch were closer allies with Britain, so by my calculations, this deal seemed to be three to one in favor of the British.

"My Grandfather is concerned that additional ownership by the d'Arcy group would not be in the best interests of Turkish Petroleum."

I had lost track of Amir and the Emir of Mohammerah. They were also not represented in the ownership of Turkish Petroleum and their land was nowhere near Kirkuk. Given their objections and connection with Wilhelm, I assumed that the Germans had asked for them to be included.

"I think young Amir has a point" Ahmed Riza Bey said. "Speaking on behalf of the empire who owns the oil, we feel British Petroleum would be a direct competitor of Turkish Petroleum and therefore a share by the d'Arcy Group would not be in our best interest."

Amir's face lit up when Riza Bey spoke. He still had much to learn about negotiations.

"We are also only a few hundred miles from completing the rail line to Kirkuk as we speak" Gustav Müller added. "We will be operational before the French could even complete negotiations for the right of way let alone lay the first rail. Besides, our friends in Constantinople have already chosen their partner for the Railway to Baghdad. We Germans will finish what we started."

Sir Mark glanced furtively at Picot. They both had peculiar smiles on their face, as if they knew something the rest of us did not. I expected them to be angry with the direction of the conversation but instead it seemed to go as they expected.

Gulbenkian surveyed the room and raised his hands halfway into the air.

"I think we have reached a good stopping point for today. I am also very happy to hear the open conversation around the challenges we face with this deal. I knew coming in that it would not be easy. This is the first step required to address the issues however, so I am pleased with our progress."

The participants seated at the table all rose as one. Amir made his way to join a conversation between Wilhelm and Gustav while Sir Mark and François Picot gravitated towards a bar cart by the entrance and helped themselves to a glass of whiskey.

I saw Riza Bey heading for a conversation with Gulbenkian and caught Khalil's attention. I motioned in their direction and Khalil understood immediately what I wanted. He walked over to browse the books on a bookshelf within earshot of the two men who had begun a conversation in Turkish.

That left Assad and me to wander out of the room and on to the veranda overlooking the lake.

"Well?" Assad asked in Persian. "Did you learn anything?"

My instincts were telling me to be cautious with Amir and Wilhelm at this point. I felt a kinship with the commander because of our shared experience in the revolution, but at the end of the day he was obligated to share what he learns with Amir.

"Just the obvious" I replied. "Germany needs this oil and does not want to give the British access. The British believe they are in control of the deal. We should know more when Khalil reports."

"Well I must get back to my *master* in case he needs something" Assad said dripping with sarcasm.

I looked out at the lake and decided to walk down to the dock to have a better look and to get away from all of the intrigue.

The view of the lake was even more spectacular from the end of the pier. The clear blue water seemed to go on forever although I could also see the mountains rising in the distance.

"It is beautiful is it not?" I heard the voice of a woman speaking Persian from behind me and knew at once it must be Gertrude Bell. I turned to find her dressed in a long skirt and white blouse. As she approached I could see that she wasn't very attractive but there was something about her that made you want to look deeper. As the French say, she had a certain *Joie de vivre*.

"Salaam! Chetori *Al-Khatun*?" I asked, hoping that she was not offended at the name we Persians used. The word meant 'Lady of the Court' but it also carried the sense of 'one who spies for the crown'. Most everyone in Asia Minor believed her to be a spy for the British.

"*Merci*! I am well Aghayeh Kashani" she replied. "Will you please call me Gertrude?"

"Certainly Gertrude" I said.

"I came down to look for my sun hat. It blew away as I disembarked earlier."

"I have not seen a hat" I replied. "But I will help you search if you like."

"No need" she said. "I asked if you thought the lake was beautiful."

"Yes" I replied as I turned to take in the view. "I am not used to such large bodies of water."

"We sailed out to the Aghtamar Cathedral today. It is on an island in the middle of the lake. It was built over a thousand years ago."

"I understand you are an archeologist. Isn't a thousand years a little too new for your taste?"

"Witty" she replied. "I like that."

"I am not as funny as Sir Mark I am sure."

"Mark Sykes is not funny. His idea of humor comes at the cost of someone else's pain. *Schadenfreude* I believe the Germans call it. If Calouste has told me ahead of time that he was here, I would have stayed in Constantinople."

"Will you return to Constantinople on your way home?" I asked trying to change the subject.

"I am not going home" she replied.

"Sorry, but Monsieur Gulbenkian said you were on your way to England."

"I am travelling to England Sayed, but that country is no longer my home. My father has summoned me and the British foreign service wishes to be rid of me. So I am bound for England."

"If England is no longer your home, then where is home?"

"The desert. Arabia, Mesopotamia, the Levant, Persia... I have more interests in common with the tribes of the middle east than I do with the English. Allah blessed you Sayed when he made you Persian."

This was something I never thought to hear from an English woman.

"There you are!" a voice called out in French from behind us.

We both turned to see Gulbenkian striding along the pier in our direction.

"Are you alright Gertrude? I was worried about you."

"I'm fine Calouste" she replied switching seamlessly into French herself. "Sorry for my behavior earlier. I will apologize to your guests at dinner tonight."

"No need for that. I simply wanted to be sure you were not injured."

"Only my pride" she said with a smile.

"Would you like me to leave you two alone Monsieur?" I asked.

"No, no Sayed Kashani. I was actually coming to speak with you and was pleased to find Gertrude here as well."

"Then would you like me to give you two some privacy Calouste?"

"Would you mind dear? I am afraid I must speak with Sayed Kashani before dinner."

"Will dinner be formal again tonight?" She asked. "Herr Müller and Riza Bey are proper gentlemen you know" she said to me with a wink.

"No black tie tonight. I am afraid Riza Bey has already left for Constantinople. He feels we are very far from having an agreement and did not want to waste any more time."

"I'm sorry to hear that" she replied. "So does that mean the negotiation is a failure?"

"Oh no, not at all. We are just getting started. Today I simply wanted to confirm the areas of contention. Now we begin the long, hard work of finding a compromise that satisfies all."

"Well if anyone can do it, you can."

Miss Bell turned towards me. "Sayed. Will I see you at dinner?"

"Yes Gertrude. My nephew Khalil will be there as well. He has an unlimited curiosity and thirst for knowledge. So if he asks you too many questions please let me know."

"If he is willing to learn from a woman, then I will be happy to answer every question he may ask!"

She touched her heart and then her forehead as the Arabs do and turned to go.

When she was out of earshot Gulbenkian turned towards the water and breathed deeply.

"She is an amazing woman and cares deeply about the people of the middle east, but I am afraid she will never be truly happy."

"How can one be happy without a family?" I asked.

"So true. I have been married now for more than twenty years Sayed and have two beautiful children. They are my true fortune."

We stood in silence for a few moments looking out over the water. I felt it was best to let him drive the conversation.

"In just a few moments you will see the sun setting over the lake. It is one of the reasons I chose this site for my house. I just love to watch the sun set!"

I got the feeling he was stalling, as if he was not sure where to begin.

"Jean-Baptiste wrote to me of your background Sayed. About your militia and the fight for Persian self-rule. He told me that you were a man of principle and a man of your word."

"I am honored to call him my friend Monsieur."

"So I was quite surprised to see you arrive at my door with Amir Ardalan from Bushehr and Wilhelm Wassmuss. May I ask what is your connection with them?"

I had been so focused on learning the connection with Gulbenkian and Jean-Baptiste that I had never considered how the reputation of my travelling companions might reflect badly on me.

"I met Amir and Commander Assad in Tabriz for the first time on our way north. Assad was a hero of the Constitutional Revolution and I respect him for his courage and sacrifices. Amir is another story. He hid his true identity from us at first and his relationship with the Emir until after he thought Khalil and I might be useful to him. I have no loyalty to Amir or to his grandfather."

"And Wassmuss? Do you know who he is? What he is?"

The way the question was asked made it clear to me that Gulbenkian knew very well who Wilhelm was. I now had to make a decision of who to trust, a German spy who was in league with my cousin the Ayatollah, or a fellow Freemason. My instincts told me to trust Gulbenkian and to distance myself from the Germans. The choice was quite easy.

"Wilhelm is a German spy who has been sent to foment unrest in the south of Persia" I answered. "I have been told that he wishes to destroy the refinery at Abadan and disrupt the flow of oil to the British."

"Destroy the refinery?" Gulbenkian asked. "I was aware of his efforts to disrupt the workers and cause strikes, but if he blows up the refinery that would be an act of war! Lives would be lost. Tensions are running high enough as it is."

"I believe he plans to use my cousin Ayatollah Abol-Ghasem Kashani to do his dirty work. So it will appear to be religious fanatics and not the work of Germany."

I was following my instincts at this point. I had crossed the line now and there was no turning back. I was no spy for the British. I felt that we deserved more of the oil production than we were getting, but I did not agree with the destruction of property. No matter who it belonged to. If nothing else, Persia needed that refinery.

"Yes. Jean-Baptiste mentioned your cousin as well."

"May I ask you why the Emir of Mohammerah is part of your negotiation?"

"It is a bit complicated and does not seem to make sense on the face of it" Gulbenkian said, "but let me explain. The Germans are trying to bring the Ottomans into their formal alliance with Austria-Hungary to divide western Europe from Asia and cut off Russia from its allies. There are many people who believe we are on the verge of a war and the Germans want to secure access to oil for their ships. The Berlin Baghdad Railroad and oil rights in Mesopotamia are critical to this."

"The Ottomans see Germany as a powerful ally against the Russians," he continued, "but they are not quite sure they can trust either Germany or Austria-Hungary. So they are also courting the French Government to establish a treaty with them. By joining the French, the Ottomans could leverage France's alliance with Russia to reach a détente. Monsieur Picot and Riza Bey met privately the day before Herr Müller arrived. That was the real reason for Riza Bey and Picot coming to Van."

"So I see why Germany is so keen to get access to the new oil fields" I said "and why they would want to cut off the British from Persia's oil, but how does the Emir fit in?"

"The Emir is an insurance policy. The Kaiser has suggested that the Emir could invade Mesopotamia and expand the borders of Mohammerah all the way to Najaf in the west, to the port of Basra in the south, and the new oil fields in Kirkuk in the north. It would triple the size of his Sheikhdom and provide an alternate route for the oil. The Berlin Baghdad railway runs through the heart of the Turkish homeland, so if the Ottoman relationship falls through, they will need an alternative."

"It would also place Najaf and Karbala under the control of a Shia government" I added. "I think I understand Abol-Ghasem's interest in this matter now, unfettered access to the two holiest cities in Shia Islam."

My head was spinning with all of the new information, but

something didn't quite make sense.

"May I ask how you know about the German plan for Moham-merah?"

Gulbenkian laughed.

"Mark Sykes may have his faults, but he is very well connected in the Cairo foreign office."

"He is a spy?"

"I would not use that term for him or for myself if that is your next question."

"I would never..."

"Oh don't worry Sayed. I would not be insulted. I know how things look, but the truth is I am a simple businessman. An oil man."

And I am a simple stamp collector I said to myself.

"If I can bring people together into a deal" he continued, "then I can make money for myself and my people."

"Monsieur five percent" I said.

"I am proud of that nickname" he said.

"If I remember correctly you would retain fifteen percent of Turkish Petroleum."

"That is true, but I will give five percent to my foundation in Armenia to help my people, and another five percent as a bonus to any Armenian workers in the oil fields. So you see I am left with only five percent for my family. I have more than enough to live comfortably now. It is time to help others."

When I heard this last comment, I felt my trust in the man was validated. He could still be lying about his intentions, but the sadness on his face was not the look one would expect from a charlatan.

"I am very honored to meet you Monsieur" I said.

He reached out and took my hand.

"I am very glad to know you too Sayed Kashani."

We both turned to look out at the water and the sunset.

"I know you must still have many questions" he finally said. "Best to let things settle a bit. I expect to meet with the Germans and Amir separately from Sykes and Picot over the next few days to understand what it would take to consummate a deal. Frankly I don't see that a deal is possible until the Ottomans make their choice."

"I believe you are correct" I offered.

"Then if you would do me the honor, I would like to invite you and Khalil to accompany me back to my home in Constantinople where we conclude our discussions. This will give us more time to talk."

"I would like that very much Monsieur Gulbenkian."

I shook his hand again and looked again into his eyes to see if there was anything I was missing.

"I insist you call me Calouste. All of my good friends do."

"If you will call me Abdulrahim."

"It's a deal."

We heard a bell ringing up at the Villa and started back.

"Wilhelm plans to travel on to Constantinople as well" I said as we walked. "He wants me to meet with someone there."

"You don't know who?"

"I have no clue."

"Then I will invite him to ride with us in my private car."

"You have an automobile?"

"No, car as in part of a train. You will see. It is the only way to travel!"

We walked back to the house in silence as I tried to digest all that I learned.

I had barely enough time to speak with Khalil before dinner. He was waiting for me in his room.

"I saw you through the window speaking to Gulbenkian on the dock uncle. Did you learn anything?"

"Quite a bit Khalil, but first let's hear what you learned."

"I was careful. I don't think they suspected I was listening, but I am also worried that I misheard their conversation. Turkish is very close to Aziri, but there are some differences."

"Just tell me what you think they said."

"Riza Bey said he spoke with Müller this morning on a walk by the lake. He said they couldn't trust the Germans, which surprised me. I thought they were already close. Then he said his conversation with François Picot two days ago was much more positive and that it appeared France was the better choice of partners. He said he received a cable from his government just before the meeting. They had uncovered evidence of a possible rebellion outside of Karbala. He called the Emir a greedy son of a dog and that if they could find proof, Enver Pasha would send troops into Mohammerah to wipe out the Emir's entire family."

This all made sense given what I learned a few minutes before.

"I don't understand Uncle. Enver Pasha sent a letter to Amir welcoming him to Van. I thought they were talking about Turkish Petroleum, but this is much bigger. They were talking about war."

"I know Khalil. You did well."

"Does it make sense to you?"

"It does."

"But Enver Pasha's note?"

"An armed guard may protect you from outside threats, but these same guards may easily become jailers who will escort you to prison."

"Are we in danger of being put into an Ottoman prison?"

"No, no, we are fine. I can't tell you everything just yet, but please keep your ears open. Riza Bey left already for Constantinople and I expect we will follow in a few days. In luxury, not in chains. Calouste has invited us to travel with him."

"So what do we tell Amir and Assad? What will happen to them?"

"You leave that to me. I expect Amir and Assad will return to Mohammerah when we leave. We tell them nothing. It's Wilhelm that we must worry about. We need to keep him guessing whose side we are on."

We heard the gong from downstairs and followed the others as we all made our way to dinner. Khalil and I were still wearing our western attire and getting more used to it by the day. Amir and Assad continued to don their Bakhtiari robes. Sykes and Picot were wearing much more formal suits than they did for the meetings earlier in the day and looked almost as conservative as Herr Müller.

We followed the others into a formal dining room with a massive table that could easily seat twenty. Just like the table at lunch, it was set with fine china, silver utensils, and crystal. There were even name cards showing us where to sit. When I saw the arrangement I understood why.

Gertrude and Sir Mark were placed at opposite ends of the table facing the same direction making it difficult for them to interact. Amir and Assad were directly across from Gulbenkian in the seat of honor even though I now understood that this was a charade. Khalil sat next to Gertrude, an arrangement made for Khalil's benefit I am sure. I was positioned close to Sykes and Picot, perhaps in hopes that I would get to know them better.

The footmen and butler served our first course and filled our glasses with white wine. Monsieur Picot made a point of examining the bottle after his glass was filled.

"A wonderful choice Calouste. I adore Viognier!"

With that endorsement we all raised our glasses and took a sip. I was not much of a wine enthusiast, but I found it very pleasing. From the look on Khalil's face, he did not enjoy it nearly as much, but then he did not have much experience with alcoholic beverages.

There wasn't much conversation and I wondered if the open disagreements of the earlier meeting was the cause.

"Sir Mark, I understand you toured the Aghtamar Cathedral today?" I asked to break the silence.

"Yes. It was 'smashing' as we say."

I didn't understand the English word he used but I gathered it was good.

"It is well preserved" Picot added. "Two hundred years older than Notre Dame, but of course not as majestic as our lady."

"Older than Westminster Abbey as well" Sykes replied. "Strange to see a church standing alone on an island in the middle of nowhere."

"The island was home to one of our most famous Armenian kings" Gulbenkian said. "At the time the island was a settlement and one of the King's residences. The other buildings on the island have long been destroyed. The church is now all that remains."

"Like many ancient sites" Gertrude added, "wiped out by the victors of war."

"It is so all over the world" Gustav Müller added. "The strongest are meant to rule and to write the history books."

"I have read Darwin and Wallace" Gulbenkian offered. "I understand survival of the fittest in the animal kingdom, but animals lack compassion. Isn't that what sets us apart? Our compassion for our fellow man?"

No one seemed ready to comment further.

"Our friend Khalil is very quiet tonight" Amir chided. "Have you read Darwin too?"

"I have" Khalil said sheepishly.

"I didn't know Darwin had been translated into Persian" Sir Mark interjected.

"I don't know if it has or not" Khalil replied then looked straight on at Amir. "I read it in the original English."

I doubt the others heard the edge in his voice, but I could tell that Khalil was annoyed by Amir's constant comments.

"You speak English as well as French?" Gertrude asked.

"And German" Assad said. He also seemed to be annoyed with Amir.

I looked across the table to catch Khalil's eye. We agreed to keep his language skills a secret. When he met my eye he nodded and then returned to his meal.

"Compassion" I said looking as well at Amir, "is a virtue that we could all use a little more of."

"I believe the most important distinction is education" Gustav said. "As victors we owe it to those we conquer to educate them so they can join us in the modern world."

"Hear, hear!" Sir Mark replied.

"It is the white man's burden is it not?" Picot added.

"White man's burden?" Gulbenkian asked incredulously.

"Kipling" Sir Mark Replied. "Take up the White Man's burden, Send forth the best ye breed, Go bind your sons to exile, to serve your captives' need."

I couldn't follow the English, although I could tell Calouste was not happy with the direction of the conversation.

"So it is the responsibility of the western world to... educate the... backward societies?" he asked.

"Most certainly!" Gustav replied. "Barbarians like Alexander the Great destroyed the cities of his enemies and killed or enslaved its people. They are extinct today just like the species Darwin writes of in his book. When we conquer a country, we establish schools and churches and the rule of law. We build new factories..."

"And drain the natural resources from the natives in payment" Assad interrupted with contempt.

"A good education is never free" Sir Mark quipped.

Gertrude stood up and threw her napkin on to the table.

"You insensitive ass! Do you even think about what you are saying before it spews forth from your mouth?"

She stormed out of the room and slammed the doors behind her.

Sir Mark looked around the table for support as if he were the injured party and then seemed to notice for the first time that Commander Assad and Amir were wearing Bakhtiari robes and that half of the people at the table would not be considered 'white'.

"I'm sorry if I offended" he offered. "I was only trying..."

His voice fell off as he realized that he was not saving himself from the faux pas.

"I am truly sorry. Please forgive me."

I glanced across the table to see Herr Müller truly enjoying the situation, almost as if he baited the younger man into a trap.

The footmen returned with another course and gave us time to recover our composure. The butler began filling our glasses with a dark red wine. Ever the consummate host, Gulbenkian tried to put the incident behind and announced that we were about to try a grand Cru Bordeaux.

Monsieur Picot announced that he was planning to attend the World's Fair in Lyon on his way back to Paris which led to light conversation for a while. Herr Müller announced that the Americans would soon open the Panama Canal which seemed like a good topic for the group until he insisted on pointing out that the Americans accomplished what the French could not.

By the time dessert was served we were all looking for an excuse to retire.

Khalil and I bid ourselves adieu and retired quickly to my room.

"Why does Amir do that Uncle? Why?" Khalil asked when the door was closed.

"He is jealous of you Khalil."

"But he is a prince!"

There came a light rap on my door. When I opened it, Gertrude Bell was standing on the other side.

"I am so glad you are not alone" she said. "May I come in?"

I stepped back and let her in.

"Khalil, I am so sorry we didn't have more time to talk. I promise we will on the train to Constantinople. It seems we will be returning together."

"I would like that Miss Bell" Khalil replied.

"For now I just wanted to make sure that you knew my feelings about my country's colonial ambitions in the middle east."

"It is not necessary Gertrude. We Persians know where you stand."

"Perhaps, but I wanted you to be sure of my position. I have worked tirelessly to ensure that the people of the middle east will be able to rule themselves, no matter what happens over the next few years. The great powers have no right to divide up Persia into spheres of influence or to take advantage of a corrupt Shah. We should be celebrating your new parliament and recognize that the Persian people are perfectly capable of putting their own house in order."

"I wish the rest of your countrymen felt the same way" I said.

"Now that you know where I stand, I need to give you some information that might help you with the remainder of your trip and then I would ask a favor of you."

"What do you know of the purpose of my trip?"

"You are going to Paris to sell some stamps. Correct?"

I thought of responding but I didn't think she would believe my answer.

"I spent the last few weeks in the Cairo office Sayed Kashani. While I was there, I overheard a conversation between Sir George Barclay and Sir Mark Sykes. They were discussing a letter received a from Sir Cecil Spring Rice."

"Sir Mark I just met, but I knew both Sir George and Sir Cecil when they were in Tehran" I replied. "I camped out on the grounds of the British consulate for months during the early days of the Revolution seeking refuge. Sir Cecil was very kind to me, but that was over eight years ago. Isn't he now the British Ambassador to the United States?"

"Yes and according to his letter, you made a lasting impression on him as well. He said that you were one of most honest and sincere men he had met during his time in Tehran."

"I lost track of Sir George" I said, not knowing how to respond to her previous comment.

"There is a reason. He has been on assignment based in the Cairo Office as Special Assistant to Winston Churchill. He spent most of his time in Constantinople. Last year they awarded him the Star of India for his work, although it wasn't publicly stated what that work was."

"So why was I the topic of conversation in Cairo?" I asked bewildered.

"I didn't hear much more, only that 'you were the man for the job'."

"Gertrude, I love my country. I am proud to be Persian. We may have a lot to learn, but we have taken the first step towards real independence."

"Of course. I understand how you feel better than most."

"Then you must know I will not be a spy for Britain."

"That is what Sir George said as well. 'Kashani will never do anything that is not in the best interest of Persia' I believe is how he put it."

"So you know nothing more?"

"About this matter? No."

"And other matters?" I asked.

"Other matters will have to wait until I confirm a few suspicions and answer a few questions."

I waited for her to continue but she simply smiled and turned towards Khalil and took his hand.

"I'm sorry that our chaperone was not a part of the conversation. I promise it will be different next time."

She turned, opened the door, and peered both ways down the hall.

"Good night gentlemen" she said and then was gone.

I turned to face Khalil.

"The more I learn about this trip the more confused I become" I said half to myself.

"Perhaps it will help to tell me. I find that explaining something to others helps focus the mind."

"Perhaps you are right" I said. "Sit down. This might take a while."

The next day Gulbenkian planned to meet with Amir and

Herr Müller alone into the afternoon so I had some free time. Much had happened since we arrived the previous morning. So much that it seemed more like several days had passed.

It was clear to me that Khalil and I would no longer need our porters, tents, or our pack animals, so after breakfast, Commander Assad and I walked out to the caravan camp to pay the porters and decide what to do about the rest.

The porters were happy to take my horses and mules as part of their payment which was good news indeed. The group divided up the rest of our equipment once we separated out the items that would accompany us to Paris. The porters carried the latter up to the house and said their farewells.

With that out of the way, Assad and I had a chance to catch up. We walked through the grounds in the late morning, enjoying the manicured lawns and the sculptured trees that adorned the property. Once we were well away from the main house we discovered a small pavilion where we could sit and talk.

"We are returning to Khoy tomorrow" Assad said. "I will miss your company greatly."

"The feeling is mutual Commander Assad. It was an unexpected surprise meeting a man of your reputation. The stories you shared with the Major! I will remember them forever. I might even steal a few for myself if you don't mind."

"You are welcome to them Sayed. I am sure I stole a few of them myself. My memory is not what it used to be."

We sat in amiable silence for a period until thoughts of Wilhelm broke into my conscious mind.

"May I speak frankly with you Assad Agha?"

He nodded.

"Please be careful of Wilhelm. I believe him to be a very dangerous man."

Assad smiled.

"I said exactly the same thing to Amir in Tabriz before we met you. Wassmuss hides his emotions and his thoughts like a sandstorm hides the sun."

"I am happy to hear you are suspicious as well."

Another matter weighed on my mind. I didn't know if Amir would carry his resentment of Khalil back to the Emir. It would be petty to do so, but then Amir did not seem to let things go easily.

"Amir seems unhappy with Khalil and me."

"He is obsessed with finding a way to put Khalil in his place" Assad replied. "He sees your nephew's superior intellect as a threat. He is not accustomed to competing for attention."

"I have counseled Khalil on this matter. He means no disrespect or harm. Khalil has no experience with people in Amir's class."

"Khalil is not to blame at all!" Assad spat. "Don't worry about this any longer. You have my word. When we return to Mohammerah, Amir will have more pressing issues to deal with and will forget he even met your nephew."

"*Merci* Commander."

"If I may speak frankly with you Sayed, it seems to me you are walking in to a pit of snakes in Constantinople. Do you have any better idea what Wassmuss has in mind for you there?"

"None at all" I replied. "He has only said that he would like to introduce me to some people and hear them out."

"Sayed, I know you have more experience dealing with powerful men than Khalil, but that was at home where people you trust had your back. In Constantinople you may find yourself face to face with one of the three Pashas. Enver and Djemal are dangerous enough, but Grand Vizier Talaat is unpredictable. Stay away from the Sublime Porte if you can."

"I appreciate your concern my friend. I truly do. What do you know of the German Alliance with the Ottomans?"

"Only that it is a precarious relationship built on suspicion and fear. The Ottomans do not trust the Germans, but they fear the Russian Bear more."

This seemed to confirm what Gulbenkian had said.

"And what of Gulbenkian?" I asked. "Do you trust him?"

Assad stared off into the distance as if collecting his thoughts before replying.

"I like the man. He seems genuine, but he is shrewd. He has a reputation for being a miser, yet he has shown nothing but generosity to us these past few days. Then you don't build an empire from nothing in this world without knowing how to keep your rivals at bay. Many powerful men covet what Gulbenkian has. If you can stay out of the line of fire, you should be safe."

Coming from a man like Assad I was comforted to hear these comments which reflected my own thoughts.

As we headed back towards the Villa I was pleased to see Khalil and Gertrude Bell walking together in the distance. I wondered what topics they were discussing, she with her Oxford education and he with his insatiable appetite for learning.

As we approached the front door, Sir Mark and Monsieur Picot were just exiting the Villa. From the valise in Sir Mark's hand and the awaiting carriage I assumed he was making his escape. They saw the two of us approaching and waved.

"I don't want to deal with them this morning" Assad said. "I think I will go and join Khalil and Miss Bell."

Sykes waited patiently for me to approach and held out his hand when I arrived.

"I hope there are no hard feelings about my unfortunate comments last night Monsieur Kashani. I feel truly awful."

I grasped his hand and smiled.

"I took no offence Sir Mark. Please forget it happened as I already have."

"You are too kind Monsieur. Now if you don't mind, I must be on my way. I hope to see you soon."

He turned to Picot and shook his hand as well.

"It was a pleasure meeting you Monsieur Picot. I will see you in Paris after I finish my business in Cairo. I think your ideas will prove to be a perfect solution and I believe my superiors will agree."

Sykes disappeared into the carriage. We watched it drive off until it was out of sight, but instead of turning towards the door, Picot faced me, seeming to size me up.

"You are a mystery to me Monsieur Kashani" he said after a few moments of silence. "I was briefed on all of Calouste's guests before I arrived and was surprised when you and your nephew joined the discussion."

I wasn't quite sure what Picot was getting at with his comment.

"Monsieur Gulbenkian was surprised as well" I replied, "but he made us feel welcome."

"Oh, don't get me wrong Monsieur. I am very happy for this surprise and you are most welcome even if it is not my place to say so. I was not fully prepared. That is all."

"What was it von Moltke wrote? 'No battle plan survives first contact with the enemy'."

"He actually wrote 'No plan of operations extends with certainty beyond the first encounter with the enemy's main strength'... but I think I prefer your translation much better. You see you have just made my point for me. A shop keep and stamp collector quoting von Moltke the Elder."

"The elder?" I asked.

"Yes. His nephew of the same name is currently Chief of the

General Staff for Germany and just as formidable as his Uncle. Sound like anyone we know?"

I laughed out loud.

"Khalil and I are hardly in the same class and we are anything but formidable."

He continued staring at me although now with a disarming smile on his face.

"Let's take a walk shall we?" he finally said.

We set out towards the lake and walked quite a ways before either of us spoke.

"I understand you led a militia in the constitutional revolution."

"Yes. We called ourselves the Fatemieh Society and I was the Director."

Picot laughed.

"From that description I would guess you were the leader of a debate club and not a militia. You published a newspaper during this time as well?"

"Yes, it was called 'The Divine Mirror'. We felt it was important to educate the public on the reasons for our opposition to the Shah. More important perhaps than taking up arms."

"In the end you did take to the barricades as we say though. Didn't you."

"Not through speeches and majority decisions will the great questions of the day be decided—but by iron and blood" I quoted.

"And now the humble shop keep is quoting Bismarck. Tell me, do you ever quote any Frenchmen?"

"Not when it comes to the art of war" I replied, intending the barb.

"Touché!" he replied and laughed out loud once again.

No matter how direct his questions I felt it would be very difficult to get angry at this man. He disarmed you with his charm.

"Would you be willing to answer a few questions of mine Monsieur Picot?"

"*Certainement!*" He replied.

"I am interested in understanding colonialism from a ... white man's perspective."

"I thought you had forgotten that unfortunate *faux pas*?" he replied.

"I have, but I find that most widely held ideas have some merit. I also find that if you can understand a situation from the *other's* point of view, you can often find a solution to even the most challenging problem."

I had the impression he was trying to decide if I was sincere, since his answer was not immediate, but perhaps he was simply trying to find the right words.

"We French have a slightly different philosophy than the British and the Germans" he began. "You know from history that each culture rises and eventually falls. Babylon, Rome, the Sassanian Empire... these were cultures that flourished and advanced civilization. They created great art, made scientific breakthroughs, and gave us philosophies that have shaped the modern world."

"Sassanid Persia was a great society" he continued, "although it languished two hundred years after the Arab Muslims invaded. Europe was in the so-called Dark Ages at this time, but in China, Oh Monsieur! The Tang Dynasty was the pinnacle of civilization. Almost completely unknown to the western world. They had mechanical clocks and wood block printing almost a thousand years before we claimed to invent these technologies."

"If you imagine civilization as a marathon, some parts of the world are always ahead of the others. For whatever reason, we Europeans have come to power and have pulled ahead of the race. We believe it is our responsibility to share our culture and knowledge with the parts of the world who are less fortunate. For the faithful, this also means bringing the good news to these remote places."

"So you see, we believe our efforts are a fair trade. We bring our modern technologies and philosophies into a place rich in natural resources and teach them how to reap the blessings God has bestowed upon them. In return, we share in the profits as any investor ought to."

I resisted the urge to argue the merits or to identify the parties reaping the largest share of God's blessing. His explanation did give me a better idea of how a civilized country could justify these actions and maintain a belief that they were a benefactor and not the antagonist.

Claiming that a cause is God's work brings its own set of challenges. How many people have died throughout history because someone was doing God's work? I fought for our right to self-government not because God told me to, but because it is the right of people to be free.

"Thank you Monsieur for your explanation. I believe I understand you better now."

Picot had the look of a dog who had heard a noise it didn't quite understand. He obviously didn't expect that response.

"Do you think your allies the Russians are doing God's work?" I asked.

"Only if God requires a warm water port for his warships" Picot retorted.

I wondered what my cousin the Ayatollah would have to say about that comment. I wondered also if God preferred destroyers or battleships in his fleet?

I know dear reader that you may think I should rot in hell for such comments, but you see that is the reason for me telling this story, to determine that very fate.

"Have you ever made a business deal with someone you did not respect Monsieur Kashani?"

"I have sold stationary to the Shah's men for many years Monsieur Picot, but I never extended them credit. Credit requires trust and trust requires respect."

"France and Russia have had a love hate relationship for centuries" he continued. "They appreciate our culture and we appreciate their good taste. With the recent unification of the Lesser Germany, France is concerned that they will try to prosecute the Franco-Prussian war once again. Russia on their eastern front makes them think twice. Make no mistake however, we trust the Czar will do only what is in his best interest."

I recognized the truth in his response, but immediately thought of the Ottoman's dilemma. I wondered if Picot would be willing to share his thoughts on this topic.

"Our friends the Ottomans might be a similar deterrent to the other German speaking empire if they were to have similar ideas."

Picot gave me that curious dog look again.

"You may be right" he replied, but that was all he said.

We had arrived at the foot of the dock, but heard a bell ringing up at the Villa.

"Lunch already?" Picot exclaimed as he pulled his watch from his vest pocket and opened the cover.

"Shall we?" I said as I motioned towards the villa.

Picot closed his watch case and returned it to his vest pocket.

"You are a very interesting man Monsieur Kashani with very intriguing ideas. I wonder if you will come to see me when you reach Paris? I'd like to continue this conversation and introduce you to a few of my friends."

"I would be delighted Monsieur Picot."

"And Khalil of course. I have an American friend Gertrude Stein who hosts a salon in Paris. All of the most gifted people are there. I think your nephew would enjoy it and fit in perfectly with that crowd."

"I am sure he would welcome the opportunity."

After a marvelous lunch I retired to my room and slept much of the afternoon. With all of the walking and conversation I needed the rest.

Dinner was much more subdued than the previous evening. Without Sir Mark everyone seemed to be on their best behavior. Wassmuss and Herr Müller uttered less than ten words between them. Amir acted the perfect prince that he was. The conversation focused mainly on the food and wine, of which I had two glasses. By the time dessert was served I was ready to sleep once again.

At breakfast the following morning, I learned that Wassmuss and Herr Müller were already on their way to Constantinople, leaving at the break of dawn. There was no note or any message from Wilhelm to arrange a meeting. Since it was well known I would stay with Gulbenkian however, I was sure he would find me if he still wanted me.

After breakfast we all gathered at the front of the villa to see Amir and Commander Assad off. The porters had their horses ready and the rest of the caravan was waiting for them at the gates. Amir surprised me with his courteous manners in saying goodbye not only to me but to Khalil as well. Perhaps Commander Assad had intervened on our behalf.

The Commander turned in his saddle and said to me "If you are ever in Bushehr Sayed, please be my guest."

"I will my friend" I replied. "I will."

They rode off towards the gate as the remaining guests gathered on the front steps.

"We leave just after lunch if that's acceptable to you all" Gulbenkian said to us all, as if we would dare object. "Please have your cases ready beforehand and I will have my staff send them ahead to the train station."

CONSTANTINOPLE

June 12th, 1914

When Khalil and I returned to our rooms I found a new flat top canvas trunk with beige and brown checkered pattern sitting on my bed. Inside was a steamer bag and a note which explained they were a gift from Gulbenkian. According to the tag attached to the handle, the manufacturer was Luis Vuitton of Paris, the foremost maker of travel goods. I had never seen craftsmanship of this quality in a trunk before.

I heard a rap at my door as Khalil pushed it open.

"Uncle he gave me a set as well! Should we accept these? They must be expensive."

"Why not" I said. "If we are travelling with the upper class we must look the part."

I transferred my personal items into the trunk with room to spare and latched the top shut. Even the sound of the latches closing made me feel that his trunk was a solid piece of craftsmanship.

Khalil and I took a walk by ourselves before lunch. He was so excited to retell his conversation with Gertrude Bell from the previous day that I didn't get a word in edgewise.

After a light lunch on the veranda, Gulbenkian informed us

that we would be sailing across the lake to Tatvan to catch the train. We all walked down the path to the dock leaving the Villa behind to the servants.

I was excited for the opportunity to sail since I had never in my life been on a yacht. The voyage was short but refreshing with the wind blowing in my face. We were gliding across the water at the speed of a galloping horse, but the only sound was from the sails fluttering in the wind. I understood immediately why men of Gulbenkian's ilk sail just for the pleasure of it. There is a peaceful feeling that approaches the sublime.

We disembarked on the other side of the lake to find a motorcar waiting for the five of us and in minutes we arrived at the station.

We were greeted at the curb by a representative of the Oriental Railway Company. Instead of entering the station, we were led through a private entrance on to the platform and into a private car that was attached to the rear of the train.

The interior of the car was reminiscent of the main dining room of the villa we had just left. Persian carpets covered the floor. Every surface crafted of leather, brass, and polished hardwood. The car provided a seating area, a dining area, and what appeared to be a miniature library complete with a writing desk.

"There is a second car through that door" Gulbenkian said as he pointed forward "where you will find a sleeping car. Each of you have a private berth for the night. We should arrive just about this time tomorrow at Haydarpasa Station if everything goes as planned."

A whistle sounded up ahead and the train began to lurch forward, the motion not nearly as smooth as that of the yacht. Khalil and I took a seat on a sofa to steady ourselves. Gertrude and Picot did the same on the other side of the car. Only Gulbenkian remained standing although he was holding on to a railing to steady himself.

As we picked up speed the jerky acceleration smoothed out somewhat and became a more or less constant vibration. I looked out the window and saw that we were travelling faster than I had ever moved before. The telegraph poles next to the track whizzed by the window so fast that just when one was lost to the rear another appeared at the front of the car.

"Focus on a point in the distance Monsieur" Picot said. "It will be easier that way."

I did as he said and felt myself calm a bit. I hadn't even noticed how tense I had become or that I was squeezing the arm of the sofa so hard that my hand had turned white. I turned to Khalil to see a broad smile on his face and no sign of fear. He was enjoying the ride.

"Would you like a drink Sayed Kashani?" Gertrude asked in Persian.

"Yes. I think that would be helpful Miss Bell. Merci!"

I turned my attention inside the car and realized that when I did, the motion seemed to cease. Aside from the vibration from the rails and a gently sway side to side, all sense of forward motion stopped.

"A physicist in Germany called Einstein wrote a paper about something he calls relativity" Khalil said to me. "I don't understand the math, but essentially he says that motion is relative. If you ignore what happens outside Uncle, you feel you are not moving at all."

"I just realized the same thing Khalil. I am better now."

Gertrude returned with a splash of whiskey in a crystal glass.

"I added some water to open it up" she said as she handed me the glass.

Whether it was the addition of the water, my repeated exposure to the strong drink, or the excitement of the ride, I found that I quite enjoyed sipping the Scotch.

Calouste caught my attention and motioned for me to join him in the library.

"How are you doing Abdulrahim?"

"I'm fine Calouste. *Merci.*"

"Please have a seat. I apologize for my lack of time yesterday, but I *was* able to conclude my discussions with the Bakhtiari and the Germans yesterday so I can now focus on my remaining guests."

I sat down in an overstuffed chair facing Gulbenkian and took another sip from my whiskey.

"It seems odd to me that you never considered running for a seat in your Parliament Abdulrahim. I am sure you would have been elected if you ran."

"Maybe one day" I answered. "I don't know if I would play that game very well. I get rather angry at times when I witness blatant stupidity and unchecked greed."

"Are the members of the Majlis such men?"

"Oh no. Most of them are like me. It's the Shah's appointed ministers I am referring to. Those that consider themselves part of the ruling class. They believe power is their birthright and not derived from the consent of the governed. They see their positions as an opportunity to redistribute wealth to the people who need it least."

"I met with your former Treasurer General, Monsieur William Morgan Schuster on his journey back to America after he was sacked."

"Schuster made a valiant attempt to eradicate the parasites from our government, but they were too deeply ensconced."

"I believe the Russians played a part as well."

I took another sip of the whiskey before replying.

"They most certainly did. I am not aware of any treaty between Belgium and Russia, but the way the Czar protected the

Belgian customs officials in Persia you would think they were taking a percentage of the profits."

"Monsieur Schuster mentioned that to me as well. How did the Shah ever turn over the responsibilities of collecting Persia's boarder taxes to a foreign government?"

"I believe the Shah and his ministers are receiving a percentage as well. From what Monsieur Schuster said to my friends in the Majlis, it appears we do not import any goods because no money ever makes it to the treasury from these customs agents."

"Indeed. I must visit your tobacco plantations next time I visit Persia" Calouste said in jest.

"I believe they are located very near the tea and coffee producing regions" I replied.

The smile on his face reassured me that we understood each other's sarcasm.

"Some of my friends in the British Parliament are worried that the Anglo-Russian Convention of 1907 has damaged our relations with Persia" Calouste said. "Do you have any opinion on that?"

"Tell your friends not to worry" I replied. "The damage was complete and likely irreversible."

"Sorry? Could you repeat that?"

"Certainly" I replied. "Prior to this agreement being made public, we admired Britain. Your country was our beacon during the early days of the revolution, but we felt betrayed by this agreement. In fact, I believe all of the countries of Europe are now tainted by this."

"But the way I read the agreement" Calouste said, "both Britain and Russia recognize Persia's strict independence and integrity."

"Yes, and then it divides up our country into three separate zones of influence without our consent. If we wish to negotiate a deal with Britain in the north, we are not allowed for that territory was given to Russia. You tell me if this fundamentally recognizes our independence and integrity."

"I can see your point" he replied, "but the intent was to stop the two great powers from fighting against each other and thereby causing collateral damage to Persia."

"So then when Monsieur Schuster requests the assistance of a British citizen with impeccable credentials and relevant experience to help us resolve our financial challenges, we are told he is not allowed to help since Tehran is in the Russian sphere of influence. Should we declare Shiraz to be our new capital in order to get the help we need from a British Citizen?"

Gulbenkian had no reply.

"And who will help us stop the ... non-collateral damage ... inflicted directly by the Russians through the shelling of our capital building and destruction of our ancient sites in Tabriz?"

I felt myself losing control and the tone of my voice reflected that. I saw the others looking at me from the opposite end of the car.

"I'm sorry Calouste" I said lowering my voice. "This has nothing to do with you. It is simply one of my pet peeves I think you call it."

"It's quite alright Abdulrahim, I should have known this would be a sensitive subject for you, but I needed to know your feelings."

"Do you have the power to undo this agreement?" I asked, hoping it was so.

"I am afraid not" Gulbenkian said then seemed to stare for a moment at Monsieur Picot who was sitting at the far end of the car, playing a game of cards by himself.

"We may be able to prevent a similar mistake from occurring

before it happens though." His voice was barely audible sitting only two feet away.

"Another treaty?" I asked, matching his level.

"An agreement that would carve up the Arabian peninsula into a French and British sphere of influence."

I remembered Sir Mark Sykes' comment to Picot as he left the Villa the day before.

"Sykes and Picot?" I asked quietly.

He simply nodded his head in agreement.

"We should discuss further when we arrive at my home in Constantinople. For now I think I've heard enough."

We dined on a meal that was just as good as the ones served in the villa and drank from several bottles of French wine. Just as I experienced with the scotch, the taste of these fine wines was growing on me. The stories told that evening by Gertrude, Picot, and Gulbenkian were just as entertaining as Major Kahn's stories on our caravan, but of a much more cultured nature. Gertrude told of her archeological expeditions in Arabia and her dangerous encounters with the Druze. I don't believe I ever met a woman as interesting or as brave as Gertrude Bell.

We retired to our berths shortly after dinner. Exhausted by the events of the day and pleasantly calmed by the wine, I slept within seconds of my head hitting the pillow.

I awoke the following morning to the gentle swaying of the train. For someone used to travelling by caravan it seemed odd that we continued to make progress while I slept. Khalil and I had a light breakfast together as the others streamed in to the car.

We still had several hours to go and while Khalil was absorbed in his new geology book, I was growing bored by the minute. Monsieur Picot taught me to play Patience, a card game that you can play by yourself, but then Gertrude and Calouste suggested I learn to play Whist so that all four of us could play. Picot and I partnered against the other two.

I have a good memory for details and the rules are not that difficult, so after only a few hands Picot and I were winning more often than not. Gertrude insisted to be my partner for a change and the two of us won seven games in a row.

"Monsieur you are a natural player" Picot declared after the seventh game. "I believe you can learn nothing more from me. Fortunately we were not playing for money."

"I am no gambler" I replied, "but I do enjoy this game."

We played a few more hands which I lost on purpose, but the others soon grew tired and we each retired to our own devices.

Lunch was served and we fell back in to our routines. I was able to look out the windows now without losing my sense of stability and I noticed a distinct change in the landscape passing by. There seemed to be more small towns along the route and many more people. The clock on the Library wall approached a full day of travel and soon thereafter we began to slow.

"We are approaching Haydarpasa Terminal" Calouste announced. "You can see the Bosporus in the distance now."

I looked through the window and saw a body of water that was quite different from Lake Van. The water appeared more restless, almost angry. The sheer number of sailing vessels anchored off the shore was the main difference however. The naked masts of the ships seemed to come together like a forest of trees. The tangle of ropes swaying in the wind appeared to be their leaves. We rolled through the outskirts of the city now with buildings flanking both sides of the track. When we finally pulled to a stop we were greeted by a massive four story building of tan stone and two majestic towers reaching to the sky.

"Haydarpasa Terminal was built almost forty years ago, but I still think it is a magnificent building!" The way Calouste spoke of the station it seemed he almost had some personal connection with the place.

We stepped down out of the private car and assembled on the platform. Calouste spoke briefly with a porter who scurried off to make arrangements for the transport of our trunks.

"I have a motor boat waiting for us at the dock" he said. "We must cross over to the other side of the straights to reach my home. We will go on ahead. Our luggage will follow."

We proceeded down the platform until we came upon a long queue of people. Calouste seemed to be confused by this and flagged down another porter.

Khalil was listening to their conversation and leaned in close to me.

"They have some kind of new customs formality for trains originating in the region around Lake Van" he said. "We will need our passports."

Fortunately I kept mine in my jacket pocket and not in my trunk. This was my first time out of Persia, so I didn't feel comfortable being separated from it.

I shared this information with Gertrude and Picot who were also prepared. When Calouste returned he opened his mouth to speak but then stopped.

"You all have your passports out already. How did you know?"

"I told them Monsieur Gulbenkian" Khalil said. "I worried they would need to retrieve them from their bags."

"So you speak Turkish as well?"

"Yes Monsieur."

"I should have guessed as much."

"What is this new formality Calouste?" Picot asked.

"I'm not quite sure. It's new and seems to be only for trains coming from the eastern provinces. I am sorry for the inconvenience. There doesn't seem to be any way around it for us."

Coming from the rear of the train we were the last group to approach. A uniformed officer sat at a table set just inside the platform gate with a pair of armed guards flanking him. The Ottoman official said something to the group in Turkish then motioned to our passports. We handed them over as a group. He looked through each in turn then handed the British and French passports back to Gertrude and Picot. He motioned for them to pass but for some unknown reason he held on to ours.

The official turned in his seat and spoke to the guard standing on that side of the table. Then he handed over our passports to him and motioned for us to follow.

"Calouste?" I asked.

He shrugged. "I have no idea. Just keep calm and we should be through in a moment."

The guard led us into the main terminal and then into a small room. Gertrude and Picot followed us but were not allowed to enter. We found ourselves in the presence of yet another Ottoman official sitting at an identical table, complete with two more armed guards.

He took the passports from our escort who saluted and left the room. This official looked them over just as the first man did, but the look on his face was disturbing. It appeared we were insulting him simply with our presence.

He stared up at each of us in turn, but seemed to focus longest on Calouste.

He asked a few questions in Turkish to which Calouste replied. Khalil turned to me with a look of despair. I had no idea what was being said, but this was not what I expected for a man of Gulbenkian's stature.

"Monsieur, do you speak French?" I asked finally.

He looked at me as if I had insulted his mother.

He didn't so much speak as grunt. "You are Persian yes?"

"Yes Captain" I replied, recognizing his rank from his uniform.

"You were staying in Van with this Armenian?" he said gesturing in Calouste's direction.

Of course I knew Calouste was Armenian, but he carried a British passport, so I didn't understand why this was relevant.

"Yes. We had a business meeting there."

"You came to our country from Tabriz by way of Khoy yes?"

"I am a resident of Tehran, but yes, we spent a week in Tabriz on the way here."

"This is the Russian zone of your country yes?"

"We do not recognize Russian or British zones" I said, very close to losing my temper. Khalil reached over and placed a hand on my arm as if to steady me. "I am a citizen of Persia."

"You come from the Russian territory into Van to meet with this Armenian and others to plot the overthrow of our government yes?"

"No, absolutely not! If that is what you believe then please contact Ahmed Riza Bey who was at that meeting as a representative of your government. Enver Pasha himself sent an escort to Khoy to collect us and sent Ahmed Bey to this meeting. Perhaps you were not aware, but this *particular* Armenian is negotiating an important deal for the benefit of *your* country."

The two names seemed to have some impact. He looked at our documents again then motioned for one of the guards to lean down. He whispered something in his ear then the guard exited the room.

"Talaat Pasha has ordered the arrest and deportation of all Armenian radicals and their known conspirators effective April twenty fourth of this year. This man is Armenian bourgeoisie. He is a subversive who plots with the Russians to overthrow our government. You are travelling with him from the Russian part of Persia. You and your nephew will be arrested as well."

I looked over at Calouste who seemed very close to exploding with rage. Khalil was looking to me for some guidance but I had none. I was at a loss for what to do next.

A long silence ensued. I could think of nothing more to say and Calouste was remaining silent so I followed suit.

Just then the door opened and a man wearing a Colonel's uniform strode into the room.

Instead of addressing the three of us he immediately began dressing down the Captain who stood at attention behind the table. The Colonel snatched the three passports from the Captain's hand and waved them in his face. The junior officer seemed to lose two inches in height as the barrage continued.

Finally the Colonel turned towards Calouste and handed over our passports to him.

"I am very sorry for the actions of this impudent dog Monsieur Gulbenkian" he said in French. "Ahmed Riza Bey has confirmed that you were indeed meeting at the invitation of our government and that these two gentlemen are your honored guests. I spoke with him on the phone just now. He wished me to send our deepest regrets for this unfortunate incident. Please accept my apologies."

"It is all a misunderstanding" Calouste said in a calm voice. "No apology is necessary Colonel."

We made our escape from the room before anyone had a change in heart and met up with Gertrude and Picot who were visibly relieved to see us.

"What was that all about?" Gertrude asked.

"A misunderstanding" Calouste replied. "Let's board the motor boat and we can discuss it further after we have had a chance to freshen up. I've been sullied and need a steam bath to remove some of this filth."

We boarded the motor boat and headed out across the Bosporus Straights. This boat was propelled by a motor providing a much different experience than the sailboat on Lake Van. We accelerated on to the waves like we were cutting the water with a knife. I held on for dear life until I remembered Khalil's advice and looked off into the distance.

What I saw was breathtaking.

The old city of Constantinople seemed to spread out over every inch of space available, but standing majestically on the hill side was the ancient Hagia Sophia Mosque and not far from there the Blue Mosque. Calouste saw me admiring the scenery and leaned in close.

"Hagia Sophia is more famous, but for me, the Blue Mosque is more spectacular. Five main domes and eight secondary domes. The six minarets reach a hundred feet up into the sky! Even as a Christian I am moved by the call to prayer."

As we docked I saw a high arched structure off in the distance that could have been a bridge or a rail line.

"What is that?" I asked.

Calouste smiled for the first time since we left the train.

"The Roman aqueduct."

"You mean that is water on the top?" Khalil asked.

"Yes. We still use it to get drinking water from the hills outside the city" Gulbenkian answered. "I will make sure you have a chance to explore it before you leave for Paris Khalil. It is an engineering accomplishment that has stood for almost two thousand years."

We disembarked from the motor boat and on to the dock. My legs suddenly felt unsteady. Strange that standing on a solid structure should feel just like a moving boat.

"The feeling will pass quickly Abdulrahim. I know it is a bit disconcerting."

We walked the length of the dock and boarded an awaiting

carriage. By the time I sat down I was feeling more under control. The driver snapped the whip over the horses and the carriage lurched forward over the broad cobblestone avenue that paralleled the waterfront. Khalil and I were turning our heads constantly trying to take in all of the scenery.

"Is your home near the Sublime Porte?" I asked.

"No. The government is closer to Gulhane Park. You will see it soon enough I am sure."

That wasn't the answer I was looking for.

The carriage turned off the boulevard and into a series of twisting winding, streets eventually arriving at the wrought iron gates of a large townhouse. As we alighted from the carriage and walked to the front steps the front door opened and a butler emerged to greet us. Like the man who ran the country house, this man was dressed in a western suit, but sported a traditional Turkish fez.

"Welcome to my home in the city" Gulbenkian said. "Please come in and make yourselves comfortable."

We all walked into the foyer and through to the library. This house was not nearly as large as the Villa, but the interior was just as elegant, although decorated in a more oriental style. It gave me the impression that the décor was like the butler's Fez, a political concession and an attempt to fit in.

No sooner did we arrive in the library than a second much younger servant arrived with a note on a small silver platter. Gulbenkian read the note and gave an order to the boy who immediately ran off to carry it out.

Gulbenkian cleared his throat to get our attention.

"Now that we are safely home I wish to tell you all how deeply sorry I am for the incident at the train station earlier. I can assure you I had no idea that this inquisition was awaiting us. I would have cabled Ahmed Bey in advance if I had."

"Calouste don't worry" Picot said, "No harm came of this. A

mere five minute delay to our journey. That is all. No?"

"Françoise is correct" Gertrude agreed.

"I am afraid for Abdulrahim and Khalil it was more than a simple delay. They got a glimpse of the ugly reality of the present Ottoman regime."

"Calouste, you forget the atrocities I must deal with in my own country" I said. "This was a small inconvenience. You triumphed in the end. This is all that matters."

In the distance we heard the bell at the front door and moments later the butler entered the room with Ahmed Bey in tow.

"Monsieur Gulbenkian, I am so sorry that you and your guests were detained. Djemal Pasha has asked me to convey his personal apologies and would like to invite you and your guests to dine with him this evening."

This was the first time I had heard Djemal Pasha's name in connection with Gulbenkian and was curious why it was not Talaat Pasha who sent Ahmed Bey. He was the Interior minister and responsible for the Armenian roundup.

"I appreciate the gesture Ahmed Riza, but we have all travelled a long way and are exhausted."

The look on Ahmed Bey's face was one of sharp pain. He switched to Turkish and had an extended conversation with Gulbenkian which given the collection of guests was quite rude. I did not understand a word, but from the tone of Ahmed Bey's voice it did not sound like an extended apology.

I looked across the room to Khalil and he nodded indicating he was following the conversation.

Ahmed Bey finally paused and scanned the room looking at each of us in turn.

"I am looking forward to your presence at dinner this evening. We will start early given your long journey."

Then he turned and faced Picot.

"Monsieur Picot, it is most important that you are able to attend. You have a unique opportunity tonight and you do not want to waste it."

He bowed slightly at the waist and left the room.

"It seems we will be dining at the Sublime Porte this evening. My staff will show you to your rooms. I am afraid we don't have much time. A carriage will be here in an hour to fetch us."

Khalil and I were shown to our rooms where we found our Louis Vuitton trunks waiting for us, but first I had to know what was said.

"There is big trouble in the east Uncle. The Russians have been recruiting Armenians to overthrow the government. Ahmed Bey says the Talaat Pasha has lost his mind and wants to arrest every Armenian within a hundred miles of Constantinople. Djemal Pasha does not agree and wants to calm things down."

"And what of the remark to Picot?"

"Enver and Talaat want to consummate a deal with the Germans right away, but Djemal believes the French can help stop the Russians and will be a better partner."

"So he is reaching out to Picot to broker a deal" I said half to myself.

"It seems so" Khalil agreed.

I considered the new information for a few moments until Khalil finally interrupted.

"Are we in any danger Uncle?"

"There is always danger when you fly close to the sun" I replied. "I learned that lesson in Tabriz with the Crown Prince. *In Sha Allah* we will be on our way to Paris in a few days, so we only have to stay out of trouble until then."

The Pasha's carriage arrived at Gulbenkian's door as promised to fetch the five of us. We navigated the twisting and turning streets for several minutes, but then Gulbenkian suddenly started to peer out the windows on either side as if something was amiss.

"Is there anything wrong Calouste?" I asked.

"We are not taking the correct route for the Sublime Porte."

"Did Ahmed Bey say we would dine there?"

"No. I just assumed ..."

He stopped midsentence and sat back in his seat although the look of worry was still visible on his face. I wondered if Gulbenkian thought we were on our way to prison the way he was reacting.

A few minutes later a broad smile replaced the worry and Calouste exhaled.

"We just turned on to Mese Avenue" he said. "They are taking us to Topkapi Palace."

"The Palace?" Picot asked. "Will the Sultan join us?"

"No, the Sultan lives in the new Palace. Topkapi was the official residence for four hundred years, but now it is home to the royal mint and sometimes used for formal events."

We drove on for a few more minutes and then made a turn towards a large entrance covered in marble and decorated with ornate gilded Ottoman calligraphy. It was difficult to read in the fading light as the sun was now below the horizon.

"This is the Imperial Gate" Gulbenkian said.

The carriage entered the tall tunnel through the outer wall of the fortress and proceeded out into a broad courtyard surrounded by a park. I expected the carriage to stop but we continued rolling across the courtyard to a second gate.

"The middle gate" Calouste explained.

Up ahead was indeed a second gate embedded in a crenelated parapet flanked by two tall towers.

"It looks like some of the German castles I have seen in books" Khalil said.

"More French than German I would say" Gertrude added. "Magnificent details in any event."

There were several buildings dotting the courtyard, all dark and unoccupied from outward appearances.

"One of these was the Harem" Calouste offered as if reading my mind. "The other held the Sultan's elite guard."

The carriage pulled through the middle gate and arrived in yet another courtyard. As before we continued forward, deeper into the inner structure of the ancient fortress. This time, as we approached yet another gate, we pulled alongside and came to a stop.

The footmen jumped down from their perch on the back of the carriage and opened the door for us to alight as the door to the final gate opened and a liveried servant emerged to welcome us.

"Please follow me" he said in French.

More gilded Arabic calligraphy surrounded the entrance. I recognized a few verses from the Quran. The most prominent read "In the Name of God the Compassionate, the Merciful". I hoped that Djemal Pasha was of a like mind.

"The gate of Felicity" Gertrude said as she passed by.

We passed through the gate to see a large square building surrounded by columns with decorative arches supporting hanging eaves to form a veranda. Light was visible on the inside of this building and as expected the servant led us into a vast audience chamber.

While the elevated throne was visible at one end of the room, our eyes were drawn to a large dining table placed closer to the other side. That end of the room was well lit by several candelabras on the table, a few suspended in the air, and still others placed on the side tables that lined one wall.

The place settings were just as regal as the ones in Gulbenkian's Villa, with the marked exception that there were no wine glasses to be seen.

As we made our way towards the table we heard a voice in the distance announce something in Turkish. The last three words required no translation. The name Ahmed Djemal Pasha was clear.

The man strode into the room with the confidence of his office. He was of medium height and build, wearing a western three piece suit and necktie. His high forehead hinted at the beginning of pattern baldness, but what hair he lacked on his head was compensated for by his enormous moustache. It reminded me of the handlebars of Khalil's bike.

As he approached he surprised me by greeting Gertrude Bell first.

"Miss Bell it is so wonderful to see you again!"

"It is my pleasant surprise as well Pasha."

"We met when I was Vali of Baghdad" the Pasha said as he turned to greet the rest of us.

"You must be Monsieur Picot" he said with a broad smile. "*Enchanté*"

"The pleasure is mine Pasha."

"Calouste, it has been too long" he said as he continued down the line.

"Pasha" Calouste said as he bowed his head. His demeanor was not impolite, but I could see that Gulbenkian was not happy to be summoned here tonight.

"And you must be Sayed Kashani. *Salaam* Sayed Kashani."

He reached out to shake my hand and I did likewise. I was taken by the man's warmth. He did not come across as one of the three most powerful men in the Ottoman Empire.

"Salaam Pasha" I replied. "May I introduce my Nephew Khalil."

Khalil greeted the Pasha in Turkish to his great delight.

"Your Turkish has that wonderful hint of an Azeri accent Khalil" the Pasha said in French.

"I'm sorry Pasha" Khalil said. "I will try to do better."

"I was not complaining my boy. Not at all! I have been told Turkish may be your sixth or seventh language? I think you should accept that not all of your languages will be perfect. Riza Bey has shared some of your accomplishments with me. Truly amazing for a man of your young age."

His smile was disarming. A true politician.

"Shall we sit? I understand you had a long journey and I do not wish to keep you longer than necessary."

"It is our pleasure to dine with you" Calouste said as we all took our places behind a chair.

We did not dare sit until the Pasha took the lead. Once he was seated, we followed suit and a staff of six immediately began serving all of us simultaneously. Plates full, they disappeared as quickly as they came.

"Thank you all for coming on such short notice" the Pasha said. "I assure you, I would not have pressed for this dinner if I had the luxury of time."

"I would like to speak openly tonight" he continued "with the understanding that everything said here tonight is confidential and not to be spoken of outside this room except as I will direct."

He scanned each of us in turn to get our confirmation.

"An emissary from Kaiser Wilhelm arrives tomorrow hoping to formalize terms for an alliance with our government. This has been widely rumored, so it should not come as a surprise. While the Grand Vizier and Minister of War are inclined to accept this offer, I believe an alliance with France and England may provide the better outcome for our empire."

I knew that Gertrude and Calouste had connections with the British government and Picot with the French, but I was dumbfounded that Khalil and I would be included in this conversation. The Pasha could have easily requested that we would remain at Gulbenkian's home.

"I believe Calouste has presented our plans for Turkish Petroleum to you Monsieur Picot?"

"Yes Pasha."

"Including the incentives we are willing to provide your government?"

"In detail Pasha. Ahmed Riza Bey and I spoke at length as well. I believe I have a complete picture of the opportunity and the benefits for France."

"Good. I am glad to hear it. We also are aware of your country's interest in the Levant, especially Lebanon and Syria."

"These are Ottoman territories" Picot was quick to say. "My government has no desire..."

"Please Monsieur Picot" the Pasha interrupted. "Our conversation will be much more productive if we speak openly. Desire ... Desire is precisely the word for France's attitude towards the Levant. This is to be expected. It is the actions in pursuit of desire where we may experience conflict. So far both of our countries' passions are under control."

"Yes Pasha. My countrymen do see opportunities in the Levant."

"Now we are making progress!" the Pasha exclaimed. "Let us forego the details for the moment. Suffice it to say if we consummate a relationship with France, we may open the door for our new friends to pursue these opportunities further."

"I see" said Picot. "And how could France repay the kindness?"

"We are very concerned about your ally on our eastern border. You may have heard they are now inciting revolt among the local population."

"We are somewhat familiar with the issue, yes." Picot replied.

"Of course you are. How insensitive of me."

Djemal Pasha turned to Gulbenkian.

"My deepest apologies for your detention today Calouste, but we have hard evidence of a revolt around Lake Van and must do what it takes to stop it."

Calouste remained silent and the Pasha continued.

"We wish not only to form an agreement with France, but to join the Triple Entente and thereby quash all hostilities with Russia."

"Your meaning is perfectly clear Pasha" Picot replied.

The Pasha smiled and nodded his head to confirm then turned to face Gulbenkian.

"Calouste, you know the tragedy I found when I took over as Vali of Adana four years ago."

"Yes Pasha. Five thousand Armenians tortured and killed."

"It was a tragedy. As the new governor of the region I had to restore order and return the Adana Vilayet to a peaceful productive part of our empire."

"It must have been a challenge" Gulbenkian said. I marveled at his self-control in the face of such a sensitive matter.

"Not half as challenging as what we are facing in the east today. If Talaat Pasha carries out his plan, the loss of life may exceed one hundred times that of the massacre at Adana."

Gertrude Bell audibly gasped at the statement.

I stared at Gulbenkian's face but could not read what he was thinking. Half a million people killed I thought. What could possibly warrant such a response?

"Calouste, I implore you to do whatever you can to help Monsieur Picot in this endeavor and to urge your Government's support for a strong alliance between our countries. As minister of the Navy, I would much rather our ships sail together than to oppose each other in battle."

"I am sure Admiral Churchill would agree" Calouste responded. "Naturally I will do all that I can to help with this matter."

"Miss Bell" the Pasha continued. "I understand you have been fighting for the creation of a museum in Bagdad to house the antiquities of the region and to prevent looting by outsiders."

"Yes Pasha. I don't know how you know of this plan, but it is true. I believe strongly that the relics of Mesopotamian civilizations should remain in the region. I propose to build the Bagdad Archaeological Museum to house these treasures before another Napoleon Bonaparte swoops in and takes them as spoils of war."

I saw Picot wince at that reference but recover quickly.

"I thought those treasures were in the British museum?" Khalil asked Gertrude innocently.

"Spoils of a later war" Djemal Pasha replied with a bit of humor apparent in his eyes.

Khalil looked at me as if to apologize for speaking out so I placed my hand on his arm to reassure him that it was fine.

"Miss Bell, our party strongly agrees with you" the Pasha continued. "If you would have a word with your father Sir Hugh in support of our cause, perhaps we could break ground on this new museum by the spring of next year."

I was somewhat taken aback by the blatant *quid pro quo* being offered so casually over dinner. I was wondering if there was anything on his wish list for Persia when he turned to me.

"Sayed Kashani do you have any thoughts on this topic?"

"Pasha I am a simple shop keeper with no political office or ambition."

Djemal Pasha laughed.

"They said you were humble to a fault. Fine. Let's say I would like the opinion of the Common Man. What does a Persian Shop Keeper think of the Ottoman Empire aligning with France, Britain, and Russia?"

I hesitated, but felt I had a unique opportunity to represent my country's interests.

"Well" I said. "If hostilities are ended between Russia and the Ottoman Empire, I would expect that Russian troops would no longer be needed in Khoy and Tabriz. The Persian people would welcome their withdrawal."

"Marvelous! Monsieur Picot, make a note. Once we are a full partner of the *Entente*, Russia must withdraw troops from the entire region, including the Azerbaijan regions of Persia."

"Yes Pasha" Picot replied in disbelief.

"So Sayed Kashani, when you hold your meetings in Paris, please keep us in mind."

My meetings in Paris? It seemed like the Pasha knew more about my meetings than I did.

"I am confused Pasha. I am going to Paris to buy and sell postage stamps."

"Ah yes! Thank you for reminding me."

The Pasha snapped his fingers and at once a servant appeared at his side. He whispered a few words and the servant disappeared for a moment into the dimly lit corner of the room, returning with a small package.

The Pasha gestured in my direction and the servant brought the package to me.

"I almost forgot Sayed. Please don't open this now, but I had my secretary put together a collection of stamps from across the empire. Some are quite old and worthless to the average citizen, but quite desirable as I understand it for collectors such as yourself."

I held the package in my hand anxious to see what treasures it might contain. I had not thought of my collection for days.

"Thank you Pasha. You are too kind."

"It is my pleasure Sayed. And for you Khalil…"

The Pasha gestured to his servant who brought a stack of three books to Khalil.

"These are three first editions from Taqi ad-Din, one of our empire's greatest polymaths and the chief astronomer who built the first observatory in Constantinople. One book is on astronomy, of course, the second is a treatise on optics, and the third on the mechanics of the steam turbine. Like you, he had an insatiable appetite for learning and was largely self-taught."

Khalil stared at the books in disbelief. It was obvious Ahmed Riza Bey had provided information on the two of us and while I was grateful for my unopened gift, I was even more delighted that he would bestow these precious works on Khalil.

I understood why the Pasha wanted the support of the other people at the table, but I was still having a hard time to understand why he even bothered with Khalil and me.

"Thank you Pasha. I will treasure these."

We had all finished our meals by this time and without missing a beat, the dessert was served. The servants brought trays of pistachio stuffed Baklava and Turkish bread pudding covered in clotted cream. A third tray was covered in a variety of dried fruits and candied walnuts. I took a small selection from each tray since I couldn't decide.

The Pasha described each of the desserts in great detail and offered Turkish coffee which everyone accepted. We made small talk among each other as it was obvious the formal reason for the dinner had been accomplished.

After another half-hour of conversation the Pasha's servant

entered the room and whispered in his ear again.

"I am afraid I must be going. There is an issue I must attend to at the Sublime Porte. Thank you all again for coming on such short notice."

Without waiting for a response from us he turned and quickly disappeared into the darkness.

We all looked around at each other as if to ask if this had been real, but before anyone could speak, the servant returned and led us all to the awaiting carriage for our trip home.

We rode in silence and when we arrived at Gulbenkian's townhouse we all breathed a sigh of relief.

"Breakfast will be served in the dining room tomorrow morning" Calouste said once inside, "but please get as much rest as you need. We all need time to recover from a most eventful few days."

I awoke the next morning to find full sunshine streaming through the lace curtains in my room. I was too tired the previous evening to examine the Pasha's gift, so after I washed my face and hands in the water basin, I went straight to the package and tore through the wrapping paper.

Inside was a stock book with the stamps carefully protected in clear velum envelopes. I expected a pile of stamps loose in a box, but obviously this collection had been assembled by someone who was a collector.

I went to my trunk and extracted my magnifying glass and stamp tongs before returning to my new samples. I emptied the contents of the envelopes one at a time, picking up each stamp with the tongs and examining it with the glass. The selection of Ottoman stamps took my breath away. They were in superb condition and some quite old for the region. As I examined the final envelope there was a knock on my door.

"Come in" I called out expecting it to be Khalil.

When the door opened it was Monsieur Picot instead.

"I am sorry to intrude Sayed Kashani, but I am leaving and did not want to do so without saying good-bye."

I stood up and placed the stamps safely on the bed before walking over to the door. He did not seem to want to enter any further.

"You are leaving?"

"Yes. I went to our embassy early this morning and cabled my superiors in the government. Prime Minister Doumergue has requested I come home immediately to discuss the details of the Pasha's offer."

"Do you think he will be open to this idea?"

"I don't really know him that well frankly. He is an interesting man, a protestant, which is unusual for France, and even rumored to be a Freemason."

"A Freemason?"

"Yes. It is a secret society which is popular with some of the most powerful men in France. It is said that in their secret meetings is where the real political and business negotiations are held."

"Who will help the widow's son?" I asked, testing to see if he was one of us.

"I beg your pardon Sayed?"

"Sorry. I was quoting an article I read recently about the socialists in your government. Something about widows and orphans."

"Yes, well Doumergue is a member of the Radical Socialist party, but has frankly moved more to the political center after coming to power. In any event, I must be off now and wanted to reiterate my offer to you and Khalil. When you arrive in Paris please be my guest. Calouste will give you my address."

He turned to leave but then hesitated.

"I almost forgot, Miss Bell and I are travelling together. She was called home by the Foreign Secretary. She sends her regards as well."

And like that he was gone.

The mention of cables reminded me that I should send a telegram to my wife and cousin now that we have reached Constantinople. I would have to think carefully about what to share. Even with our code, I had a strong sense that the Pashas were monitoring every message leaving the city. If they decoded the message and I revealed anything about last night's discussion, I would find myself in a prison for sure.

I knocked lightly on Khalil's door and found him absorbed in one of his newly acquired books.

"Uncle, this book is three hundred years old! They all are!"

"Take good care of them then" I said. "Are you hungry?"

"Not yet. I'll be down in a little while. Optics is a fascinating subject. I want to build a telescope!"

I made my way down to the dining room and found a selection of dishes being kept warm by candles underneath trays full of water. I helped myself to a hearty selection and had a seat by myself at the table. It was odd being alone after so many days on the road with such a large group of people.

Calouste entered the room and sat across from me after he poured himself a cup of tea.

"What are your plans for today Abdulrahim?"

"I need to send a telegram to my wife later this morning letting her know I made it safely to Constantinople."

"If you like my man can take care of that for you. Simply write out the message and place it in an envelope on the desk in your room. He will bring you back the confirmation."

"Thank you Calouste. That would save me trying to find the office."

"Of course" he responded in a despondent manner.

"Is there anything I can do to help?" I asked, knowing there was not.

"What?" he asked. "Oh. No. I'm sorry I have a lot on my mind."

"I can see that" I replied. "Would it be helpful if Khalil and I left today as well? We have relied on your hospitality far too long."

"Oh good heavens no" he replied. "My mind is elsewhere this morning that's all. In fact I was hoping to show you around the city later today if we have time."

He looked around the room to make sure we were alone.

"I also want to introduce you to a few fellow travelers at our lodge before you leave. These are connections that will benefit you on the road to Paris and even when you return to Tehran."

"Picot made an interesting remark earlier about the Prime Minister of France. He indicated that he might be a brother."

"But Picot is not one of us."

"I know. He knew nothing of the widow's son. Yet there are rumors in Paris."

"There are always rumors in Paris. The French live for rumors and innuendo. In this particular case they are based in fact. Doumergue is a member of L'Ordre Grand Orient in Paris. I expect to take you there as well when we reach Paris."

"You want us to travel together to Paris? I think this would be too much of an imposition Calouste."

He waved his hand in the air.

"I am afraid you don't understand Abdulrahim. It is not a matter of choice. I have my instructions from on high. Even so, it is my pleasure. I really enjoy your company."

"Instructions from on high? Do you know who I am supposed to meet in Paris? Do you know what this is all about?"

"I am afraid I know little more than you do Sayed. Whitehall wants you in Paris so I am to deliver you to Paris. The original plan was to meet you in Constantinople when you arrived, but you made my life much easier when you showed up on my doorstep in Van."

"Whitehall?" I asked dumbfounded. "The British Government wants me in Paris?"

"So I am told."

"Gertrude told me of a conversation she overheard between Sir George Barclay and Sir Mark Sykes. They were discussing a letter received a from Sir Cecil Spring Rice."

"I know Sir George and Sir Cecil" Calouste responded. "This may have started with them, but my instructions come from higher up. You are to help settle a dispute between Lloyd-George and Churchill."

I was dumbfounded. "But I have never met these great men."

"I know nothing more than what I have told you. I'm sorry. I have booked us passage on the Orient Express in three days. That should give us time to recuperate and make the introductions at the local lodge. I hope this is acceptable to you and Khalil."

"Of course. May I ask you a related question that has been bothering me?"

Calouste nodded his consent.

"If Khalil and I had not arrived at your Villa with Amir, how would you know we had arrived in Constantinople? This is a big city and trains arrive many times a day."

Calouste stood up and motioned for me to join him by the window. He parted the drapes and pointed towards the street corner where a man was leaning against a building, wearing a three piece suit and a fedora hat pulled down to cover most of his face. He was reading a newspaper but occasionally looked over towards the front door of the townhouse.

"You have been followed since you arrived in Tabriz."

"By who?"

"The Germans for one" he said indicating the man on the street. "And the British Secret Service Bureau for another" he said as he indicated a window on the third floor of the building across the street. "The MI6 branch more precisely."

I looked up to where he was pointing in time to see the curtains fall back into place.

"The Brits are a bit more subtle than the Germans, but make no mistake, they both know where you are. They were following us last night, but did not dare enter the old Palace."

"Are Khalil and I in danger?"

"Not from these low level operatives. The Germans are to keep an eye on you and record where you have been. The Brits are there to spy on the Germans and protect you if they feel you are in danger. C wants you delivered safely to Paris."

"C?"

"Oh sorry. Sir Mansfield Cumming. He is head of the new Bureau. Signs all of his documents in green ink with a capital C for Cumming or for Chief, so everyone calls him C."

Khalil walked in to the room as we turned back towards the table.

"What are you looking at Uncle?"

"Nothing Khalil. Calouste was pointing out an interesting character on the street. Are you hungry?"

"Famished! I never knew research could work up such an appetite."

I retired to my room after breakfast and wrote out the message to my wife and cousin using my code book. I did not mention any of the information I had learned from Calouste or Gertrude. I simply told my cousin the truth, that Wilhelm met with me in Van and that I expected to meet him now that I was safe in Constantinople.

Once written I rang the bell in my room and handed over the envelope to Gulbenkian's butler when he arrived. I tried to give him money but he refused saying Gulbenkian had an account with the office at a negotiated rate.

I spent the remainder of the morning engrossed in my stamp collection, trying to incorporate the new additions into the existing arrangement. Presenting a collection to maximum effect is part logical organization, part symphonic orchestration. The lesser stamps must be grouped together into passages that build to a climax with the presentation of the truly important specimens. The pages must turn themselves in anticipation of the payoff.

When I heard the knock on my door I looked up at the clock on the mantle above the fireplace and realized I had been at it for almost three hours. The butler presented two envelopes on a silver tray. The first was the envelope with my telegram and the second addressed to me with my name written in Persian.

The envelope with the telegram contained a copy of the form from the office, complete with time sent and confirmation of receipt in Tehran. Two large official seals were stamped over the telegrapher's signature and the account number charged.

I opened the second envelope to find a note written in Persian. Wilhelm informed me that my presence was required at two meetings the following day and that a carriage would be sent for me at nine.

I informed Calouste at lunch at which point he suggested we spend the remainder of the day at *Aga Hamami*, for a steam bath and massage.

It was a short carriage ride made more interesting by the two parties following us at a distance. Several times Calouste instructed the driver to take sudden turns and double back. Twice we waved at our German tail as we passed him by in the opposite direction.

"Why did you taunt him?" I asked as we pulled up in front of the bath house.

"So they know that we know" he answered. "Otherwise they believe they have the upper hand."

We entered the three story bath house through an elaborately carved door that proclaimed that the establishment was built in 1454. We were directed to the second floor where we found a spacious changing room for men. We removed our clothes and donned a loose fitting garment designed to protect our modesty while enjoying the experience of the bath. Not quite a robe but more than a diaper.

"Have you taken a steam bath before Abdulrahim?"

"Once before in Tehran, but if memory serves it was somewhat different than this."

"We will start with the warm room to adjust. Just try to relax and enjoy."

We spent hours moving from room to room, each more sweltering than the previous until I was covered in perspiration. The walls and floors were clad in marble with seating banks constructed along the walls. On the top floor a translucent skylight dome admitted the afternoon sun which seemed to give the entire space an ethereal beauty.

Between rooms we reclined in a semi-private niche where we enjoyed cool drinks and a respite from the intense heat. Twice we were joined by friends of Calouste. He never said so directly, but I am sure these were the Ottoman Freemasons he wanted me to meet.

Towards the end of the afternoon I was led into a room and instructed to lie face down on a stone table where a young man first covered me in fragrant soap and scrubbed me clean with a rough mitt. Then he rinsed off the soap and massaged my back and shoulders with more force than I expected from his delicate looking hands. He repeatedly dipped his hands in perfumed oil, working it into my back until I became accustomed to the kneading and pulling. Eventually I felt all of the stress in my muscles recede and began to enjoy the manipulation. I'm sure I even dozed off at one point.

I rejoined Calouste in the final room where we stood in a cool water fountain and washed away the last bit of oil and soap from our now flaccid muscles.

As we dressed I could see that Calouste had enjoyed the treatment more than I.

"You seem recovered Calouste."

"I am much better now *merci*. I needed that after the ordeal at the train station and our surprise audience last night."

We found our carriage waiting for us at the front door and in moments were heading home. I was so relaxed I didn't even bother to look for our surveillance.

"I'm not sure I could handle a large dinner tonight" I said.

"I anticipated as much" he replied. "I've asked the staff to prepare a light meal so we can make an early night of it. A little food and a large glass of Claret will be the perfect end to this day."

I awoke the next morning feeling more rested than I had since I left home and with a much bigger appetite than expected. Breakfast was served as usual, buffet style, and I took full advantage of it eating much more than I should.

Khalil and Calouste left early to tour the Valens Aqueduct with a professor from the Imperial School of Naval Engineering who was an expert on its construction. Gulbenkian never seemed to do anything half-way and I was grateful that he took such an interest in Khalil's education.

I was finishing my third cup of coffee when the butler announced that my carriage arrived. I was not particularly looking forward to the day's events and therefore not in any hurry to get started. I decided to linger a little while longer and make the carriage wait.

When I was ready I told the butler that I was leaving for the day. He escorted me out to the carriage a full fifteen minutes behind schedule.

The carriage was empty which surprised me a bit. I expected Wilhelm to be lurking in the shadows.

We set off and eventually turned onto the wide avenue that fronted the sea. The collection of ships anchored off the coast with all of their various shapes and sizes was a feast for the eyes. We continued to hug the waterfront but soon I noticed a large green park on my left. Some of the structures seemed familiar. I stared at one tower in particular until I realized I was seeing Topkapi Palace from the water side.

Up ahead I saw a gathering of military men dressed in uniform walking briskly in the same direction I was headed. As the carriage turned I saw a grandstand constructed on what appeared to be a broad boat dock. I could hear the excited voices of the crowd carried on the wind. It seemed they were speaking in many languages, most unintelligible to me except now and then I caught a bit of English. I thought they were saying 'any moment now' but I wasn't quite sure.

The Carriage came to a halt just short of the grandstand and when the door opened, I found Wilhelm standing in full dress uniform of the German Army.

"You are late Sayed, but fortunately you did not miss the main event. Please come with me."

I alighted from the carriage and tried to keep up with the German as he strode towards the grandstand. He led us to a spot on the lower level near the end. I took a moment to scan the other seats and saw the VIP box near the top in the center. I recognized Djemal Pasha and Ahmed Riza Bey, but the others I had never seen before.

"Have a look out there" he said and pointed off into the distance up the straight.

I focused my attention in the direction he pointed and saw two warships steaming in our direction, side by side. They appeared to be moving quite fast on the water.

Wilhelm handed me a pair of binoculars and showed me how to use them. When I raised the glasses to my eyes and focused the lenses I found the two ships steaming straight for me, seemingly close enough to touch. On the first ship I counted five main gun turrets each with a pair of long guns. An explosion of fire and smoke erupted from the guns as I watched. A second later the sound hit us all like thunder from a distant lightning strike. It stunned the crowd into silence for a moment but immediately they jumped up out of their seats as one and began cheering.

A second volley sounded from a smaller set of guns in the bow just forward of the conning tower. This time the sound followed much closer to the spray of smoke and fire.

"SMS Goeben" Wilhelm shouted over the cheering crowd. "A Moltke-Class Battlecruiser. And her companion is the SMS Breslau, a Magdeburg Class Cruiser."

I turned my attention to the Breslau and its four stacks billowing thick black smoke. A large wave was being thrown off each side of the bow. It was then I noticed most of the crew standing in full dress uniform, lined up on the side of the ship.

The ships were now close enough that I did not need the field glasses. Moments later they were passing in front of the grandstand at full steam. Another round of guns fired and the midshipmen all snapped to attention and saluted which drew further cheers and a standing ovation from the audience.

"Do you see the third ship?" Wilhelm asked with a sly smile on his face.

I scanned the horizon back to where these two ships had come from using the binoculars but to no avail.

Wilhelm pointed to a spot on the waterfront much closer to us than the other ships. I saw a small mast of some kind emerging from the water, but no evidence of a ship.

Then suddenly a two hundred foot long boat shot out from under the water not a hundred feet from the shore in front of us. The shocked crowd was silent for a moment and then roared as one.

"SM U-21. One of our newest Underwater Boats."

On the opposite side of the grandstand a military band began playing a rousing tune I had never heard before. Wilhelm along with half of the crowd snapped to attention and began singing in unison.

"Deutschland, Deutschland über alles, Über alles in der Welt..."

I had no idea what the words meant but it seemed they were all proud of the events. They sang as one for several stanzas with the Turkish crowd watching in silence.

The music settled down and the crowd hushed. An official stepped out onto the raised dais by the water and announced something in Turkish and then in German.

"The final demonstration" Wilhelm said in my ear as he pointed off to the middle of the straight.

I saw an old rickety sailing vessel being towed by tug boat to a position about three hundred yards away. The tug released the line and the decrepit looking boat slowed to a stop, adrift now in the currents of the straight.

The master of ceremonies made another announcement in Turkish and then again in German as the tug boat sped away. The crowd gasped as Wilhelm pointed back to the U-Boat.

A pair of long thin tubes shot out from the front of the boat. A trail of bubbles seemed to follow the tubes as they picked up speed. They appeared to be powered by some type of propulsion system that pushed them forward towards the old ship that was still drifting in the straight.

They converged on the ship and when they did a huge explosion demolished the old wooden vessel throwing splinters of wood a hundred feet up into the air. It caught fire in no time, the pitch-soaked wood catching like kindling. When the main mast broke in half and fell into the water the crowd cheered even louder than before and the band began to play. This time the Turkish members of the audience were singing so I assumed it must be their national anthem.

"What was that?" I asked Wilhelm over the music.

"They are called torpedoes" Wilhelm replied with a broad smile on his face. "That is what makes the U-Boat such a powerful weapon. They can sail up to any ship undetected and fire torpedoes at the unsuspecting target from point blank range."

I was tempted to say that this was not a very fair fight, but then I knew that war was about winning and stealth was a tactic employed for millennia.

Wilhelm turned my attention to the VIP box.

"Djemal Pasha you know from dinner last night. Talaat and Enver are standing by his side."

Enver and Talaat were applauding politely but were not as enthusiastic as the others. As I studied them Talaat looked directly at me. I held his gaze for a few moments at which point he said something in Enver's ear causing him to look in my direction as well. When Enver replied to Talaat he nodded his understanding and then looked away.

I guessed that Wilhelm's casual mention of our dinner with Djemal Pasha was meant to show me that he was still in control.

"The Englishman to the right of Enver is from Vickers Limited. They manufactured the Whitehead torpedoes you just saw demonstrated. He is here to sell arms to our friends the

Pashas, although he has yet to realize they have no money."

"And the man in the Navy uniform on the other side?" I asked.

"*Konteradmiral* Wilhelm Souchon of the Mediterranean Division Squadron. He is commander of the ships you saw here today and responsible for their great victories in the two Balkan Wars. Thanks to men like Souchon and Tirpitz, we now have the second most powerful Navy on earth. With Britain's Navy spread out across the seven seas we are free to concentrate our forces in the place of our choosing to create an overwhelming advantage. The Kaiser has even offered Admiral Souchon to the Turks along with these ships to bolster the Ottoman Navy."

Yet another incentive I thought to myself.

"Is there anything you wish to share about your dinner conversation night before last Sayed?"

"Do you think this is an appropriate place to discuss this?"

"Look around Sayed. No Persian speakers for miles."

"Haven't you learned that is not a safe assumption yet?"

"Ah yes. I see what you mean. How is Khalil by the way? Is he enjoying the Taqi ad-Din manuscripts he received from the Pasha? They are quite valuable."

Knowing that we dined with the Pasha was one thing. Knowing details about the books was another level of information altogether.

"And your stamp collection is now much bigger I understand."

He obviously had someone either inside the dinner or perhaps his information came from one of Gulbenkian's servants.

"It seems Djemal had something for all of you in Topkapi Palace that night. If my superiors would have given me the latitude I requested, Monsieur Picot would never have boarded that train yesterday. We cannot allow the Ottomans to join the Triple Entente Sayed. It will not happen."

I wondered if this line of conversation was intended as a threat.

"You and Gulbenkian made a mistake yesterday humiliating my man. This is not a game Sayed. The future distribution of power in Europe is at stake here. The fate of nations will be determined in the next few months before the first shot is fired."

Definitely a threat.

"What do you want from me Wilhelm? If this is not a game then tell me what you expect and stop dodging in and out of shadows with your thinly veiled threats!"

He snickered to himself.

"This is much better Sayed and you are correct. It is time."

He stood up and turned towards the two war ships which had pulled alongside the dock while we were speaking. The crews were busy securing the vessels with lines to the bollards.

"The Pashas and their entourage will tour the ships once they have completed docking, but we have an appointment across town."

We returned to the carriage in silence. If I thought I could have begged off of the next meeting I would have, but at this point I did not think I had a choice.

We proceeded around the Golden Horne that made up the old city and arrived at the foot of a wide bridge.

"This is the Galata Bridge" Wilhelm said. "It is a floating bridge, an engineering marvel built by Hüttenwerk Oberhausen AG. Up ahead you can see Galata Tower."

"Is that where we are going? I asked"

"No. We are going to Dolmabahce Palace to meet with Sultan Mehmed the fifth."

I was somewhat surprised by this to say the least. Calouste had given me the background of the Ottoman power structure in our conversations at the bath the day before. Sultan Mehmed was now seventy years old and did not become sultan until he was sixty five. By that time the Young Turks had moved all governing into the Parliament and vested the three Pashas with most of the real decision making power. The Sultan was a figurehead. So why did he want to meet with me?

We entered the palace gates and proceeded on to the ceremonial hall where we were treated to a display of alabaster stonework and crystal chandeliers that put every Persian palace I have seen to shame. Even the carved stone staircases were inlaid with crystal.

We were ushered through the grand hall and out through the back towards the southern wing and in to a smaller representation room where we found a relatively subdued conference table and chairs.

A pair of servants presented us with cut crystal goblets of water and then disappeared from view.

"Now we wait" Wilhelm said in Persian.

"Not for long" came a response also in Persian as the old man himself entered through the side door.

"Heir Wassmuss it is good to see you again."

Wilhelm snapped his heals together and bowed.

"And you must be Sayed Kashani?" the Sultan said.

I had no idea of the proper term to greet a Sultan so I improvised.

"Yes Your Highness" I said and bowed following Wilhelm's lead.

"Please take a seat and have some refreshment. Travelling all this way must have been tiring."

I waited for the Sultan to sit and then took my place at the table.

"Your Persian is flawless Your Highness. May I ask where you learned?"

"Reading the great Persian Poets of course. I spent the first thirty years of my life in seclusion at Topkapi Palace. Nine of those in solitary confinement you might say."

This confused me and evidently it showed.

"Oh I was not under arrest. It is simply our custom. Future sultans are confined to the Harems well into adulthood. I studied the great Persian writers and philosophers and spent years developing my own style of poetry. I left Topkapi at age thirty and never had a desire to return."

"His Highness the Sultan has written several marvelous poems Sayed. They read like works from Omar Khayyam."

"You are too kind Wilhelm, but if you don't mind, I have a busy schedule this afternoon and would like to get straight to business."

Wilhelm bowed his head. "Certainly Highness."

"Sayed I am sure you are wondering why I would call for you and why I have insisted on keeping this meeting such a secret."

"Yes Your Highness" I answered.

"I am not happy with the current state of our Caliphate Sayed. My own government is engaged in negotiations with both the Central Powers and the Entente to choose an ally. I say that neither of these choices are in the best interest of Islam. We must resist the influence from the West. They are on the verge of occupying the entire Islamic world. My Caliphate!"

"I am sure your cousin the Ayatollah would agree with me" he continued. "We must restore the ways of our ancestors to the holy lands of Arabia and beyond. Sharia law is the law of Allah. Blessed be his name. We must resist the secularism that is rotting our country from the inside. Don't you agree?"

This was not quite what I expected to hear and not something I agreed with, but I knew when to keep my opinions to myself. I chose to answer a different question.

"I am sure Abol-Ghasem would strongly agree with you Highness."

"The challenge has been that we are ourselves divided against each other. I have read a quote from the American President Lincoln that a House divided against itself cannot stand. A very wise man. This saying is true for Islam as well."

I did not dare tell him that this quote was actually from the Christian Bible. I shot a glance a Wilhelm who very softly shook his head no as if reading my thoughts.

"You have studied American history Majesty?" Wilhelm asked.

"I studied their civil war and their struggle with cultural change. Their notions on slavery are a bit naïve, but I did learn a few things here and there."

I waited for the Sultan to return to the original topic on his own accord.

"I believe we must first heal ourselves from within and unite in a common cause against the West."

"You mean Sunni and Shia Majesty?" I asked.

"Yes. Sunnis and Twelver Shia alike. I would like you to carry a proposal back to your cousin and to all of the Imams in Persia. In return for their support, we will establish a special administrative zone around Bagdad that includes Najaf and Karbala. I would appoint Ayatollah Kashani the protector of the Holy cities of the Shia faith. We will create a group of learned elders that combine both Sunni and Shia clerics to act as my Rightly Guided Caliphs. Together we will re-establish Sharia law throughout the Ottoman empire and eject the infidel British and French from our holy lands!"

His voice rose to a fevered pitch at the end. He took a moment to calm down and after a brief respite turned to me and said in a much calmer voice "With the permission of your parliament, we will help you eject the British and Russians from Persia as well."

"You would like me to bring this message to Ayatollah Kashani" I confirmed.

"Yes. Right away. Leave today if you are able. We have no time to lose."

I looked at Wilhelm for guidance. Did the Sultan know that I was on my way to Paris? Did he know of my other connections with the British and French?

"Yes your Majesty."

The words were out of my mouth before I realized I had said them.

"But first Majesty" I continued, "I need to determine where my cousin is at the moment. He was in Qom when I left on this journey, but I believe he was also preparing to travel himself."

The last part was a lie, but not one that was easily found out.

"You sent a cable to your wife yesterday, you can cable Qom to enquire about the Ayatollah."

Even if my privacy meant nothing to these people, couldn't they at least pretend that it did?

"I will take him to the telegraph office straight away Majesty" Wilhelm offered.

"No need. We have a telegraph and telephone in our communications room. I will have my secretary take you there now. We will know his whereabouts before you leave the Palace."

I knew Wilhelm was trying to help me out and I was certainly grateful, but now what was I to do?

"I will do my best Majesty" I said as he rose from his chair and walked toward the door.

"I expect your best Sayed" he said without turning. "I am counting on you."

He turned and stared directly at me.

"So do not disappoint me."

The Sultan left and before I could say a word to Wilhelm the Sultan's secretary appeared. We were ushered through the palace and down into a basement level office just near the entrance. The door to the room was flanked by armed guards but once inside we found a simple desk with a telegraph key on one end and a desk telephone on the other.

The secretary explained what we were after in Turkish and moments later the telegrapher was keying in a message as Wilhelm and I stood by, powerless to stop it.

After several minutes of waiting, the receiver began clicking while the telegrapher scribbled his notes. This was followed by another burst of clicks as the man pecked out yet another message. We waited patiently in the room for what seemed to be a half hour although I am sure it was only a few minutes of actual time. The receiver sprang to life again as another message was received.

After a brief conversation between the secretary and the telegrapher we were ushered outside the room and up the flight of stairs to the entrance.

"Ayatollah Kashani left Qom a few days ago on his way to Karbala" the secretary said in French. "We will book passage for you on the Berlin-Bagdad rail line to the end of the line and you can hire a caravan from there to Karbala."

I was about to open my mouth when Wilhelm stepped forward and shook the secretary's hand.

"Thank you. We will return to the city and await your instructions."

With that the two of us left through the door and made our way slowly down to our carriage.

"Don't say anything until we are out of the gates" he told me in Persian.

Once safely outside Wilhelm sat back in his seat and exhaled.

"Did you know he would ask me to turn around and head for Mesopotamia?"

"No Sayed I did not. This was most unexpected."

"What are you playing at Wilhelm? I thought you were trying to negotiate a deal with the Emir of Mohammerah? And another deal with Gulbenkian? Then there is the display of German military might this morning. How many ways are you going to hedge your bet?"

"As many as it takes to succeed!" he screamed.

The look of hatred in his eyes frightened me. For the first time I saw Wilhelm out of control and confirmed what I already expected. He was a dangerous man.

"I need some time to think" he said under his breath. "This was most unexpected."

"You said that before. I can't go back now. I am expected in Paris."

"You won't have to go back Sayed. I will work this out. Gulbenkian booked you on the Orient Express for the day after tomorrow right?"

"I'm sure you know better than I do."

"You will be on that train."

"But how about the train ticket they will book for me for tomorrow?"

"You will be on that train as well."

"I don't understand."

"Just trust me. I will work this out" he spat. "I need access to the time tables and to connect with some of my colleagues, but I should have this worked out by tonight."

We rode on in silence for a mile or so until we approached the Galata Bridge once again. Wilhelm rapped his knuckled on the roof of the carriage and it slowed to halt.

"I will get out here. I have much to do and little time. Go back to Gulbenkian's and wait for further instruction."

He spoke to the driver in Turkish and then disappeared into the crowds.

The driver delivered me safely to the front of Gulbenkian's townhouse and as the butler shut the door behind me, I breathed a sigh of relief.

Calouste emerged from the library to find me standing in the middle of foyer, trying to decide what to do next.

"Are you alright Abdulrahim? You look as if you have seen a ghost?"

"I have spent the day with one I am afraid. I need a drink and your council if possible."

Calouste led me into the library and poured a generous glass of single malt. I filled him in on the events of the day and as expected, he was as worried as I.

"I thought the Pashas had all of the power?" I asked

"They do, but Mehmed is still the Sultan. He still controls the Palace guards, the modern equivalents of the Janissaries, and is very dangerous in his own right."

"So it seems Mark Sykes' information on the German plan for Karbala and Najaf was correct" I said.

"Not entirely. It looks like the Sultan's plan has similar aspects, but cuts out the Emir of Mohammerah... and the Germans for that matter."

"I hadn't considered that. If the Sultan's plan is to eject the western powers from Arabia, that means the Germans would be ejected as well. No more Berlin-Bagdad Railroad. No more access to the oil. My cousin would prefer that over some deal brokered by the Germans and the Emir."

"Precisely. That is what upset Wilhelm. That is why he is willing to help you escape."

"Escape from where Uncle?"

We both turned to see Khalil standing in the entrance to the library. I filled him in on the highlights and reassured him that nothing was wrong. When I finished he was quiet for a moment and then smiled.

"Do you have any idea of what Wilhelm is planning?" Khalil asked. "Because I think I know."

"Only that he said I would be on both trains" I replied.

"Makes sense" he said. "Here is how I would do it."

He walked across the room and joined us.

"I studied the rail system maps when we arrived. It looks like there is a stop in Soma, about five or six hours after you leave the Haydarpasa terminal. If you sneak off the train there, you can catch the afternoon train back to Constantinople and be back in time for dinner. Of course we will need a trunk that we are willing to sacrifice."

"A trunk?" I asked then answered my own question. "Right, if I board without my trunk then they will be suspicious, but I won't be able to reclaim it in Soma, so I will have to abandon it."

"And you probably should not return here to my Villa" Calouste added.

"Right" Khalil agreed.

"Do you think the Germans and Brits will continue to follow me?" I asked Calouste.

"Very Likely" he replied. "In fact, I would expect the Sultan to put a man on you as well, just to ensure you are following his command. That's the person we need to worry about now."

"So I will have three people on my tail?"

"Yes, but maybe that will work to our advantage. Let me reach out to MI6. They may be able to help conceal your departure in Soma."

Calouste went off to make his arrangements as Khalil and I discussed more details.

An hour later a messenger from the Sultan delivered my ticket and itinerary followed shortly thereafter by a second messenger from Wilhelm.

"The ticket out of Haydarpasa is for the seven thirty train in the morning" I announced to Khalil after reading the message from the Sultan's Secretary.

"Perfect!" Khalil said. "That will get you to Soma just before one, plenty of time to catch the two o'clock train back to Haydarpasa. What does Wilhelm say?"

I read the note and laughed out loud.

"You anticipated his plan to the letter. I am to exit the train at Soma and catch the return that afternoon."

I noticed something else in the envelope and withdrew a second ticket.

"Two o'clock train from Soma to Constantinople" I read. "I'm all set."

"Not entirely" Calouste said standing at the library door. "MI6 are arranging a double for you. He should be ready in time for the train."

"A double?" I asked.

"A man that looks like you" Calouste replied. "Same height. Same build. You will meet him and exchange clothes. He will ride in your place to the end of the line."

I rose early the following morning and packed my Luis Vuitton trunk with my clothes and stamp collection and left it on the bed. I would not be returning to the townhouse, so I had to get that ready for the trip on the Orient Express.

I put on my traditional Persian robes and turban for the train ride south into the Levant and Mesopotamia. Not only would the contrast be greater when I swapped clothes with my double, I didn't want to lose my best western suit to the ruse.

I packed a second trunk with a few old bed sheets and carried it downstairs to wait for the charade to begin.

The sultan provided a carriage for me as expected and even a ferry across the Bosporus to Haydarpasa terminal. The footman from the carriage accompanied me across the straights to help with my trunk.

When we arrived at the terminal, the porters took my trunk from the footman. I boarded the train after a brief stop at the newsstand twenty minutes before departure.

So far so good.

As I boarded the train I noticed that the footman from the carriage stood watch on the platform. He didn't board the train with me, but I am sure he had instructions to watch me until the train left the station.

I showed my ticket to the conductor and was escorted down a long narrow hallway to a semi-private compartment. A man and a young child were sitting on one side as I settled in to face them.

"Do you speak French?" I asked them.

They shook their heads then said something in Turkish.

I indicated that I didn't understand and was relieved to discover that I would not need to carry on any type of conversation.

I heard a flurry of activity on the platform and felt the train start to move. It appeared I may have gotten lucky with my accommodations. I doubted an agent for the Sultan would bring their child into a potentially dangerous situation.

As we picked up speed I relaxed, knowing I had five hours to kill before the action started. It was then that the door opened and a large man in his mid-twenties entered our cabin and pointed to the seat next to me.

"This seat is empty?" he asked in French.

He did not appear to be Turkish or Armenian for that matter. He had sandy blonde hair and green eyes, with a nose that had apparently been broken at least once. How he knew I spoke French when I was dressed in my robes and turban was a mystery. He might have known I was Persian and assumed I spoke French, but I thought the more likely answer was that he knew which languages I spoke before he even boarded the train.

He sat down next to me and settled in. Within minutes he was leaning against the wall apparently fast asleep.

I picked up the copy of *Le Temps* I bought at the newsstand and suddenly felt like a fool. Perhaps the French newspaper I held was the reason this man spoke to me in French.

I needed to calm down.

After reading the newspaper for an hour I decided to reconnoiter the train. My seat mate was still sleeping as was the father and child opposite. So I rose and exited the compartment as quietly as I could. Then I headed off to find the toilets and the dining car.

The train's decor was certainly not up to the level of Gulbenkian's private cars, but it was clean and serviceable. I found the toilets at the front end of the next car and the dining car three cars ahead of that. I ordered a coffee and light snack then settled in to a table facing the rear of the train.

It didn't take long for my seat mate to appear in the dining car. He seemed a little surprised to see me staring at him as he surveyed the car. He passed through without stopping though so I relaxed a bit and enjoyed my refreshments. At this point I had to believe he was a tail. Better safe than sorry.

A few minutes later a gentleman in a three piece suit entered the car and ordered. When his food was ready he made a show of scanning the available seats as if deciding where to sit. He walked to my end of the car past my table then turned and headed for the other end.

I don't know how he did it, because I didn't see him make any move towards my table, but after he passed by, a small envelope appeared on the corner of my table. The famous Harry Houdini could not have performed better.

There were very few other passengers in the car and none seemed to be paying attention to me, but I retrieved the envelope and held it under the table for a moment before examining its contents. There was a simple note written in French which read "fifteen minutes prior to arrival, car number four, forward toilet."

I looked up at the man who was now seated at the far end of the car facing me and nodded my understanding then placed the note in a pocket of by robe. He gave a barely unperceivable nod in return and went on about his business.

My seat mate reappeared a few minutes later and bought his own refreshment then surprised me by approaching my table.

"May I join monsieur?" he asked.

Now that I was paying attention I noticed his French had a very strong accent.

"*Mais oui*" I replied.

As he sat down I peered over his shoulder to the man who passed the note. He touched the side of his nose with his finger which I interpreted as asking me to notice the new arrival's broken nose. If I needed confirmation, I now had it.

"You are going to Bagdad?"

"To Karbala" I answered. "And you?"

"To the end of rail line" he said simply.

"You are from Karbala?" he asked.

"No. I am from Tehran, but I have business in Karbala."

"Ah, Persian. You are Muslim?"

"Most of my countrymen are" I replied, not really answering his question.

"I am Muslim" he said with a big smile. "*As-Salaam-Alaikum.*"

"*Wa-Alaikum-Salaam*" I replied, not wanting to spoil his enthusiasm.

"Forgive me" I said, "but I have not met many light haired, green eyed Muslims."

"I am Bosniak" he said, his smile disappearing from his face. "I live in Constantinople for my life, but my Mother is from Sarajevo."

"And your father?"

"*Allah* is my father" he said flatly. "My mother escapes from Bosnia when Austrians force her husband to army. We have good life in Constantinople. My Mother she is happy. So I am happy."

I was surprised by his bold admission that he was a bastard child. His blonde hair and eye color suggested that his father was probably an Austrian soldier and that he was not a product of immaculate conception as he suggested.

"My name is Kashani" I said, trying to change the direction of the conversation.

"I am Tarik. Please to meet you."

I was finished with my refreshments and not really interested in continuing the conversation, but with a few hours left in the journey, there was not much I could do.

"What is your line of work?" I asked Tarik.

"I was boxer" he replied. "Champion of my weight class."

He did a phantom double punch into the air and brought his fists back up to a defensive position. The pride was back in his voice and the smile back on his face.

"And you?"

"I have a stationary store in Tehran, but I am on a trip to trade stamps."

"Stamps?"

"Yes. You know, postage stamps."

"Like use on letters?"

"Yes. I collect them. New, used, from all countries."

"I never hear people collect stamps" he said. "Wait!"

He reached into his jacket and pulled out an envelope. He removed the letter from inside and placed it back in his jacket.

"You have stamp from Bosnia?"

"No, I don't."

He handed me the envelope with a broad smile on his face.

"Now you have stamp from Sarajevo. Letter from my cousin."

I examined the stamp in the sunlight from the window. It was cancelled of course, but still in good condition.

Merci beaucoup" I replied. "I don't think I will ever forget how I acquired this." I doubt he heard the sarcasm in my voice.

The smile on his face was infectious. He appeared to be quite a powerful man, but there was something about his demeanor that was almost child-like. I am sure that if he lost his temper, he could be quite dangerous, but I quite liked the young man.

Tarik finished his snacks as well and there was a lull in the conversation, so I decided it was time to return to my compartment and hopefully get a little sleep before the real excitement began.

As expected, Tarik joined me and we both settled down into our seats. The man and boy that shared the room were still fast asleep themselves.

I woke from a deep sleep with the sudden fear that I had overslept. The man and his son were fully awake now, the boy leaning against the window looking like he wanted to escape from the confines of such a small space. I checked my pocket watch and found that I had cut it close, but if we were on time, we still had twenty five minutes to go.

A conductor walked down the hallway calling out "Soma. Next stop is Soma."

I rose from my seat and opened the door to the compartment.

"Excuse me, are we on schedule?" I asked the conductor.

"Five minutes ahead Monsieur" came the reply.

So I had indeed cut it close. I sat back in my seat and saw Tarik awake, looking at me with his boyish grin. I took up my newspaper and tried to focus on a story or two that I had read before, but after a few minutes I couldn't wait any longer.

"I think I will go to the Toilet" I said. "I will be right back."

I left the paper and found my way to car number four and then all the way to the forward part of the cabin to find the toilet. I entered and closed the door behind me. Not twenty seconds later someone rapped on the door. I cracked it open to find a man dressed in a western business suit and fedora hat peering in.

"Monsieur Kashani?"

I opened the door wide to let him in and closed it behind him. It was not a very spacious room but it was large enough for two men of my size to stand comfortably. Indeed the man standing in front of me was my exact size, right down to his generous belly.

"We have plenty of time Monsieur so do not panic" he whispered. "You were not followed, but I expect your watchdog will come looking soon. So let's first exchange clothes."

We both stripped down to our underclothes and exchanged garments. The final step was our shoes and headwear.

With him wearing my robes and turban I was struck by the

resemblance. Even his moustache was the spitting image of mine. In fact, when I looked into the mirror on the wall behind the man and at my own face, I was amazed at the similarities.

"Let's make sure you didn't forget anything" he said reaching into the pockets of my robe.

"I believe these are yours" he said, handing over the contents.

My brain was not working at full speed it seemed. If he had not reminded me, I would have been left without my father's watch, my ticket to Iraq, my return ticket to Constantinople, and my new Bosnian stamp.

"I think I should keep this" he said as he plucked my outbound ticket from me.

I placed my watch in the suit where it belonged and the ticket and envelope in my new breast pocket.

"Nice suit" I said.

"Savile Row" he replied although I had no idea what that meant.

I heard the whistle and felt the train slowing as we approached the station in Soma. I was anxious to make my escape.

"So what next?" I asked.

"The train will stop in Soma for ten minutes. It is set to depart at twelve forty. We wait until Twelve thirty five and I will leave the toilet and head for the dining car. If all goes well, your tail will follow me and you will exit the door just beside the Toilet just prior to the train departing the station."

"Tarik" I said. "My tail's name is Tarik. He is from Bosnia and he was a Boxer."

"I know all about Tarik" he said. "Dangerous man. He tell you anything else?"

"He's a Muslim."

"Of course he's a Muslim" my double whispered. "He is a member of the Sultan's personal guard. And he broke his nose fighting, but not as a boxer."

"He is a good liar then" I said. "And the story about his mother being from Bosnia?"

"That was true" my double replied. "The Sultan has taken in many refugees and orphans from the Balkans into his Ordered guards. He doesn't kidnap Christian boys and convert them to Islam like the Janissaries of old, but he is fond of brain-washing his troops from an early age to follow him and no one else."

I had mistakenly assumed the child-like demeanor was a result of an inferior intellect and one too many punches. Thinking back though, it did remind me of the vacuous smile you see on the face of young true believers, people with such deep faith that nothing in this world could harm them and if anything did, it must be Allah's will.

I felt the train grind to a stop and heard the telltale sound of steam releasing from the boilers.

We were quiet for a long moment until a knock came on the door.

"It's occupied" I said.

"Kashani?" the voice called out. Tarik was obviously uncomfortable that I was gone for so long.

"Yes Tarik. I'm afraid I must have ate something bad for breakfast this morning. I will be here for a while longer."

"I am sorry my friend. I was worried for you."

"*Merci mon amie.* Why don't you wait for me in the dining car. I will be out soon."

"I will wait in dining car" he said.

I heard the sound of footsteps and the door to the car open and close. I pulled out my watch. Twelve thirty six.

"We'll give it two more minutes" my double said checking his own watch.

Those two minutes passed in silence and were the longest two minutes of my life. We heard the sound of several people pass by the door to the toilet as we lingered. Finally my double was ready.

He cracked opened the door and peered out into the hall. Then he turned back to me.

"Wait until I am standing in front of the door to the next car. Then exit the toilet and on to the step. Wait for me to go through the door and then exit the train. Go immediately towards the rear with your back to the dining car and when you are a good distance away pull the hat low and turn for the waiting room. Once inside go to the toilet and wait there another fifteen minutes. Got it?"

"Yes."

"*Bon Chance!*"

He peeked out the door one more time and then he was gone.

I saw him wait at the door and with his right hand behind his back, signal me to move.

I made for the train exit, then on to the platform as he opened the doors to the next car.

I pulled my hat low on my head and walked slowly towards the back of the train. Anyone watching from the dining car would see a well-dressed businessman exiting the train.

I walked until I was across from the last entrance into the terminal and headed for the door. As I entered the waiting area I spied the signs for the toilet and made my way to the safety of a private stall next to the wall.

When I closed the door behind me I let out a long sigh of relief. I had not been paying attention to my breathing but it seemed like I had been underwater for a long time and was just now catching my breath. I hadn't been afraid during this entire maneuver, but now that it was over I was shaking. I held out my hands and by the light of the window I could see they just would not stop trembling.

I heard the whistle from the train and the chuffing sound from the platform. I stepped up on my tip toes and peered out the small window. The train began to move and then picked up speed.

I leaned against the wall and caught my breath as people came in and out of the washroom. I could see through the crack of the door that others were waiting, but I stayed in the stall quite a while.

I pulled out my watch again. One ten. I had been hiding for thirty minutes.

I exited the stall to an empty room, washed my hands and then pushed open the door to the waiting room of the station. The central room was full of people waiting for the next train, my train back to Constantinople.

I scanned the crowd looking for Tarik, just to make sure he didn't discover my ruse and alight from the train himself. Not seeing anyone remotely like him, I looked for anyone paying attention to me. So far so good.

I bought a copy of *Le Figaro* from the newsstand and settled down into a seat to wait for boarding time. When I brought the paper up to read, it provided a nice shield for my face. A few minutes later I felt rather than saw someone sit down in the chair next to me.

"Well done Kashani" he said.

I turned to see the man who slipped me the note.

"Tarik remained on the train and is now sound asleep, thanks to a drug placed in his coffee. When he wakes up in twelve hours, he won't be able to tell your double from the real thing. He will be woozy at least until he hits Aleppo and likely to the end of the line. That gives you a good eighteen hours before he realizes we made the switch, if he does at all."

"My double said Tarik is a dangerous man" I said.

"Very" he replied.

"Then I thank you for your assistance."

"Just doing my job. You are a very important man. We must get you to Paris safe and sound."

"It seems like everyone I meet knows more about my trip than I do!"

"I know nothing about the reason for your trip Monsieur Kashani. Only that C wants you in Paris and that is what I intend to see happen."

"Then you will accompany me back to Constantinople?"

"Then put you up for the night, see you on to the Orient Express and then through to Paris."

"What do I call you?" I asked.

"Some call me... Tim" he said with a grin.

"Your name is Tim?" I asked.

"No, but that will do" he said.

Our train was announced and we boarded without incident. The trip back to Haydarpasa terminal was uneventful as well, but when we pulled into the station, Tim and I waited for a long while before alighting. I saw a man walk down the platform from the terminal and stop outside our car to examine his watch. It seems that must have been the all clear signal because everything went at full speed after that.

We made our way down the platform, out the side exit to the docks where a motor boat was waiting for us. Instead of heading south this time, we made course for the Galata Bridge and once under it motored on for another fifteen minutes before docking at a mansion that fronted the water.

I followed Tim into the house and found a collection of servants there to greet us.

"I'll send word to Gulbenkian that we arrived safely" Tim said. "The staff will show you to your room. We've taken the liberty of providing you with the necessities for the night. Freshen up and then join me for a drink before dinner if you like."

I did as instructed and found myself shortly thereafter with Tim in the library enjoying a single malt.

"Today went as well as I could have expected" he said.

"I appreciate your help. I must admit I got a little worried at Soma."

"Don't mention it. I remember my first few operations. I was a bundle of nerves after each. You get used to it."

"May I ask where you are from?"

Tim smiled.

"Sure. I grew up in Oxford England, but I studied at Cambridge. I joined the service when it was started in oh nine."

"Your French is quite good. Did you live there?"

"Now you are getting into delicate territory, but I will answer your question. I spent several years in France and the past two in Cairo and the various parts of the Ottoman Empire."

"So you know Sir Mark Sykes" I ventured.

"I know Sir Mark very well" he replied. "Funny man."

"I just met him in Van" I said.

"I know Monsieur Kashani. I was there in Van as well, although not very visible at that time."

"Was it you in the apartment across from Gulbenkian's townhouse?"

"Guilty as charged" he said raising his free hand. "I told you, I have been sent to protect you."

"And when we were detained by the Ottomans at Haydarpasa?"

"I was also unaware that they had set up the screening process. As soon as we saw what was happening we phoned Riza Bey and he got word to the station to let you all go."

"What is happening with the Armenians?"

"It's awful I'm afraid. I have seen baggage cars packed with people being sent out east like cattle. Best we can tell they are being slaughtered and buried in mass graves a hundred miles east of the city."

"Who is responsible for this?"

"Talaat Pasha" Tim replied. "Enver and Djemal resisted at first, but Talaat showed them evidence that the Russians and Armenians from Van are colluding so they went along."

I tried to imagine how an entire group of people could be held accountable for the actions of a few. It was a tragedy. Then I remembered that gaze from Talaat Pasha on the reviewing stand by the water and realized that if the Germans had their way, they would provide the man with a fleet of ships and U-boats.

"Do you know a company called Vickers Limited?" I asked.

"I do. They supply our armies with most of their weapons."

"Why would the King allow them to supply Whitehead Torpedoes to the Ottomans and Germans?"

"Are you being serious?" Tim asked.

"I saw a representative of Vickers at the Naval review a few days ago. He was standing with Talaat and the other Pashas. Wilhelm Wassmuss pointed him out."

"Naval review?"

"Yes, the SMS Goeben and Breslau? How could you not hear them firing their guns in the straights? Then the U-Boat destroying that old wooden ship with torpedoes. I would have thought everyone in the city was aware of that."

"I was out of the city on other business at the time" he said. "We don't have enough men to handle everything."

I could tell this was news to Tim from the look on his face. He placed his scotch on the table and walked to the far end of the library where a telephone was sitting on the desk. He made a call speaking in hushed tones but in a very animated manner. When he returned he was visibly shaken.

"Thank you for that" he said. "It was very helpful. Now how about dinner?"

I helped myself to another scotch followed by a wonderful meal. The two of us dined alone at the big formal table and spoke about more palatable subjects. The glass of wine on top of the scotch and the exciting day sent me to bed early.

We were out of the house at first light the following morning and into a carriage for our ride across the city. Tim and I arrived at the Sirkeci Terminal with plenty of time to spare before the departure of the Orient Express. While Gulbenkian did not have his private car attached to this train, he did buy out all of the compartments in our car, so it was for all intents and purposes our own oasis. When Tim and I boarded the train, Khalil and Calouste were already there.

"Uncle! I am so happy to see you!"

"We got notice last night you were safe" Gulbenkian said, "but it is good to see you arrived safely Abdulrahim."

"Everything went like clockwork Calouste" my handler said.

"Thank you Clive" Gulbenkian said. "What is the status of our friend Tarik?"

"I got a telegram this morning. He is awake but still groggy. We should be well out of Ottoman territory before he is able to report back."

The man I knew as Tim turned and nodded in my direction. "Monsieur Kashani."

"Clive" I said as I nodded back.

He smiled and left our compartment leaving me with Calouste and Khalil.

A porter appeared dressed in a crisp white uniform and carrying a silver tray with coffee and croissants.

"What was that all about uncle?"

"I will tell you later Khalil. We have a long trip ahead of us and plenty of time to catch up."

The train lurched forward as I heard the whistle blow. We were on our way once again.

BUDAPEST

June 17th, 1914

The first big test came a few hours into our journey when the train slowed to a stop at the border with Bulgaria. The conductors arrived at our compartment and took all of our passports for customs formalities. If we made it past this crossing, we would be out of the Ottoman Empire and into the sovereign territory of a nation with no love lost for the Turks.

We held our breath for half an hour, hoping that the Sultan had yet to discover I was not *en route* to Karbala. Our fears were quickly assuaged though when our passports were returned, stamped with the proper seals.

We were on our way again.

We passed the time in conversation, playing Patience, and reading newspapers. I even got a chance to practice my English by attempting to read Calouste's copy of the Financial Times. Khalil sat with me during this exercise and acted as my tutor. He was a wonderful teacher.

The food service on the Orient Express was marvelous. The chef de cuisine was well known and the meals lived up to his reputation. I tried Italian pasta and chicken à la chasseur for the first time in my life. I couldn't decide which was my new favorite. Khalil told me after my second trip to the dessert buffet that my dear wife would not be happy if I returned from this trip even heavier than I started.

Did I mention Khalil was a wonderful teacher?

We crossed into Romania without incident at the border and pulled in to Bucharest almost 10 hours after leaving Constantinople. The train took on more passengers and supplies at the station and we all took the opportunity to stretch our legs on stationary land. We were now well outside the reach of the Sultan.

Once underway again it was time for another meal. We shared a bottle of wine from Châteauneuf-du-Pape and enjoyed a wonderful filet of beef with vegetables. I was so content from this meal that within an hour of returning to our compartment I was ready for bed.

The following morning we were told that we had crossed in to Hungary during the night, passport formalities again being performed by the staff. Just after breakfast we arrived in Budapest.

That is where everything turned upside down.

The soldiers arrived at our compartment before we had a chance to exit the train, dressed head to toe in the powder blue uniforms of the Austria-Hungarian army. The officer in charge wore a blue flat topped cap with black brim, black leather gloves, and knee-high black leather riding boots. He had a pistol in a holster on his waist and was flanked by four enlisted men, each armed with swords.

"Sayed Kashani?" their leader asked.

"I am Sayed Kashani" I confirmed.

And that is when I was arrested and taken off the Orient Express.

We were fortunate that I was the only one taken. Calouste, Khalil, and MI6 agent Clive were left on the train as I was loaded into the back of a van and driven away to a local jail.

I didn't speak Hungarian and not one of the soldiers spoke French, so I could only assume that the Sultan was behind this. Austria-Hungary was historically an enemy of the Ottomans. They had been at war over the Balkans less than forty years before. The Germans however were pushing hard to make them part of the Central Powers.

I sat in my barren cell for several hours wondering what to do when just after noon Calouste appeared at the Jail and was allowed to see me.

"Is it the Sultan?" I asked.

"Yes" Calouste replied. "I don't have much time Abdulrahim, so please listen."

"We were able to get our trunks unloaded and checked in to a hotel while we sort this out. I went to the British embassy and cabled London for assistance. Clive is there at the embassy waiting for the reply."

"Khalil?"

"He's worried but otherwise handling this well. I asked him to stay at the hotel to wait for instructions if we need him."

"What am I being charged with?" I asked.

"Nothing. You are being held at the request of Franz Joseph, Emperor of Austria and King of Hungary."

"Is there anything I can do besides wait?" I asked.

"I'm afraid not. Just sit tight. If we turn over your passport and get a guarantee from our ambassador, we might be able to get you out of here and held under house arrest at the hotel until this is sorted out."

"Good. Because I doubt this establishment serves Chicken à la chasseur, let alone Italian pasta."

"I am glad to see you still have your sense of humor Abdul-rahim."

That was the last I saw of anyone familiar until the following day.

Sometime in the mid-morning Calouste arrived with a well-dressed man carrying an attaché case. We were shown to a bare meeting room with a small table and three wooden chairs.

"Monsieur Kashani, I am Sinclair Dodgson, undersecretary and assistant to Sir Maurice de Bunsen, Ambassador to Austria-Hungary."

"I am pleased to meet you Monsieur Dodgson" I replied.

Both men sat down as Dodgson pulled several papers from his case.

"Monsieur Kashani, can you tell me how you know Mohamed Mehmedbasic?"

"I don't know him" I replied. "I have never heard that name before."

I looked at Calouste for help but he just sat silent with a worried look on his face.

"Then why were you carrying an envelope sent by him to Tarik Gujic?"

"I collect stamps" I said flatly.

"Stamps?" Dodgson asked.

"I shared a train compartment with Tarik recently and when he discovered I collected stamps, he gave me the empty envelope which had a stamp from Bosnia. It was a gift."

"How recently?"

"Two days ago" I said. "That's why the stamp is still on the envelope and not properly secured in my collection."

"So he was on the Orient Express?"

"No. We were on the Berlin-Bagdad railroad."

"I'm sorry? You mean you were coming in to Constantinople on the Berlin-Bagdad railroad? I thought you were staying with Monsieur Gulbenkian for the week prior to your trip."

"I was" I said. I looked at Calouste for guidance but he was just shaking his head in disbelief.

"I was" I repeated. "But I was asked by the Sultan to carry a message to my cousin in Karbala, so I pretended to make the trip. You see I had to be on the Orient Express the following day ... so I returned to Constantinople when I reached Soma, the first stop."

"I see" he said. "So why did you have to pretend?"

"Because I was being followed. I had to make it look like I was actually going to Karbala."

At this point I finally realized how unbelievable my story was sounding, but I didn't know how to get out of the predicament without lying and getting caught.

"Who was following you?" he asked.

"Tarik. He works for the Sultan."

"This man was following you, yet you had a conversation with him and he gave you a gift?"

"I know how this sounds, truly, but if you met Tarik you would understand. He is not the brightest candle in the sconce."

I waited for the next question, but it was not forthcoming. So I asked my own.

"What is so important about this envelope to warrant all of these questions?"

"Have you heard of the Black Hand or Young Bosnia?" Dodgson asked.

"No."

"They are terror organizations in the Balkans who want to overthrow the government and gain independence from Austria-Hungary. Mohamed Mehmedbasic is a prominent member of both. He recently attended a meeting in Toulouse, France where they made plans to assassinate Arch Duke Franz Ferdinand, the Governor of Bosnia, and others. He addressed the envelope in your possession after he returned from that meeting and mailed it from Sarajevo. The Austria-Hungarian government believes an attack is imminent and now believes you are somehow linked to these anarchists."

"This is bad" I said to myself. "This is very bad."

"Look Monsieur Kashani, Monsieur Gulbenkian has vouched for you and says you are an honorable man, but I am afraid I will need more than that."

"You are attached to the British Embassy?" I asked.

"Yes" he replied.

"With high security clearance?" I asked.

That question caused him to look to Calouste for guidance.

"You can tell him" Calouste said.

"Yes. I have high security clearance" he said.

"Then please wire your embassy and ask them for confirmation of my story. Two agents from the British Secret Service Bureau were on the train with me and witnessed the whole thing. Including the part where Tarik handed me the empty envelope."

"I see" said Dodgson. "I will certainly look into that, but I have to tell you, on the surface, this story is preposterous."

He stood up and returned his papers to his attaché case.

"In the mean-time, I need you to keep this information to yourself. We don't want the locals to ask too many questions and frankly, to think that you are trying to deceive."

"I will try to see you again tomorrow Abdulrahim" Calouste said as they left the room. "Don't worry."

The jailers returned me to my cell where I spent the next two days wondering if I would ever see the end of this fiasco.

My answer came mid-day on the second day after my interview with the undersecretary. I was escorted out of my cell and out to the front office of the jail. Calouste was waiting there, this time with Clive and a man unknown to me by his side. The jailers said something in Hungarian to the stranger who smiled, shook their hands, and then replied.

The jailers returned to the back rooms of the Jail and the stranger turned to me.

"Right. You are free to leave the jail, but not yet free to leave Budapest" the stranger said in English. "Here are your personal effects."

He held out a small paper bag to me. Inside were my pocket watch, wallet, and the stamp from the envelope. Surprisingly, the corner of the envelope had been cut off carefully such that the stamp was not damaged.

As we exited the jail and stood on the street, the newcomer departed on foot, leaving the three of us waiting for a carriage.

"Translator from the consulate" Clive said. "Hungarian is a difficult language to master."

"Where are we headed?" I asked.

"The Grand Hotel Royal" Calouste responded. "Khalil is dying to see you and I believe you need to freshen up."

After a short carriage ride I was reunited with Khalil at the hotel and had a chance to wash for the first time since arriving in Budapest. Calouste had purchased a three bedroom suite which was quite a contrast from my most recent lodgings. When I emerged from the washroom I found a full meal waiting at the table.

"It's called room service Uncle" Khalil said. "We just call them on the phone and they bring us whatever we want."

I didn't much care how the food was ordered as much as how delicious it tasted. I tried to take my time, but after nearly four days in jail I was famished.

"This hotel is amazing Uncle. They have an exhibition downstairs from the Lumiere Brothers. A motion picture. When you watch it, it feels like you are really there."

"Maybe I will get a chance to see it before we leave" I replied between bites.

"And there was a concert that Monsieur Gulbenkian and I attended from a man called Bartok. It was very strange music, but very moving. I can't describe it. Everyone says he has been influenced recently by Debussy, but I don't actually know what that means."

Calouste chuckled from the other side of the room.

"Khalil, I think you are the most unpretentious person I have ever met. It means that this new French composer Claude Debussy's music has given Bartok new ideas for his own music. These composers feed off of each other for new ideas. It's like Einstein reading Heisenberg and having his own thoughts taken in a new direction."

"I see" said Khalil. "Thank you Monsieur Gulbenkian."

"So I am still unable to leave Hungary?" I asked Calouste.

"I'm afraid you are correct, but we received some good news from Gertrude Bell."

"She has reached London safely?"

"She made it to Paris, but she wired us good news. It seems while she was a student at Oxford she met a doctoral student called Istvan Tisza, or Stephen as she calls him."

"And this Stephen is important because...?"

"He is currently the Prime Minister of Hungary, and we have an audience with him tomorrow."

"It helps to have friends in high places" I said.

"He is an interesting man. Studied international law in Heidelberg and political science at Oxford. He was a bank president before joining parliament and a strong supporter of the English School of Economics. I think he will be sympathetic."

"Is he a supporter of the Sultan?"

"No. In fact, rumor has it that he is only a reluctant supporter of Emperor Franz Joseph and an open advisory of Prince Franz Ferdinand."

"So that might help us out of Hungary, but isn't Vienna the next stop on the Orient Express? We don't want to anger the Emperor do we?"

"Quite right. So this morning I cabled Djemal Pasha and informed him of our predicament. He then sent a message to Count Leopold Berchtold, the Austrian foreign minister in Vienna. He gently reminded the Count that the Three Pashas were making the decisions as to joining the Central Powers and that the Sultan was working against that alliance."

"But Djemal has sent Picot to France to work against the alliance himself" I reminded.

"Which they know nothing about" Calouste replied. "It's all about illusion and misdirection."

"Like Harry Houdini" I said.

"Yes. Speaking of famous Hungarians!"

"So what do we do now?" I asked.

"Now we rest and prepare for tomorrow."

"Khalil, do you think that room service could provide some dessert?" I asked. "I can't seem to find any on the table."

Khalil looked at Calouste and then back at me.

"I'm sorry uncle. They were all out when I ordered. Maybe tomorrow."

I saw Calouste force back a smile so I knew I was being played. It was only because Khalil cared so I let it go.

"Yes. Maybe tomorrow" I said with a smile. "Now tell me all about this motion picture exhibition."

The following afternoon we were taken to the office of the prime minister. I originally wanted to leave Khalil behind at the hotel, so if things went wrong he would not be involved, but Calouste felt that it would be a good experience for him. It seemed the longer they were together, the more Calouste treated Khalil as his protégée.

We were made to wait in his outer office for more than an hour past our appointed time, but that was to be expected for a Prime Minister. When it was finally our turn, we were escorted by his aide into the heart of the minister's inner sanctum.

Istvan Tisza appeared to be in his mid-forties with a bushy moustache, deep set eyes, and receding hairline. He removed a pair of spectacles from his nose and came around the desk to greet us.

"You must be Calouste Gulbenkian!" he said warmly. "I have long wanted to meet you!"

"The pleasure is mine Minister. May I introduce Sayed Kashani and his nephew Khalil Redjaian."

"Monsieur Kashani. Monsieur Redjaian. I understand there has been a big misunderstanding regarding a small envelope."

"Nice to meet you Minister" I replied. "If I had removed the stamp and discarded the rest when I received the gift, I would have saved us all a lot of trouble."

"You collect stamps I am told."

"Yes. From all over the world, but mostly from Persia, my home. I have published a book on the subject."

"Well maybe you will have time to acquire a few specimens from Hungary on your brief stop in Budapest. I will introduce you to our post master while we are waiting to clear up this misunderstanding."

"I would be honored" I replied.

"Gertrude Bell sends her best wishes to you all" Tisza said. "We were friends at Oxford."

"Gertrude was recently a guest at my place on Lake Van" Calouste said. "Sayed Kashani and Khalil were my guests as well."

"She mentioned that in her cable. She vouched for the good name of Monsieur Kashani and mentioned that Khalil was quite a bright student, as well as an inventor. Perhaps you can invent a time machine like the one HG Wells has written about. Then I could go back and correct some of my mistakes when I was Prime Minister the first time."

"You have read HG Wells Minister?" Khalil asked.

"I read his early works to relax and clear my head. After reading John Stuart Mill and Auguste Comte I needed something a little lighter and more fanciful."

"I know what you mean" Khalil said. "I read Comte's 'A General View of Positivism' right after Darwin's 'Origin of the species' and felt like my brain was unable to hold any more. Then I read 'The Island of Doctor Moreau' for fun. But all three books shared common themes so I was more confused than ever ... and Doctor Moreau gave me nightmares!"

The Prime Minister studied Khalil for a few seconds and then smiled broadly.

"You know, I have read all of those works myself and until now I had not considered how they relate. You have given me something to think about."

I placed my hand discretely on Khalil's back to reign him in a bit.

"Minister, what will it take to clear up this unfortunate situation?" I asked. "I will answer any questions and cooperate fully. I have nothing to hide and have truly done nothing wrong."

"I believe you Sayed Kashani" the Prime Minister replied. "Otherwise you never would have been invited to my office. Your story was corroborated by eye witnesses so the matter of the envelope has been resolved. We still have the request from Sultan Mehmet to Emperor Franz Joseph however. I have received word from our Foreign Minister that this request is being dealt with, but due to the internal schism in the Ottoman government and our two country's history we must tread very carefully. We wouldn't want to create a 'storm in a tea cup' as the British say."

"We Persians say making forty crows out of one" I offered.

"Forty crows?" Tisza asked.

"It's from a story about a mother crow who accidentally raised a baby chicken..." Khalil began.

I didn't think the Prime Minister of Hungary wanted to hear the full story so I interrupted.

"It's a long story Minister. Basically it is a storm in a tea cup."

"I see" he said politely. "I expect that in a few days you will be free to resume your journey to Paris. Until then, please enjoy our beautiful city and spend some time with our Post Master."

It was obvious from his tone that our audience was over. We all bowed our heads and followed the Minister's aide out of the inner sanctum and through the outer offices to the street.

As we stood there waiting for a carriage, I glanced across the street and saw a familiar blonde haired hulk of a man with a broken nose.

Tarik was looking right at me and raised his hand like he was pointing and firing a gun. I turned to get Calouste's attention but when I turned back he was gone.

"Tarik is here" I said to Gulbenkian.

"Here in Budapest?"

"Here right across the street" I answered. "He's gone now, but he was standing right over there waiting for us."

"Right. So let's not tarry."

We hailed a carriage and decided to make for the British Consulate instead of the hotel. Clive was staying there and would need to be alerted.

After meeting with Clive and filling him in on the meeting with the Prime Minister, we decided it was best that he accompany us back to the hotel. We hailed another carriage and circled the streets for a while. After we were sure we weren't being followed, we made our way to the hotel.

"I have three men on their way to help establish a perimeter" Clive said. "The hotel detective will be alerted as well. Don't worry."

We returned to our suite and tried to relax. As the sun was setting outside Clive returned and assured us that everything was under control. A man would be stationed by our door throughout the night.

Shortly after that I received a message from the Post Master of Hungary, asking to meet with both me and Khalil the following afternoon. I was happy to include Khalil, but somewhat curious as to why the invitation was addressed to both of us. Khalil did not share my passion for collecting stamps.

Everyone agreed that it would not be proper to decline the invitation and that with our extended security, we were in no real danger.

We ordered dinner to our room and spent the night speculating as to when we would be cleared to leave. With all of the commotion I forgot to order dessert.

The following morning, Khalil and I explored the hotel. He delighted in showing me the motion picture demonstration. It was just as he had described. Very lifelike.

We returned to our suite where I retrieved my stamp collection from my trunk and finally added the Bosnian stamp in its proper place. I hadn't paid a single *Gheran* for the specimen but it was the most costly of my collection.

Khalil and I took a carriage to the Post Master's office with Clive and one of his men in tow. They escorted us into the building and outer offices and stood guard while we waited.

They were very discreet. To the casual observer they appeared to be waiting for meetings themselves.

We were shown into the office of Laszlo Kiss, Postmaster General for the Royal Post of Hungary. We even started at the prescribed time. No power games for this man.

"Monsieur Kashani, Monsieur Redjaian I am so happy to meet you."

"The pleasure is ours Postmaster" I replied.

"Please. I hope we can do away with formalities. Otherwise you should be addressing me as Count and that would be awkward. Please call me Laszlo."

I was embarrassed that I did not properly address a Count.

"I am so sorry Count... I mean Laszlo. Shall we start over? I am called Abdulrahim by my friends."

"And I am Khalil."

"Welcome" the Postmaster said warmly. "Khalil, do you know why I wanted to include you today?"

"We were curious about that" Khalil replied.

"It is because we do more than deliver mail. We are responsible for the Telegraph and Telephone service in Hungary as well. We even have a Post and Telegraphy College to train the engineers and technicians we need to create and maintain new services. We drive innovation for the kingdom. But I am getting ahead of myself. I see you have brought your collection Abdulrahim."

"I have" I replied.

"Wonderful. Let's have a look at that first."

He showed us to a table by a large window where the light was good and we went through my collection page by page. Laszlo asked more questions and showed more interest than anyone I have ever spoken to, but then the mail was one of his responsibilities.

"Marvelous collection" he said as I closed the book.

"Our postal system has a long history. Ferdinand the First established a formal courier service in 1526. Mail coach delivery started in the 18th century. We introduced public mail boxes almost one hundred years ago. We combined our service with the Austrians after the compromise, but we have been fully independent for the past six years."

"Compromise?" Khalil asked.

"Two countries, one ruler. Franz Joseph is ruler for both, but we still keep that which makes us Hungarian."

He pulled out a small envelope from his coat pocket and gently emptied the contents onto a blotter which was sitting on the table. Then he pulled out a pair of tongs and picked up a specimen.

"Here is a twenty five Kreuzer from the 1870s. It's not that rare, but one of the earliest stamps of the Hungarian Kingdom."

Laszlo handed the tongs to me and I examined it with my magnifying glass. It was cancelled but still in great condition.

"This one however, is very rare."

He took the tongs back and picked up a yellow colored stamp with the number two and Kr which I assumed was Kreuzer. This one was not cancelled allowing all the detail of the lithography to come through.

"This one is from 1871 and was part of our first printing with a new lithography process. A large part of that print run was so poor my predecessor destroyed them, so only a very small portion of them were released and only a small portion of those are unused."

This was an example of something we collectors lived for, a rare stamp that few have ever seen, let alone held in their hands.

He went through the rest of the package, two dozen in total, and told me the story of each. Some, he explained, were newspaper stamps, a special type used to pay the cost of mailing newspapers and magazines.

When he finished he pulled out a second envelope and brought out a selection of printed cards, the size of my hand.

"Do you have Postal Cards in Persia Abdulrahim?"

"I don't believe so. What are they?"

"They are printed cards which include prepaid postage. Instead of buying a stamp, the postage is printed on the card. They also don't require an envelope. The buyer writes his message on the card and drops it into the mail box. Some of them have return postage pre-paid and are perforated so that the recipient can simply tear them in half and write their response. They are less expensive to make and to transport."

I picked up one with my tongs and examined the printing. I didn't have anything like this in my collection, nor had I seen anything like this in Persia. I decided I would try to buy one and take it back to show our own postmaster.

"Uncle we could print these in Persia and sell them in the shop" Khalil said.

"I was just thinking the same thing."

"The message is plainly visible to anyone though" Khalil added. "Some of our customers would not like that, but the government would."

Laszlo laughed.

"You're right. These will never replace the privacy of a letter in an envelope. They are mostly used for invitations and other quick messages."

He paused for a moment.

"You could use these for secure messages if you wrote in code I suppose. It would have to appear natural. Otherwise the fact that you were using a code would raise suspicion."

Talk of codes reminded me that I had been out of jail now for a few days but had yet to cable home. It appeared I would have plenty of time to do that. Then I realized how lucky I was that Calouste had retrieved my trunk from the train and that it had not been searched. How much more trouble would I have if they had found my cousin's code book?

"Where can I purchase one of these Postal Cards?" I asked to change the subject. "I would like to take one home and introduce these to my country."

"Why do you need to purchase one? These are yours. They are my gift to you."

"These postal cards?"

"And the stamps I showed you. I thought you understood that?"

I had accepted stamps from Djemal Pasha and from Wilhelm, but in both cases I felt that they were more of a bribe than a gift. Laszlo's offer was somehow different. I was the one who needed help this time.

"The cards I can accept, but the stamps are too valuable."

"Abdulrahim you are welcome to them. Please. It is a small

thing."

"Not for me. I cannot accept them... but I will trade for them."

A broad smile formed on Laszlo's face.

"I see. So I will select stamps from your collection in return for these?"

"Yes."

"Any stamps I like?"

"Of course not! We will negotiate. It is my job to get the better part of the deal but give you enough value for your stamps so that I do not feel like a thief."

He laughed again.

"But I was willing to give them to you for nothing."

"Yes, and that would make me feel like a charity case, which I am not. It is all about balance."

"A balance where you get the better part of the deal?"

"Yes. I am a Persian businessman. That is the only kind of balance we know."

He opened my collection and went through it page by page once again. Then starting from page one he selected two dozen stamps and placed them on the blotter in front of the collection. He had a very good eye and seemed to be selecting stamps that I could easily replace. In fact I already owned replacements for most.

I reviewed his choices, returned five to the collection and replaced them with five of my choosing. One because it was too precious and the others because he was being too generous.

He countered my selection, leaving the rare stamp in my collection, but replacing two of my choices with better stamps. I was impressed with his knowledge and sense of fairness. He was respecting my wishes, but not letting me take advantage of him.

I examined the selection and decided it was appropriately

balanced in my favor. I still had to go through the motions though. I shook my head and took a few loud breaths through my mouth as if I was in pain.

"You did understand the concept of Persian Balance didn't you?" I asked.

"Yes, but we are in Budapest, and we Hungarians know how to get a good deal as well."

He held out his hand and I put on a show of reluctantly shaking it. He placed his newly acquired stamps into the envelope and put that back in his coat pocket while I placed my new stamps in a similar envelope and closed them up in my specimen book. I was truly excited by the new acquisitions and could not wait to get back to the hotel to rearrange the collection.

"Now for something I think Khalil will appreciate" Laszlo said as he rose from the table.

"You can leave your collection here. We will come back for it."

We stood and followed the postmaster out of his office and through the building, finally arriving on the ground floor in an enclosed courtyard.

"We are always trying to innovate as I said. Twenty years ago we designed a motorized tricycle for our couriers."

We crossed the courtyard and entered a garage workshop where one of the three wheeled cycles sat. Khalil immediately knelt down by the machine and started to examine it.

"Look how the engine is mounted uncle. And look at the drive train. There is a tension control there and some sort of clutch mechanism over there."

"And when the cover is placed over the engine you would see where the mail bags are stored."

"This is very interesting" Khalil said. "You've used these for twenty years?"

"We used them for about ten years, but now we have a fully

enclosed automobile designed by Janos Csonka. From what I have heard, you two have a lot in common. He is a self-educated man with no university training, yet master of many fields of study. He owns many patents for his inventions, including something called a carburetor, whatever that it."

"It's a device that mixes air and fuel in the proper ratio for combustion" Khalil said to no one in particular as he studied the tricycle.

"Of course you would know that" Laszlo said. "He finalized the design of his car nine years ago and proved it out by driving it over two thousand kilometers through the Kingdom. We had a fleet of them built and became one of the first countries in the world to use cars for delivering mail."

Laszlo led us over to a second bay where one of the cars was being worked on. Khalil ran ahead to examine the engine as soon as he saw it.

We gave Khalil time to study the car but eventually the postmaster was out of time and led us back to collect my specimen book. He saw us out to the reception room and thanked us for the visit before returning to his next meeting.

Khalil seemed to be lost in thought. I am sure I would not understand any of what was going through his mind.

Clive and the other agent met us near the front door and assured us that there was nothing to worry about. Not one sighting of Tarik.

Traffic on the streets of Budapest was a mix of automobiles and horse drawn carriages. Clive hailed a hansom cab for our trip back to the hotel. The weather was fair and the sun was close to setting so the driver had lowered the top providing a wonderful open air view of the city.

We crossed a bridge over the Danube and drove along the river front on a broad boulevard before turning back towards our hotel. I recognized the area as we approached, but suddenly traffic stopped just short of our hotel. It was not obvious what the issue was, but horse drawn carriage and motor vehicle alike were stopped dead on the street.

Clive motioned for his man to run up ahead and determine what the issue was. Just as he disappeared from sight we heard the shouts on the street and turned towards the sound.

Tarik stood on the sidewalk with a pistol in his hand pointing at me in the back of the car while people all around were scattering away.

"Kashani!" he shouted. "You come to me!"

I was sitting on his side of the car with Khalil in the middle and Clive on the opposite side.

"You think you are smarter than Tarik? You think I let you humiliate me and run away?"

I raised my hands in front of me and tried to calm him down.

"Put the gun down Tarik. Let's talk. You want me to go back to Constantinople? I will go with you."

It was not the first time a gun had been pointed at me. I was concerned for my safety, but frankly more worried about Khalil. If Tarik missed me he could hit Khalil by mistake.

"Get out of car!" he screamed. "Now!"

I heard the gun shot but did not see any flash from Tarik's pistol. When I saw the confused look on his face and the dark stain forming on his shirt I understood why.

Tarik was still pointing his gun in my direction when a second shot rang out, hitting him in the head and knocking him to the ground.

The gun dropped from his hand and bounced off of the stone sidewalk, discharging the weapon. The bullet hit the tire of the car which caused it to pop, sounding almost like a fourth shot.

Several women screamed. Men were shouting *"Rendorseg! Ren-*

dorseg!"

As I was coming to my senses Clive jumped out of the car and rushed around the back to secure the weapon and ensure that Tarik was neutralized. It was then I saw our second guard walking slowly down the sidewalk with his gun pointing at Tarik.

Clive placed his finger on Tarik's neck and then motioned to his partner to lower the weapon.

Tarik was dead.

"Abdulrahim, you and Khalil should proceed to the hotel. It is two blocks ahead on the left. We will take care of this."

"You are sure he was acting alone?" I asked.

"We're sure. Get back to the room and wait for me there."

Khalil and I stepped down from the car and walked briskly down the side walk to our hotel as uniformed police officers rushed in from all directions. We made it to the front door and through the lobby to the elevator without being stopped. Moments later we were safely in our room.

Calouste was there waiting. When he saw us he became alarmed.

"What's wrong?"

"Tarik ambushed us on the street and pulled a gun" I answered. "One of Clive's men shot him dead."

"My God! Are you two all right?"

"We are fine. Just a little shaken. Can we get a whiskey from room service?" I asked. "Or does it only work for food?"

Calouste walked over to the phone and picked it up.

"Yes. I'd like a bottle of Macallan eighteen year old scotch whiskey sent up please."

There was pause.

"What do you mean you don't have it? What kind of Scotch

have you got?"

Another pause.

"Fine. Fine. Send it up please."

Calouste returned to where we were standing and shook his head.

"I'm sorry. I thought this was a good hotel, but evidently they only have blended scotch. Something called Johnnie Walker."

I went to my bedroom to freshen up and store my stamp collection. I returned to find the scotch had been delivered and poured over ice.

"It's quite good actually" Calouste remarked. "I've never had it this way before."

I took a glass and settled onto the sofa. Khalil returned from freshening up and decided to try a glass of wine instead.

"You know uncle, I just had an idea. Did you see how the bullet blew up the tire of the car?"

"I heard it and felt it more than saw it" I replied.

"Now that they are using automobiles for police and army vehicles, it seems to me they would be easy to disable by shooting the tires. What if I could invent a tire that was bulletproof?"

"How big would the market be?" Calouste asked.

"I don't know, but every army in the world will want them" Khalil replied with glee.

"I think it's a good idea Khalil, but can we talk about something else. I've had enough of guns for one day."

The following morning I slept in. The excitement of the previous day combined with my newfound appreciation for scotch whiskey made it difficult to get out of bed at a respectable hour. When I did rise I found a selection of fruit and bread on the dining table along with a hot pot of coffee. Calouste was sitting at one end of the table with his face buried in his hands. Khalil was sitting at the other end watching honey drip from the end of the honey dipper back into the pot.

"Good morning" I said softly to Calouste.

"Is it?" he asked just as softly.

"Uncle! I think I know how to do it!" Khalil shouted.

Khalil did not partake of the whiskey the night before and spoke just a little too loudly from my point of view. I raised my hand and motioned downward.

"Please. A little less enthusiasm Khalil. What problem have you solved?"

"Bullet proof tires. I know how to make them. Honeycomb!"

"I see" I replied although I most certainly did not.

"The structure of a honeycomb is very strong but light weight. If I can figure out how to pressurize the individual cells so that the bullet only deflates a small portion..."

"This sounds very promising Khalil. Why don't you think about it some more and let's talk after lunch."

"Yes Uncle. It seems I do have a ways to go before my idea is fully baked."

After a few cups of coffee and a light breakfast both Calouste and I began to feel like ourselves again. Room service delivered two messages in the space of an hour.

The first was from Prime Minister Tisza to Calouste and me.

> *My dear friends. I am saddened to hear about your further troubles yesterday. I have informed Sultan Mehmet that such behavior by his personal guards on Hungarian soil will not be tolerated and that his request to further detain Sayed Kashani was now impossible. You are now free to resume your journey. Godspeed.*

The message was accompanied by my passport, so we were now truly free to move on.

Calouste phoned Clive at the embassy to give him the good news and to request booking for the following day on the Orient Express.

The second message was a telegram from my cousin Abol-Ghasem Kashani. After decoding the message it read:

> Heard of your betrayal. Sultan sent second messenger with proposal. Am considering. Will await your explanation when you return. Very disappointed.

Of course my cousin's happiness was not my most pressing matter, so I wondered why he would bother to encode and pay to send such a message.

I did feel badly that I had not informed my family of our progress, so I sent a message to my wife in the clear telling her we would leave Budapest the following day for Paris.

I was tempted to add *In Sha Allah* but I was confident that God could not possibly want to throw even more hurdles in my way.

We had a quiet night in our suite with a traditional Hungarian meal of beef goulash and chicken paprikash. I was beginning to like this smoked paprika that they put in everything here, but what I really liked was the Gundel Palacsinta. The crepe-like pancakes filled with nuts and chocolate sauce were light and sweet and satisfied my craving for sugar that had been building for some time.

I told the waiter when they came for the dishes that I was happy to see they did not run out of dessert on my last night in Budapest. Of course he replied that their desserts were made upon request and that they never ran out. Khalil then quickly excused himself from the table and retired for the evening.

We rose early the next morning and made our way to the station. The Orient express pulled in as expected and minutes later we were safely ensconced in our compartment with

Clive watching over us from the end of the car.

We pulled out of the station on schedule for our three hour trip to Vienna. If we were lucky, we would pass through Austria without any further delays, make Munich by nightfall, and would arrive in Paris the following morning.

PARIS

We held our collective breath while stopped at the station in Vienna. Khalil suggested during this tense time that if we got detained here, he would try to meet some fellow named Sigmund Freud. I told Khalil he should have his head examined for even thinking the thought and he just said 'exactly'.

Sometimes I really don't understand that young man.

We left Vienna without incident though and made good time out of Austria and into Bavaria where we stopped in Munich. Thoughts of Wilhelm Wassmuss danced through my head as we waited patiently for new passengers to board and the train to take on more coal and water.

When the train did not leave on time we became a little worried.

After an hour's delay the conductor arrived at our compartment and apologized for the inconvenience. We were told that there were mechanical difficulties, but I learned much later that we were held up by the German government so that a very important passenger could board the train.

After a second hour's delay we were on our way to Paris and all of us retired for the evening without further incident.

We pulled in to Paris *Gare de l'Est* just after breakfast where we were met by Calouste's man, Maurice. We were taken by private car to his home at 51 Avenue d'Iéna, a ten minute walk from the *Arc de Triomphe* to the north and Thomas Jefferson Square to the south. The massive three story town home was simply beautiful to behold. The elaborate stone carvings and delicate iron work capped by the typically French mansard roof was as stunning on the outside as it was on the inside.

"Please make yourselves at home my friends" Calouste said as we entered the house. "Maurice will show you to your rooms. Please relax and freshen up. I have some business to attend to but I will meet you downstairs for lunch so we can make our plans."

The rooms of the ground floor were covered in oil paintings. Statues of all shapes and sizes stood on the floors, occupied niches, and adorned the tops of the antique furniture that filled the house.

As we ascended the stairs I noticed a statue of a naked woman, on her knees, weeping. It was beautiful aside from black stains on her backside. Maurice noticed my gaze and stopped for a moment.

"It is boot polish Monsieur Kashani. The statue is of Eve, just after she was expelled from the Garden of Eden. Monsieur Gulbenkian told his son that it was Eve who was responsible for the fall of Man. So when he visits, he kicks her backside every time he descends the stairs. The maid refuses to clean it off."

Our rooms were more than comfortable. They were luxurious. So much so that I suddenly felt homesick for the first time on the trip.

We had been on the road for months now. For most of that time I was so busy and worried about first one thing and then another that I had not really thought about my wife and my children. Now that I was safe and sound in Paris, I had the time to truly miss them. I wondered what it would be like if we were all enjoying these marvelous surroundings together. How could we ever share the experience with them?

I was interrupted from my thoughts by a knock on the door.

"Uncle! You will not believe this but Calouste has given me another gift! A Brownie!"

"Really? I like chocolate very much. Would you share a piece with your uncle?"

"Not fudge brownies Uncle. A camera! An Eastman Kodak Brownie model two to be precise. Now we can take photographs of our trip and bring home pictures to show our friends and family."

"I was actually just thinking about that when you knocked" I said.

"Do we have any plans yet for Paris? When do you meet with the collectors?"

"I don't really know Khalil. I assume we will find out at lunch."

"The Eiffel tower is not far from here. It's just on the other side of the river. I hope we can see that while we are here. I hope I can climb to the top!"

"I'm sure you will have a chance" I said. "I expect we will be staying in Paris for a while before returning home. I must make several business connections for Ali Ladjevardi even after this meeting with the so-called collectors."

Khalil returned to his room to learn all he could about his new camera and I sat down with my stamp collection to incorporate all of the new specimens I had acquired in Budapest.

When we went downstairs for lunch and entered the dining room, of which the walls were covered by four ornate tapestries. I had no time to appreciate these however as we were surprised to find Gertrude Bell seated with Calouste at the table.

"Gertrude!" I said. "What a surprise."

"Miss Bell!" Khalil exclaimed.

She stood and gave us both kisses on the cheek in the Parisian style which further surprised and flustered Khalil.

"I would ask if you enjoyed your trip on the Orient Express" she said, "but I already know how that went."

"The time on the train was just fine" I replied. "It was the time in jail that I could have done without."

"Yes, well you are safe now in a more civilized country and that is all that matters."

We sat down at the table and began lunch as Calouste pulled out a note from his coat pocket.

"Your meeting with the collector is set for next week. I am to accompany you if that is acceptable?"

"Of course" I replied.

"I'm afraid things are heating up quite a bit. There is some sense of urgency now. The only reason the meeting is pushed to next week is to allow time for their travel."

"Yes. The market for stamps is rather volatile lately" I said in jest. "Now that I have arrived in Paris, can't you tell me a little more about the people I am meeting with?"

Calouste wiped his mouth politely with his napkin before replying.

"I suppose it's time" he said. "Do you remember I mentioned Sir Mansfield Cumming when we were in Constantinople?"

"The man who runs the Secret Service Bureau" I replied.

"Yes. Well, originally you were to meet with his man in Paris, but after your report on the naval demonstration and Vickers Limited, C felt it was important to meet you in person."

"My report?"

"You spoke to Clive about the SMS Goeben and Breslau? The

Torpedoes?"

"Yes. I remember. After my return from my first encounter with Tarik. Clive made a phone call as soon as I mentioned it."

"Yes. He called me and I relayed the information to C. Lord of the Admiralty Churchill was livid that we didn't know about it sooner. Part of C's responsibility is to report on the Naval and Military readiness of the Central Powers."

"I'm glad I wasn't there when he heard the news" Gertrude said. "Winston is not very pleasant to be around when he is disappointed."

"Does that mean I spied for the British while in Constantinople?" I asked.

"Does it really matter what you call it?" Calouste asked.

"It most certainly does" Gertrude said before I could respond. "People have called me a spy because I travelled throughout the Arabian Peninsula and learned what I could about the people and the situation on the ground. When I saw something that needed to be addressed I said something about it to the Foreign Office. Newspaper reporters do that and they don't call them spies! I spy for no one but myself and I resent others saying that!"

"Miss Bell and I are of like minds. I will never betray my country Calouste" I said. "I thought I made that clear."

"You didn't betray Persia uncle" Khalil interjected. "You provided information about the Germans and Ottomans to the British. A scene that was witnessed by thousands of people. Persia's interests were not impacted."

"I would never ask you to betray Persia's interests Abdulrahim just as I would never do anything myself to hurt the Armenian people. C has many people in his organization that feel the same way. One of his men in Austria provides information about the German fleet but would never reveal information about his homeland."

"That man has honor" I said.

"You felt it was important to share what you knew about Vickers because you felt what they were doing was wrong."

"I did."

"You published stories in your newspaper during your Constitutional Revolution because you felt what was happening to the people was wrong and the public deserved to know."

"I did."

"So meet with C and determine for yourself if you can make the world a better place while still maintaining your honor and dignity."

"I will" I replied, "as long as he understands the ground rules."

"Thank you" Calouste said. "That's all I ask."

"So we meet next week?"

"He will meet with us as soon as he can break away from his other commitments. The War Office and Admiralty demand quite a bit of his time at the moment. It's surprising he can even find the time to get away."

Calouste referred to his notes and continued.

"Next on our agenda, Monsieur Picot has asked if we would join him out on the town tomorrow night. Dinner at the Ritz Hotel and Drinks at the Olympia Hall."

"Oh you will love the Ritz Abdulrahim!" Gertrude exclaimed. "Auguste Escoffier is the preeminent Chef in all of France. Kaiser Wilhelm called him the Emperor of Chefs!"

"Do they serve dessert?" I asked.

"Have you ever had a Chocolate Soufflé?" she asked.

"Not unless they served it on the Orient Express."

"You would remember if you had one" she replied.

"The Olympia. This is a cabaret?" I asked. Paris was famous for risqué performances that never would be allowed in Persia.

"Yes. The same creators as the Moulin Rouge" Gertrude replied. "Olympia is considered more chic at the moment and much closer than going all the way out to Montmartre. In fact it is not far from the Ritz."

"Do you think it appropriate for Khalil to attend such a show?" I asked.

"Khalil is a grown man Abdulrahim" Calouste replied. "I know you don't think of him that way, but he is. Consider it part of his further education."

"I will trust your judgment" I relented. "But I will have to explain to the family if anything goes wrong."

"You mean like explaining to them how you were arrested for attempting to overthrow the Hungarian government?" Khalil asked in jest. "Or how you made three trips to the dessert bar on the Orient Express?"

I opened my mouth to respond but I realized immediately that I was not in a position to judge.

"The Olympia sounds like fun" I said simply.

I sent out a cable the following day to my dear wife and children, telling them that we had safely arrived in Paris and would be staying here for a while. I requested an update on the situation at home by post since I would be in one place long enough to receive it.

Khalil and I walked the streets of Paris and tried out his new camera. We exposed an entire roll on our adventure and sent the film off for prints when we returned to Calouste's home. I was exhausted by the time we retired that evening.

Dinner at the Ritz was quite a surprise, not because of the food and the wonderful Chocolate Soufflé, but because of the friend Gertrude brought along with her.

Khalil's life was never the same after that evening.

Monsieur Picot, Calouste, Khalil and I were seated at our table when Gertrude and her friend approached.

"Sorry we are late everyone" Gertrude said. "May I introduce you to my friend Barbara Nowak."

I must tell you dear reader that I was taken by her beauty from the moment I saw her and I was a happily married man. Her hair was blonde but with a hint of light brown tone and done up in a style they called the colonial. Several long curls draped seductively across her neck and onto her shoulders. Her eyes were somewhere between green and gray. She was slender, but not fragile looking. Her complexion... I think that is what truly set her apart. She had smooth alabaster skin that looked so soft... As I said. I was a happily married man.

I had no doubt that Khalil fell in love with her the instant they were introduced. We never actually discussed this, but I could tell by the look in his eyes that he was somehow changed after that night.

We all stood to greet the new arrivals although Khalil seemed to be stuck in his chair for a few seconds. When he finally extricated himself, he stood up too fast and bumped the table, spilling the water from his tumbler.

"Enchanté Mademoiselle" Picot said as he bowed and kissed her hand.

When he did this Barbara smiled and blushed. Her entire face seemed to glow.

"I'm afraid Barb is not accustomed to our Parisian ways yet" Gertrude said. "She arrived from Poland only a few weeks ago."

"So your name is quite apropos!" Khalil exclaimed.

"Barbara, this is Khalil" Gertrude said. "He is the young man I was telling you about."

"Pleased to meet you Khalil" Barbara said. Her French was understandable but with a noticeable accent. It added to the mystery.

"What do you mean her name is apropos Khalil?" Calouste asked.

"Just that the name Barbara comes from the Greek meaning traveler from a foreign land and if I remember correctly, Nowak means newcomer in Polish. So her name literally means newcomer from a foreign land."

"Like I told you" Gertrude said to Barbara, "he is full of surprises."

Two waiters converged on the table from nowhere and helped the newcomers into their seats. It was no coincidence that Gertrude had Barbara sit next to Khalil.

"So what brings you to Paris Mademoiselle?" I asked.

"I am on my way to London to become a nurse" she replied.

"Like Florence Nightingale and Clara Barton?" Khalil asked.

"Yes. You know of them?"

"I have read about them and admired their bravery and dedication. Why nursing?"

"My father is… was a doctor. I assisted him in his practice until he passed last year."

"I am so sorry to hear that" Khalil continued. "So why not become a doctor instead of a nurse?"

"As if that is possible in this day and age" Gertrude interjected. "A woman doctor."

Barbara looked at Khalil with interest.

"You believe I can be a doctor?" she asked.

"Why not? You trained with your father. With the right education you can do anything you want."

"I am afraid our friend Khalil is still young and idealistic Mademoiselle Nowak" Picot said. "He does not yet understand the limitations society places on the fairer sex."

"I am aware of them" Khalil said with a hint of anger in his voice that I had never heard before. "I just do not accept them. Look at Miss Bell here. Consider all she has accomplished."

Finally he turned towards Barbara. "Don't give up on your dreams Mademoiselle and do not let other people set limits for you."

"Hear, hear!" exclaimed Calouste as he raised his water glass in the air. "Waiter! A bottle of Champagne please. Tonight we are celebrating unlimited possibilities."

I saw the look in her eye as she turned towards Khalil and I knew right away that she was taken by him as well.

"Khalil, I believe you are the most interesting man I have ever met in my life" Barbara said as she extended her hand.

It took him a few seconds, but he finally realized he was expected to kiss it. He did it with just as much panache as Picot had done previously, but he held her hand for a few moments longer than necessary. They both appeared to be unaware that the rest of our group even existed, let alone that we were watching them.

"It seems both Khalil and Mademoiselle Nowak are quick studies when it comes to the customs of French society" Picot remarked.

That meal turned out to be the best of my entire life. The food and wine exceeded all of Gertrude's praise. The Chocolate Soufflé was so light and … well… chocolaty.

We took a carriage to the Olympia for the second half of the evening. There was an excitement in the air from the moment we arrived to the moment we left the building. It was as if something was in the very air that we breathed. The singers and dancers on the stage were only part of the attraction. The people in the audience contributed just as much to the electric atmosphere.

"You see the gentleman and lady at that table?" Gertrude said to Khalil and Barbara who were once again seated next to each other.

"The woman in the beautiful hat?" Barbara asked.

"Yes. She is also the woman who designed and made that hat. That's Coco Chanel with one of her two lovers."

"Two lovers?" Khalil asked.

"Yes. One is the heir to a textile empire and the one with her tonight is Boy Capel. He financed her clothing shops and fashion line."

"And everyone knows this?" Barbara asked.

"Oh yes. The two men are close friends. And both married I might add."

"I may be liberal in some of my thinking" Khalil said, "but not when it comes to love. The Quran says we may marry up to four wives if we can support them. That is not for me. I want to find the one person that I can love for the rest of my life."

"You don't know how happy I am to hear you say that" Barbara said.

She must have realized too late how revealing that statement was because she blushed again and took a deep drink from her champagne glass.

Just then a woman approached our table and held out her arms towards Picot. She had raven hair and wore much too much makeup for my taste. Unlike the makeup, the dress she was wearing revealed much more than it should. In fact the parts that were barely covering her body were almost transparent.

"Monsieur Picot! How wonderful to see you after all this time. Won't you introduce me to your friends?"

Picot seemed a bit flustered by this new arrival, but stood up and embraced the woman.

"Margaretha it has been ages! Where have you been?"

"Performing here and there. I have just returned to Paris."

Calouste cleared his throat to get Picot's attention.

"Oh I'm sorry. Everyone this is Margaretha Zelle, better known by her stage name Mata Hari. She is a dancer."

"Pleased to meet you all" she said. "And who is this powerful looking gentleman?"

She placed her arms around me and kissed me on the cheek as if I were already quite familiar. As she pulled away I felt her hand brush across my inner thigh. I didn't know whether to be aroused or insulted.

"May I introduce Abdulrahim Kashani from Tehran Persia" Picot said.

"Persian! Oh! I just love Persian men" she replied as she gently stroked my face with the back of her hand.

Up close I could tell that at one time she had been a stunningly beautiful woman, but the years had not been kind.

"And my friend Calouste Gulbenkian" Picot continued.

"Monsieur five percent! Oh my! What a pleasure sir."

She strolled around my chair and approached Calouste who stood and held out his hand to take hers. While it appeared at first that he was being forward, I realized his action was more of a deft defensive move to keep her at a distance.

He kissed her hand politely and then returned to his seat.

"This is Gertrude Bell and her friend Barbara Nowak" Picot said, but Margaretha ignored them and walked straight towards Khalil.

"You must be Persian as well! Such a handsome young man. Are you related?"

"I am his nephew" Khalil said.

"There is so much an experienced woman like me could teach you Monsieur Khalil."

"I beg your pardon!" Barbara suddenly exclaimed.

"Oh my! I am so sorry. I did not realize you two were a pair."

Barbara backed away and looked towards the ground in embarrassment until Khalil stepped closer and placed his arm around her waist.

"We are" Khalil said defiantly.

"Yes. I can see that" Margaretha said. "Pity."

She returned to Picot's side held out her arms for a hug.

"I'm afraid I am unable to join you *Mon Cheri*. I must prepare for my show."

"You are performing tonight?" Picot asked almost choking on a sip of Champagne.

"Yes, but not here. I am opening at a new club not far from here. I know the owner and agreed to help him with his grand opening. It will be the event of the season!"

"I see" Picot replied. "Well, break a leg!"

"Oh darling Picot that saying is for actors! We dancers say to each other *Merde* for good luck!"

"Yes. Well ah ... shit then."

He kissed her on each cheek and she disappeared into the crowd.

"That was Mata Hari?" I asked. "I have heard of her."

"Yes. In the flesh" Picot commented.

"A little more flesh than there was when she was at her peak" Gertrude said a bit perturbed.

Calouste ordered another bottle of Champagne and we all settled in to our seats for the next act on stage, a young black woman singing songs she called the blues. Her voice was as beautiful as her face and the music strangely moving. It was like nothing I had heard before.

Sometime after midnight the crowd thinned and the level of excitement waned. I caught Gertrude suppressing a yawn then noticed that Khalil and Barbara were still engaged in conversation, oblivious to the rest of the world. I'm sure that if she were out alone Miss Bell would have already retired for the evening.

Calouste stood and turned towards Monsieur Picot.

"What a marvelous evening François. Thank you for your hospitality."

"It was my privilege" he replied. "Abdulrahim, I would like to invite you and Khalil to a salon next Saturday night if you are available. My other friend Gertrude, Miss Gertrude Stein."

"Only if you will allow us to host you before then François. We owe you a great debt for this evening."

"Don't be silly. You are in Paris. This is my home. When I am in Tehran you can return the favor."

"It is a deal" I replied. "I hope it will be soon."

We exited the Olympia and found a line of carriages waiting to take the patrons home.

"Barbara and I will take our own carriage home" Gertrude said. "It is out of your way."

"Miss Nowak" Khalil said. "May I see you tomorrow?"

"You mean later today" Calouste said with a smile.

"Yes. That's what I meant. Later today."

Barbara looked at Gertrude who smiled back at her.

"I have no plans for the day" Barbara replied.

"Wonderful!" Khalil said a little too loudly. "Let's have lunch then we can explore the city together."

"I'd like that very much."

Khalil escorted her to the waiting hansom cab and helped her up into the seat.

"Tomorrow then" he said.

"Tomorrow" she replied as she bent down to kiss him on the cheek.

The cab drove off with Khalil still watching it drive away.

"Do you want to join us Khalil?"

He finally turned and noticed that we had already climbed into our own carriage. He had the look of a man who was completely smitten.

"You will see her again in less than eleven hours Khalil" Calouste said then turned towards me. "Hopefully he will survive until then."

Khalil left shortly after breakfast, evidently not wanting to be late for his lunch date.

"I remember being that much in love" Calouste said to me when Khalil was gone.

"It changes when we get older doesn't it" I replied. "Not as intense, but somehow much deeper at the same time."

"New relationships are certainly more... intense, as you say" Calouste said.

Maurice entered the room bearing a note which seemed to trouble Calouste.

"Something wrong?" I asked.

"A note from Clive. Arch Duke Ferdinand and his wife have been shot in Sarajevo. They're both dead."

"Was it the Black Hand like the Hungarians suspected?"

"It appears so. The shooter was a Bosnian Serb called Gavrilo Princip. He was a member of the Black Hand and a confederate of that man who wrote the letter to Tarik."

"If I was still in Budapest, I doubt they would let me leave after these events."

"You're right. Clive says the Emperor is livid."

"What plans for today then?" I asked after a long silence.

Calouste stared out of the window in thought for a long while. I thought perhaps he might not have heard my questions.

"I will meet with Clive today but tonight we visit the Lodge" he finally replied. "With luck, Prime Minister Doumergue will be in attendance and we can learn more about this assassination."

I spent the morning relaxing and reviewing all of the new additions to my stamp collection. After lunch I made several new business connections suggested by Calouste and returned home barely in time to prepare for the lodge meeting that night.

We arrived at the Lodge just after sunset. The meeting room was slightly larger than our hall in Tehran, but the layout was identical. The Worshipful Master sits in the east, the Senior Warden to the west, and Junior Warden to the south. The floor was dominated by the familiar black and white checker board pattern.

All of the members wore their aprons as did I, mine having been hidden inside the lining of one of my robes for months in case someone on our travels got a little too curious. The symbols on the apron identified one's rank and previous offices. Anyone with a trained eye and knowledge of our customs could wake up in a new lodge and understand the power structure with one scan of the room.

The meeting proceeded as usual with business completed in just over an hour. There was a sense of unrest in the hall as everyone's mind seemed to be on Sarajevo. As Calouste had hoped, Prime Minister Doumergue was present.

"Prime Minister may I introduce my good friend Sayed Kashani from Tehran Persia."

I shook hands with the grip proper to my level of indoctrination.

"My pleasure to meet a brother from so far away Monsieur Kashani. Jean-Baptiste La Mere has informed me that you were en route. Welcome to Paris and to L'Ordre Grand Orient de France."

"My honor Minister."

"Minister, if I might be so forward" Calouste said in hushed tones, "I was hoping to ask what you know about the situation in Sarajevo?"

Discussion of politics and religion is expressly forbidden in most lodges, especially in Britain, but the French had adjusted their rules in a very liberal direction. While most Masonic organizations require members to believe in a supreme being, the French no longer required it. There were even splinter groups in Paris that included elements of the occult in their rituals. This lodge was more liberal in the discussion of politics, but I saw no evidence of a mystical influence.

"The situation in Sarajevo is not good" Doumergue replied. "Franz Joseph has demanded an explanation of this murder and compensation from Serbia."

"But Princip is a Bosniak and a subject of the Austrian Empire" I said.

"The Emperor has determined that the Serbs were behind it" the minister replied. "They have always wanted a reason to attack Serbia."

"If they threaten Serbia then Russia will be pulled in to the situation" Calouste added.

"And Germany will be required to assist Austria" he added.

"And France will be asked to support Russia" I said.

"And Britain will be pulled in as well" the Prime Minister concluded.

We all paused to consider this likely chain of events.

"Certainly they will not let things spin out of control like this" I said in disbelief.

"It all depends on Franz Joseph" the Prime Minister replied. "If he backs down then the other dominos will not topple."

"Then let us hope he will find the strength of character to back down" Calouste replied.

The conversation turned to issues facing the Lodge, so I left to meet some of the others in attendance. There were several members of the National Assembly and business men who all seemed to know I would be in Paris. As Calouste promised, I made several additional connections that would pay off for myself and Ali Ladjevardi in the future. If my visits this afternoon were any indication, I would be busy for weeks just following up on these leads and the introductions they would bring.

I also met several actual stone workers and master carvers in the membership. I learned that over the past fifty years, Paris had been transformed by Napoleon the third's order. It had been a boom time for the true Masons of Paris but the funds and therefore the work was coming to an end. The few remaining projects were either being cancelled or scaled back.

On the carriage ride home Calouste was lost in his thoughts. We arrived after ten, but according to Maurice, Khalil was not yet home. Given that Parisian life extended late into the evening, I was not that concerned, but I did hope he would be careful.

The next morning Khalil came down for breakfast on time, but I could tell right away something was off.

"Good morning Uncle. Good morning Calouste" he said to us.

"Late evening?" Calouste asked.

"I don't know where the time went" he replied. "When I am with her it seems like the clocks all run twice as fast."

Calouste gave me a knowing look.

"Plans for the day?" I asked.

"Can I go to England Uncle?" he suddenly asked.

"Today?" I asked.

"Barbara is leaving for England in two weeks and I want to accompany her."

I wasn't prepared for this sudden request. It was only a few months ago that Khalil wanted to stay in Tabriz and work on the wheelchair design with Tim at the American school.

"My business will require at least a month and then we return to Persia" I replied. "Can Barbara stay in Paris a bit longer?"

"Her nursing classes start in two weeks. She has to be in London by then. Gertrude is travelling with her. She said I could join them."

"Let me think on it for a while" I said even though I knew what my answer would be.

"You will consider it?" he asked.

"Yes. I said I will think about it."

This answer seemed to satisfy him for now, but I knew I would have a difficult decision to make.

"Thank you Uncle. Do you need me today?"

"I don't think so" I replied.

"Good. I will see you tonight then."

"Likely not" I said under my breath.

He left in a hurry without eating any breakfast or even having a cup of coffee. When he shut the door to the dining room I looked to Calouste for help.

"Don't look at me" he said. "I don't have any advice on how to deal with a love sick young man."

"My biggest challenge is that I think they are a perfect match. She is smart and beautiful. How could he do better?"

"I agree, but does he have the means to support a wife?"

"This is one of the details I believe he is forgetting. He lives in the back room of my shop in Tehran and has no money to speak of."

"Perhaps her father left her money? He was a doctor after all. She obviously has money to travel and for tuition to nursing school."

"Perhaps. I will talk to him about this when I can. If I can get him to sit with me for more than ten minutes."

Calouste just laughed at this last remark and offered no reply.

"Do you have plans for today Calouste?"

"I must update the Ambassador and send another cable to C. This business in Sarajevo may change everything."

"I see. I have a meeting with a possible supplier for Ali Ladje-vardi. I should be back in time for dinner."

We went our separate ways and as expected reconnected late in the afternoon.

"What news from the embassy?" I asked.

"Just as I expected. C is no longer able to come to Paris. Would you consider a trip to London in say ... two weeks?"

"Do you and Khalil have some secret arrangement I should know about?"

"Sometimes fate will have its way."

Khalil was thrilled to learn that we would be making the trip to London together. He ran out of the house without eating breakfast again to share the news with Barbara. In fact, I didn't see him again until Saturday, when we were all invited by Monsieur Picot to the Salon at 27 Rue de Fleurus. Even then, Khalil arrived separately with Gertrude and Barbara.

On the carriage ride over, Picot made it a point to warn me

that I would likely see and hear many strange things. He asked that I keep an open mind and not to judge anyone too harshly. With that warning in mind, we arrived at the residence of Gertrude Stein and Alice B. Toklas in the 6th arrondissement on the Left Bank of Paris.

We arrived just after dark and were greeted warmly at the door.

"*Bonsoir* Gertrude!" Picot said as he kissed her on both cheeks.

"*Bonsoir* François! It has been ages since you have been here!"

Miss Stein was a rotund woman whose figure was not enhanced by a purple corduroy dress. Her dark hair was cropped short, almost like a man's. She seemed happy to see Picot but there was no joy in her face.

"It was difficult to attend when I was assigned to Beijing, and now they have just reassigned me to Beirut. I had some business in Paris before I return to Lebanon and so here I am."

"How marvelous for you. I hear Beirut is a lovely city."

"It is. It is. Gertrude, may I present my good friends Calouste Gulbenkian and Sayed Abdulrahim Kashani."

Gertrude turned and examined us head to toe before breaking into a forced smile.

"Of course Monsieur five percent. Your reputation proceeds you. I must say we don't get many millionaire oil barons visiting this salon, but your prestigious art collection and generous charity work sets you apart, so of course you are very welcome here."

"Miss Stein" Calouste said in English as he bowed. "I am looking forward to seeing your collection, especially the Cézanne five apples."

"Well I am afraid you will be disappointed. My brother Leo just recently moved to Italy and took half of our collection with him. Five apples was the only Cézanne he wanted, but I still have all of the others. Fortunately for me he didn't care for Matisse or Picasso, who I adore."

"Then I am looking forward to seeing them. This is my friend Abdulrahim Kashani from Tehran, Persia."

"Monsieur Kashani. Welcome to Paris. Are you in oil as well?"

"No Mademoiselle" I replied, "but I *am* a collector. A collector of postage stamps."

"How quaint" she replied with not much enthusiasm. "Please come in and introduce yourselves to the gang."

We entered the salon which resembled an art museum more than a residence. Paintings were hung on the high walls in three levels, floor to ceiling. A few of them immediately caught my eye and frankly confused me.

"Does she have a small child who paints?" I said quietly to Calouste. "Some of these are very nice, but some are... well, like a bad dream."

He smiled broadly and leaned in towards my ear.

"Some of these artists are an acquired taste and a bit avant-garde, but rest assured they are all truly talented painters. Her collection will be worth quite a bit one day."

We made our way into the adjoining room where most of the other guests were speaking in small groups. A young woman offered us each a flute of Champaign and I gladly took one.

It was then I saw Khalil and Barbara standing near two women engaged in conversation. There was something different about Khalil. He was wearing a new suit of clothes and his hair was different. He seemed more ... like an adult and not like the adolescent I took in as my assistant.

As we neared I realized one of the women was Gertrude Bell. The other I did not recognize.

"Uncle! You are here!"

Khalil's face seemed joyful. I had never seem him so happy.

"*Salaam* Uncle Kashani" Barbara said. "*Chetori?*"

I didn't understand the implication of how she addressed me for a few moments, or that she spoke partially in Persian.

"Barbara! I am well. Thank you. How nice to see you again"

"Gertrude" Calouste said.

"Oh Calouste" Gertrude replied. "You're here. I want to introduce you to Alice Toklas. She is Gertrude's companion."

"Mademoiselle Toklas" Calouste said. "What a lovely house. Your collection of furniture seems to be as well chosen as the art on the wall. It is all Renaissance period?"

"It is Monsieur Gulbenkian. What a keen eye you have. Barbara was just telling us that she will be leaving for London to study medicine."

"Nursing" Barbara interjected.

"Did you know Gertrude studied medicine at Johns Hopkins University for three years before realizing it was not her thing."

"You see" Khalil said. "You can be a doctor as well if you put your mind to it."

"She better be prepared for resistance" a voice said.

I turned to see Gertrude Stein approach our group.

"It was an uphill battle the entire way, even though I graduated magna cum laude from Radcliffe and had the backing of a world renown professor. As I have always said, men expect women to adapt to their abnormal sex drive and be a woman first and always, instead of a human being first and then a woman."

Nobody in our group knew quite what to say to that. Barbara's pale skin showed her embarrassment as she took Khalil's arm and escaped from the group.

"Oh how wonderful" Stein exclaimed. "Pablo has arrived. Please excuse me."

She was gone as fast as she came.

"Pablo?" I asked.

"Picasso" Calouste responded. "The man who paints bad dreams" he said under his breath.

I saw Khalil and Barbara across the room speaking to a man who was shuffling cards on a small table. It seemed like a good idea to join them rather than risk making an honest remark about the paintings in front of the new arrival.

"The cards are called Tarot cards" the man was saying as I approached.

"And they can really tell the future?" Barbara asked.

"In the hands of one who has been properly trained" said the stranger.

"Uncle, this is A.E. Waite, from Brooklyn New York. He was just telling us about these Tarot Cards."

Waite appeared to be in his late fifties. What was left of his hair was mostly grey and wildly unkempt. He had a bushy grey mustache to match and an overall look that he was thinking of some far off land even though he was looking right at you.

"Mister Waite this is my Uncle Kashani."

"Pleased to meet you Monsieur Kashani. I was just telling this young couple about these Tarot cards. I had them designed and printed after many years of systematic research into the occult and membership in several secret societies."

"Secret Societies?"

"Like the Freemasons and the Hermetic Order of the Golden Dawn.

"You say the Freemasons use these cards?" I asked.

"No, no, that is a false rumor. The Freemasons are not a magical society. It was through my membership in the Free-masons that I met the people who inducted me into the Golden Dawn."

"And what does this Golden Dawn teach?" I continued.

"Well, it is a philosophy based on the Hermetic Kabala and teaches personal development through study of Astrology, Geomancy, and of course, reading the Tarot."

"And the cards tell you the future by communicating with spirits?" Calouste asked over my shoulder having gravitated in our direction.

"Actually there are some that believe this, but I believe the cards are a door into our subconscious mind. Are you familiar with Freud?"

"Sigmund Freud from Vienna?" I asked.

Khalil turned to me in surprise. I still didn't know who he was or what he was famous for, but I had a good memory for names and if Khalil wanted to meet him he must be important.

"Yes. Doctor Sigmund Freud. He has worked out a theory that your mind has a hidden part called the subconscious that knows many things that your conscious mind cannot access. When you shuffle and cut the cards of the Tarot, your subconscious is actually ordering the cards to represent that untapped knowledge."

"So how does it work?" Barbara asked. "Can you show us?"

"Certainly. Please sit down."

He motioned towards the seat opposite his and placed the cards on the table in front of her.

"Take the cards and mix them up like I was doing before. Do it as long as you wish and think about a question you would like to have answered."

Barbara took the cards in hand and began shuffling, slowly at first, then faster as she got the hang of it.

"Now cut the deck three times."

"I don't know what you mean" she said.

"Like this" Khalil said as he picked up a portion of cards, placed them on the table, and capped them off with the remainder then repeated the action twice more.

"I'm afraid we must start over" Waite said. "The deck is now a blend of your subconscious and of Khalil's."

"That should be fine" Barbara said. "My question is actually about the two of us."

"It is highly unusual but we can give this a go" he said. "Your question is about the two of you?"

"Yes. Our future together."

Waite turned over the deck to reveal an image of a naked man and woman standing in front of a great winged figure with the sun shining overhead. The title of the Card was 'The Lovers'.

"How Marvelous! It is here just waiting for me."

He placed the card face up at the center of the table and placed the remaining deck face down at his right hand.

"This card is the significator. It represents the two of you. This couple is like Adam and Eve in Paradise" he said. "This is the card of pure human love, before it is contaminated by the material world."

Barbara was blushing but did not take her eyes off of the card.

Waite picked up the remaining cards and turned over the first one on top of the Lovers.

"This card covers you. It shows the influences on your present situation."

"The Fool?" Barbara said. "We are foolish for being in love?"

"No mademoiselle, this is not the way to interpret that card in this context. You are in the intoxicating first days of love. It is like a mania. Nothing seems as it used to be. Am I right?"

"He is right Barbara" Khalil said. "These last few days I feel intoxicated. We giggle at the simplest things. It feels wonderful."

He took her hand and kissed it gently.

"If I may continue" Waite said. "This next card crosses you. It represents your obstacles."

He turned over a card with seven stars hanging on a small tree with a man, but the card seemed to be upside down.

"This is the seven of Pentacles" Waite continued. "It is a card about money, but since it is reversed it represents lack of money, or a challenge with money. In your quest to be together you must overcome a need for monetary support."

"We know this will be a challenge" Khalil said to Waite. "So far the reading is very accurate. Let's keep going."

"This is your crown, your ideal outcome."

Waite turned over a card to expose 'The Sun'.

"Oh my!" he said with a smile on his face. "You turned the best card in the deck for your crown! It represents a fortunate marriage and contentment."

Barbara looked towards Khalil and giggled like a little girl.

"Here is your foundation, your base" Waite continued.

The card showed a picture of a man and woman walking through an arched doorway with a child, two dogs, and an old man. Ten golden stars seemed to be raining down, but on closer inspection they formed a pattern.

"This card is the ten of Pentacles. When it is turned up as your foundation, it means you have both had a solid home and family support in childhood. This prepares you well to become parents in the future."

"I never asked you how many children you wanted darling" Barbara said to Khalil.

"As many as we can afford" Khalil said with a broad smile.

He turned toward me at that moment and I saw such a look of joy on his face.

I will remember that look forever. I never saw him smile like that again.

241

"This next card is behind you, your recent past."

The card showed a woman wearing only a red scarf surrounded by a garland of green. There were animals in the four corners. The title of the card read 'The World'.

"This is obviously a very appropriate card for both of you. It's meaning connotes a long voyage."

Waite turned over the next card to form a completed cross.

"The Page of Pentacles is your near term influence, what is just about to happen. It represents study and scholarship. Would either of you be on your way to a college or university?"

"She is on her way to study nursing!" Khalil exclaimed. "How could the cards know that?"

"I don't see anything related to scholarship in the picture" I whispered to Calouste. "He must have overheard their plans."

Next he placed a card to the right of the cross, aligned with the bottom.

"Ace of Cups shows your current attitude that will define your present actions. It is a very good card. It represents love, joy, abundance, and fertility."

"So we will be rich and have lots of children!" Barbara exclaimed.

Waite held up a hand in caution.

"This card does not predict the outcome, only the actions you will take in the short term towards your goal."

"But it is still a good sign, isn't it?" she asked.

"A very good sign" Waite responded.

"The next card represents your environment. The world around you that will shape your fortune."

He turned over the card and placed it above the Ace of Cups.

I could tell immediately that this was not a good card. A man's body lay dead on the ground with ten swords piercing his back. Barbara and Khalil both let out a gasp when the card appeared.

"What does it mean?" Barbara asked as she covered her mouth with her hand.

"Violence, pain, affliction, and tears" Waite replied. "It does not necessarily mean violent death, but it is a card of suffering."

Khalil placed his arm around Barbara's waist to reassure her.

"When you finish your study, you will be working in a hospital darling. Maybe this card refers to the patients you will care for."

"I suppose you are right" Barbara said. "It isn't the final card. It isn't our future."

"Now we have the penultimate card. This represents your hopes and fears."

The card was titled 'Knight of Wands' and it showed a knight in a suit of armor on horseback, carrying a club in his hand.

"This knight is on a journey. He is looking to the future, expectant."

"But is it a good card or a bad card?" Calouste asked.

"It depends on the next card to some extent. It could be simply a card of departure or a change in residence."

"We are moving to London" Khalil said. "It must be a change in residence."

"And if the next card is bad?" Calouste asked.

"A card of absence, fleeing the scene of a tragedy."

"It all depends on the next card?" I asked.

"Yes. The nature of the next card reveals the true meaning of the knight of wands and the answer to this young lady's question."

Waite turned towards Barbara.

"And now it is time to ask your question. The final card will reveal the answer."

"Will we be together as man and wife within the next year?" Barbara said.

Waite turned over the final card and hung his head.

It was a dark card. A woman sits on her bed weeping in sorrow with nine swords on the black wall behind her.

"I am so sorry" he said. "Perhaps we should try this again. I don't believe that shuffling and cutting with two different people provides a truly legitimate reading."

"What does it mean?" Barbara asked.

"Mademoiselle, truly. Let me take up the cards and ..."

"Tell us!" she screamed. "Tell us!"

The room around us suddenly went quiet at the outburst. After a moment the others continued their conversation and Waite picked up the card from the table.

"Death, Mademoiselle. Death and despair."

Tears flowed from her eyes as she sat motionless, staring at the remaining cards on the table before her.

"Barbara, you heard the man. We didn't do it the right way. It's my fault for cutting the cards. I should have let you do it."

She began shaking her head slowly and then wiped the tears from her eyes.

"A Romani woman came to our house one day asking for food" she began. "My father was always compassionate and gave her a basket full of bread and fruit. She thanked him and offered to read his fortune with cards like these."

She wiped the tears from her eyes and then fanned herself with her hand.

"She was very happy with the cards until the end. She turned over the last card and began to cry. She said that such a good man did not deserve this fate."

"What fate?" Khalil asked.

"She would not say. She left the basket of food on the table and fled. Three days later my father died."

Khalil held Barbara close as she placed her head on his shoulder.

"Well, are we having fun yet?" Gertrude Stein chortled as she approached the group.

She surveyed the group and seemed to realize something was not right.

"A.E. I told you the only good thing about those cards was the artist who painted them for you" Stein continued.

"Let's get another glass of Champaign" Khalil said as he helped her up from the table.

"I want to go home" Barbara said. "If you don't mind."

Khalil looked at me and at Calouste for help, but I thought her idea was probably the best so I simply nodded my agreement.

The couple made their way through the crowded room and out of the door to hail a cab.

"They will be all right" Calouste said. "She just needs a little time to get over the shock."

"I am terribly sorry about that" Waite said. "She really should have tried again."

Khalil and Barbara left the Salon and returned to the flat where Gertrude Bell was staying. The rest of us stayed for only an hour more. We met some very interesting people that night, but none of us had the mood to enjoy the evening after the Tarot reading.

The meeting with C was confirmed for July 28th. After we booked passage to London, I spent the next two weeks meeting with potential business suppliers while Khalil and Barbara stayed mostly to themselves. Calouste invited them over for dinner several times but they always had other obligations.

One of my new contacts in Paris suggested that I make connection with a firm in Hamburg Germany concerning a new luxury fountain pen called the Mont Blanc. It had been shipping now for a few years and had gained the reputation as the finest writing tool in the world. Calouste enthusiastically recommended the product, but warned that relationships with German companies might prove difficult in the coming months. I was able to buy a few dozen specimens from the dealer in Paris. If they sold well in my shop, I would find a middle man, no matter the state of relations with Germany. That's what we Persians do best.

The night before we were set to leave for London, Calouste succeeded in arranging a final dinner for the group. Barbara seemed fine although Khalil was much quieter than usual. The dinner seemed to revive at least some of the joy we experienced that first night in the Ritz.

Gertrude and Barbara left early after dinner to begin packing for the journey. We had an early start the next morning and women just seem to need more time when it comes to travel preparation.

When Khalil and I were finally alone I shared with him the letter I received from home. I saw a glimmer of happiness in his face as he read. He even laughed out loud at a few spots.

"It seems nothing much changes back there" he said. "I will miss Persia Uncle. I truly will."

"What are you saying Khalil?"

"That I won't be returning home with you Uncle. I can't."

"I don't understand?"

"I've been doing a lot of thinking over the past few weeks. When I first fell in love with Barbara, I dreamed of walking with her in the garden back home and showing her the mountains outside of the city, but in my mind it was like we were walking the streets of Paris. I realized that this is impossible. Can you imagine asking her to wear a *chador*? To cover that beautiful face and hair?"

I laughed thinking of the image.

"She's Catholic Uncle. She will never become a Muslim and I would never ask her."

"Will you become a Catholic?" I asked in disbelief.

"No. Neither of us is very religious. We both grew up in places where belonging to your church was just part of growing up. It was not a choice. We both believe in God, but our God is able to accept all religions. Even if the Church will not marry us, we will find a way."

"So if you do not live in Persia will you return to Poland with her?"

"We don't know. It doesn't really matter. What matters now is that she finishes her nursing school and then we can figure things out."

"What about money?" I asked.

"Her father left her enough for school and to live for a few years.

"And you? What will you do?"

"She asked me if I wanted to go to university" he said with no enthusiasm.

"That sounds like a wonderful idea" I replied.

"Maybe" he said. "I told her about some of my ideas. About the delete key for the Persian typewriter and bullet proof tires. That's what truly excites me. She said I could stay home and work on my inventions until we find something that will sell."

"It may not be easy" I offered.

"I know. There are no guarantees in life except that if you don't pursue your dreams you will never realize them."

"True" I replied.

"I do have one request though" he said timidly.

"Yes?"

"If I am able to invent something that everyone wants, I won't know how to market it properly. Would you be willing to help me Uncle? For a share of the company of course."

I looked at him and saw the tears swelling in his eyes. I realized just how important this was to him and that he was making a very difficult decision. So I took him in my arms and held him tightly.

"You are family Son. You will always be family, no matter where you live, no matter what you do."

He was sobbing openly now. I could feel him shaking. The last few weeks must have been very stressful for him. He had been thinking through all of the decisions and their implications by himself.

"I don't know what to do Uncle. I love her, but I don't know how I can make it work. There are so many issues to resolve. It's impossible!"

He pulled away from me and wiped the tears from his eyes. He seemed ashamed that he had let his emotions loose.

"I want you to be happy Khalil. You deserve to live your life your way and if Barbara loves you half as much as you love her, you will find a way to make it all work out."

"You really think so?" he asked.

"Khalil, you are one of the smartest people I know. I don't know Barbara that well yet, but I can tell she is your match. Together you are unstoppable."

"It's true. She is much smarter than I am about some things."

"So together you will figure it out. Besides, tomorrow we all go to London and she starts nursing school, so it seems like there isn't much to decide tonight, is there?"

"Actually no. The next few weeks are all planned."

"Exactly. So let me introduce you to a single malt I found in Calouste's library. I'll cut it with a little water for you. Get a good night's rest and the world will be the same when you wake up tomorrow."

LONDON

July 27th, 1914

We arrived in London after an uneventful journey from Paris. Two short train rides separated by a ferry across the channel took less than a day. We arrived at Calouste's town house in Kensington just in time for dinner.

Calouste's wife and children were at their home in the country, but he sent word as soon as we arrived that they should join us in London.

Gertrude Bell retired early to her place in Knight's Bridge with Barbara in tow. Barbara was due to start nursing school the next day and would have little time for anything else over the next six weeks. She promised to keep in touch and to send for Khalil when she had any free time.

When they left, Khalil stood looking at the front door for more than a minute without moving a muscle. He then retired early to his room without saying a word, leaving Calouste and me to our after-dinner drinks.

"What is the plan for tomorrow Calouste?"

"We meet with C at his office in Whitehall at ten. What happens next depends on his offer and your decision."

"What can you tell me about this man?"

"Well, let's see. He joined the Navy when he was young, but unfortunately over time he became quite seasick, so he left active service and moved into a desk job."

"I can appreciate his distaste for the water. I enjoyed your yacht on Lake Van, but my brief rides across the Bosporus in Constantinople was enough to tell me I wouldn't like the open sea."

"I remember you looked rather uncomfortable. The odd thing is, C loves to go fast and to pilot any vehicle with a motor. He was an early member of the Royal Automobile Club and the Royal Motor Yacht Club. He even just recently got his pilot's license and joined the Royal Aero Club. This for a man of age fifty four."

"He sounds like a man who enjoys a thrill. Maybe Gertrude should take him to climb a mountain."

"Perhaps you should suggest that when you meet him."

"I think I will wait until I know him a little better. So he's in charge of all of the intelligence services for Great Britain?"

"Now we are getting into a sensitive area. Publically MI6 does not exist and neither does MI5."

"There are two organizations or six?"

"In the beginning there were many more military intelligence sections, but MI5 and MI6 are the ones that have survived. MI5 operates inside the United Kingdom and MI6 everywhere else in the world."

"So C runs both?"

"Oh no, although that would make things much easier. A man called Vernon Kell runs MI5. Very bright man. In a way K and C should swap jobs. K speaks seven languages including Russian and Chinese. Oh, and Polish, so we should keep him away from Barbara."

"Surely he wouldn't be interested…"

"I was only joking Abdulrahim" he interrupted. "You really should work on your sense of humor. Captain Kell is a military man as well. Army. There is a bit of a rivalry between their organizations. In fact, the War Office, Admiralty, and Foreign Office can't agree on who's in charge of the budget for the organizations."

"I know a bit about the inner workings of a new government organization" I said. "Everyone wants control but nobody wants to fund the day to day."

"Exactly. So to date C has had to work with people of independent means, who don't require a paycheck. In fact, in the beginning he had to rent a flat out of his own pocket to serve as his office."

"So he doesn't pay his spies?" I asked.

"He does not. In fact, can you call someone a spy if they are not selling secrets?"

"That is a good question. It explains why you are working for him" I said.

"I don't work for the Secret Service Bureau" Gulbenkian said. "Everything I have done on this trip was simply because I was in the right place at the right time and willing to help. Your arrival at Lake Van was serendipitous, but I would have met you in Constantinople nonetheless and seen you safely to Paris."

"And Budapest?"

"I am a man of my word. Once you were in my care, it was my responsibility to see it through. The assassination of the Archduke was definitely not in the plan either. I will need to meet with the Foreign Secretary, Sir Edward Grey to understand how all of this will impact the Turkish Petroleum Company. If war does break out, that deal may be on permanent hold."

We both sat in silence for a moment considering the gravity of what was happening in the world. Great changes were in store.

"You know I never really thanked you for your hospitality.

You seem to truly enjoy welcoming guests into your home."

"My wife and children will be surprised to hear you say that my friend. Do you remember the statue by Auguste Rodin in my house in Paris?"

"The one with the rope around its neck about to be hanged?"

"Yes. It's one of his Burghers of Calais. I told my wife and daughter it was meant as a warning of what may happen to those who try to come into my house. You see I don't like to be surrounded by strangers and people who want to insinuate their way into my life."

"But the gathering in Van? Your friendship with Gertrude Bell?"

"Van was a business meeting. Sykes and Picot and the Germans were there because I needed to learn what they wanted. Gertrude is indeed a friend, but she has earned my respect."

"So Khalil and I are strictly business?"

"At first perhaps, but I am a good judge of character Abdulrahim and you are a Brother Mason. I have truly enjoyed the journey over the past few weeks. You have more than earned my respect, you have earned my friendship. Thank you my friend."

I didn't know what to say to that so I decided not to reply. I raised my whiskey glass in a toast and drank it dry.

"There is another reason I have felt a connection to you and Khalil" he said. "My mother is a Persian citizen. So you see, I have a good reason to hope for your success in building a free and independent country."

"Where is your mother now?" I asked.

"With my wife in the country. You will meet them all tomorrow."

"It looks like we have a big day tomorrow" I said, "so I think it's time to retire."

"Good night Abdulrahim. God bless you."

I still remember the change that came over Calouste when we reached London. He seemed to be lost in thought for much of the next few weeks. Even when surrounded by family he appeared to have much on his mind. It almost felt like his mission was complete and it was time to move on to the next job.

We arrived at Whitehall the next morning on time and were shown into the waiting room outside of Mansfield Cumming's office. There were no markings on the door save a room number, no evidence that this was the head office of a global spy network. It appeared to be the domain of a typical English Bureaucrat.

Just as we entered the outer office the door to the inner office opened and several men emerged.

"Ah Gentlemen, let me introduce you to Calouste Gulbenkian and his friend Abdulrahim Kashani from Tehran."

The man who spoke had grey hair, wore a monocle in his right eye, and had very thin lips. It seemed his mouth was simple a slit in his face.

"Calouste, it's good to see you again" said one of the men in French.

"Likewise Vernon" Calouste responded.

I assumed this was Vernon Kell, from MI5.

"Salaam Aghayeh Kashani" he said to me.

"You speak Persian as well Monsieur Kell?" I asked in French.

"Only enough to be polite."

"May I introduce Sir Alexander Bethell from our Naval Intelligence office."

The man in full Naval uniform bowed slightly and smiled.

"Mister Kashani, I want to thank you for your report on the German maneuvers in Constantinople. This was a critical piece of information for us and further evidence of how woefully understaffed we are in that part of the world."

"And finally" Cumming said, "Let me introduce William Melville and Basil Thomson from New Scotland Yard. They are part of the Criminal Investigation Department for the Metropolitan Police. They were just telling me about some amazing new technologies they are developing to help solve crimes."

"Mister Kashani" Basil said.

"*Tanks* for *yer* time Cumming. We'll be in *tooch*" said Melville.

With that the four men left the room and closed the door behind.

I looked at Calouste and as if to read my mind he said "Melville is Irish. The accent takes a little getting used to."

"Come in Gentlemen. Make yourselves comfortable."

We entered the sparsely decorated office and sat in two of the four chairs that were vacated by the previous visitors.

"Well Monsieur Kashani, you have travelled quite a long way to be here, so I will not beat about the bush as we like to say. I need your help."

"That is my understanding" I replied.

"Three days ago the Russian Army mobilized and is on the move to their western borders. As a result, this morning we received word from Vienna that the Emperor has declared war on Serbia and has warned Czar Nicholas to stand down."

Calouste and I looked at each other and shared the same thought. The dominoes had begun to fall.

"Do you know what that means?" Cumming asked.

"It means within a few weeks most of Europe will be at war" I replied. "God help us."

"Exactly right. Do you have any sense for what that will mean for Persia?"

"I can't speak for my government, but I expect we will remain neutral. There is no compelling reason for us to join either side. Especially if the Ottoman's remain neutral or join the Entente."

"Do you think there is still a chance they will join us and not Germany?" Cumming asked.

"There is a chance. The three Pashas seem to be split, but the Germans are making a very generous offer."

"Your friend Wilhelm Wassmuss has been behind much of that, hasn't he?"

"Wilhelm is no friend of mine."

"Sorry. Just a figure of speech. Mister Kashani, can I speak frankly with you under the strictest of confidence?"

"Of course. I expect it goes both ways. What we say here is not to be shared unless the other party agrees."

"Quite Right. Good. Good. Good" he said and then drew a deep breath.

"The gentlemen from Scotland Yard were here because we have uncovered a plot between German Intelligence and members of the Indian Revolutionary movement. They are based out of a Barber shop here in London owned by a man called Karl Gustav Ernst. They're trying to convince the war lords in Afghanistan to partner with the separatists in India to overthrow British rule. This would tie up a large number of our troops and disrupt the flow of goods from the subcontinent."

"So what will you do about it?"

"We will cut the head off of the snake here in London, but we cannot be sure that this is the only snake. We believe Wassmuss has agents operating out of Southern Persia that are part of this effort, but we have no eyes and ears in that area, let alone Afghanistan."

"You want me to help with that?"

"Precisely. We need to establish a network of trusted individuals to gather information about German activities in Persia and your neighbors to the east. You ran a newspaper didn't you?"

"Yes. For a time."

"So think of this assignment as being a foreign correspondent for a global newspaper."

"And what exactly would you want me to report on?"

"Report on things that you think would be interesting to us. German activities of any kind. Russians misbehaving in the north, not living up to their agreements with us."

"You want me to spy on your allies?"

"The word spy is so overloaded. I prefer the word report. We are in the business of collecting information, understanding it in the context of what happens on the ground, and reporting it to the consumers who will benefit most."

"And yes" he continued, "we are on the same side as the Russian Empire in this matter, but you must have noticed that since Bloody Sunday, the Czar has had his hands full with the Bolsheviks. Have you been following the news of this Marxist called Lenin or Joseph Djugashvili who caused the labor strikes in the oil fields at Baku?"

"I am not familiar with them" I replied.

Dear reader, Djugashvili is not a name you will likely have heard of, but after he adopted the family name of Stalin the whole world learned his name.

"They are actively trying to foment a breakup between the Bolsheviks and the Mensheviks in the Duma" C continued. "If a war breaks out, we suspect it will provide Lenin with just the diversion he needs to return to Moscow and lead the revolution from inside."

"My cousin has advocated some of his Marxist ideology" I

offered. "but most Persians are believers in free trade."

"Yes. Your cousin the Ayatollah is a key piece to the puzzle. We believe the Germans may try to stir up trouble within Persia using Bolshevik sympathizers like your cousin. That is in addition to their attempts to disrupt our supply of oil from Abadan."

I remembered sharing the information about my cousin's desire to sabotage the refinery and looked to Calouste who simply nodded, confirming that he had *reported* on this as well.

"Because of your warning, we were able to thwart that attempt and restore morale among the workers. You see you have already been a very important asset for us. We simply want to formalize the relationship."

"I'm listening. What else would you ask of me?"

"Run for Parliament. It will give you access to more information on the inner workings of the government and give you power to change the things you believe are wrong."

"Power? The true power still lies with the Shah. Until we get him under control, we will not be able to make the deep reform required."

"What if there was a new Shah? One that believed as you do? Someone you could trust to do the right thing for the people of Persia."

"That would not only take the right leader" I replied, "it would take money and the promise of power to many people in order to gain the support required for a coup."

The image of Major Reza Khan in his Cossack uniform suddenly flashed through my mind. What if a man like that were leading the country, someone who understood right from wrong, who had a sense of justice?

"Why would you want to see a change anyway?" I asked. "Wasn't it his father that sold off the oil rights in the first place?"

"Do you trust your present Shah?" he asked simply.

"I see your point. The man has no honor. If he reneged on his father's agreements to the Parliament he can renege on the Oil leases as well. He cannot be trusted."

"If you did have someone in mind who understands the meaning of honor, someone we could work with over the next few years, then we could see to it that all the right pieces would fall into place for him. With you providing support from Parliament and our financial support and political assurances, it would simply be a matter of time before the change becomes inevitable."

Alarm bells were going off in my head. I was feeling like I was sinking deeper into a conspiracy that I did not want to be part of. Images of Arch Duke Ferdinand's assassination flashed through my mind. Did C expect me to assassinate our Shah?

"I will not be party to any kind of assassination!" I blurted out without thinking first.

"Who do you take me for Kashani? My team is not in that business. If you were the type of man who would do something like that you would not be sitting here in my office."

It was the first sign of true emotion I saw from him since I walked into his office.

Then it struck me.

C was not trying to bribe me personally. He was promising monetary support for a regime change. He was not telling me who should be the new Shah. He was asking me to choose the man I wanted. He was not asking me to spy on my own people. He was asking for reports on the Germans, the Russians, and the Bolsheviks, three groups I considered to be a threat to my country's future.

"How would I be able to help you in the south when I live in the capital?"

"Your membership in Parliament and business interests will

provide cover for your travel throughout Persia, but you will also need to establish a network of like-minded men throughout Persia, especially if you are to be successful in overthrowing the Shah."

I cringed when I heard him say the words out loud. Was I really planning to overthrow the Shah? How did I go from listening to his ideas to owning them so quickly?

"And my cousin?" I asked almost without thinking.

"Our Persia experts tell us that this will be the stickiest wicket of them all as we say. The support of the mullahs will be useful in opposition to the current Shah, but the Imams will want an unfair share of power if the change is successful."

"And they may insist on expelling your government from Persia while they are at it" I said.

"It's a chance we are willing to take. If we get that far, there may be some incentives we can offer to help smooth over the issues."

"Najaf and Karbala?" I asked

Cumming looked surprised.

"Yes as a matter of fact. How did you know?"

"Because you are not the only ones offering up that territory as part of a deal. Even the Sultan is trying to broker a deal with the Shia leadership. That's why I needed rescue from that train to Karbala."

"Yes. I forgot about that."

"Then there is the unfortunate reality that the Ottomans control this area at the moment."

"Certainly. Although François Picot and Mark Sykes have proposed a plan that would be put into play if the world goes to war as we suspect. We haven't worked through the details, but they are preparing to present it to Foreign Secretary Sir Edward Grey in a few weeks. The French diplomat Paul Gambon has given his support for the framework."

I thought back to the day on Lake Van when Sykes was leaving. Was it the idea they had just hatched together at the conference?

I sat back in my chair and thought through the enormity of his proposal. Now I understood why he wanted to have this meeting in person and why I had to come to Paris and London to hear it.

"Why me? I am a simple businessman."

"I told you he was modest" Calouste said.

"Most truly great men are" Cumming said.

"Monsieur Kashani, we have been following you since you and your militia camped out on our embassy lawn in ought six. You have a reputation of doing the right thing even when your self-interest would have you do otherwise. You are a natural leader who formed a militia and saw them safely through the constitutional revolution. Then instead of parlaying that into a political career you stepped back into your old life and let others bask in the glory."

"And you are a tough negotiator" Calouste added. "What is it you said to the Hungarian Postmaster? 'It is my job to get the better part of the deal but give you enough value for your stamps so that I do not feel like a thief'."

"How do you know that? You weren't with us that day."

"Khalil. He worships you Abdulrahim. He told me all about your visit with such pride."

"What would my friends and family say if they knew I was working with you? I cannot be branded a British spy."

"If anyone finds out about our relationship then we have failed. Your first objective is to operate in complete secrecy. Our friends at Scotland Yard have developed some techniques that will help you communicate with us in a way that will protect you from exposure. If you accept, we would like you to stay on a few weeks to get trained."

"Can I have a few days to think over your proposal?" I asked.

"Of course. I don't expect you to jump into this without careful consideration. That's why we chose you. Take some time to consider it, but if the answer is no, I would appreciate making it quick. We will need time to invite our other choices to Paris."

"Other choices?"

"Do you ever go into a negotiation without alternatives?" Cumming asked.

"Of course not."

"Well neither do I. Don't get me wrong. You are the man we want, better than all the others combined. But if you are unwilling to help us, then we will be forced to go to our best alternative."

My first reaction was that I was being forced into a decision and that did not sit well with me. Then as I thought about the possibility of not being involved in the choice of our next Shah, I realized that C was offering me a unique opportunity to shape the future of my country.

"Thank you" I said. "My decision won't take long."

I remembered Calouste's comment from the day before about working on my sense of humor.

"So I guess you don't want to have a look at my stamp collection" I said.

"So glad you reminded me!" he exclaimed then reached into his coat pocket and removed an envelope.

"I took the liberty of assembling a collection of British East India Company stamps along with some more interesting samples from the Convention States. If it's variety you are looking for in postage stamps, India is your place!"

"I was only joking about the collection" I said feeling a little embarrassed.

"Think nothing of it. Consider it part of maintaining your cover. You came out here to trade stamps and by Jove you will have significant new pieces to show your friends back home."

"Thank you ... pardon me but what should I call you?"

"C will do. If you come on board we will call you P1. P for Persia and one for the head of country. All of your recruits will have their own numbers. We never use names. Names are dangerous. Remember, secrecy is job one."

He reached out to shake my hand so I assumed the meeting was over.

Calouste and I left the office and waited until we got our handsome cab before either spoke.

"His ask was much bigger than I was expecting" Calouste said. "You have a lot to think about."

"Yes I do."

"Would you mind accompanying me to meet someone about a new project of mine before we head home?"

"Of course. What is it?"

"I'm thinking about building a church for my fellow Armenians here in Kensington. I am meeting with Mewes and Davis, the firm that designed the interior of the London Ritz Hotel. They have some ideas to show me."

"There is a Ritz hotel in London?" I asked.

"Built a few years ago. My wife and I should take you for tea in the Palm Court."

"Do they have chocolate soufflé there as well?"

"I'm sure they do, but not with afternoon tea."

"Oh. I see." This was truly disappointing.

"But they do serve some wonderful biscuits and scones with tea. I'm sure you will like them."

"You won't tell Khalil will you?"

"You have my word Abdulrahim."

"Good. Then I would love to accompany you to tea at the Ritz."

I was surprised at the level of details that went in to the building of a church. I was even more surprised to hear the budget and to learn that Calouste was donating all of the money for the construction. My friend was an enigma of sorts. He was a hard driving businessman who fretted over every penny spent on the project, but in the end was willing to pay large sums of money on his art collection and charitable causes.

We arrived home after the meeting with Mewes and Davis to find a house full of family. It was one o'clock and the family was gathered around the dining table when we entered the room.

"Papa!" exclaimed a young teenaged girl who immediately popped up out of her chair and grabbed her father in a bear hug.

"Rita darling. You have grown at least an inch since I saw you last! You are turning in to a beautiful young lady."

"Hello Father" a young man said as he stood politely by his chair.

"Nubar. My people were expecting you for your summer internship last week. Why didn't you show up?"

"I know father, but I wanted to spend a little time with Mother while you were still away. You can dock my pay for the time lost."

"But we aren't paying you anything?"

"Exactly" responded Nubar. "So the calculation won't be challenging."

"Nevarte darling" Calouste said as he kissed his wife on the cheek.

"You are looking fit dear" she responded then looked at me.

"Aren't you forgetting something?"

"Oh yes. Yes. I am so sorry. Abdulrahim Kashani, let me introduce my wife Nevarte, my son Nubar, and my daughter Rita."

"Pleased to meet all of you" I said.

"Won't you join us for luncheon Mister Kashani? I assume my husband won't eat until later as is his custom."

"I will be happy to join you" I replied.

"And I as well" Calouste joined in.

Nevarte simply looked in the direction of a footman who immediately began setting two additional places.

"Have you met Khalil yet?" Calouste asked.

"There was nobody else here when we arrived. We have another guest?"

"My Nephew Khalil" I said. "He is only a little older than your son."

"But much more mature" Calouste said half under his breath.

"Your son graduated from Harrow and will start at Trinity College Cambridge this fall. I think he has shown quite a bit of maturity."

"And his frequent visits to North London Collegiate in the middle of the night?"

"Can I help it if the girls there found me totally irresistible?" Nubar said with a smirk.

"Oh please!" Rita said.

"I'm sure Mister Kashani isn't the least bit interested in the challenges of raising a young man."

"My boys are still in primary school" I told her. "So I have time to prepare."

"Did you enjoy the country?" Calouste asked.

"Yes dear, but you must realize that running a house that size is a full time job. Even with the staff, I am constantly called on to make decisions and settle disagreements."

Calouste chuckled and wiped his mouth with his napkin. "I told you if you married me I would build you a Palace. I never promised you would enjoy it."

"Well for now I left your mother with that responsibility. She stayed behind at the country house."

"And who will cook for her? Certainly not old Misses Sanders. She hates English food."

"Oh no. She will be eating Turkish as usual. Nusret stayed behind with her."

"What? I was looking forward to ..."

"Don't worry darling" Nevarte interrupted, "your other chefs travelled with us. You can enjoy French and Greek cuisine until your mother decides to return your favorite Turkish Chef."

"How many chefs do you have at your house in Tehran Monsieur Kashani?" Nubar asked.

"Only two" I answered. "But they both cook Persian Cuisine."

I would have to tell my first wife and house keeper that they had been elevated in status to Executive Chef and Chef de Cuisine. They might demand an increase in their allowance, but I would take that chance.

"After enjoying the fine food on this trip though" I added, "I expect I will look for my own French Chef when I return."

Or have my housekeeper learn to make a chocolate soufflé at the very least I thought to myself.

We finished our luncheon and I retired to my room to examine the stamps C gave me. To my amazement, the envelope contained a detailed description of each specimen, which in some ways was more valuable than the stamp itself.

Khalil returned in the mid-afternoon and we decided to take a walk in Hyde Park. I wanted to discuss C's offer, but I also needed to get an update on his plans. We walked and I talked for more than an hour, sharing my thoughts with the only person I trusted had my best interest in mind.

"So if you accept their offer" Khalil asked as we walked the pathways of the park, "you won't have to share any information you don't want to share?"

"Correct."

"And they expect you to choose the next Shah?"

"Yes. It would be my decision."

"Uncle, do you think Major Reza Khan would make a good leader?"

"Reza Khan was the first person I thought of. He certainly has the trust of his men and the presence of a leader."

"And when he learned the truth about the bicycle lesson, he stood up for justice even against the Crown Prince."

"Yes" I replied, "but I need to be sure. This is a decision that will take time. I need to get to know him better."

"So does that mean you will do it?"

"I don't see that I have a choice. If I don't then someone else will and I can't be sure they will have Persia's best interest at heart."

"I wonder if Scotland Yard will give you invisible ink... or a code book."

The mention of code book reminded me that I needed to update my dear cousin. Not only would I have to send a telegram that would give him something he could use, I would have to meet him on my way home and try to rebuild our relationship. I would need to keep him close if I worked for MI6.

"Invisible ink?" I asked. "Like writing with lemon juice?"

"You know about that?"

"Invisible ink has been around since the ancients" I replied. "Every military man knows about the importance of secret communications."

"I read about ultraviolet light at the Library at the British Museum this morning. There are some chemicals that are only visible when you shine UV light at them."

"So that's where you were all day."

"Yes uncle. Barbara has no time for me. She is either in class or studying. So I have been spending my time in the Library."

We walked for a while longer until Khalil broke the silence.

"Uncle, how can it be that someone you have only known for a few weeks can become so important that you can't endure being without them even for a few days?"

"Enjoy it while you can" I said. "This intense feeling won't last forever."

"Enjoy?" he asked in disbelief. "I am in pure agony without her!"

"I know son, but you are only in agony because you are so intensely in love. You will be together soon and that feeling of joy when you are with her will pay for all of this misery."

He stared at me for a few moments without speaking then looked towards the ground and shook his head.

We continued walking in silence for a while until I had worked through my remaining issues.

"Well, I don't know anything about UV light" I finally said, "and I have no idea what the Metropolitan Police can teach me. I only know that I need to make up my mind about MI6 and give Cummins an answer so I can get on with my life."

We walked in silence for several minutes more before Khalil finally spoke up.

"Uncle, they are asking you to become a King Maker, like the Queen Mother Atossa for King Xerxes or the Earl of Warwick in the War of the Roses. These were respected figures who changed the course of history. They are giving you significant power to decide for yourself the direction of our country's future. I think you should do it."

I realized I had already made up my mind, but was struggling to find a way to feel good about the decision. I may be no Earl, but Khalil was right. I had a once in a lifetime opportunity here. It would be dangerous, but I had never walked away from a challenge in the past.

"I think I will" I replied. "I will do this."

I told Calouste the news when we returned home and he immediately called C to arrange our next meeting.

"We will meet C tomorrow after five at the Royal Automobile Club at Pall Mall. It's close to the Ritz, so I think we will have tea with the family, then you and I will continue on to the club afterwards."

The following afternoon, Khalil and I joined Calouste and his family for afternoon tea.

We Persians drink tea, or *Chai* as we call it, but the upper class in Britain has turned a mid-afternoon refreshment into a formal event. When that event is held at the Ritz Hotel, it is transformed into a display of decadence fit for royalty.

The walls and ceiling and floors of the Palm Court competed with one another for notoriety. The gilded chandeliers vied for attention over the stained glass faux skylight. The light from the gold plated wall sconces reflected off of the polished marble floor. I felt like we were entering the palace at Versailles instead of a hotel restaurant.

We were seated on a collection of upholstered chairs and settees around a small table, Calouste and his wife Nevarte opposite of Khalil and I, with Rita and Nubar opposite of each other in the chairs.

"Have you had high tea before Monsieur Kashani?" Nevarte asked.

"I have not Madame Gulbenkian. This is a new experience for Khalil and me."

A member of the staff welcomed us and gave Calouste a small menu that listed the selection of teas to choose from.

"Abdulrahim, do you have a preference between the Darjeeling or the Orange Pekoe from Ceylon? Or maybe you would like to try an oolong tea from China?"

"Why don't you choose Calouste. I am not really a connoisseur and your choice of wine has always been good."

Calouste ordered the Orange Pekoe and we all settled back into our seats. It wasn't long before the tea was brought out followed by a multi-level silver serving tray filled with small sandwiches and scones.

Khalil and I held back to watch how the others behaved before diving in to partake. Everything tasted wonderful, including the tea, but I was certainly left wanting more. I understand that afternoon tea is not a meal exactly, but I was just getting started when the last scone was gone and nothing was left but the crumbs.

Just then, a well-dressed man approached our table. He was short but had a powerful self-confidence. The first thing you noticed though were his eyes. They were wide open and fully engaged, not quite like a mad man but somewhat startling. He smiled broadly showing all of his teeth.

"Calouste! What a pleasant surprise!"

"Henri." Calouste acknowledged the newcomer but seemed somewhat uncomfortable with the turn of events.

"Mister Deterding" Nevarte added. "Where is your lovely

wife?"

"At our place in the country Mrs. Gulbenkian, I will send her your regards."

"Monsieur Kashani, this is Henri Deterding, chairman of Royal Dutch Shell Petroleum and my good friend. Henri, this is Abdulrahim Kashani and his nephew Khalil Redjaian from Tehran."

"Ah really? Are you with the Anglo-Persian Oil Company Monsieur Kashani?"

"I am afraid not Mister Deterding. I am only a humble merchant, not affiliated with any oil company."

"Well don't make the mistake of calling Calouste a merchant of any kind. I did that once. He prefers to be known as an architect of corporations!"

I looked at Calouste and could tell he was uncomfortable, but had no idea why. I knew Royal Dutch Shell was somehow involved in the Turkish Petroleum deal, but it wasn't clear if that had any bearing on his reaction.

"Nevarte dear, would you mind taking Khalil and the children home. I believe Henri and I have some business to attend to before our meeting at Pall Mall."

"Of course darling" she replied.

They all took their leave as the three of us sat back at the table. The waiter brought over a new place setting for Deterding and poured out a fresh cup of tea.

"If this is about the three hundred thousand pounds again" Calouste said as the waiter retired, "I told you I would see it through."

"Yes, but Cartier are insisting on their money by the end of this week or they will ask for the necklace back. I can't possibly ask Lydia to return the emeralds. She adores them."

"You should have thought about your cash flow problem before you bought the necklace."

"Yes, Yes I know, but Catharina is returning from the country in a few days and I want to enjoy the last few nights with Lydia while I can. She has been especially accommodating since I gave her the jewels."

He looked around to ensure nobody was listening

"A man of your appetites will surely appreciate my predicament."

I understood the implications all too well and felt very uncomfortable witnessing this conversation.

"I said I would see this through and I will. My banker in Paris wired me yesterday that the funds will be available tomorrow. So don't worry. Your mistress can keep her jewels."

Deterding's relief was visible. He looked as if a great weight had been lifted from his shoulders.

"Thank you my good friend. You will not regret it."

"I will expect my five percent of your next big deal as we agreed, so perhaps you might come to regret it."

"Of course. Of course. So you are meeting someone over at Pall Mall?"

"Yes. At the Royal Automobile Club."

"I bet I know just the man. Thomas Boverton Redwood. He's a member there."

"Yes. That's right. He is on the Admiralty's Fuel Oil Committee and has asked my opinion on the matter."

"Right. Well, I shall not detain you any longer. Thank you again for your assistance Calouste. Monsieur Kashani it was very nice meeting you."

"Mister Deterding" I replied as he walked away.

I was struck by how easily Calouste had just lied about our meeting. If I hadn't known we were meeting with Cumming I would have believed this Boverton Redwood *was* our next meeting.

"I am sorry you were put in the position of hearing that conversation Abdulrahim. Henri really should have chosen a better place and time."

"Think nothing of it Calouste. Shall we go?"

It was then I noticed the maître d' hovering at a discreet distance.

"Andrew, can you put this on my tab please?"

"Certainly Monsieur Gulbenkian. There is another matter that the manager asked me to enquire about."

"Yes?"

The maître d' looked discreetly in my direction as if asking for permission to speak in my presence.

"Well go on."

"The manager wishes to enquire if the young guest staying in your suite will be here longer than originally planned?"

A look of recognition spread across Calouste's face.

"Yes. I see. Please have the accommodations extended for another two weeks Andrew. I should have arranged this sooner. Thank you."

"My pleasure Monsieur."

Calouste looked at me and smiled.

"Too many pieces on the chess board at the moment. I've lost track of a few. I thought she was in my suite at the Carlton. Now I have to remember which one is there."

I decided there was no appropriate reply to this.

"You are fortunate Abdulrahim. Your culture allows up to four wives as I understand it."

"Yes, but only if you can afford to support them" I replied. "In fact I have a second wife myself."

"I see. Well, our church does not tolerate this practice, so we are not allowed to make our other relationships … official as it were."

"I understand."

"Good. I am glad to hear it."

We walked the short distance to Pall Mall and entered the Royal Automobile Club right on time. Cumming gave our names at the front desk and we were shown directly into the main lounge where several gentlemen were engaged in a lively conversation. Cumming was sitting alone at the other end of the room reading a newspaper and sipping a drink.

"Gentlemen. Welcome." Cumming said. "Can I interest you in a whiskey?"

We both agreed as we took adjoining seats across from the head of MI6. A waiter appeared to take our order then disappeared through a door nearby.

"Well Mister Kashani, do you have good news for me?"

"I believe I do Mister Cumming. I have decided to become your man in Tehran."

"Capital! I am thrilled to hear that. This calls for a toast."

As if on cue the waiter returned with two cut crystal glasses of single malt on a silver try. Calouste and I took our glass and raised them in a toast.

Calouste pulled a folded piece of paper from the inside pocket of his coat and handed them over to C.

"What is this?" Cumming asked.

"My invoice for the expenses incurred seeing Monsieur Kashani safely to London."

Cumming reviewed the pages and then went through them a second time.

"But there are line items for nights of lodging at your place in Van and Constantinople. And one here for two Louis Vuitton steamer trunks."

"Yes. They were required for the journey."

Cumming said nothing further. He simply shook his head in disbelief and pocketed the papers.

"So what is next for me?" I asked trying to break the awkward silence.

"Ah Kashani. Will it be possible to extend your stay in London another month?"

I thought of Khalil and Barbara and realized another month would enable me to watch over them for a while longer. I would also have time to make some business connections.

"Another month would be fine. It might give the great powers a chance to settle down before I have to travel."

"Yes, well I am afraid that might be wishful thinking. The situation is grave I am afraid. The optimists believe there is still a chance to pull back from the brink, but the pessimists believe full scale war is eminent."

"So why do you need me to stay for the month?"

"Oh right. Yes. Well... do you remember the gentlemen from Scotland Yard? I have arranged for them to educate you in what we call trade craft and to outfit you with some equipment which might come in handy."

"Such as?" I asked.

"They have developed a very small camera for one thing. There will be times when you will want to take photographs of documents and this camera is designed for that purpose."

"I see."

"They have several designs for miniature handguns as well in the works but those may not be ready for use. We will want to provide you with a quality pistol before you go however and ensure you are properly trained to fire it. I know you have a military background, so these classes will likely be a review for you."

"And finally, we would like to teach you a few techniques concerning disinformation and propaganda. You ran a newspaper, so I am sure these techniques will come as no surprise to you as well."

"And when do I begin these classes?"

"Next Monday. Basil will send a car for you and ring Calouste's man with the details."

At that moment a new man entered the room and met the gaze of Calouste and Cumming.

"Thomas" Calouste exclaimed. "I thought I might run in to you here."

The gentleman acknowledged the others in the room and then walked over to our small group.

"Abdulrahim Kashani may I introduce Baronet Thomas Boverton Redwood. Thomas is the man who literally wrote the book on Petroleum Engineering."

So Calouste was not technically a liar.

"I am pleased to meet you Monsieur Kashani. You must be pleased that Great Britain now owns fifty one percent of Anglo-Persian. To me this is an indication in the faith we have in the future of your country."

"Abdulrahim is not directly connected with APOC Thomas" Calouste interjected. "And he is likely not aware of the recent parliamentary vote confirming the purchase."

"I'm sorry" I said trying to understand what was being said. "The government of Great Britain has purchased a majority portion of the Anglo-Persian Oil Company."

"Yes" Calouste replied. "The deal was negotiated just before you arrived in Van and was ratified by our parliament while we were in Paris."

"Churchill presented the deal himself and won the vote with

a huge majority" Redwood said. "Now that he has committed our navy to fuel oil, there is no turning back."

I knew immediately that when my cousin heard the news he would redouble his efforts to undermine the company.

"Calouste, you and Kashani must join us for the motor race next week."

"Do you have room for one more?" Calouste asked. "Abdulrahim's nephew is a mechanical wizard that would love to see the state of the art in racing engines."

"Of course. The more the merrier!"

Redwood took his leave and I turned my attention back to C, who seemed to be evaluating me.

"What Thomas didn't say" Cumming said, "was that this deal guarantees the crown access to the oil as a preferred customer. With the German Navy's rise, access to oil and free passage through the Suez canal is becoming more important by the day. I think it would be a good idea if you became more interested in the internal politics of oil when you return home."

"I understand" I replied.

"You might want to become familiar with some of the geological indictors of possible oil fields as well. Abadan is not producing at the level we need to sustain our fleet, so additional wells will be required."

"Hence the deal with the Ottomans" I replied looking at Calouste for confirmation.

"I will look after Mesopotamia" Calouste said, "But C is correct. As you grow your network back home you should teach your associates to look for potential new fields. We will make sure they are properly compensated. Khalil has the makings of a first class petroleum engineer if he wants to pursue it."

"I agree, but Khalil will not be joining me on the return trip. He would like to stay in London for a while."

"I see" said Calouste. "That does change things doesn't it."

We finished our drinks and dined together at the club, but the conversation turned to racing of all kinds and my thoughts turned to second guessing my decision.

The next morning I received a call as expected from Scotland Yard. I was to meet with Sir Edward Henry, commissioner of the Metropolitan Police Department on the first of August to begin a four week training.

When I arrived at New Scotland Yard I was shown to a small room in a wing of the building that resembled a chemical laboratory more than a police headquarters. After waiting a fairly long time by myself, Sir Edward Henry arrived with an assistant in tow.

"I am so sorry for the delay Mister Kashani, but there is a lot going on at the moment."

"I am at your disposal Sir Edward." I replied.

"Yes. Thank you for your understanding. Let's get on with it."

Sir Edward's assistant sat down at the table in the room to take notes. I followed suit as my host started pacing the small space as he spoke.

"Over the next four weeks you will be given the tools and techniques we have developed for our detective force. You will be able to put many of these techniques to good use when you return home. Some require support from a laboratory full of chemists and technicians and will not be practicable for your own use. However, you should be aware of them."

"I will be teaching you what I can about fingerprints and will give you a copy of the book I wrote on classification several years ago. I understand you are a stamp collector and have a keen sense of observation for minute details."

"Yes" I replied. "I do a lot of work with magnifying glasses and have even noticed fingerprints on the back of some stamps."

"Good. Well those skills will come in handy. You will not have access to a large database of prints like we do, but you will be able to secretly lift prints of a subject and compare them for a match when necessary."

"We will spend some time with codes and secret writing techniques. This will be followed up by a class on concealment devices and dead drops."

"Dead drops?" I interrupted.

"All will be revealed in time. For now, a dead drop is a technique you will use to communicate with someone when you don't want anyone to know you have a relationship with. I believe you have met William Melville?"

"Briefly, yes."

"A few years back we had the pleasure of a visit from Harry Houdini, the escape artist."

"I am familiar with him as well" I replied.

"Our Mister Melville locked up Houdini as best he could and within two minutes he was free. Melville demanded Houdini teach him everything he knew about picking locks and escape. Mister Melville will be passing along that knowledge to you."

"We will teach you how to tell when someone is lying and how to lie convincingly yourself."

"This will help me in our Parliament as well" I said, trying to lighten the atmosphere.

The comment at first confused Sir Henry, but then when he understood my meaning he laughed.

"Yes. Quite right. Although politicians often believe the lies they are telling and that makes them especially hard to detect... Where was I?"

He paused for a moment to collect his thoughts.

"Right. We will spend quite a bit of time in the field learning how to follow someone without being detected and how to spot someone following you. This latter technique we call dry cleaning. If done well, you will be able to spot multiple tails without letting them know you are on to them. We will practice this on the streets of London until you are proficient."

I thought about the list so far and realized there was a lot to learn.

"We will wrap up with several standard techniques for recruiting informants and evading detection including honey traps, false flag operations, and limited hangouts."

I was about to speak when he raised his hand to stop me.

"I know these are strange terms, but they will make sense once you understand the principles."

I nodded my head and he smiled.

"Wonderful. Well that's all for me. My assistant will be your guide throughout the next month and will make sure you know where and what time. Do you have any further questions of me?"

"No Sir Edward."

"Well then, let's get on with it."

I shook hands with Sir Edward and bid him farewell as his assistant showed me to my first class of the day. It had been a while since I was in school and took some getting used to, especially since English was not my strongest language. I found the subject matter interesting though and my first day ended before I even had a chance to get tired.

The next class was the following day, a Friday, and the last day of July. That weekend Khalil and I joined Calouste and Boverton Redwood at the motor races. I believe it was the first time I saw Khalil think of something other than the beautiful Barbara for an extended period since they met. Sir Thomas offered Khalil a chance to take the car around the track after the race concluded, but Khalil was more interested in watching the mechanical team disassemble the engine to inspect for damage.

The following week all hell broke loose on the continent. Germany attacked Luxembourg and then declared war on France. Belgium tried to resist but then fell. Germany declared war on France then as expected, Britain and Russia honored their treaties and joined the fray.

More importantly, the Ottoman Empire formally ratified their alliance with Germany and the Austrian-Hungarian empire. The lines were now drawn.

The war made completing my training even more urgent. C dropped in several times over the next few weeks to ask if my instructors could hurry the process along so I could be on my way back home. Each time he was met by the response; 'proper training takes time'.

I learned from Khalil that the pressure on Barbara's class at the nursing school was even more intense. The early battles were proving to be more horrific than any previous war. Casualties were higher than ever due to tanks and mustard gas and other new inventions which made it easier to kill and maim. There was a shortage of medical staff on the front with not enough trained nurses to fill the need. Barbara's class was accelerated from six weeks to four and every student nurse in her class was expected to join the Red Cross upon graduation.

That second week passed quickly for me and as Friday classes came to a close, I was summoned to Whitehall again for a late meeting. I expected to meet with C in his offices, but at the last minute my carriage stopped outside of the Admiralty building. I presented myself at the reception area and moments later was shown into a sparsely furnished room with a large table. Huddled near the opposite end were Gertrude Bell and a group of men examining a map spread out before them. I recognized three of the men; Mark Sykes, François Picot, and Sir George Barclay, former ambassador to Persia. They flanked a distinguished man in the center who wore the uniform of a Naval Officer.

"Ah Sayed Kashani. How wonderful to see you again!" Sir George exclaimed. "Winston may I introduce you to Sayed Abdulrahim Kashani."

I walked across the room to the group who backed away from the table and turned to greet me.

"Sayed, I would like to present the First Lord of the Admiralty, The Right Honorable Winston Churchill."

Churchill reached out and shook my hand with a firm grip.

"Mister Kashani, thank you for joining us on such late notice. We are hoping to get your opinion on a proposal from Sir Mark and François Picot. I believe you know them both."

"We have met sir. Yes."

I looked down at the map on the table and immediately saw a line stretching from the Palestine Lebanon border across the northern part of Arabia. A large letter A marked the area to the north and a large letter B marked the section to the south. Looking more closely I noticed the whole region of Mesopotamia colored in Red. Finally I saw a dotted arc drawn across the bottom below the B. It immediately reminded me of the maps that defined the British and Russian Spheres of influence in my own country.

"You are carving up Arabia and the Levant" I said to no one in particular. "Into spheres of influence I assume."

"Yes" Sir Mark said, "that's correct."

I studied the maps more and imagined the Bedouin tribes that inhabited much of these regions. While at first the line seemed arbitrary, the division seemed to take these traditional territories into consideration.

"And how did you determine the split?"

"That was Gertrude" Sir George replied. "She said this division would do the least harm to the status quo based on her first-hand knowledge of the local tribes."

"And this shaded section at the bottom?"

"That territory will become a new country unto itself called Iraq. It will join Transjordan and Syria as newly formed self-governing states."

"Self-governing?" I asked looking to Gertrude for confirmation.

"A monarchy to begin with" Gertrude offered. "Then over time a parliamentary government like you put in place for Persia."

"It will take a strong leader to shepherd the tribes in the early years" I remarked. "This shaded area includes Sunnis and Shia and Kurds, not to mention the Yazidi, Babi and other minorities. You think a single leader will be able to pull them all together."

"With the right financial and military support" Sykes offered.

The mention of the military made me wonder whose army he was referring to, or did Sir Mark think that weapons provided to the right side would win the day.

"I have recommended the Hashemite family and not the house of Saud as the best choice for leaders" Gertrude added. "The Sharif of Mecca has agreed to an alliance against the Ottomans now that the Three Pashas have sided with Germany. The Sharif's sons would be the rulers of the three new countries."

I thought about this for a moment and then looked up to Churchill.

"Tell us what you think Sayed Kashani" he said. "It is the reason we brought you here."

"How soon?" I asked.

"It will take a year or more to work out the details reach an agreement between France and Britain. By then our forces should have established control of the middle-east. Russia will be preoccupied with the Ottomans and Germans in the North. We will present the deal to them as a fait accompli once we have control of the territory."

"So two years from now?" I offered.

"Most likely" Picot replied.

I studied the map again and tried to imagine how this endeavor would ever be successful. I didn't want to say anything that might jeopardize my new position.

"Out with it Kashani" Churchill bellowed as he lit up a cigar. "Tell us what you think."

"If you can keep the needs and desires of the people in mind and start laying the groundwork now, then you may have a chance. You will need to give everyone a voice, especially the minority factions in each area. Otherwise there will be unrest from within no matter which group has the best weapons and training."

I said the last bit looking straight at Mark Sykes.

"The new Kings must understand this from the very beginning. Theirs is not a mandate from heaven, if there really is such a thing. Loyalty must be earned." I said in conclusion.

"The Sharif is fully in agreement" Gertrude said. "He brought up the same issue himself."

"And how would your cousin the Ayatollah see this move?" Churchill asked.

"My cousin will have two main concerns" I began. "His first priority is to protect the Shia faith which means the holy cities of Najaf and Karbala. Will the Sharif of Mecca be willing to protect these cities and allow free access to Shia from all countries in the area?"

"Jerusalem may be a challenge in that regard as well" Sykes said to Picot. "We need to account for that in our plan for Palestine."

"The Sharif has protected Shia in their pilgrimage to Mecca throughout his tenure" Gertrude said ignoring Sykes. "It's part of the reason I chose him. He should extend this tolerance at least to the Moslem minorities."

"And the second concern?" Churchill asked.

"Money" I said simply. "Abol-Ghasem is not happy with the way profits are currently shared from the Anglo-Persian fields. If he thinks Britain is receiving an unfair share from the new Iraqi fields..."

"Does he not grasp how difficult it was to find the oil and build the infrastructure necessary to transport it to the refinery?" Churchill roared.

"My cousin is a follower of Marx" I replied, "and would like nothing more than to nationalize the oil fields. Reality is not his concern. We are dealing with perceptions here."

"Yes. Yes I see" Churchill replied turning towards Sykes and Picot. "You need to think this through more. I think Kashani has the right idea here. Perception is key."

"There is another player you must consider" I offered. "Emir Khazal Khan of Mohammerah."

"Surely he cannot think he has a claim to the new oil fields?" Sir Mark said. "Besides, he has no standing army to take territory of this size."

"He has Commander Assad" I ventured, "with his Bakhtiari tribes in Khuzestan and all the Germans Wilhelm Wassmuss can muster. Now that Germany and the Ottomans are aligned, they may squeeze out Calouste Gulbenkian and Royal Dutch Shell entirely and throw the deal to Deutsche Bank and perhaps an American company like Standard Oil. The Americans haven't taken a side and Standard certainly have the expertise."

"Good God he's right" Churchill said under his breath. "Wilson has declared that they will remain independent for the foreseeable future and god knows every major oil company in that country would jump through fire to get their hands on oil fields in this hemisphere."

Sykes and Picot looked troubled by the last comment, as if they had not considered the possibility at all.

"Well, I can see I was right to call you in to this conversation Kashani" Churchill said switching his cigar to the left hand and holding out his right to me.

It was obvious I was no longer needed, so I shook hands with everyone and said my farewells. I found a cab and headed back to share what I had learned with Calouste.

Khalil spent his time in the library of the British Museum during the day and with me during the evenings. He wanted to know everything I was learning in my tradecraft class. I tried to get permission for him to join me, but to no avail. In the end I think I learned the material better since each night I had to teach him what I had just learned myself.

Each morning the papers would report on the latest battle of the Frontiers. Unfamiliar names like Mulhouse, Haelen, and Lorraine became the talk of the town as the war raged on. Embedded reporters took photographs and filed reports from the front. The World was seeing evidence of destruction within hours of the actual event for the first time in history, sights that had been exclusively reserved for the participants in past wars.

By the end of August my training was complete. My private graduation ceremony was held in C's office with Sir Edward Henry, William Melville, and Basil Thomson from New Scotland Yard.

"Director Cumming" Sir Edward said once we were all present, "I am pleased to report that Sayed Kashani has passed our training with flying colors. He did especially well in dry cleaning and lock picking. He seems to have a real talent at spotting a tail."

"And don't forget his marksmanship" Basil Thomson added. "He could handle a sniper rifle just fine when we got him, but I never saw anyone take to a handgun the way he did."

"Yes, well it seems that you will know how to use this then" C said as he pulled a small wooden box from a desk drawer and handed it to me.

I opened the box to find a Webley Mk. 1 semi-automatic pistol and two new boxes of cartridges. It was the same type of weapon I had trained with.

"The cartridges are the new nitrocellulose type" Thomson said. "We discovered that the cordite bullets left a residue in the barrel which caused it to jam. Hopefully you won't need to use this that often, so two hundred rounds should do you for a while."

"Specially if you keep shootin' as well as you 'ave" Melville chimed in with his thick brogue.

"Got *yer* this as well" he continued as he handed me a holster for the gun. "Shoulder strap. Should do well under *yer* robes for when *ya* get home."

C reached out his hand and I shook it warmly.

"You're all set on transportation to Abadan" he said. "And you understand what's expected from the Emir?"

"I'm clear" I answered simply and shook hands with Thomson and Melville.

It was the last I saw any of them for several years.

As I completed preparations for my trip home, Khalil received the news he was dreading to hear. I learned about it on our daily walk through the park.

"Barbara is going to France" Khalil blurted out without warning. "She joined the Red Cross with her class mates. They're going to the front."

We stopped walking and turned towards each other.

"How soon?" I asked

"Tomorrow" he said fighting back the tears. "She doesn't even have time to be with me. She's already said good bye. I will never see her again."

"Don't worry" I replied. "Nurses and doctors are protected in battle zones. The Germans will never shell the area around a hospital."

"She told me the same thing. She is not afraid at all, but I can't get those Tarot cards out of my head. Everything was foretold in those cards."

"Khalil, you don't believe …"

"Death and Despair Uncle" he interrupted. "The final card was Death and Despair."

"And she will certainly be surrounded by Death and Despair at the front, but that doesn't mean she will not return."

He hung his head low and stared at the ground.

"I have lost her. The only woman I have ever loved."

I took him by the shoulders and shook him.

"Listen to me. I may not be able to see the future, but I am confident that everything will turn out alright. For now you need to focus on the present. She is off to France and I am planning to return to Tehran. Will you come with me and wait for word there?"

"How could I?" he said as he stared blankly at me.

"But you can't do anything further to protect her here?"

"I could volunteer to help with her hospital unit."

"An able bodied young man like you? The moment you volunteered they would have you in training for the front. You don't get to choose your orders when you are in army."

"Look Khalil, Calouste has been our host now for far too long. I know he likes you, but you can't stay at his house when I leave."

"I know Uncle. I have found a flat near my new job. I am moving my things there tomorrow."

"Your new job?"

"I haven't been completely open with you about my studies these past few weeks. I have been reading at the library as I told you, but I have been reading with a tutor. When he found out I had finished all the books he gave me in Van, Mister Gulbenkian put me on an accelerated study in Petroleum Engineering. He said the paper I wrote on scaling fractional distillation processes surprised even the head of his lab."

"So he offered you a job?"

"Yes Uncle. In fact I started last week when you were finishing your last classes at Scotland Yard."

I was not surprised that Calouste had hired Khalil. He knew all too well that my nephew was a diamond in the rough. And if I knew Calouste, Khalil was worth much more than they were paying him as well, but until he established his credentials, Khalil was lucky to land this position without a degree.

"Congratulations Khalil. I am very proud of you."

I embraced him and gave him a warm pat on the back. I was truly happy that he had found a way to support himself. If Barbara was able to make it back from the war, then the two of them would have a prosperous life.

"So you are leaving soon Uncle?"

"Tomorrow" I said. "The admiralty has arranged a berth on a battle cruiser heading to Port Said. From there I am on an oil tanker through the Suez canal down to Abadan."

"To the refinery?"

"Yes. It seems that you are not the only oil man in the family."

"But then you are going home to Bagh Ilichi right?"

"Eventually. First I must meet my cousin in Najaf. We have a lot of catching up to do."

When we said goodbye the following day, it was the last time I ever saw Khalil. I just didn't know it at the time.

MOHAMMERAH

September 1, 1914

I left South Hampton on the first of September aboard the HMS Invincible and arrived in Port Said a week later just after sunrise.

The journey was uneventful, even though I never truly got comfortable travelling on the open sea in a war ship. Images of the German U-Boats off of Constantinople played in my head anytime I heard a suspicious noise and there were plenty of unrecognizable sounds inside a battle cruiser. The sheer size of the ship minimized the motion though, so I was able to persevere and did not suffer the motion sickness I felt on the train when we first left Tatvan.

Port Said was a thriving international community with inhabitants from all religions and nationalities. It was built out of thin air by Vicomte Ferdinand de Lesseps only fifty years before as the entrance to the Suez Canal. Like Constantinople, the city straddles the border of two continents with Asia on the East. Unlike the Ottoman capital, Port Said has Africa to the west.

The Suez Canal cut more than four thousand miles off the journey from the Atlantic to Indian ocean. The feat caused such a change to the world market, that it contributed to the economic depression of the 1870s. Prices plummeted instantly, depreciating the value of those goods stored in warehouses throughout western Europe. Merchants who had bought high, had to sell low. Fortunately I was not around at the time.

The Canal was considered a neutral zone by the Treaty of Constantinople and open to ships of all countries, even during times of war. It was protected by the British and thus far there had been no attempts by the Ottomans to take control.

The HMS Invincible was to remain on patrol in the Eastern Mediterranean, so I was escorted to an empty Royal Dutch Shell oil tanker that was waiting its turn to make the one hundred twenty mile journey south to the Red Sea.

The sun was only an hour above the horizon but already I could feel the familiar heat of September. As we walked the docks I congratulated myself on the decision to change out of my western attire and in to my flowing robes. Not only would they be more comfortable, they would help me blend in with the locals. That is once I left my naval escort behind.

"You must be Sayed Kashani" the English captain of the tanker said as he welcomed me aboard. "I have received orders from chairman Deterding that you are to be his honored guest while aboard. You are close friends with Sir Henri?"

"I am surprised he even remembers me" I said, truly baffled by the welcome. "I only met him once. Calouste Gulbenkian introduced us while we were having tea at the Ritz."

"So you are friends with Mister five Percent as well. I see I am in the company of a true oil man."

I decided there was not much to be gained by setting this man straight so I allowed him to think what he wanted. I followed him to the bridge of the ship which provided a wonderful view of the canal in front of us and the eruption of activity on the deck below as our ship was released from its moorings.

"The canal has only one shipping lane" the captain commented. "Ships are arranged into three convoys a day, two travelling south and one north. We're in the first group and will pass the north-bound convoy in the Great Bitter Lake."

"How long will it take?" I asked.

"We make eight knots throughout the passage and should arrive at the Red Sea in a little over twelve hours with the current tidal flows."

"And from there we set out immediately to Abadan, or will we put in somewhere else first?"

"We took on supplies when we docked here in Port Said."

The captain led me over to a map table and pointed down to our current position.

"It's only two and half days to transit the Red Sea and into the Gulf of Aden at French Somaliland here" he said as traced his finger on the map. "Another two and half days to the Strait of Hormuz and into the Persian Gulf."

"Abadan should be less than a day from there" I ventured, estimating the relative distance remaining from there.

"Not a bad guess" answered the captain. "We usually plan six days all told from the time we leave the Mediterranean."

If we arrived early morning at Abadan I thought to myself, I would have time to find a boat heading up the Shatt al-Arab waterway to Mohammerah and from there to the Karun River to the Palace before nightfall.

"Captain, are you aware of any U-Boat activity along our route?"

I could tell from his sudden change in expression that I had struck a sore subject.

"Not this far south" he replied, "and they have yet to attack a civilian vessel. The admiralty has warned us to be on the lookout in the Med and especially the Atlantic and to report any sightings."

"I guess you have more to fear on the return trip" I said.

"Why is that?" he asked.

"Because you will be fully loaded" I replied. "Greater economic damage."

"*In Sha Allah* that will not happen to one of my boats."

"You speak Arabic captain?"

"I am a sea captain" he chortled. "I know how to pray to God in more than a dozen languages."

A waste of time no matter what language I thought to myself.

A crew member called the captain away as we were towed into the channel by a tug and took up our position near the front of the convoy. I kept out of the way and watched the teamwork of the captain and his men maneuver the ship through the entrance to the canal. After only a few minutes the captain turned the helm over to his first mate and returned to my side.

"Take a look Sayed, the view will be exactly the same for the rest of the day. Barren land to the left and right with the pilot boat out in front. Let me show you to your quarters and then to the mess hall. We'll have a bite to eat."

My English had been getting stronger every day after arriving in London, but nothing had prepared me for the terms used aboard ship. When I was invited to the *mess* aboard the battle cruiser, I thought for a moment I was being asked to clean something up. I also learned that one could drink port while looking through the port hole on the port side of the ship as it was sailing into the next port of call. English was indeed very confusing.

The captain proved to be a gracious host. I dined with him for most of my meals during the six day journey. I was called to the bridge several times during the journey. The first time as we passed into the Red Sea and again the following day.

When I joined the captain the second time, he pointed off to the eastern horizon to a large port city.

"Jeddah" he said, "the gateway to Mecca. From our current position you are less than seventy miles from the holy city."

He gave me a pair of binoculars which made the city of Jeddah seem within an arm's length of the ship. As I was taking in the view I heard the Captain bark a command.

"All ahead slow Mister Johansen"

"All ahead slow Captain" the first mate repeated and immediately I felt the ship slowing down.

"Is everything alright Captain?" I asked.

He pointed off the starboard bow to a motor yacht making good time across the water on an intercept course with our ship. I brought up the binoculars in that direction and saw a light haired young man wearing a western suit, standing in the bow with his hands grasping the rail.

"I got a message on the wireless from the home office that we would be taking on another passenger."

The incoming boat changed course to come along side as a long cargo net was thrown over the side.

"He's not actually planning to climb aboard that way is he?" I asked.

"If he wants to come aboard he is" the captain replied. "He's lucky I agreed to slow down."

"Mister Johansen once he clears the railing all ahead full."

"Aye Captain"

I wondered how difficult it was to climb a cargo net up the side of a moving ship this size and why it was so important that this new passenger come aboard.

"All ahead full Captain" the first mate called out as the young man's head popped up over the railing.

Two crew members helped him up and over and began pulling back the cargo net as the ship slowly regained speed. I tried to get a good look at the young man with the binoculars but he was gone. In fact, that was the last I saw of him on the ship. He didn't dine with us or spend time with the rest of the crew. If I hadn't seen him climb aboard I would have never known we had a new passenger.

The remainder of the trip was spent reading a book I found in the ship's tiny library and playing whist with the crew. My luck was just as good as before so I won a little spending money, but limited my wins so as not to make any enemies.

Just after breakfast on the sixth day the tanker docked at the refinery in Abadan to take on its liquid cargo. As expected, I would have plenty of time to make the short trip to Moham-merah before the sunset made travel more difficult.

Prior to leaving my cabin, I took out the Webley Mk1 from my trunk and strapped on the shoulder holster. I made sure the gun was fully loaded and that the safety was on before putting on my outer robe. While I didn't expect any trouble, river bandits were a common problem in this area, especially for travelers like me.

What I did not expect as I disembarked was the familiar face I saw on the dock. There dressed in the typical Bakhtiari knee length cassock with white sash belt and rounded felt hat was my fellow comrade from the revolution.

"Commander Assad!" I exclaimed in Persian. "How did you know I was on my way?"

"Good news travels fast my friend. We received a cable from Cairo last week announcing your visit and confirming your arrival this morning."

Commander Assad looked over my shoulder and scanned the docks before returning his gaze to me.

"Where is your nephew?" he asked. "I assumed he would be with you."

"Still in London. He's working for Calouste and pining for his new lady."

"Khalil in love?" he said with a smile. "How wonderful! Is she a good match?"

"A perfect match" I replied. "But not a good situation. She is a nurse and is now serving at the front in France."

As a career military officer, Commander Assad knew what that meant.

"Well let's hope it is the will of Allah that she will find her way back to a long and happy life with our Khalil."

A porter loaded my travelling case on to a small cart as we began walking away from the ship.

"I have one of the Emir's motor yachts moored just over there. It will be a short ride up to Qasr al-Failiyah palace."

"Does he know why I am here?" I asked, also wanting to know if Assad knew as well.

"He has some idea. The British Consul came down from Ahvaz yesterday for a private meeting. It seems you impressed Winston Churchill in London, but I thought Paris was your final destination."

The way he said it made it sound more like a question.

"As did I" I replied. "The war changed all of that."

"How is Amir?" I asked changing the subject.

"He is well, but still up to no good if I am reading the situation correctly. He has continued his association with Heir Wassmuss even though the Emir has decided to support Britain and expressly forbidden him to work with the Germans."

"Is Wilhelm here in Khuzestan?"

"He met with Amir last week in the south at Bushehr. After he returned from the meeting, the prince said he wouldn't be surprised to see the boy genius again soon. This was just about the same time the Emir received word of your arrival."

I had not considered that I might already be under surveillance again. In fact, once we left Budapest, I thought I was free of that burden. More likely the Germans intercepted the telegram from Cairo to Emir Khazal.

"I have received reports of him as far east as Shiraz" Assad continued, "and other reports that say he is in Najaf on his way to Karbala."

"I wouldn't be surprised to find him in Karbala. When I leave here I am hoping to see if my cousin is still in residence there" I said.

"You met with Wassmuss in Constantinople as planned?" Assad asked.

"As *he* had planned" I clarified. "His plans backfired somewhat though. We met with the Sultan who then ordered me to Karbala straight away to offer a partnership with my cousin."

"But you continued on to Paris and London. So you expressly disobeyed the Sultan of the Ottoman Empire."

"It's a long story and Wassmuss was complicit in the plan as well. What's important to me now is to finish my business here, find my cousin, and get home to my family. Speaking of which, you said you received word from Cairo. Does the Emir have a telegraph in the Palace?"

"Yes he does."

"Can you help me send word to my wife that I have arrived safely back in Persia?"

"I can certainly help send a message, but I suggest you say that you arrived in Khuzestan. The Emir believes this to be a special zone due to its mix of Arab and Persian population."

"Which is no doubt reinforced by his direct relationship with Britain" I said under my breath.

"Precisely" Assad said. "And the wealth generated by the oil fields and refinery have made him the richest Sheik in all of greater Arabia."

I wondered if the Shah or the members of the Majlis knew the true extent of the disparity in cash flow from the oil concessions.

We arrived at the motor boat and headed up the river. It was too noisy to carry on a conversation and I was glad for the opportunity to think through what I had learned. I only had a few hours with the Emir before I moved on to the meeting with Abol-Ghasem and had to establish an alliance with Khazal before I could make an offer to my cousin. There was no room for error in the next few hours.

We passed by the docks of the city of Mohammerah and turned up the Karun river another six miles to the Palace, a grand two story building with soaring arches across the front and two towers on either end. Three tall flag poles adorned the roof looking more like the masts on a sailing ship with all of the additional ropes and riggings. Small flags and bunting adorned all available space giving the Palace a festive air. As we drew closer a cargo boat passing by in the opposite direction sounded his horn.

"Is there some celebration today?" I asked.

"No. You will find most of the larger vessels salute the Emir as they pass by the Palace. He is loved by the people of Khuzestan. They sound their horns out of respect."

"Loved?"

"Oh yes. He is truly a great leader. He makes quite a bit from the oil concessions but he has shared the wealth throughout the land. Business is thriving up and down the Karun, from Abadan up to Ahvaz. He holds court four or five times per week and knows the private business of every prominent family in the Emirate. He has settled quarrels between Sheiks and their families and eliminated the violence between tribes. They all come to him as arbiter instead of fighting."

I had been told in my briefings to expect a flamboyant ladies man who enjoyed parties and having a good time. Khazal Kaabi was reported to be a collector of automobiles, yachts, and beautiful women, not a wise leader of the people. Could both of these stories be true?

"I was under the impression he was a rich playboy" I ventured.

Commander Assad laughed from deep down in his belly. "That he is! Which makes his ability to govern and the way he cares for his people even more impressive."

"I can't wait to meet him then" I said as we pulled up to a dock behind an enormous yacht.

"Well you won't have to wait long. I will have your trunk sent up to your room. The Emir insists you stay in the palace while you are here. You and I will be joining today's audience in progress."

We disembarked and made our way down the dock to an awaiting automobile. I had never seen this type before and wished that Khalil was with me to enjoy it. After a short ride to the palace proper we entered through a side door and moments later found ourselves just inside a large throne room filled with people.

A dozen Sheiks stood along the front of the room with Emir Khazal Kaabi seated in a rather ordinary chair just in front. The Emir was dressed in a military style tunic, complete with epaulets, a white and red striped sash crossing his body, and several large medals pinned to his chest. He wore knee high riding boots over his riding pants. His beard was closely cropped and his moustache trimmed into an imperial style with just the slightest hint of handles on the ends.

A woman with a child stood in front at a respectable distance away pleading her case. I couldn't understand what she was saying and guessed that she was speaking a Lurish dialect. The Emir listened intently and asked her a few questions in that same dialect. After her last answer he raised his hand and turned to a sheik who was standing on his right. A conversation ensued and then suddenly the Emir cut him off with another gesture with his hand.

From the reaction of the woman and child, they seemed to have prevailed. She rushed to the Emir's throne and kissed his hand before taking up her child and rushing out of the room.

The next supplicant approached from the rear of the room. He appeared to be a white man in a western business suit.

"Doctor Van Ess it is so good to see you again!" the Emir said in flawless English.

"Your Excellency! Thank you for seeing me."

Commander Assad leaned towards me and spoke quietly in my ear.

"This is John Van Ess, a missionary and founder of a western high school in the area."

"I understand the new term is now under way with a record class Doctor Van Ess."

"Yes. Yes, we are blessed to have grown our class size quite a bit in Basra and even more in Mohammerah, with your help Excellency."

The man spoke English, but not with the same accent as I heard in England.

"It is only fitting that we provide our sons with a proper education is it not? Now we do not have to send them off to boarding school in Europe. Especially desirable with the outbreak of war."

"Yes Excellency. Our timing was quite fortunate."

"American?" I whispered in Assad's ear.

He nodded yes.

"So how can we help you today Doctor Van Ess?"

"I have come to announce that my wife has just opened a school for girls in Basra and that we are accepting applications."

I could hear a collective gasp from the audience in the room then a smile slowly form on the face of the Emir.

"When did you first come to our lands Doctor?"

"I have been here for twelve years now."

"You are aware it is not our custom to educate our daughters?"

"I am aware your excellency" he replied with little enthusiasm.

"But you would like to change that custom?"

"Yes Excellency, I would."

A collective murmur erupted from those in attendance and I could see several of the Sheiks behind the Emir quietly consulting with one another.

"Quiet please" the Emir said with a calm voice and the room again fell silent.

"Your Excellency, I have learned much about your culture, but after consulting with several Islamic scholars in Bagdad, I learned there is nothing in Islamic law to prohibit the teaching of women. In fact, during the eighth century in the Abbasid Caliphate it is written that 'women became renowned for their brains as well as their beauty.' Many women of that time were trained from childhood in Poetry, Music, and Dance. The greatest example of her time was a slave girl called Tawaddud, who was bought by Harun al-Rashid because she had possessed great knowledge of astronomy, medicine, law…"

"And chess" the Emir interrupted. "Tawaddud was said to be a grand master of the game of Chess."

"You know the story of Tawaddud Your Excellency?"

"Certainly. You did not think I became Emir of Mohammerah

simply by virtue of my handsome face did you?"

The room broke out in laughter, the humor having the effect I guessed the Emir was hoping for.

When my gaze returned to the Emir I noticed he was looking in my direction.

"Doctor Van Ess" he continued turning back towards the doctor. "I for one will be happy to enroll my brightest daughters in your wife's new school on one condition."

"Certainly. What is the condition?"

"That this new school is kept separate from the boys school and my daughters are to have no interaction with the boys. For the Quran also says of women 'Abide in your houses and do not display yourselves as was the display of the former times of ignorance'."

There was a murmur of agreement across the room. I wasn't quite sure what his quote had to do with education, since one had to leave the house to buy food in the market as well. And if I was not mistaken, that particular verse was addressed specifically to the wives of the Prophet going into public, not to women in general. Only scholars of the Quran would know that though and any quote at all from that book would do when an Emir is making a point.

"Doctor Van Ess, we should discuss this further tonight over dinner. I am throwing a small party for a new friend who has traveled a long way to be here with us today."

"Of course Excellency. It will be my pleasure."

With that the Emir stood up causing everyone seated in the room to do the same.

Khazal turned to speak with a few of the Sheiks as the room cleared. Moments later there were only a few people left trying to get a word with Emir. Commander Assad and I waited patiently while the final subjects were herded away by the Emir's staff.

"I am sorry to keep you waiting Sayed Kashani" the Emir said in Persian as he crossed the room toward us. "I trust your journey was uneventful?"

"Your Excellency it is my honor to meet you" I replied.

"Let's dispense with the formalities Kashani-Agha, I believe you have met with leaders well above my status on the world stage during this journey of yours. Mohammerah is a humble backwater when compared to Britain, France, and the Ottoman empire. And I am certainly no Sultan or Prime Minister of a world power."

I was not surprised that he knew of my meetings in London and Constantinople. His meeting with the British Consul and connections with Wassmuss explained London and my encounter with the Sultan. Did he know I met with the French Prime Minister at the Masonic Lodge in Paris and if so how?

"As you wish" I said simply. "May I ask if your grandson is well?"

"As well as can be expected I suppose. I have lately clipped his wings to protect him from his own blind ambition... and his petty jealousies. Speaking of which, is your nephew not accompanying you? I was hoping to meet the young man who so frustrated my Amir."

"My nephew has remained in London and has taken a job with Calouste Gulbenkian."

"Excellent! Good for him. A lot of money to be made in oil. Just the thing for a bright young man."

Khazal turned toward Commander Assad.

"Thank you for fetching my guest Commander. Could you ask my assistant to ensure that Doctor Van Ess will join us this evening. I will drive *Aghayeh* Kashani back to the dock so we can discuss business over lunch on my yacht."

Assad bowed slightly and accepted his dismissal without a word.

"Let's go shall we" the Emir said as he gestured to the door.

The automobile that Assad drove was no longer outside. I followed Khazal around the side of the palace to a large building located behind the main house. It seemed at first to be a residence of some kind, but as we drew near I heard the sounds of horses.

"This building is home to two of my greatest passions" Khazal said as we approached. "Horses and automobiles. I designed it after the Royal Mews at Buckingham Palace."

I saw a groomsman leading a fine Arabian stallion out of the building and into the fenced area in front. Khazal made a bee line through the gate and straight to the animal. He stroked its head and began speaking to him in Arabic the way a father would to a young child.

"This is my favorite and my finest stud."

The Emir turned to the groomsman and said a few words in a dialect I did not understand before giving the horse one last stroke.

"Let me show you my latest acquisition" he said with an almost childish glee.

We walked into the building and turned down the long central corridor. The first stalls held more horses, but halfway down open parking spaces replaced the stalls and a collection of automobiles replaced the horses.

Khazal approached a space on the left and placed his hand on the bonnet in almost the same loving manner he had used to stroke the horse just moments ago.

"This is a Morris Oxford Bullnose. It has a 1018 cc four-cylinder side-valve engine, which I admit is small, but provides plenty of power for a two-seater."

The vehicle was quite beautiful, even for someone like me who is not an enthusiast. The radiator and head lamps were polished brass. The body was painted a light grey color with the fenders painted a shiny black. The top was down revealing just enough seating for two people.

"It is marvelous" I said. "Beautiful."

Khazal was beaming like a proud new father.

"Let's take this one up to the docks."

We climbed in and Khazal fired up the engine. He slowly maneuvered out of the space and through the double doors of the building. As we approached the road the Emir suddenly turned right instead of left towards the docks.

"Aren't the Docks behind us?" I asked.

"You wouldn't be able to fully appreciate the ride if we went straight to the boat."

He was grinning from ear to ear as he faced forward and accelerated onto the narrow lane. By the time he changed into third gear it seemed like we were flying. I held on for dear life as he rounded curves and crested small rises in the road. We came close to hitting a heard of sheep at one point and slowed only a little as we crossed over a small stream splashing water in all directions. The next thing I knew we were sliding to a stop in front of his yacht with the car spinning one hundred eighty degrees on the wet grass.

"Do you want to take a turn *Aghayeh* Kashani?"

I tried to speak and decline his generous offer, but I was breathing so hard and still in shock so I simply shook my head no.

"Maybe on the way back then" he said as he casually climbed down to the ground.

It took me a little longer to alight and regain my balance on the solid ground.

The crew seemed to know that we were on our way. Everyone seemed to be at their station and everything was at the ready for an immediate departure.

We cast off from the dock and headed up river toward Ahvaz as we made ourselves comfortable at a teak wood table set up on a wide open deck at the rear. Even though the crew was scurrying all around us, this spot proved to be a quiet, peaceful setting for a private conversation.

I was pleased to see a glass of water and took a long drink before sitting down. It was enough to calm my nerves.

"Winston Churchill asked me to give this to you" I said as I handed over a sealed envelope to the Emir.

He opened the letter and read it twice before sitting back in his chair and staring at me for a long while.

"You really are a mystery to me Aghayeh Kashani. I had never heard of you until Amir returned from Van. So I had my people in Tehran do a little investigating and now I wonder how you have been able to keep such a low profile for so long."

"I am a simple merchant Excellency. I served my country when it needed me and was content to leave politics to other more ambitious men."

"Was?" he asked.

"I'm sorry?" I replied.

"You said you *were* content... which implies you are no longer willing to leave politics to the others."

A small slip of the tongue and he picked up on it immediately. I needed to be more careful.

"I was offered a seat in the Majlis after the revolution, but I never felt I had the stomach for politics."

"So what has changed?"

I sat back in my chair and thought about how I would answer that question for a while.

"It has been more than five years since we gained a voice in our country's future. During that time I left the hard work of governing to other men. I have recently come to realize that the revolution was the easy part. Establishing a system of government appropriate for Persia is much more difficult than I had originally thought. We must eradicate the parasites that feed off of the men of the Bazaar and the people that actually do the work. There should be no ruling class. The working class are perfectly capable of representing themselves. I may not have the right answers, but I believe it's time I shoulder my share of the work."

The Emir laughed.

"You may not have the stomach for politics, but your mouth seems to be naturally suited for it."

"It's my mouth that often gets me into trouble" I said.

"Changing the Status Quo always brings trouble. It is part of the process."

We sat in silence, staring out at the other boats on the waterway. The Karun river was the major transportation route for Khuzestan province, connecting the capital in the north to the Persian Gulf at Abadan. Horns continued to sound occasionally as the larger boats passed the Palace just downstream.

"What do you know about the offer they are making to me?" the Emir asked finally breaking the silence.

"None of the details really. I know how important the flow of oil from Mohammerah is to the British Navy. So I know they are willing to send troops to protect that interest. I know that the Germans would like that oil for themselves and if that's not possible to prevent it from reaching Britain. They will destroy the refinery and pipeline if they can't take the oil. And I know that Calouste Gulbenkian believes there is just as much oil if not more at Kirkuk, just waiting to be discovered. As soon as this war is over, they will find it and double the output from this region."

"May I ask a blunt but critical question?" the Emir asked.

"Certainly" I replied. "I prefer to be direct."

"Where do your loyalties lie? How much of your soul did you sell to the British?"

This question was more direct than I had anticipated and one I have been asking myself off and on for the past few weeks. If I hadn't heard from Commander Assad that the people of Mohammerah loved this man and hadn't seen for myself the way he conducted the audience earlier, I would have been more cautious with my answer. Whitehall said I could trust him as well and I certainly didn't have time to develop a relationship with the Emir, so I had to make a quick decision.

"My loyalties lie with Persia and my children's future. As for my soul... I have made no promises to Britain that would endanger my afterlife, although my cousin may disagree. Like you, I have received assurances of support. So when my priorities and theirs align I will do what I can."

The Emir looked me in the eye and then turned his attention to the boats out on the river before replying.

"It seems we share some of the same challenges... and attitudes. Mohammerah is rich and my people are happy because I made the agreement with D'Arcy and Anglo Persian Oil years ago. I cannot un-ring the bell as the lawyers say without severe consequences. All of my decisions going forward are now effectively limited by that choice."

"Persia has so far remained neutral" I said, "but you have publically declared support for the Allies. The Shah must not be too happy with that."

I knew this was a touchy subject, but his answer would help me determine next steps.

"We are a long way from Tehran, both in distance and in culture. We have more Arabs living here than any other part of Persia. Bakhtiari, Lurs and Afshar. The majority of my people are Shia but a strong minority and most of my family are

Sunni. I don't have a unified province here, I have a loose collection of minorities."

What started as an explanation quickly escalated into a rant. The frustration in his voice was evident but so was the anger. It was the first evidence I saw of how dangerous this man could be.

"I am more a Sheik of Sheiks than the Governor of a Province. How am I supposed to enforce laws made six hundred miles away by a group of ethnic Persians beholden to the Shiite clerics? The mullahs are just biding their time, waiting for a chance to turn that country into an Islamic Republic ruled by a Grand Ayatollah. Your cousin Abol-Ghasem would have no compunction about becoming the supreme leader. Is that preferable to an alliance with the most powerful country on earth?"

"I do not envy your position" I said. "And I share your concerns about my cousin and the mullahs. Persia must become a modern secular society that is tolerant of all religions and ethnic backgrounds. I will do what I can to make that a reality. Khuzestan is a microcosm of Persia as a whole. Perhaps you can be the example that helps us find our way."

I saw something change in his eyes. He was no longer angry. There was a tinge of curiosity there.

"I have heard that you openly disobeyed both the Sultan and your cousin" Khazal said. "With the help of Wilhelm Wassmuss."

I remembered my conversation when I first met Calouste in Van. He was also confused by the company I kept.

"I am no friend of the Germans, especially Wassmuss. He approached me in Tehran and Abol-Ghasem asked me to hear him out. It was Wassmuss who arranged the meeting with the Sultan. He was taken by surprise when the Sultan ordered me to Karbala to negotiate with my cousin. For a brief moment our priorities aligned and so I accepted his help."

"And you have not seen Wassmuss since your left Constantinople?"

"Correct. I heard from Commander Assad that he was sighted in Bushehr but may also be in Najaf. I am hoping he is in the South so I will not have to deal with him."

"What are your plans from here?"

"Before I return home to Tehran I need to confront my cousin and convince him not to cooperate with the Ottomans and Germany. "

"Do you have any alternative to offer him?" Khazal asked, his interest seemingly piqued.

"Did the letter I carried to you mention anything about the plan that Sir Mark Sykes has proposed?"

"No, but I have heard rumors of an independent country ruled by the Hashemite Family. Can you confirm this?"

I thought back to the meeting I had with Churchill and tried to recall if they ever asked me to keep the plan secret. After a moment of thought I realized they did not. Sharing a few of the details might accelerate my primary objective for this visit.

"You are hearing about a plan that is still in its early stages" I replied, "and has not been formalized or even presented to the French government. Churchill asked for my opinion and I shared my concerns about the Sharif's son governing a multiethnic society of Shia and Sunni and Kurds. I told him it would take a skilled ruler to govern such a country."

I saw the smile form on his face as he realized I understood what he lived every day. I also knew he had a better alternative in mind to the Sharif of Mecca.

"Exactly my friend! Exactly! I believe you and I would make a good team Sayed Kashani. Mesopotamia needs a skilled ruler who has experience governing a coalition of minorities, who understands how to share oil profits with his people, and who knows how to maintain the British at arm's length while still reaping the benefits of their protection. You will need friends in the South and West to support your political career. If you can provide cover for me back in the Majlis, I can give you that support and we can execute our plan before anyone knows what is happening."

The bait had been offered and taken. Now the tricky part of the game began.

"I see what you are suggesting Excellency and I believe you are right. Abol-Ghasem cannot support the infidel Germans if he has a faithful follower of Islam as a viable alternative."

"He will want clear control over Najaf and Karbala" the Emir said.

"And a share of the oil revenues to support the spread of the Shia faith" I added.

"Which he will have once we take control over western Mesopotamia and tap in to the oilfields of Kirkuk."

"If there is truly oil to be found" I replied.

"Oh there is oil my friend. I am sure of that. My people have been secretly exploring the region for the past two years and establishing relationships with the local Turkmen and Kurdish leaders. We have identified at least five likely locations to drill test sites."

Khazal was now sharing information that MI6 did not have yet and confirming that our plan was the right one.

"Give me the afternoon to draft a proposal for your cousin" he continued. "Then you can be on your way tomorrow morning to Karbala and deliver it to him."

Khazal called for food and wine to celebrate our deal. There was no more talk of strategy, only tales of the Emir's exploits with horses, cars, and women. So far the dossier on Khazal from C and his team had been right on the money.

I sat back in my chair and relaxed. Step one seemed to be a

success. Now I just had to keep up appearances and prepare for the meeting I was truly dreading in Karbala.

We docked once again at the palace just after noon. I was pleased to find the Emir had other business in a nearby village so he drove off in the Morris Oxford and handed me off to a servant who showed me back to the Palace and my room. I was able to rest most of the afternoon and ventured out only as the guests were arriving for the dinner party.

As I entered the large ball room I found Commander Assad and Amir speaking to Doctor Van Ess.

"Kashani-Agha? What a surprise!" Amir said when I approached. From the expression on his face he truly had no idea I was in Mohammerah.

"Your Highness" I said simply.

"Commander" Amir said, "did you know Kashani-Agha would be joining us tonight?"

"Yes Highness. I escorted him to the Palace, but your Grandfather asked me to keep the visit quiet until they had a chance to speak."

The look on the young man's face was priceless. It was obvious he was not accustomed to be left in the dark. Then his countenance changed completely and he suddenly surveyed the room.

"Khalil did not join me" I responded, anticipating his next question.

He looked relieved for a moment and then seemed to realize that we were watching.

"That's too bad" he lied. "I was looking forward to seeing him again."

Doctor Van Ess had been waiting patiently to be introduced and finally could wait no more. He offered his hand to me and introduced himself.

"Kashani-Agha I am John Van Ess" he said in Persian.

"Doctor Van Ess" I responded in kind. "It is a pleasure to meet you. I was at the audience this morning and heard the news about your wife's new school for girls. Congratulations."

"We expect it will be a long hard road" he said.

"Very likely. I wish you success. We need to educate our women if they are ever to fully participate in society."

"That is an attitude shared by very few of your peers in the Arab world" Van Ess said.

"I like to think we Persians are a little more progressive than our Arab neighbors."

I could tell by the look on their faces that Amir and Assad did not share my sentiments, but were both holding the comments in respect to the Emir's decision.

"Speaking of Islamic customs and law, how is your cousin Ayatollah Kashani?" Amir asked with a smirk on his face.

"I haven't seen him in months" I replied honestly, "but I hear he is in Karbala and since I have never done the pilgrimage to the Imam Husain and Abbas Mosques…"

"Isn't it more common to visit on the day of Ashura?" Doctor Van Ess asked. "or on Arba?"

"You are familiar with Shia customs?" Commander Assad asked.

"Certainly" Van Ess replied. "How can I relate to people if I know nothing of their beliefs and culture?"

"A refreshing attitude Doctor" I replied. "To be very honest, I am not a religious man. So I would not fit in with the self-flagellating crowds that pack the streets during the month of Muharram. I'm just being practical. I may never find myself so close to Najaf and Karbala again."

"If you are *en route* to Karbala then perhaps you will travel with me to Basra tomorrow and share a meal with my family."

I had not yet planned the next stage of my journey, although I knew I would have to make my way back to the Shatt al-Arab waterway and from there up to the Euphrates river.

"I would be honored" I replied.

"I understand you took the Orient Express to Paris" Amir said. "So I guess Khalil got to spend plenty of time with Gertrude Bell."

Amir seemed intent on showing how much he knew about my journey after being caught by surprise.

"Gertrude was called back to London as soon as we reached Constantinople, so she and Picot left a few days ahead of us."

"You know Gertrud Bell?" Doctor Van Ess asked.

"Yes" I replied. "In fact, she introduced my nephew Khalil to his fiancée in Paris."

"Well then you *must* travel with me to Basra. Gertrude is an old friend of the family and I would love to hear what she has been up to these past few months.

Amir rolled his eyes, evidently disappointed in the way the conversation had gone.

We were called to dinner then and to my good fortune, Amir and Commander Assad were seated at the far end of the table while Doctor Van Ess and I were seated across from the Emir near the center.

"There is another piece of news that I did not have a chance to share with you earlier Excellency" Doctor Van Ess said in a low voice to the Emir.

"I have been appointed as the American Consul to the Ottoman Empire in Basra."

"Congratulations" the Emir said warmly. "I trust this will not adversely impact your teaching responsibilities."

"I don't believe so. In fact, it is only a temporary assignment and thus far my duties have been quite light. I bring this up because I have begun meeting with a very different class of people lately, friends of yours from Ahvaz and Cairo, so I wanted to ensure you knew the reason behind it."

"Yes. I see" the Emir said between bites. "That would have been curious had I not known of your new role already. Arnold Wilson paid me a visit a few days ago and told me the news."

"How is Captain Wilson?" Van Ess asked. "I haven't seen him for ages."

"He is well. Still working much too hard and trying to change the world singlehandedly."

Van Ess turned to me and said "Arnold is with the India Political Department, a political officer, and another close friend of Gertrude Bell."

"He is someone you should get to know Sayed" the Emir said to me. "You share many of the same opinions on ruling a multi-cultural society although he does not agree with me on independence. He believes Britain should rule Iraq like they do India, with an iron fist.

"He is also well acquainted with the entire operation at Anglo Persian Oil" Van Ess added. "He lead the team of Bengal Lancers sent to guard Masjid-i-Suleiman when George Reynolds struck oil. Gertrude calls him the 'epitome of a British Oriental Secretary'."

"I expect before too long the Captain will rise even higher in the ranks" the Emir continued. "Perhaps one day he may be the successor to Sir Percy Cox himself. He could even become the very model of a modern major general."

Van Ess laughed heartily at the last comment.

"I didn't know you were a fan of Gilbert and Sullivan?"

"Oh yes! Pirates of Penzance especially" the Emir relied.

I had no idea what they were talking about so I replied as best I could.

"I look forward to meeting him."

We enjoyed several courses of local dishes which made me realize just how long it had been since I had eaten Persian food. It had been months since I tasted perfectly cooked saffron rice. No matter how much I liked French and Turkish cuisine, nothing could compare to the dishes of one's childhood.

The conversations turned toward news from the war and speculation about the Ottoman response. Thus far they had not declared war on Britain but everyone was sure it was simply a matter of time.

Van Ess offered his opinion on any and every topic we discussed, a trait I learned over time that was typical of Americans. The Emir was very guarded in his responses, never quite committing to a firm stance on any topic. I felt I knew less about him after hearing this conversation than I knew before.

By the end of the evening I was exhausted and ready to sleep in a real bed on dry land for the first time in weeks. I thanked the Emir for his hospitality and agreed to meet Van Ess after breakfast for the short Journey up river to Basra.

Before I could leave the table though, the Emir took out a sealed envelope from his robe and handed it to me.

"For your cousin" he leaned in and said quietly. "And please be careful. Once you leave Khuzestan I am afraid you will find yourself in dangerous territory. Both the enemy you can see and the enemy you cannot."

BASRA

T he following morning after breakfast, I walked with Doctor Van Ess to the Palace Docks and boarded his small motorboat. With its humble canvass awning and stained cloth seats, It was not quite a yacht, but not quite a traditional fishing boat either. I was relieved to see my Louis Vuitton trunk secured near the front, placed there by servants while we were having breakfast.

The modest boat did provide a comfortable ride. The first part of the journey was familiar as we retraced the route I took the previous day. Once in to the main river though we turned up stream for the short ride into Basra.

The river was broad here and the traffic heavier as this was the main shipping route for cities on both the Tigris and Euphrates for hundreds of miles to the north. The waterway here also acted as the border between Persia and the Ottoman Arabian territories, and by convention, the line cut right down the center of the channel.

As I scanned the river I noticed a two hundred foot long warship off our stern flying British colors. I tried to focus my eyes to the distance and counted what appeared to be at least ten large guns.

Van Ess saw this as well and leaned in close to me.

"HMS Odin" he shouted of the noise of the motors. "Just arrived from Bahrain to protect the refinery."

I turned and shook my head to acknowledge that I had heard when I saw a small gunboat off of our port bow flying Ottoman flags. While the Odin was not a full dreadnaught, it dwarfed the smaller gunship and with its long guns, could fire on the smaller boat from its current distance while the smaller Turkish guns would barely be able to hit our boat.

It was then I realized we were right in the cross fire if they decided to test each other.

I pointed out the gunboat to the Doctor who had the pilot steer a course out of harm's way. A few minutes later I saw that the Odin was making for the dock at Mohammerah on the Persian side while the Ottoman gunboat was steering well towards the Ottoman side of the river. Just another day on patrol.

As we neared the city proper the boat slowed and we changed course into a small tributary. Van Ess leaned close to make himself heard over the engine noise.

"This is Ashar Creek" he said. "We're almost home."

The narrow waterway was suddenly tangled with boats of all shapes and sizes, from small canoe-like craft to high prow transports capable of venturing into the open sea. People and pack animals were everywhere, moving all at once, each to their own pace and purpose. Boxes and bags of cargo were being unloaded onto rickety docks and sometimes onto the muddy riverbank. The smells were just as varied as the sights and many of them unpleasant.

Ten foot tall brick embankments lined both sides of the waterway. Steps spaced every hundred feet or so provided an escape up from the riverbank to the row of warehouses on one side and coffee houses on the other. From this vantage point the cafes seemed packed to capacity with men calmly smoking their hookahs and occasionally sipping coffee from small cups. They were almost frozen in time compared to the activity on the river.

The pilot cut the engines on the boat as we glided towards the café side of the river and softly bottomed out near the bank.

"Welcome to Basra Sayed Kashani" Doctor Van Ess said as I stepped carefully off the side of the boat and on to the riverbank.

We called for a porter to help with my trunk. Doctor Van Ess gave him instructions on where to deliver it and paid him in the local currency.

"One less item to worry about" he said as we labored up the closest stone stairway and out onto the street.

We headed down an alley way between shops and on to a broad packed dirt street with not a cobble in site. The buildings were constructed from crude bricks that appeared to have been made from the same clay found on the riverbank. The whole scene was a monotone color of café au lait. The people on the street were mostly Arab with their dusty robes and distinctive *keffiyeh* headdress held in place by a simple piece of rope. I saw very few men wearing a Turkish fez, even though we were officially in Ottoman territory.

Windows on the street level lacked any glazing, replaced with simple iron bars that let in the breeze, along with dust and insects. Upper floor windows were open as well with simple shutters that hinged from the top and were propped open with a stick of wood from the bottom. The contrast with London and Paris made me understand why the British and French viewed this region as barbaric and backward.

As I turned to survey the street something caught my eye. Someone wearing a Bakhtiari white sash around a dark cassock and white felt hat was standing at the mouth of the alley we just emerged from. Just as we made eye contact the man disappeared into the front of the coffee shop. There was something familiar about him but it was only a split second before he was out of sight.

Only Bakhtiari tribal leaders wear white hats, so that limited the possibilities to someone who was likely with me at the palace last night.

My MI6 training kicked in then and I quickly scanned the other side of the street looking for another potential tail. I needed to know if I was being followed by an individual or a team. I also reached in to my robe to feel for the grip of the Webley Mk1 secured in my shoulder holster.

"It's not much" Doctor Van Ess said, "but it's home".

"How far to the school?" I asked.

"Not that far, but too far to walk. The streets are not very sanitary either so I prefer to ride."

The Doctor called out to a man with a donkey cart who pulled forward and stopped in front of us. The cart was fitted with two backward facing seats for passengers. Again I was reminded of the contrast with the horse drawn handsome cabs in London and just laughed softly to myself.

"Welcome home" I said.

"What was that?" Van Ess asked?

"Nothing important" I replied as I climbed aboard the donkey cart and we pulled out into the flow of foot traffic on the street.

The one good thing about the seats facing backwards, I didn't have to turn my head to watch for my tail. The slow speed of the donkey however made it easy for someone to follow on foot without fear of losing us.

I looked around at the storefronts as any newcomer would, making sure to return to the front of the coffee shop often. My tail was showing some level of patience by staying out of sight, but as we began our turn off the main street I saw him make a dash across the road and hurry to close the distance. So far it looked to be a single pursuer.

We rolled along on our current path for a quarter hour, heading further away from the river into an area where houses were spread farther apart. This made it much more difficult for my tail to hide.

"And here we are Sayed" Van Ess said. "The School of High Hope."

I turned one last time to locate the man in the Bakhtiari dress when I caught a glimpse of another man wearing a white sash a short ways back on the opposite side of the road. He wore a dark felt hat though, had a full moustache, and seemed to be more interested in my tail than me. Just as I got a clear look at the second man, both disappeared from sight.

I slipped off of the donkey cart and followed Doctor Van Ess through a gated fence that surrounded the property. I saw a collection of students doing exercises in a small field beside the main building and a few others taking a path to a second building near the rear of the compound.

The structures appeared very similar to the ones I saw in town, constructed with that same light brown clay. The architecture was more elaborate here though, with high arched windows and several brick columns that were somewhat reminiscent of the turrets from a castle.

The ground floor windows had the same iron bars but in addition, mosquito netting to keep out the pests. The second floor rooms were also thus protected.

"Is that mosquito netting I see in the windows?" I asked.

"Yes. It was one of the first things we did when we arrived. Malaria and other diseases are rampant in these swampy areas. We must protect the children as best we can."

"That building is the dormitory and hospital" he continued

pointing off to the right. "The main building here is where we teach classes and house our administrative offices."

We continued up the path towards the main entrance and into the building. Once inside I could see that the school was a western mission school. The furnishings were all in the English style with crosses adorning the walls in several locations.

"You teach Christianity here or only academic classes? I asked.

"In the school proper we stick to mainly academic courses. On Sundays we have a church service, but it is completely optional. Few of the students attend. The children of Sheiks almost never. But these children are curious by nature and eventually want to understand why we would travel half way around the world to their back yard."

We continued walking through the building towards the rear as Doctor Van Ess continued.

"We start by teaching about the common themes and history of the two religions, that Jesus was acknowledged as a profit in the Quran. Mostly we try to undo years of misunderstanding and emphasize that God wants us to love one another, treat each other with respect, and forgive those who sin against us."

"So nothing about the magic tricks of turning water into wine, feeding the multitude from a few loaves of bread, or raising people from the dead?"

Doctor Van Ess stopped and looked at me for a long while before a smile broke out on his face.

"No. We save the magic tricks for the university level studies."

We walked into what appeared to be an administrative area where we were greeted in turn by several people busily organizing files and writing notes. Eventually we landed in the Doctor's private office where he took a seat behind his desk and I took one of the two chairs on the opposite side.

"You haven't asked me about Gertrude Bell" I said.

"I was saving that conversation for dinner when our mutual

friend Thomas Lawrence will join us. He and Gertrude are good friends and both archeologists. They met in the dig at Carchemish in Syria."

"Gertrude and I had several discussions in Van about her work" I said. "She is a fascinating lady."

"I agree whole heartedly" Van Ess replied.

"But that is not why you wanted me to join you in Basra" I ventured.

"No it is not. It is most definitely not."

He seemed to be agitated, as if he had forgotten something important or didn't know how to begin a difficult conversation. I gave him the time he needed to find the right words.

"As you know, I am a school teacher and a minister of the Church. I never sought a life in politics and I am sure that I am not cut out for it."

"If it helps, I know exactly what you mean" I said trying to ease the tension. "I was offered a seat in our Parliament, but turned it down. I am not very good at deception."

That seemed to help as Doctor Van Ess took a deep breath and settled back in his chair.

"Then let me get right to it. As I told the Emir last night, I have recently hosted several emissaries from both the British India Office, but what I did not share was that I have also hosted representatives of the Ottoman Vilayet."

"Basra is under Ottoman jurisdiction" I said. "Why would this be a sensitive subject?"

"Because they were here to get information about the British plans for protecting the refinery and knew of my close relationship with the Emir and members of the British India Office."

"So how can I help?" I asked.

"I understand that you have just arrived from London" he said.

This surprised me, since I was careful not to talk about that part of trip with anyone but the Emir.

"Did the Emir share that with you?" I asked.

"No. Captain Arnold told me you were on your way and that you had even met with Churchill while there."

I wondered how many more people knew about my journey.

"That is true. I became very close with Calouste Gulbenkian over the past few months and he asked me to spend time with him in England after my business was concluded in Paris."

"And how did you come to meet Churchill?"

"Through Calouste" I lied, "and only briefly. You can see by the arrival of their warship that the refinery is very strategic. Churchill wanted to learn my countrymen's opinion regarding the continued sale of oil to the British."

"Which is?"

"Which is that we Persians see very little of the profits and feel that we deserve more."

He smiled at that.

"Perhaps if they knew how much was going to the Emir" Van Ess said, "their opinion of the British would change."

"Just another sign of a broken system" I said half to myself.

"And your meeting with the Emir?"

"Was a courtesy to Mister Churchill. He knew I was heading home and asked that I deliver a letter to Mohammerah in exchange for safe passage back to Persia."

"So you were simply a courier?"

"A messenger is perhaps more accurate" I said. This word somehow felt less like a lie to me.

Van Ess seemed to be confused by my response, as if he expected more.

"Forgive me for being so direct. It's just that Captain Arnold implied you had a larger role than a simple messenger."

"I can't account for why Captain Arnold would be so misinformed. I am a simple shopkeeper and stamp collector who is returning home after a very successful and enjoyable trip to Paris and London. I have made several new acquaintances along the way and added some wonderful new specimens to my collection. All in all it has been a very fruitful journey."

I had rehearsed that answer many times in my mind over the last two weeks of travel and delivered it well if I must say so myself.

Van Ess still had the look of a dog that couldn't quite understand what happened to the rabbit it had cornered.

"I see" he said finally.

My explanation seemed to satisfy him for now. He looked around at his desk and picked up an envelope from a pile.

"So you collect postage stamps?" he said. "Like this one?"

He handed me an envelope and I examined the postage affixed in the corner. It was from America.

"Yes" I said. "As a matter of fact, I don't have many American stamps in my collection yet."

"These are all cancelled" he said pointing to the stack on the desk, "so they are of no value to me. Do you collect stamps that have been cancelled?"

"I do if I can't get one that is unused."

Van Ess picked up the small pile and removed the contents of each envelope before handing them to me.

"Do you have a pair of scissors?" I asked.

He produced a pair from one of his desk drawers at which point I methodically cut off the stamp and other portions that were of interest to me. I made extra sure not to get any of the return addresses. I learned the hard way that these were a liability.

When I was done I handed the envelopes back to Van Ess.

"Thank you very much for your gift" I said simply.

The change of subject seemed to help the man's mood. He abruptly stood up and motioned for me to make my way to the door.

"I'll have one of the boys show you up to your room and introduce you to the facilities. I am sure you will want to freshen up and rest before dinner."

I peered out the window to the grounds behind the school and wondered for a moment if my tail was waiting for me out on the street.

"Thank you Doctor, but I might want to have a look around and stretch my legs. May I ask about the grounds behind the school?"

He turned to look in the direction I was looking and pointed through the window.

"There is an athletics field behind the school that is big enough for a football pitch and cricket. We've played both back there when the weather permits."

The athletic field as he called it appeared to be a broad area of packed dirt with not a blade of grass in sight.

"And behind the back gate?"

"An alleyway that parallels the street, but I don't suggest you go there. The street in front is much safer and certainly more scenic."

A young boy appeared wearing a western style school uniform with short pants, high knee socks, a button up shirt and neck tie.

"Ali please show this gentleman to the dormitory, room seven. He will be our guest tonight."

I bid farewell to Doctor Van Ess and followed the young student over to the dorm. He pointed out the kitchen and student dining area as we entered and explained the rules concerning when I was allowed to dine. We made our way up to the second floor, past the washrooms as he called them, and to my door where he immediately turned and left without a word.

When I entered my room I found my trunk waiting for me by the bed. I selected a white robe and changed out of the black robes I had been wearing. Then I removed my customary black turban and exchanged it for a white one as well. I needed to blend in with the locals but more importantly, the men who were following would be looking for a Persian man in black robes.

Once dressed I checked that my gun holster was still in place and easily accessible then I rummaged in my trunk for my dagger. I withdrew the blade from the sheath to make sure it was serviceable and then tucked it under my belt beneath my outer robe.

My room faced the street although it was a good thirty yards or so from the fence. I peered out of the window and could barely see the outline of the white Bakhtiari hat standing in the alley between two buildings across the road. I scanned the road for the second man, but was unable to locate him from this vantage point.

I slipped out of my room and down the stairs to the first floor kitchen area where I exited the building on the back side. I milled around outside for a moment getting my bearings and searched for any signs of the other Bakhtiari tail covering me from the back. I saw no signs of anyone in that direction, so I crossed the athletic fields and slipped out of the compound into the back alley.

I followed the alley parallel to the front street in the direction of the river. When I felt I had gone far enough to get behind the two men, I began looking for a way to cut back to the main street.

I came upon what appeared to be a deserted house with a

missing back gate and made my way up to the house. I circled around it keeping the run down structure between me and my tail. After waiting and listening for a moment I peered around the corner.

The front of the house was closed off to the street with a four foot tall adobe brick wall that had seen better days. An iron gate set in the center had popped one of its hinges and leaned precariously on the other side of the wall. I scurried over to the gate keeping below the wall and positioned myself to see through the opening back towards the school.

This proved to be a good position. Not only could I see white hat in his hiding spot across from the school, I could see black hat taking up a position behind him on the same side of the street.

I observed the black hat for a few minutes and never once saw him take his eye off of the other Bakhtiari. This led me to believe that instead of a two main team following me, I had one tail who was in turn being followed himself.

A donkey cart appeared on the road heading the right direction. I waited for the cart to come even with me and for both of the Bakhtiari to assess the cart and turn their attentions back to their prey before casually walking out into the road behind the cart. I walked a little ways up the street towards black hat making sure he was still occupied with his target, then casually turned into an open gate on his side of the road. I waited briefly inside the gate to ensure I was not noticed then surveyed the ground in between, looking for a path.

I was now only three houses away from his hiding place. I peered down the side of the dwelling and decided to loop around behind the buildings that separated us without any of the residents giving me away.

I climbed over first one wall and then another until I was about to scale over the wall of the final house that stood between us. That's when I saw the woman and her child hanging the wash out to dry.

I decided it was best to bypass her altogether, so I went over the back wall and into an alley that was very similar to the one I found behind the school. There were a few children playing several houses down, but they did not seem to pay me any attention. I would have been much happier trying to pull this off under the cover of darkness, but I didn't want to lose the advantage I had already gained.

I scaled over the short back wall and made my way to the back corner of the house where Black Hat was hiding. I quickly looked through the open windows and listened carefully for any signs of its owners. After catching my breath and waiting for a long while, I realized Black Hat had chosen his position well. There was nobody home.

I pulled my dagger from inside my robe and used the polished blade as a mirror to peer around the corner. Black Hat was still crouched down in his hiding spot with his attention focused up the street, so I crept around the corner and moved silently down the side of the house until I was within 3 feet of my target.

He suddenly turned and pointed a pistol directly at my center of mass.

I was about to leap forward when I recognized the man's face.

"Commander Assad" I whispered.

"Kashani?" he said softly as he lowered his gun.

I breathed deeply and returned my dagger to its sheath as Assad lowered his weapon.

"Now I know who it is you are tailing" I said as a lowered myself down next to him and peered up the street.

"That idiot Amir fancies himself an accomplished spy" Assad replied. "He would not have lasted an hour in battle with his lack of skills. When did you spot us?"

"I saw him coming out of the Alley from the river. Not many

white Bakhtiari hats in Basra."

"And me?"

"You were much more difficult my friend. I just caught a glimpse before entering the school."

He looked me up and down quickly.

"He should take a lesson from you. Changed out of the black and in to something more like the locals."

"So what is he playing at? He knew I was travelling with Doctor Van Ess. Why follow me?"

"My best guess? He wants to learn everything he can about who you are meeting with here so he can report it to Wassmuss."

"I thought Wilhelm was in the south, in Bushehr?"

"Most likely" Assad replied. "I truly do not know, but I believe Amir would follow you to the moon if it would win favor with the Germans."

"Khazal has already made his position clear. Why would Amir go against his grandfather's wishes?"

"The same reason Khazal betrayed his own father and older brother. When you are not the first in line to the throne, you have to find your own path to success."

That made everything fall into place for me and I saw Amir in a new light. While I had dismissed him as irrelevant before, I now realized he could make big trouble if left to his own devices.

"So you are here to bring him home?" I asked.

"I am here to ensure he doesn't get himself killed. You almost took me and I am seasoned solider. That young whelp is over his head and doesn't know it."

"You think I would have killed him?"

"Not if you recognized him first, but In the heat of the moment..."

I unconsciously started scanning the streets looking for others when Assad noticed and chuckled.

"He is alone. Don't worry. You are having dinner tonight with Van Ess?"

"Yes. And some fellow named Lawrence."

"Thomas Lawrence" Assad said nodding his head. "He works for British Foreign Office. Anyone else?"

"I don't know. He is the only one I was told of."

"I believe Arnold Wilson may be there as well."

"Captain Wilson?" I asked

"Yes. He is the one that is piquing the interest of the local Ottoman officials. You saw the warship?"

I nodded.

"We hear the British are planning an invasion of Basra in order to protect Mohammerah. Some say they will push north all the way to Bagdad and Kirkuk province. We believe Wilson must coordinate with Doctor Van Ess as the representative of the American government before this takes place."

The only evidence I had seen of an offensive was the HMS Odin and they appeared to be taking a defensive posture. But then my journey to Karbala and back would take several days, which is plenty of time to bring up troops from Bahrain. Could it be that I would return to Basra just as the British were invading? My dinner this evening just became a bit more important.

Amir did not likely pose a threat in the near term. My cousin was just as likely to share the details of our meeting with Wassmuss in any event, so what difference did it make if he were playing hide and seek for the next few days.

"I plan to leave tomorrow morning for Najaf" I said, "and then continue on to Karbala. Once I have concluded my meeting, I expect to return to Mohammerah to consult with the Sheik one last time before returning home."

"Then I will escort you to see Khazal" Commander Assad replied. "I will wait for you here in Basra now that I know Amir is safe. Doctor Van Ess will know how to reach me."

I took one last look at Amir keeping watch on the school and simply shook my head.

"See you in a few days Commander."

I retraced my steps back across the road and into the alley. I was back in my room with time for a short nap.

Just before sunset one of the students arrived to escort me down to the faculty dining room where Van Ess was waited with two other western gentlemen.

"Sayed Kashani" let me introduce you to Major Arnold Wilson."

The man standing before me stood ramrod straight as if at attention. His bushy eyebrows protruded from his forehead almost as far as his bushy black moustache, but did nothing to diminish the intensity of his eyes.

"And this is my good friend Thomas Lawrence who has just completed a dig at Carchemish in the Levant."

"Well not so much completed as kicked off the site by the Ottomans."

His tanned skin looked somewhat out of place with his blond hair and blue eyes. I assumed he spent a lot of time in the sun as an archeologist.

"Pleasure to meet you" I replied. "I understand you are both well acquainted with Gertrude Bell?"

"Yes. Quite" Lawrence replied. "I hear you recently met her at Gulbenkian's place up in Van?"

"And spent a few days with her in Paris as well" I replied.

"How wonderful. I can't wait to catch up with her when she returns to Bagdad."

We were all seated at a simple table that paled in comparison to the lavish settings I enjoyed with Calouste. I realized then that the experiences of the past few months had raised my expectations somewhat.

We made small talk during dinner, Lawrence and Wilson both sharing stories of Gertrude Bell and her trips into some of the most dangerous areas of the region. My estimation of her grew with each and every tale.

Wilson also regaled us with stories about driving helter-skelter through the desert with Sheik Khazal in one of his automobiles and the years he spent protecting William D'Arcy's crew during their oil exploration in Masjid-I-Suleiman.

"Is it true that D'Arcy actually told them to give up and come home?" Van Ess asked.

"I saw the letter myself" Wilson replied. "I was in the process of preparing my men for travel when they struck oil. Four o'clock in the morning, a plume of oil fifty feet high gushed out of the ground waking everyone. George Reynolds danced around, bathing himself in that slick black liquid as if were the finest French perfume!"

When the final dishes were removed from the table, the atmosphere became more serious as the subject turned to the present situation.

"Sayed, I understand you intend to travel up river to Najaf and Karbala?" Wilson said, more as a statement than a question.

"That is correct. I have business with my cousin that I must conclude before I return to Tehran."

"Have you made arrangements for the trip yet?"

"I have not. I planned to hire a boat tomorrow."

"Then I must insist you join me on my yacht at least as far as Najaf" Wilson offered. "I have business there as well."

"I wouldn't want to impose…" I began.

"It would be no imposition, truly. In fact, I received a message from Whitehall asking that I show you every courtesy during your stay here. I am at your disposal."

I was at first surprised by this turn of events, but then realized that this wasn't the first time that the path had been prepared for my mission.

"It is rather important that you conclude your business quickly" he added. "I am not at liberty to share many details, but it would be best that you are safely back in Persia before the middle of October at the latest."

This seemed to confirm Commander Assad's belief that an invasion was imminent.

"I am anxious to arrive home as well, so that timetable will suit me well."

"Glad to hear that" Wilson said. "We all want you to arrive home safely as soon as possible."

"I understand you made a stop in Mecca on the way here" Van Ess said to Lawrence, changing the topic.

"I did. I met with the Grand Sharif to discuss his views on the region and to solicit his help against the Ottomans."

"I also heard you boarded an oil tanker moving at full speed like a pirate attacking his foe." Wilson said with a smile.

"Guilty as charged" Lawrence replied with a broad smile.

"That was you?" I asked.

"You were on board that tanker Sayed?"

"On the bridge watching you through a pair of binoculars" I replied. "You were as agile as a monkey on the cargo nets. I don't believe I could have found the nerve."

"Well. One does what one must."

"And what say Hussein, Sharif of Mecca?" asked Wilson with interest. "Will he work with us?"

"Hard to tell" replied Lawrence. "Says the right words, but I am never quite sure with him."

"I don't trust him one iota" Wilson responded. "But I trust Ibn Saud even less."

"Their families will eventually contend for rule of this whole region" Lawrence offered. "But perhaps both are too old and set in their ways. Gertrude and I feel Hussein's sons Faisal and Abdullah might make good leaders in their own right."

Although Major Wilson did not reply, I could see he was not in agreement with that last statement.

"What do you see as the future for this region?" I asked Lawrence.

"Self-determination if I have any say in the matter" he replied. "Gertrude and I have debated the subject at length. We believe the only way to stabilize this region is to establish a representative government of the various tribes leading themselves into the twentieth century."

"This is a pipe dream" Wilson responded. "They may eventually learn to govern themselves, but in the near term, they will need much help and guidance. I believe they want to be led."

"And we should take responsibility for that?" Lawrence asked. "How much more of a burden do you think the exchequer can withstand? This war will be costly. India has been costly."

"Which is why we must improve the lands and turn this region into a money making enterprise. I have proposed to Sir Percy that we relocate some of our Indian subjects to this area to cultivate the land. They are accustomed to the sweltering heat and are hard workers. With proper irrigation, we could return the lands between the Tigris and Euphrates into the paradise it once was and at the same time relieve some of the population challenges in India."

Lawrence turned towards me and asked "What is your opinion Sayed? Would you be willing to accept a foreign power ruling Persia if they could bring prosperity?"

"The reality in Persia today is that multiple foreign powers have already insinuated themselves into our business. The Belgians run our customs offices like we are an imperial possession. The Swedes control our gendarmerie and the only two banks in Persia are British. That said, when we brought in an American to run our treasury, he made great progress until he stepped too hard on the Russian's toes. I am inclined to think that we should do the hard work ourselves, but I am afraid that a hundred years of Qajar rule has created a layer of corruption that may not be easy to eradicate from within. We might just need a benevolent change agent to help get us on the right path."

"So you would accept foreign rule?" Lawrence asked.

"I would accept foreign assistance and mentorship, but we must rule ourselves" I said flatly. "I believe that self-rule may be a muscle that needs constant exercise to maintain its strength. It may take some time for that muscle to develop."

"Well said Sayed!" Lawrence exclaimed. "I can see why Gertrude and you get along."

We spoke about politics and the future of the region into the night, further exposing the rift between Wilson and Lawrence. They were both too polite to let their disagreements get out of hand, but it was obvious that there was no common ground.

I adjourned to my room for the evening after making arrangements to meet Major Wilson the following morning at the docks.

I arranged with Van Ess to leave my trunk at the school so that I could travel light up to Najaf. I took a small haversack with the few essentials I would need for a few days, which included my pistol and knife.

I left early and found my way down to the docks as planned. I felt Amir on my tail and caught a glimpse or two along the way to confirm.

When I saw Wilson's boat, I wondered how Amir would be able to keep up his tail. The vessel looked like a cross between Sheik Khazal's pleasure yacht and a smaller version of the Ottoman gunship I had seen the day before, minus the guns. I surveyed the deck and saw several mounts, but there were no weapons to be seen.

"Welcome aboard Sayed" Major Wilson said as I crossed the gang plank onto the deck.

"Good morning Major Wilson. This is an interesting vessel. It appears to be a gunship, but I don't see any guns."

"You are very observant Sayed. They are stored below in case we need them. The Ottomans are sensitive to a British flagged vessel on their river as it is. Openly displaying the firepower would only fan the flame."

"Won't this boat be too big for the shallow water up river?"

"This craft is designed to patrol shallow rivers" Wilson replied. "Very shallow draft and very powerful engines. We can make twenty to twenty five knots when necessary. Long enough to stay out of trouble until the guns are mounted and ready to fire."

He said the last bit with a smile on his face like a proud father introducing his favorite son. Even though Wilson was not dressed in a military uniform, it was obvious he was a soldier through and through.

"Najaf is almost three hundred miles up river. With the current against us, we should arrive about this time tomorrow morning. So make yourself comfortable and enjoy the ride."

As we pulled away and headed up river I caught a glimpse of Amir standing on the docks with his hands on his hips, watching us power away. I couldn't quite see his face, but I am sure from his body language that he wasn't happy. I wondered how long it would take for him to hire a boat that could make the trip at half the speed of this yacht. If I was lucky, I would find Abol-Ghasem in Najaf and business with him concluded by the time Amir arrived.

We went below decks and settled into a small state room where Wilson ordered tea and some light food from a cabin boy. When the servant left Wilson relaxed noticeably.

"Now that we have some privacy, I wanted to let you know that any help you need with Sheik Khazal you simply have to say the word. Sir Mansfield Cumming cabled that you are negotiating with Khazal on our behalf and asked that I provide whatever assistance you might need. That goes for Lawrence as well. He has been briefed."

"Thank you" I said. "Our initial conversation went well. So I am hopeful that after this upcoming meeting with my cousin, I will be able to reconnect with the Sheik and make my way home."

"Splendid. Speaking of your cousin, our people in Najaf report that the Ayatollah is currently in residence at the Imam Ali Holy Shrine. I took the liberty of sending a cable after our dinner last night to verify."

"Thank you" I said again. "There is something you may be able to help me with" I added. "How well do you know the Khazal's grandson Amir?"

"Quite a challenge that one" he answered. "His activities with Wilhelm Wassmuss have not gone unnoticed. Mostly harmless I would say, but worrisome. He looked rather upset as we pulled away from the dock just now don't you think?"

"You were aware he was tailing me?"

"Yes. As I said, you are under our protection."

That was comforting to hear but at the same time disturbing. I had detected Amir and Assad, but there was obviously an additional observer that I knew nothing about.

"And Commander Assad Bakhtiari?"

"Splendid fellow! And quite loyal to the Sheik and his tribe. We intercepted his cable back to the Sheik reporting on the situation in Basra. It was through this that we became aware that Amir was lurking about."

So perhaps I did not actually miss anyone yesterday.

"I don't suppose you happen to know where Wassmuss is at the moment" I asked.

"He is currently in Kut al Mara on the Tigris just below Baghdad. He seems to be planning some sort of mission to block the river from commercial traffic. We have him under watch so I wouldn't worry too much about him."

That news satisfied the last bit of concern I had about my trip to Najaf. With both Wassmuss and Amir out of the way and my cousin located, I could relax for a while and enjoy the ride.

NAJAF

September 17, 1914

The trip up river proved uneventful and quite entertaining. Major Arnold regaled me with stories of his adventures among the Arabs and of his time in India. Despite his radical political views, I found him to be a very pleasant companion.

We docked in Najaf and I made my way to find my cousin. I was not looking forward to the conversation.

I found him as I hoped at the shrine.

"You made the Sultan quite angry with your betrayal" he said when he saw me standing there.

"Peace be unto you as well Cousin" I replied.

"Now the opportunity may be lost" he continued.

"I was not impressed by the Sultan's offer. Besides, as a Persian citizen, the Sultan has no authority over me outside of his lands."

He said nothing in response, simply stared at me with a sullen look on his face.

"I believe there is another way to achieve your goals Cousin" I ventured. "One that will enable you to maintain more direct control."

"What exactly are you offering?"

"An alliance with Sheik Khazal."

"He is a British stooge."

"He is an opportunist for sure, but he cares about his people more than the British and puts their welfare as a close second to his own interests."

"Why should I help him?"

"Because he has extracted more money from the British oil fields than the Qajars and given a large portion of those spoils to his people. He is offering a portion of the revenues from the new oil fields to fund the Shia interests. To be directed by you of course."

"You think you can buy me?"

"I think that real change will require financing. I think that people can only accomplish so much on an empty stomach, no matter how devoted they are to their cause."

"And what does the Emir get in return?"

"The expansion of his domain to include the new oil fields at Kirkuk."

"I am not aware of any active oil operations in Kirkuk."

"That's because they have not yet been established yet. The situation is very fluid at the moment."

"Kirkuk is rife with Kurds" he said with disgust.

"Which is why we need your help. Together we will create a special Shia religious zone from Persia to Najaf and Karbala, ensuring access to our holy sites and a steady supply of resources to maintain this control."

"Our holy sites cousin? When was the last time you attended prayers?"

I ignored the barb and waited for him to think through the offer.

"This may be the answer" he said after a long silence.

I took the letter from within my robes and handed it to Abol-Ghasem.

"This is a letter from Sheik Khazal. It should confirm everything I have just told you."

Abol-Ghasem took the letter but did not bother to open it. He looked off into the distance for a while before speaking.

"I have learned that during next year's Hajj, Abdullah, son of the Sharif, is planning to imprison the pilgrims. If this year is like others, that would include leaders from the Ottoman Empire, Egypt, and even Java."

"What ransom would he ask for?"

"It's all part of a plan to set up Hussein as Caliph of all Islam. Abdullah would demand support from the leaders of all Muslim countries."

I wondered if the British knew of Abdullah's plans and if that would change Gertrude's mind about the family. I also wondered how much I could share with Abol-Ghasem.

"The British want to split up the Ottoman territories and establish Hussein's sons as rulers of a new country called Iraq and a second called Transjordan" I said, hoping my gamble would pay off.

"That would give Hussein and his family enormous power!" the Ayatollah exclaimed.

"Which is why we must move quickly. If we work together with Sheik Khazal, we can pit Ibn Saud against Hussein and buy time to establish control before the British are able to make their move."

I saw in my cousin's eyes that his resistance was yielding.

"Can you find a way to stop this?" Abol-Ghasem asked.

"I believe I could buy us some time" I replied. "I have influence with the people who are backing this proposal. Their plan is in the early stages but they still have to get the French government to agree. We may have a year before they can come to an agreement."

"And Abdullah's plan?"

"I will send word back to London right away. They will see to it that this extortion never happens."

"Are you now a British stooge as well?" he asked with disdain.

"I am most certainly not. I care only for my family and my country. But I will use whatever connections I have to protect them."

This seemed to satisfy him for the moment. His whole body seemed to relax although this left him looking exhausted.

"Are you well cousin? I asked."

He did not answer, but looked at me for a long time until the call to prayer sounded.

"Peace be unto you cousin" he finally said. "Go tell the Sheik that I am interested in a conversation. I must return to Qom soon so I will travel through Mohammerah and meet with him on the way."

With that he turned and left.

It was all over so quickly that I had to stop and gather my thoughts. I had expected a prolonged conversation over several days, but it appeared that my business in Najaf was complete.

I returned to the docks and Major Wilson's boat. He returned shortly thereafter, but we had to wait for several hours before our supplies for the journey back south were loaded.

The trip down river back to Basra was much faster going with the current. I had no idea if we passed Amir on the river along the way. I hoped he would make the trip to Najaf and spend time trying to track me down so I could get on with my journey unmolested.

We arrived in Basra late in the evening so Major Wilson suggested that I spend the night on board and wait until morning to return to the School of High Hope.

I found Doctor Van Ess and Commander Assad enjoying breakfast in the faculty dining room the next morning.

"Welcome back Sayed" Van Ess said as he saw me enter the room. "I trust everything went well?"

"You met with your cousin?" Assad asked.

"Yes. Everything went better than I expected."

"Please join us" Van Ess said as he motioned to an empty seat.

I had enjoyed breakfast with the Major before coming ashore, but I was never one to pass up an offer of food. I sat down and helped myself to some dates and nuts.

"So what are your plans?" asked Van Ess.

"Major Wilson has offered us passage back to Mohammerah as soon as we are ready" I replied, gesturing toward Commander Assad.

"I hope he will be willing to go as far as Ahvaz" Assad commented. "Khazal cabled that he would await word of your meeting in his palace there."

"The Major has been very helpful so far" I replied. "I am sure that will not be a problem."

Van Ess sent a boy to retrieve my trunk after we finished breakfast and arranged for a donkey cart to take us back to the boat.

Once we were on our way and out of earshot, I asked Assad about Amir.

"He followed you up river a few hours after you left" Assad replied. "From the looks of the boat he hired, he is probably arriving in Najaf as we speak."

"I wish I could see the look on his face when he realizes I am long gone" I said.

We met Major Wilson at the docks and in no time were on our way. As I expected, he was more than happy to make the trip further up river to Ahvaz.

AHVAZ

September 18 , 1914

The journey to Ahvaz was uneventful. At one point we saw an Ottoman patrol boat in the distance, but they did not approach us while in the Shatt al-Arab and certainly did not follow us into the Persian territory of the Karun river.

We arrived at the palace just before sundown and were met by the Sheik's staff at the docks. The three of us were invited to dine with the Sheik that evening and shown to our rooms where we could rest and recover from the journey.

Major Wilson regaled us with a story of his travel across Europe on a bicycle that had us all laughing by the end.

The subject turned to my cousin and I reported on the meeting using the broadest of terms considering the group. Khazal was very happy to see us and even more excited to hear that Abol-Ghasem was willing to discuss the deal.

"How likely is he to move forward" the Sheik asked.

"I believe there is a good chance. If you can emphasize your independence from both the British and the Qajars, I believe he will find a way to move forward."

"But this is simply the truth" replied the Sheik with a sincere look of surprise on his face.

"So what is next for you Sayed Kashani?" Major Wilson asked.

"I will return home to my family and my business."

"And a new career in politics" Khazal added. It sounded more like a command than a question.

"Have you made any arrangements for travel?" Commander Assad asked.

"None" I responded. "I suppose I will make my way to Isfahan and from there to my ancestral home in Kashan."

"Then you must allow me to accompany you as far as Isfahan" Assad replied.

"You will take one of my automobiles" the Sheik said. "And one of my drivers."

"I'm sure I can…"

"I will accept no objections" Khazal interrupted waving his hands in the air. "It is settled."

This would save me quite a lot of time so I was very happy to accept his offer, especially knowing that Assad would accompany me on the journey. The territory between Ahvaz and Isfahan was controlled by the Bakhtiari tribes and Assad was one of their leaders. Even though I did not expect any trouble, I knew with him by my side we could count on the hospitality of the locals along the way.

"Thank you Sheik Khazal. I am grateful."

"Major Wilson what are your plans?" the Sheik asked.

"I am afraid I must return to Basra tomorrow" he answered. "I have to deal with a pesky German plot to block the Euphrates river."

"Wassmuss again?" the Sheik asked.

"I am afraid so. The man is relentless."

"Let me know if I can be of any help" Khazal replied.

We continued our conversation into wee hours and retired

to our rooms. The next morning Commander Assad and I bid farewell to the Sheik and Major Wilson and set out on the three hundred mile journey to Isfahan.

ISFAHAN

September 19, 2014

T he automobile provided by the Sheik was quite spacious and very comfortable for much of the ride. Sometimes we drove over actual roads, but much of the time we travelled over the hardpan soil of the open ground. Not that the open ground was flat mind you. We were either heading up or heading down, but almost never level.

We made good time to the town of Izeh, arriving in the mid-afternoon. Commander Assad insisted that we take the time to visit the Kul-e Farah rock reliefs from the ancient kingdom of Elam. I was amazed to see these carvings which had survived for thousands of years. I could not read the cuneiform writing myself, but Commander Assad was happy to tell me the stories etched into solid stone.

After touring the site we were welcomed by the headman of the local tribe and dined like kings before bedding down for the night in a comfortable guest room.

We were off early the next day and made it as far as Borujen before loosing light. Travel was once again uneventful. As we headed into the Zagros mountains Commander Assad and I spent long stretches of time simply staring out at the landscape. I had never journeyed to this part of Persia before. Seeing it with my own eyes made it almost worth the time I spent away from my family. As soon as we reached the Choghakhur wetlands, the world turned green again and the sky was filled with birds of all kinds. The mountains in the background were still covered with snow which provided a majestic backdrop to the lagoon.

The temperature was already cool by the time we arrived in Borujen, which is more than seven thousand feet above sea level and one of the coldest cities in Persia in winter. It seemed to me I was in paradise.

When we pulled into town, Commander Assad made a stop at a small inn and inquired within. He emerged from the establishment with a broad smile on his face.

"You look as if you have some good news" I said when he returned to the automobile.

"I do indeed" he replied.

"Are you willing to share?"

"You will find out soon enough."

He gave the driver directions and within a few minutes we parked in front of a large residence. Before we even had a chance to get out of the car, we were greeted by a middle aged woman who bore a striking family resemblance to Commander Assad. Just on her heals was someone I recognized immediately, our former prime minister and older brother of Assad, Najaf-Qoli Khan Bakhtiari.

"Ali-Qoli!" the woman shouted as she ran into the arms of Assad. "I thought you were in Ahvaz with Khazal!"

"*Salam Chetori* little sister! You look well?"

"I am so happy to see you brother!"

As I looked closer at Assad's sister it suddenly struck me.

"You are Bibi Maryam Bakhtiari!" I said in awe.

"Yes. That's right. And you are?"

"I am Abdulrahim Kashani."

"Leader of the Fatemieh Society? You fought with us in the revolution."

"I played a small role. Nothing like you. My wife is still talking about the woman who saved Tehran. Your skills with a rifle are legend!"

"You should see her ride a horse" Commander Assad interjected.

"I have met some very famous people on my trip" I continued, "but I am sure Farrokh Lagha will be most impressed that I got to meet you."

"Even more than a former Prime Minister" Najaf-Qoli said with a smile on his face. "I am afraid the men of our family will never be able to measure up to our fearless little sister."

"Minister Najaf-Qoli, it is a pleasure to see you again" I said. "You are living here in Borujen?"

"We are visiting friends."

"Please come inside! Have some tea and something to eat." Bibi said.

We followed them into the house and into the front parlor. A servant appeared with a tray of tea and snacks and placed them on the table in front of us.

"Minister, you left Tehran last January if I am not mistaken" I said. "I never learned why you resigned."

"You could say I was frustrated with our lack of progress. Frustrated with the way the British and Russians continue to manipulate the central government."

"And Ahmad Shah? I asked. What do you think of his leadership?"

"What leadership?" Bibi spat. "His uncle held the real power until Ahmad reached his majority in July. It has only been two months, but there is no indication that anything will change."

"He is just like all the Qajars before him" Najaf-Qoli continued, "more interested in lining his own pockets than making any real change. I am too old to continue the fight. It is time for the next generation to step up and take the reigns."

"Is there anyone you think is worthy of the job?" I asked.

"My little sister of course" the minister replied with a broad smile, "but I am afraid our society is not yet ready for a woman to lead us."

"If the Ayatollahs gain any more control" Bibi offered, "we will never see a woman in power."

"Is there anyone else you have seen that could unite us?" I asked.

"I am afraid not" Najaf-Qoli said after some thought. "But I am sure he is out there somewhere."

"Have you met Major Reza Khan of the Cossack brigade?" I asked.

"I know of him by reputation only. I have heard good things about him. Self-made. Fearless. But a military man? Are you sure that's what we need now?"

"I can tell you more about the man when I return from Isfahan brother" Assad added. "We travelled with him for several days. He seems to have a good sense of what is fair and right."

"I think you should make it a point to get to know him" I suggested. "Then I would love to hear your opinion."

"I will do that" Najaf-Qoli replied.

"What do you think of the Germans?" I asked. "Their weapons were important to our success in the revolution."

"That is true" Assad offered, "but is that because they truly wanted to help or simply wanted to disrupt the British?"

"I trust the Germans as little as I trust any foreign power" Najaf-Qoli said. "We are simply pawns on their chess board. They will use us when it suits them and sacrifice us when we are no longer useful."

"This fellow Wassmuss is a fine example" Bibi said. "He takes on Persian ways and speaks Persian, but in his heart he is still a German agent."

"You have met Wassmuss?" I asked.

"Yes. In fact I saw him lurking around in Kashan a few days ago."

"Kashan?" I asked. "We were told he was in Iraq only a few a days ago."

"I don't know who told you that, but I saw him with my own eyes in Kashan on my way here to Borujen."

"He is in Kashan" I said to myself. If true I am sure he will know it when I arrive. He seemed to have limitless sources of information.

"Perhaps you should reconsider your route home" Assad said.

"I believe you are correct" I replied. "I plan to give that man a wide berth."

"You and Wassmuss have history?" Bibi asked.

"A brief history. Let's just say I do not wish to deepen our relationship."

I allowed the conversation of Wassmuss to end there when Bibi changed the subject.

"Where do you plan to stay in Qom?" she asked.

"I don't know. I will try to find a reputable inn."

"We have a cousin in Qom who owns a very nice inn" Najaf-Qoli said. "We stayed there on our way to Borujen. You must lodge there."

"Yes" Assad added. "I forgot to share that with you Abdulrahim. I have already sent a cable to him to save a room for you. He will take very good care of you when you arrive."

"But I don't know how long it will take to get there from Isfahan" I said.

"It doesn't matter. When you arrive there will be a room for you" Assad replied.

We continued our conversation through dinner and late into the evening, reminiscing about events from our victory against the previous Shah. These three siblings were a major reason for our success and like all veterans, we loved to share stories about our past with people who were actually there. With civilians, not so much.

The following morning we shared breakfast with out hosts and said our goodbyes. Isfahan was only seventy miles away, mostly down hill. As expected we arrived well before noon.

Commander Assad arrived at an inn in the heart of the city. The driver helped me unload my Louis Vuitton trunk, which now looked worse for the wear.

"I am sure we will see each other again" I said to Assad. "I am very grateful for all of your help."

"And I am thankful to have met you as well my friend. I'm sure your future business with Sheik Khazal will bring us together soon."

He turned to climb aboard the Sheik's car when I remembered something else.

"Commander! Please give my best to Amir when you next see him."

He smiled at that and nodded.

"I will be happy to pass along the well wishes."

I spent the afternoon arranging my travel plans. I struggled to find a team of porters who was willing to take me directly to Qom, bypassing Kashan. Everyone pointed out that my preferred route would take us off the beaten path. I was tempted to buy a horse and set out on my own, but travelling in open country was dangerous even with a group of well armed men. I was finally able to hire a team when I agreed to pay an outrageous premium.

I was less than three hundred miles from home now, but I still felt a million miles away.

I sent a telegram to my wife before retiring, giving her an update on my progress. If we made good time, I would be home within a week.

QOM

September 22, 1914

Wwe made good progress during the first two days of our travel, although it seemed so much longer crossing the hardpan desert on horseback. This part of my journey was not nearly as comfortable or as scenic as the past few weeks had been. That and it's easy to become spoiled when travelling as a guest of powerful men in yachts and automobiles.

The following few days were slower, just as the porters had predicted. We had issues with one of the horses on day three and lost another half a day trying to locate a way station with water the following day. When the lead porter declared that we would reach Qom the next day I was elated. Not only with the prospect of sleeping on a real bed again, but also because I had a sudden craving for *Sohan*, the delicious toffee brittle made with saffron, almonds and pistachios that is Qom's famous delicacy. Just thinking about it made my mouth water.

Qom is the center of religious scholarship in Shia Islam. It was home to my cousin the Ayatollah, although I did not expect he could have arrived before I did. Then again, it would be a mistake to underestimate his resources.

When we arrived at the inn, Assad's cousin greeted me as if I were family. He put me up in his best room and invited me to dine with his family. I even got to satisfy my craving for *Sohan*.

I slept well that evening on a comfortable bed and full stomach but it proved to be the last good night's sleep I would have for a while.

When I arrived at the stables to rejoin my porters I was told by the hostler that they had packed up and left an hour before. Only my horse remained in stalls.

"It is so difficult to find reliable help" a voice called to me in English from the shadows.

Wilhelm Wassmuss walked out of the stable and into the light. His face was haggard and his robes were dirty as if he had slept with the horses.

"I paid off your porters" he continued. "They have returned to Isfahan."

"I would say you look well Wilhelm, or that I am happy to see you, but I think we both know both would be a lie."

"You have not only caused me much pain these past few weeks" he said, "but you cost me a good night's sleep. I had to ride all night from Kashan when I learned you were here."

"I'm sorry you wasted the effort" I replied. "But I don't think we have any further business to discuss."

He pulled a pistol from his robe and pointed it at me as several large men appeared from all sides. I felt rather than saw the man who approached me from behind. Even if I could draw my weapon and shoot before Wassmuss, I could not escape from the goons who had me surrounded.

"I will tell you when our business is concluded Sayed" he said. His normally pleasant features were drawn up into a pained expression.

"I received a cable from your cousin two days ago" he continued. "It seems that each time I put a plan in place, you find a way to disrupt it. I am frankly a little tired of this."

"And I am tired of you meddling in my business as well. Germany and Persia are not at war. We have declared our neutrality. So I do not understand what business you have in my country."

He smiled at this.

"Your country" he said. "That is interesting coming from an agent of MI6."

I was sure the subtleties of my arrangements with C would be lost on Wassmuss and wondered just how much Wilhelm knew about my assignment. He could simply be making an educated guess based on reports from his comrades in London.

"What is it you want from me?" I asked.

"For now, I want you to be my guest in Qom until Abol-Ghasem arrives from Najaf. The three of us need to have a conversation about the future."

I realized that I was in no position to resist at the moment. I could only hope that I would have a better chance to escape from wherever he planned to hold me. Even the most diligent person will become complacent after a few days.

"I always wanted to spend a few days in Qom" I lied. "Lead on!"

Wassmuss pointed to one of his men, who searched me and confiscated my handgun and dagger.

"A Webley Mk 1" Wassmuss said with a broad smile. You know that model has several design flaws. This Pistole 08 on the other hand was designed by Herr Luger and has none of these shortcomings. Even the nine millimeter Parabellum ammunition is superior."

"Parabellum?" I asked.

"*Si vis pacem, para bellum*" Wassmuss responded. "Latin. It means 'If you seek peace, prepare for war'."

"I see. So this is you seeking peace?" I quipped.

"We Germans are always prepared Sayed. Now let us be on our way."

My captors tied my hands and helped me up on my horse.

We rode to a house on the outskirts of Qom. Several times I was tempted to goad my horse into a gallop and try to outrun my captors, but with Wassmuss riding behind me I knew I would have to outrun a bullet as well. So I maintained my composure and stuck to the original plan of waiting until the crew became complacent.

Wassmuss put me into a bedroom with a window on the south wall that was much too small for me to fit through and a solid door which was locked the moment I entered the room. My trunk was eventually given to me after being searched as well, so I resigned myself to settle in and pulled out my stamp collection to pass the time. I estimated it would take a few more days at least for my cousin to arrive in Qom, so I used the first day to catch up on my sleep.

By the end of the second day I had a good feel for my jailers' routine. I was fed on a regular schedule but forced to use a chamber pot rather than allowed to use the outhouse. I was able to predict which guard would come on duty at any given time and managed to strike up a conversation with two of them. One was a rather large man named Hamid who seemed to be the leader of the group and the other an older fellow named Farhad, who was from Kashan.

"Where did you meet this German?" I asked Farhad before he left me on the third day.

He hesitated, but turned and studied me for a moment before replying.

"I don't really know him" he replied. "Hamid does."

Farhad carried himself like an educated man even though I heard him pray twice a day during his watch. I had to find a way to appeal to his better nature if I could.

"You know I am returning from a trip to Paris" I said.

This seemed to grab his attention.

"Paris? But there is a war."

"Yes. The fighting started just after I arrived in France. Do you know who I met on my trip? A very famous family."

He seemed more interested now, but did not speak.

"I met Commander Assad Bakhtiari in Tabriz, and his brother, Prime Minister Najaf-Qoli, and their sister Bibi Maryam Bakhtiari just last week on the way home.

"They are true heroes" Farhad said in awe. "Is it true that Bibi Maryam can shoot a rifle better than most men?"

"Yes. She is a truly amazing woman."

I seemed to be on the right track.

"And when I was in Tabriz I also visited my friend Sattar Khan."

"Really? You are a friend of that great man?"

"We fought together" I added as if it were just a passing thought.

He appeared to be confused by my comment.

"So if you are a soldier with friends in high places, how did you come to be captured so easily by this German?"

I realized that Farhad was not among the group that captured me at the stables. Maybe I had a chance.

"I guess I let my guard down" I said shaking my head. "I was so close to home I became careless."

My guard seemed to consider that but did not offer any further comment.

"I'm very disappointed" I continued ,"that we fought to gain freedom from one tyrant and now have foreign powers like England, Russia, and Germany meddling in our business. I wish they would all just leave us alone."

I hoped that would plant a seed that I could harvest the following day. For now I thought I had said enough.

Farhad looked me over for a few moments longer as if contemplating a riddle, then abruptly left.

The following day he returned as usual in the late afternoon with my meal, but seemed to have something on his mind. He lingered for a few minutes after I began eating my supper.

"I spoke to Hamid about your capture" he said. "He told me you were outnumbered eight to one and surrounded at the stables in the inn."

"Yes" I replied simply.

"When Hamid asked me to help him, I was told you were a dangerous criminal, but this is just not true. You are a patriot being held against your will by a German spy."

"Also true" I replied.

He stared at me for a while until I found the silence unbearable.

"Can you help me?" I asked.

He looked over his shoulder back into the other room and then down at the floor.

"It would be dangerous for me" he said. "The others would not understand."

"I would not want you to do anything that put you in danger" I said. "Is Wassmuss near?"

He glanced over his shoulder again and then shook his head.

"I haven't seen him since he delivered you here."

"He is waiting for my cousin Ayatollah Kashani to arrive in Qom" I said.

This seemed to disturb Farhad.

"The Ayatollah is your cousin?"

"Yes. The German captured me to blackmail my cousin. Wassmuss is waiting for my cousin to return from Karbala to negotiate my release."

The blood drained from Farhad's face.

"He wants to force my cousin to convince the mullahs to help Germany. Abol-Ghasem refused, so now Wassmuss is applying pressure through me."

"What am I doing helping this *Farangi*" he said staring at the floor and shaking his head.

I let him think a while longer, sensing he was almost ready.

"Perhaps you can get word to the mosque that I am being held?"

Farhad looked around again at the door then approached closer.

"I have watch duty tonight. I will return then."

He turned and left the room without further word. I heard the door lock a moment later.

If he was willing to let me escape, I would need to travel light I thought. How far did we ride after my capture? What direction was the town?

If I could find my way to the mosque I could enlist the help of my cousin's colleagues. But what if Wassmuss was watching the mosque for my cousin's return? I would have to be careful on my approach.

I searched my trunk for anything that would be helpful on my trek to the city and realized I would have to come back for my stamp collection and other personal items. There was also the matter of my handgun and knife. I could not leave Qom without my gun.

There was still a few hours of sunlight left and nothing to do but wait.

The hours passed very slowly once it was dark. The moon was visible in the sky providing some light through the window. I realized my black robe would help me to blend in better during my escape and keep me warm in the cool evening air. I put it on and sat back on my cot to wait, hoping that Farhad would come through.

Just as the moon was setting I heard the door unlock and push in.

"I have water and food for you" he said as he handed me a small rucksack. "You must be quiet. The others are sleeping."

I followed him out the door and through the main room. I could hear snoring coming from one of the other rooms, but otherwise everything was quiet.

We exited the house through the front door and scurried quietly away from the house to a small formation of rocks a few hundred yards away.

"You are on your own from here" he said with barely a whisper.

"Qom is to the east" pointing in that direction. "The hills are to the west" he said pointing in the opposite direction.

I nodded.

"You are exposed here on the plain. I suggest you make your way west and then north along the edge of those hills. They will provide some cover. Circle around and approach the town from the north. They will expect you to head due east from here."

"Merci Farhad" I said. "I will not forget this act of kindness."

There was still enough light to see the worried look on his face.

"The next watch begins in 2 hours. I will lock your door when I return. Hamid will not bother to look in on you. If we are lucky, they will not notice you are gone until breakfast. Good luck. Please tell your cousin what I did and have him pray for my soul. I do not want to give up my place in paradise because I helped an infidel."

He took off around the rocks and headed back towards the house. I watched for a long while to make sure the others did not stir before leaving my hiding place. When I was certain we had not been discovered I headed west to the hills as Farhad suggested.

I made it to the base of the hills and turned north, walking for several hours across uneven terrain. The moon had set by this time, so the only light in the sky was from the stars. My eyes adjusted to the low light, but that didn't make the travel any less dangerous. Several times I almost stumbled in to one of the many shallow ravines.

As the sunrise was just lightening the eastern horizon I took a rest and ate some of the rations Farhad had provided. I looked back towards the south and realized I had not come all that far. I would have to step up my pace.

I returned the remaining food and water to the rucksack and set off at a brisk walk, cursing the extra pounds I had put on during my journey.

An hour later the sky was now fully light in the east. I gazed at the horizon expecting to see the sun peek over the horizon any minute.

That was my mistake.

I stepped on a small rock and rolled my ankle. As I tried to recover my balance I slipped on the scrabble and started sliding down into a deep ravine. I tried to compensate by putting more weight on my other foot, but pain shot up my leg and I tumbled forward out of control, sliding down the slope twenty feet into a dry river bed.

I must have lost consciousness, because the next thing I knew, the sun was fully up and shining into my eyes.

That's when I heard the jangle of stirrups and looked back up the slope to the south.

"You will never learn Sayed" Wassmuss said with contempt.

I shaded my eyes and found him sitting on his horse at the top of the ravine.

"Did you not realize that your tracks would be easy to follow once the sun was up?"

I saw a disgusted look on his face as he pulled his handgun from a holster and pointed it in my direction.

"I am so weary of the trouble you have caused me. I should have eliminated you when you doubled back to Constantinople. The Bosniak would still be alive, the Sultan would be in my debt, and your cousin would already be aligned with Germany. I will not allow you to get in my way again."

He raised his arm into firing position.

"So my Cousin has arrived in Qom then?" I asked trying to buy a little more time.

"He arrived late last night. I went to retrieve my bargaining chip only to discover the house completely empty."

"Good help is so hard to find" I quipped.

"As I said" Wassmuss replied. "It is time to say goodbye."

"I don't think you want to do that" I said in desperation.

He smiled at that remark.

"And why is that?"

"Because we will not allow it" I heard a familiar voice say from behind Wassmuss.

I saw Major Reza Khan and his Cossack Brigade ride into view behind the German, every one of the Major's men aiming their rifles at Wassmuss.

I marveled at their stealth and noticed their harnesses and stirrups were all rigged to eliminate the noise.

"Put your weapon down Wassmuss" Major Reza Khan said. "I will not ask a second time."

Wassmuss tossed his Luger to the ground and put his hands in the air.

"Are you well Sayed Kashani?" he called to me. "It seems you had a little accident."

Major Reza Khan motioned to one of his men to help me out of the ravine. It was then I noticed he was leading my horse.

"It is good to see you again Major" I said. "How did you know I needed help?"

"Commander Assad received a cable from his cousin the inn keeper. The man who runs his stables witnessed your capture but they were too late to do anything about it. Assad cabled me in Tehran and we rode out to help. We found the German in Qom, but he didn't lead us to you until today. I apologize for the delay."

I rubbed my ankle to restore circulation as the soldier brought my horse down to me. I stepped up into the saddle with my good leg and prodded my horse forward until I was up and out of the ravine facing Wassmuss from a safe distance.

Major Reza Khan took up a position next to me surveying Wassmuss.

"What would you have me do with this man?" the Major asked. "We can ensure he never bothers you again if that is what you want."

I saw Wassmuss turn to look at me when he heard that I was now about to determine his fate. I understood the implication of the Major's comment, but I didn't believe it was my place to put a man to death. Even though I was not religious, I had enough sense of right and wrong to know that was not a choice.

"He held me prisoner for several days" I said. "I think I should return the favor. We might need to hold him a little longer than a few days if we want to stop his meddling in Persian business."

"One of my companies is scheduled to travel to Behbahan in the south" the Major offered, "to deal with a local chieftain there. I have heard there are British troops in the area. Perhaps we should deliver Wassmuss to the British and let them deal with him now that Britain and Germany are at war."

The look on Wassmuss' face was almost worth the trouble.

"I believe that is just the right thing to do Major" I replied.

"Good. It is settled then."

Reza Khan gave orders to a pair of his soldiers who promptly secured the German's hands and tied them to his saddle.

We led Wassmuss back to the house where I was held captive and placed him in the same room where I was held. It seemed Farhad had convinced the others to run away. They were no-where to be found and I found my trunk in the front room waiting for me with my handgun and knife sitting on top.

"A few of my men will hold the German here until the second company arrives" Major Reza Khan said when I rejoined him outside.

"So what is next for you Major?" I asked.

"The rest of us are returning to Tehran if you would care to join us."

"I am very happy to hear that. I would be honored."

We first rode back to Qom where I found my cousin at the entrance to the mosque and explained the situation.

"He held you captive for all that time?" he asked.

"Yes and I must thank a man named Farhad from Kashan. He arranged my escape."

"Perhaps you can thank him by naming your next son after him" Abol-Ghasem replied.

"I will have Abbas or Hassan name one of their sons Farhad when they have families. I do not think there will be any more sons for me."

"I would tell you to put your trust in Allah cousin, but I know it would do no good. Peace to you and safe journey home."

"For that I will put my trust in Major Reza Khan and the Cossack Brigade cousin."

He shook his head slowly as if to say there was no hope for me and returned to the mosque.

TEHRAN

October 2, 2014

O ur trip back to Tehran was uneventful and gave me more time to become acquainted with Reza Khan. The more I got to know him, the more I felt he was the right man to lead our country. I never let on to him that he was in a job interview of sorts and he never gave me any indication that he suspected.

We entered the city proper and made our way to my shop on Nasserieh Avenue so that I could be sure I still had a business. I trusted Ali Ladjevardi to look in on my caretaker, but one can never be too careful in these matters.

"It seems your shop survived your long absence" the Major remarked.

"From the outside it appears so" I replied. "I won't know the extent of the damage until my good friend Ali and I do an audit of the inventory and review the books."

Major Reza Khan sat on his horse in silence and I knew it was time to say goodbye.

"I can not thank you enough for your assistance and your companionship on this last leg of my journey."

"It was my pleasure Sayed. Perhaps after you have recovered from your journey you will invite me to dinner. To hear your description of your wife's food made my mouth water."

"It is a promise" I replied.

The Major gave me a salute and led his men off to their next mission, wherever that would take them. As for myself, I suddenly felt the need to see my family. So I rode the last few miles alone to my home.

When I arrived at the gate of Bagh Ilchi I was exhausted from the trip, but when my children ran into my arms all thoughts of the past few months disappeared.

I was finally home.

I looked up to see my wife standing at the door with tears in her eyes.

"I hope those are tears of joy *Khanoum*" I said then noticed the letter she was holding in her hand.

"Tears of Joy for your safe return and of sorrow for Khalil" she replied as she held out the letter to me.

> *Dear Uncle and Aunt,*
>
> *I hope this letter finds you safely united back home in Tehran. I never realized how important a loving family was to one's happiness until now.*
>
> *Shortly after you left Uncle, I received a letter from Barbara telling me of the horrors she had witnessed on the battlefield. I was beside myself with worry for her safety. I do not understand how men can do that to each other.*
>
> *The following day Gertrude Bell arrived at my office to tell me that the Germans fired artillery into the medical field hospital where Barbara worked and killed all of the doctors and nurses who were saving lives there. The love of my life is dead uncle. I guess the Tarot cards were correct after all.*
>
> *I had no choice but to leave London and the bad memories of that place. Mr. Gulbenkian was very generous and booked passage for me on one of his company's freighters*

to America. I will work for him in the New York office until I decide what to do with my life.

I have lost everything that was important to me. I do not know what to do.

I will write you again when I have a permanent address, for now you can write to me using Mr. Gulbenkian's London Address.

I miss you both very much and hope that one day I will see you again.

Khalil

It broke my heart to learn of my nephew's loss, but I was sure that he would recover. He was young and resilient. Time may not always completely heal, but the pain would surely fade over time and become bearable.

I returned to my shop the following day and met with my friend Ali Ladjevardi to learn how my business had fared over the past five months.

To my great surprise, the profits were more than what I experienced myself the same period in previous years. I told Ali that perhaps I was better off selling the business to him. Of course he was too much of a friend to agree.

If I ran for the Parliament I would still need someone to mind my business. Ali agreed to continue the arrangement that had worked so well while on my journey with a percentage of the profits.

So it was that within hours of returning home, I found myself with no day to day responsibilities.

The following morning I received an invitation to dine with Sir Walter Townley, the British Ambassador. It was to be a private dinner at his residence and I was to come alone. This did not come as a surprise. I was confident that he had been informed of my arrangement with MI6 and expected that someone on his staff would be assigned to ensure I kept my part of the bargain. What wasn't clear was whether he understood the limits of my participation.

"Welcome home Sayed" Townley said as I was shown into his library. "I am very happy to see that you have recovered from your travels."

"Thank you Sir Walter" I replied. "I am happy to be home."

He motioned for me to sit in one of the chairs by the fire place and took his place on the settee opposite.

"Would you care for a glass of claret before dinner?"

Before I could answer his servant appeared with two glasses on a tray. I could not refuse and was happy that I did not. My first sip revealed it to be a wonderful glass of wine.

"I understand you made quite a few new acquaintances in London" he offered.

"I made many new connections" I replied, "and learned quite a lot while in England. You come from a very lovely country Sir Walter."

"Yes. Quite right. I do miss home. Foreign service is a calling that requires many sacrifices, but one does what one must. You understand that more than most, do you not Sayed?"

This question was the real reason I was here.

"Service to ones country is a noble cause" I offered. "Sometimes it puts us in difficult situations. Sometime it puts our lives in danger, but we do as our conscience directs and sacrifice what we must to the greater good."

I hoped that this answer would satisfy.

"Yes. Well I can see we are of a similar mind. I am very happy to hear that."

He held up his glass in a toast then made a show of smelling the fragrance of the wine before drinking. I followed suit and was rewarded with a wonderful surprise. The experience of smelling the wine was almost as nice as the tasting.

Sir Walter may have heard what he wanted to hear, but I needed to make sure he understood my position clearly.

"Sir Walter, may I speak plainly?"

"Of course Sayed. We are alone."

I took another sip from my wine before starting.

"I am sure you are aware of my arrangement with Sir Mansfield Smith-Cummings, but I am not sure that you are privy to some details that I feel are important."

"I was told you agreed to work with us, but you are correct, I was not appraised of the finer details."

"I want you to understand that my allegiance is first to my family and then to my country. I am a proud Persian Sir Walter, and I will do nothing that is not in their best interest. Furthermore, I will never take money for my assistance."

Townley smiled at that.

"Sayed, when my superiors asked about you, I told them that above all, you had integrity. We never would have invited you to Paris if we felt you could be bought. Men who seek money will always look to the highest bidder. We were looking for a man of conviction."

"You knew the reason for my journey when we met at the wedding last November?" I asked.

"Yes. I asked Jean-Baptiste Lemaire to approach you with the opportunity. Naturally he was unaware of the true reason behind the request, and in fact I felt it was best if you discovered that when you arrived in Paris as well."

I thought back to our conversation at the wedding and my response when asked about Wassmuss.

"And your questions about Wassmuss and my cousin?"

Sir Walter shifted in his seat, a small indication of discomfort with my question.

"I must confess I knew about the German's visit to your shop. We were not watching you Sayed, but we were keeping Wassmuss under tight surveillance. So when you answered my question about him I listened carefully to your answer. I knew you were walking a fine line. You didn't actually lie to me however, so I decided to let it go. In a way that confirmed for me that you were ready to handle yourself in difficult conversations."

Townley seemed to relax, satisfied with the direction of the conversation for now. After a comfortable silence he continued.

"What are your plans now that you're home? Are you content with your business?"

I guessed that the interview was not quite complete.

"It is odd that you should mention this. My travels have given me a new perspective you might say. It is time for me to do something about the situation in our Parliament and not just sit on the side and criticize. When we hold the next election I will run for office. I think it is time we had the right kind of leadership in this country and I intend to do everything in my power to place Persia on the right path."

"I am thrilled by this news Sayed. You can count on me and my staff to help in any way we can."

Sir Walter smiled warmly and closed his eyes as he sipped his wine. It appeared he had just heard everything he needed to know.

After dinner I was driven home in one of the embassy's carriages. The house was dark so I quietly made my way to the bedroom. My wife was awake and waiting for me when I got into bed.

"You are working for them now." It was a statement and not a question.

"I am working for Persia" I replied. "If they can be helpful I will use them to get what I need."

"And your business?"

"Ali Ladjevardi will continue to run my shop. I plan to run for a seat in the Majlis in the next election and will need to build my support base over the next few months. It will not be easy, but I must."

"Will you still collect your little pieces of paper?"

I smiled at that as I thought back to how my collection had grown over the past five months and all of the people I met who contributed. Friends as well as foe.

"Of course *Khanoum*. I may be changing jobs, but I will always be a stamp collector."

I blew out the lamp and rested my head on my pillow. I was finally home and had a plan for the foreseeable future. It was time to get some much needed rest.

EPILOGUE

I promised you a story dear reader and I believe I have delivered. Those of you who know the history of my country will have an idea of what happens next, but not the story behind the story. I will certainly tell that tale one day, but just as Scheherazade saved a bit for the next telling, so must I.

Farewell until next time.

ACKNOWLEDGE-MENTS

The authors would like to thank the following people for their help with editing the book. Alex Matini, Goli Kashani, Barbara Brooks, and Kamran Kashani.

Thank you to Termeh Bertina for the cover design as well.

Without the efforts of these individuals we could not have delivered the book you have just read.

AFTERWARD

The Stamp Collector is a fictional book based on the life of a real person. Many of the events in the book are based on fact. Some are completely fabricated. There is no solid evidence that Abdulrahim worked for MI6. A British handgun was found in his personal effects at his death which was a surprise to his family.

Abdulrahim and Khalil made the trip to Paris sometime during World War I. Here is a photograph from that journey including Khalil's bicycle. Abdulrahim is holding the umbrella. Khalil is standing next to him in the dark jacket.

Abdulrahim's participation and leadership in the Constitutional Revolution is documented as well. We don't know whether he ever met Sattar Khan and the other patriots, but he did fight and publish a newspaper.

He was also the first person to publish a book on stamp collecting in Persian and he was truly a Freemason as well.

Khalil was an inventor who patented the idea of bullet proof tires and the delete key on typewriters along with many other ideas. He did fall in love with a Polish nurse who died in the war. He never returned to Persia and immigrated to New York where he lived the remainder of his life. The story of his bicycle being stolen by a relative of the Shah is true, although it happened in Kashan and not in Tabriz.

Ayatollah Abol-Ghasem Kashani was the cousin of Abdulrahim and played a significant role in the history of Persia during Reza Shah Pahlavi's time and beyond. Here is a family photo of the two together. Abdulrahim is in the front row on the right and Abol-Ghasem is third from the left.

Abdulrahim met Reza Shah when he was a Major in the Cossack Brigades. Here is a picture of them together in front of Abdulrahim's stationary shop in Tehran.

Gertrude Bell, Calouste Gulbenkian, Mark Sykes, and Françoise Picot were real people. Although some anecdotal observations were applied, much of the accounts presented here are documented in the numerous books written about them. They were important players in the history of the middle east during this time period.

The story of the statues of Eve and the Burghers of Calais in Gulbenkian's house in Paris is from a video interview of Calouste's grandson that can be found on-line.

Churchill's decision to convert the British fleet from coal to oil changed the world in many ways. The history of Royal Dutch Shell, British Petroleum, and the discovery of oil in Persia by D'Arcy is fascinating and well documented. All of the machinations presented in The Stamp Collector are based on these sources and are accurate.

Wilhelm Wassmuss was a real person who was considered the German Lawrence of Arabia. There is a great story about his capture by the British and a suitcase that we could not work into the book, but we recommend the reader look into the life of this colorful character.

We hope you enjoyed this story. The story of Reza Khan's ascension to Shah and how Abdulrahim played a part in his rise will be in our next book.

ABOUT THE AUTHORS

D. Andrew Brooks and Farhad Kashani met in the late 1980's while working for a high tech company in Silicon Valley. Over the decade they worked together, they travelled often to Asia and became good friends.

Farhad returned to Iran to start a business and published several books in Farsi for the Iranian market. At the time of this writing, he will have travelled to 160 of the countries recognized by the UN and 200 Traveler's Century Club's Countries and Territories including Antarctica. He has visited all 50 states of the US, seen all 30 provinces of Iran, and been to half of the provinces in China.

Brooks has worked as a product executive at various High Tech companies in the valley including Salesforce for eight and a half years. He has worked in six startups over the years with three successful exits. He has written two other historical fiction novels set in China and Taiwan that will be published in the near future.

Abdulrahim Kashani was Farhad's Grandfather. As Farhad was compiling a photo album on the Kashani family history, he sought advice for publishing the album for the American Market. As Brooks began to dig into the story behind the photos, it became clear that the life of Abdulrahim Kashani and his trip to Paris was extraordinary. Why would a Persian man travel to Paris in the middle of a world war? Someone had to write a book about this man, even if little was known about the de-

D. Andrew Brooks

tails of his trip.

Printed in Great Britain
by Amazon

14771674R00222